# ONE and ONLY

**KARLA SORENSEN**

Copyright © 2023, 2026 by Karla Sorensen
Cover and internal design © 2026 by Sourcebooks
Cover design by Stephanie Gafron/Sourcebooks
Cover photos © svrid79/shutterstock, Ollphotograph/Shutterstock, FrentaN/Shutterstock, Artkio/Shutterstock, Larek/Shutterstock, LiliGraphie/Shutterstock, Annanomaria/Shutterstock, alexkoral/Shutterstock, Elena Shtei/Shutterstock, Edge Creative/Shutterstock

Sourcebooks and the colophon are registered trademarks of Sourcebooks.

All rights reserved. No part of this book may be reproduced in any form or by any electronic or mechanical means including information storage and retrieval systems—except in the case of brief quotations embodied in critical articles or reviews—without permission in writing from its publisher, Sourcebooks.

No part of this book may be used or reproduced in any manner for the purpose of training artificial intelligence technologies or systems.

The characters and events portrayed in this book are fictitious or are used fictitiously. Any similarity to real persons, living or dead, is purely coincidental and not intended by the author.

All brand names and product names used in this book are trademarks, registered trademarks, or trade names of their respective holders. Sourcebooks is not associated with any product or vendor in this book.

All biblical verses are used as reflected in the New International Version (NIV) of the Christian Bible unless otherwise noted.

Published by Sourcebooks Casablanca, an imprint of Sourcebooks
1935 Brookdale RD, Naperville, IL 60563–2773
(630) 961-3900
sourcebooks.com

Originally published in 2023 by Dutch Girl Publishing, LLC.

Cataloging-in-Publication Data is on file with the Library of Congress.

The authorized representative in the EEA is Dorling Kindersley
Verlag GmbH. Arnulfstr. 124, 80636 Munich, Germany

Printed and bound in the UK and distributed
by Dorling Kindersley Limited, London
001-362182-Mar/26
CPI 10 9 8 7 6 5 4 3 2 1

*To my boys.*
*I hope you never read this, but if you do, you are the very best encouragers in the world and that's about the only reason I finished this book on time.*

# CHAPTER 1

# Greer

**In my own defense, the decision to hire a husband wasn't** *actually* a bad one. It was the execution where I stumbled.

Yes, I could've thought things through better (my tendency to act first and think second *was* one of my personality flaws) and sure, I could have tried to do it the old-fashioned way (really though, who has the time).

The truth was that I never should have scheduled *interview possible husband candidates* and *last-minute design consultation for my stupid brother's teammate* on the same night.

Convenience—the location of the restaurant to my hotel, getting both of these things out of the way at once—and cravings—I would fight someone over baked ziti—were the drivers for that decision, and no doubt, I could look back on my desire for cheesy carbs as the thing that caused my downfall.

The walk from my hotel to the restaurant didn't take as long as I thought, so I showed up plenty early and paused before I told her my reservation name.

In hindsight, this would've been the moment to call the entire thing off.

Before giving her my name, I was the only person involved.

Before sitting down in that booth, no one knew what I was attempting. In my mind, I could see the proverbial door of my escape sliding shut.

My chest went a little tight at the ramifications, but instead of walking away, I hitched my chin higher and approached the host stand.

"Reservation for Greer Wilder," I told her.

She gave me a polite smile and grabbed two menus. "Of course. Follow me, please."

The booth I requested was in the farthest corner from the entrance, curved for privacy. In the center of the table was a tasteful arrangement of short, squat candles flickering with warm light and a bud vase filled with a single rose.

Perfect.

I gave her a frank look and pulled a fifty out of my purse. "I will need this table all evening," I told her.

She arched some seriously perfect eyebrows. "Okay?"

"I've allotted a very specific amount of time for each guy I'm meeting, and as long as no one shows early, it should be just fine."

Her mouth fell open. "How many dates do you have tonight?"

First, they weren't *actually* dates, and for a moment, I

considered explaining that to her. But then there would be questions and judgment, and I really didn't feel like pausing for either option.

Second, whatever they were called, I had way too many of them to be considered sane.

"A few," I hedged. "I have something very specific I'm looking for."

A nice smile.

Taller than me.

Relatively sane.

Moderately attractive.

Willing to fake marry a stranger for money.

I didn't *say* any of that, of course. But nonetheless, when she gave me a wide-eyed look that straddled the line between worry and awe, I felt a hysterical bubble claw its way up the back of my throat.

The front of the restaurant was a long uninterrupted stretch of windows, so I specifically chose a seat in the booth that had me completely hidden from view. Normally, I'd want the opportunity to study any approaching male specimen—especially given my current situation—but for the sake of any early arrivals, I wanted to make sure they couldn't see me from the host stand.

A server approached with two glasses of water and a speculative gleam in his eye.

"Hi," he said. "I'm Rocco, and it looks like we're in for a fun evening."

Someone had warned her coworker.

I sighed, reaching into my purse for another fifty. "Rocco, you have no idea."

"What can I start you off with?"

"Fresh waters after every guest, please," I said with a tiny smile. "And a chardonnay."

He exhaled a laugh. "You got it, boss."

I'd taken a small sip of my ice water, trying to decide whether it was rude to eat half the basket of bread before my first appointment arrived when my phone screen lit up with my sister's name.

"Sorry, Poppy, don't have the time right now," I muttered and hit ignore.

I let out a slow breath, tucking my hair behind my ears while I waited. My hand reached out to straighten the perfectly straight silverware, but I pulled it back and set my clenched hands in my lap.

I could do this.

I had really good reasons and great gut instincts.

The hostess approached. "Here you go," she said to gentleman number one. Her face gave nothing away.

Pasting a polite smile on my face, I turned to face my first… contestant? Option? I wasn't quite sure what to call them yet.

"Greer," he said, snatching my hand for an enthusiastic handshake. "It's such a pleasure to meet you."

It was a testament to my sheer force of will that I didn't lose my smile.

He was at least forty years older than his profile picture.

"Mike?" I asked slowly, my eyes darting to his thinning white hair and the reading glasses tucked into his plaid shirt.

He took his seat, pulling the glasses out and settling them on his nose as he studied the menu. "Well, this looks wonderful."

Oh gawd, what did I get myself into?

"I only have time for one drink," I reminded him.

"Of course, dear," he said. "My granddaughter told me that drinks are the way us singles do things now."

I took a healthy swallow of my chardonnay.

Contestant two was not much of an improvement. His age bracket was nearer mine, and he smiled nicely. He was an inch or two taller than me in my heels, and I let out a quiet sigh of relief as he took a seat. It was just as I registered the nice, dimpled smile, the broad shoulders underneath his tailored shirt that I also saw the wedding ring.

"You're married?" I asked him. That was conveniently absent from his online profile.

He grinned. "We're…adventurous," he said silkily. "And you are just our type."

I cleared my throat and flagged down Rocco.

Contestant three was friendly. Funny. Only one year younger than me, and his hand was ring-free.

But the top of his head hardly cleared my tits, and there was no *universe* in which my family would buy into that.

When he left, I walked to the bathroom and slumped against the wall by the restroom. Rocco met me in the hallway with a basket of bread.

My general demeanor must have screamed exhausted and cranky and full of second-guessing thoughts.

"He was short," he said.

I ate two pieces before I answered. "Too short, Rocco."

"Who's next?" he asked.

"I don't even remember," I answered glumly.

Rocco snapped to attention. "Incoming."

I pinched my eyes shut. "Tell me."

His facial expression was cautiously optimistic. "A seven. Maybe an eight if you can get him to fix the clothes."

"Really?" I smoothed a hand over my hair and snatched one more piece of bread. "You're a godsend, Rocco."

Contestant four was, unfortunately, a complete pig.

Even though he gave me a warm, thorough study from head to toe as I approached the table, it didn't take long to knock him off the list once he opened his mouth.

"Normally, I like my girls short"—he leaned forward, eyes locked on my mouth—"but I think you could convince me to try to wrangle those legs around my shoulders pretty easily."

"Rocco," I called out. "We're done here."

Contestant four sat back with a shocked grin. "What's that mean?"

Rocco appeared at the table. "Sorry, man, I'm gonna have to ask you to leave."

"Bitch," he muttered as he stood.

"Have a good night, asshole," I called after him. I slumped in my seat.

Hostess Miranda approached. "Do you have some time to eat before the next one?"

Wearily, I glanced at my watch. "Yeah, maybe something quick." Then I sighed, setting my forehead in my palm. "Next guy isn't a date, thankfully. It's a business meeting. Shouldn't take much longer than thirty, though. Then one last guy after him."

Miranda patted my arm. "Rocco's getting you some food."

"Thank you." I lifted my head and smiled. "You two are the best."

She rolled her lips together, eyeing me curiously. "You're like…hot. And you seem really nice. I don't understand what you're doing with these guys."

*Don't cry.*

*Don't cry.*

I hated crying. My family had done enough of it the past few months, and I always kept my shit together when everyone else was falling apart.

Crying wouldn't help anything. Not tonight.

My shoulders slumped, weariness cutting down to the bone. "Have you ever been willing to do something insane…just to make someone you love happy?"

Miranda nodded slowly.

"That's what I'm doing. I'll probably regret it," I added. "If that helps."

A group arrived at the restaurant, and Miranda gave me a regretful look. "Sorry, I gotta go seat them."

"Go ahead." I watched her walk away. Maybe I'd invite Rocco and Miranda to my fake wedding.

I pulled my phone out and saw two more missed calls from Poppy and a text from an unknown number.

> **UNKNOWN**
> It's Parker's friend, Beckett. I'm running a couple of minutes behind, but I'll be there.

I didn't answer because Rocco set a small plate of bruschetta in front of me.

"Bless you," I told him. I demolished two before my phone rang again.

When I saw my little sister's name, I glanced at my watch to check the time, then hit the button to answer the call. Before I could even say a word, she was talking over me.

"Where are you? I just stopped at your apartment and you're not here."

"It's a Saturday night. Aren't I allowed to be gone?"

"You never go out on the weekends," she said. "You're either at your place or home."

"That is categorically false," I told her. "I do things all the time and don't tell you. Besides, why are you stalking me at my apartment?"

"Erm, just dropping something off."

At her tone, I narrowed my eyes. "Dropping what off?"

"That blue sweater."

"You mean the blue sweater you said you didn't borrow when I asked how it disappeared from my closet?"

Poppy was quiet for a moment. "Yes?"

I rolled my eyes. "I'm in Portland for a couple of days."

"Why?"

*Hopefully finding someone who will pretend to marry me for financial compensation because I didn't know how else to feel in control of a very uncontrollable situation.*

I cleared my throat. "Meetings."

"Are you seeing Parker?"

At the mention of our brother's name, I snorted. "No. He's still playing hard to get, but he texted the other day to see if I'd do a favor for one of his teammates." I glanced at the face of my watch. "He should be here any minute for our initial design consult."

"Oooh. Which teammate?"

"Does it matter?"

"Yes." Poppy laughed. "You're not even a little interested in who you're meeting?"

I toed off my heel under the table and arched my foot, groaning at the stretch after wearing them all day. "Of course I'm interested in who I'm meeting, but also…it doesn't really matter, you know?"

She sighed, one of those little sister sighs that made me feel like I was old and beyond help in her eyes.

"What?" I asked. "I'm just helping him with a design for his daughter's room, and that's it. It doesn't really matter to me who he is or what he does."

"Oooh, a daughter. So he's one of the unmarried ones."

"How on earth do you know that?" Despite the bruschetta, my stomach was still grumbling unhappily. I took another bite.

"If he was married, or dating, his significant other would help with the room, wouldn't they?"

"I suppose," I said, words muffled through the food in my mouth.

"Gawd, Greer. Please don't talk with your mouth full when he gets there."

I laughed. "I won't."

"What are you wearing?"

"Clothes."

She groaned.

With a sigh, I glanced down. "Dark jeans, nude heels, and the black wrap top that you said makes my boobs look good."

Poppy hummed. "I'll accept it."

"It's not a date, Pops." I actually wasn't sure what my activities could be called, other than a night trapped in a hell of my own making.

Curse my soft gooey heart who would do anything for my family.

Curse it up, down, and sideways.

She ignored me. "I can't believe you don't know who it is."

"I didn't say I didn't know. You're putting words in my mouth."

"Greer."

I rolled my eyes. "Why, do you have the entire roster memorized?"

"Yes."

I laughed even though I damn well knew my little sister was serious. The Portland expansion team was still relatively new in the league, and our brother Parker had transferred in the off-season.

He was close to home, just a few hours west of Sisters, Oregon, where our family lived. And our family…well…that was a touchy subject at the moment. We were all a little raw and, judging by my current state of affairs, not making the best decisions.

"Text me when he gets there. I wanna know who it is."

"I'm not going to text you once my meeting starts," I said offhandedly, turning to look at the front of the restaurant. Miranda shrugged. If he was too late, he might run into contestant five's time, and I was not trying to make this night harder than it already was. "But his name is Beckett. There. Now you can go about your evening and leave me to mine."

"Wait," Poppy said, "Beckett Alvarez or Beckett Coleman? They are both *cute*. Alvarez is their center. Coleman is a tight end with Parker."

I rubbed my forehead. "I don't know, Poppy."

"I can't believe you're so blasé about this!"

With another glance at my watch, and the realization that he was now even later than I'd thought he would be, I shifted irritably in my seat. "Poppy." I sighed. "Let it go."

"What? It's a big deal that Parker asked for your help. He's not talking to any of us right now. The dick," she muttered under her breath.

I pinched the bridge of my nose. "He's not a dick. He's grieving."

"We all are," she pointed out. "But he's the only one grieving *and* avoiding us."

"I know." I took another bite of food. A really, really big one.

"They have to be friends if Parker asked you to help."

There wasn't enough bruschetta in front of me. I stared at the remaining pieces and tried not to pout when Rocco swooped in and cleared the plate before Beckett Unknown Last Name arrived.

Emotional eating was so real, and the more Poppy talked about why Parker was ignoring our family, and why I was in Portland, I was gonna need a loaf of bread the size of my face.

"Poppy, I'm not dragging a new client into our family drama."

"I'm looking at the Voyagers website now," she said absently. "There is another Beckett on the defense. He's not a starter."

"Please stop."

"Too late, I'm already googling. Alvarez is married. Maybe it's Coleman."

"Poppy." I sank my forehead into my palm and stared down at the table. "I will find out who it is in about two minutes, so please stop."

"Gawd, I hope it's Coleman. He is gorgeous. This opportunity is *wasted* on you."

"Because it doesn't matter," I burst out. "He's a football player! So fucking what?" Okay, I was yelling a little. Hunger and me and bad dates and big scary emotions that were driving me to Portland to try to find a husband apparently made me a wee bit edgy. Poppy went quiet on the other end of the phone.

My heart was pounding. I didn't really mean it, but all I could think about sitting in that stupid booth was my dad's gaunt face and hearing his tired voice saying how badly he wanted to walk a daughter down the aisle before he died.

My chest started caving in the longer I thought about it. Caving into something hollow and sad and scary.

All the little bricks holding my emotions into place started crumbling, one by one by one.

I blew out a hard breath, ruthlessly shoving them back into place.

"I don't *care* who it is, Poppy, because he's just a man who wears tight pants and tackles dudes over a stupid leather ball for a living, and I don't *care* about that. There are so many other things I care about more."

A throat cleared above me.

I pinched my eyes shut.

Shit. Shit. *Shit*.

"Poppy, I have to go," I whispered. Slowly, I set the phone down on the table and wondered if it would be an obvious evasion to crawl under the table and hide there until he left.

My gaze tracked over to a big hand hanging loosely at his side, mapped with veins and free of a ring. Then it kept going up, and up, over a trim waist, a white button-down shirt covering a very nice chest and shoulders, to a truly, incredibly spectacular face.

Symmetrical and firm-jawed, with the kind of dark hair and golden skin and stubble and piercing dark eyes that would cover a magazine.

I swallowed. "You must be Beckett," I said quietly.

Slowly, so very slowly, he arched an eyebrow.

Gathering the tattered shreds of my dignity, I stood from the booth, let out a controlled breath, and extended my arm toward him.

Beckett eyed my hand for a beat, then his palm slid over mine, his big, warm fingers curling over my own in a firm grip.

Something ominous trailed up my spine, warm and quiet.

"Greer Wilder," I said. Then I cleared my throat. "I apologize for what I said. It was...unprofessional. And untrue."

He made a low humming sound.

Things I never, ever experienced: nerves in front of a man. Not because I was impervious to nerves. But I'd been around a lot of impressive men in my day. I had two brothers who were professional football players. The whole chiseled abdomen thing didn't cause me any tummy flutters.

But as Beckett eased his long body into the booth, legs sprawled open, hand drumming on the table, and eyes locked onto me, I felt a foreign kind of unsteadiness.

I didn't like it. Not one little bit.

"I like football. I don't think it's stupid." I swallowed. "Love it actually. I've been watching Parker and Erik play my entire life, so it would be ridiculous for me to judge someone negatively for something like that."

"Okay."

That was it. Just the one word. It was steady and low.

Rocco stopped by the table, eyes widening incrementally when he caught sight of Beckett. He recovered quickly when I kicked at his foot under the table.

"Anything to drink, sir?"

Beckett glanced at my empty wineglass, and I found myself clenching my jaw at the slight glimmer of a frown in his eyes. "Just water, I think," he said.

The slight edge to his words had my jaw tightening.

"I had a meeting before this," I found myself saying. "Just... trying to make the most of my evening while I'm in town."

"Okay."

I managed a nervous glance at my watch and blew out a slow breath. "Shall we get started?"

His eyes—dark and fathomless—narrowed incrementally. "I don't know if this is gonna work."

A hysterical bubble of laughter pressed up my throat, and I desperately tried to swallow it down. Mr. Tall, Dark, and Handsome had no clue just how right he was.

# CHAPTER 2

# Beckett

Greer Wilder, who looked absolutely nothing like her younger brother, was trying not to laugh. I could see it in her eyes and in the way she pressed her lips together.

For a moment, I considered getting up and walking out. Canning the idea altogether.

I hated it when I felt like I was being laughed at, and it set my jaw rigid with tension while she tried to hide her reaction with a sip of water.

But I thought about Olive. And I reminded myself why I was doing this in the first place. I took a deep breath and set my hands on the table. Our gazes met and held.

"I'm sorry," she said. "Normally, I'm much more…"

"Professional?" I added helpfully.

Oh, she didn't like that.

Her eyes flashed. "Yes."

"Then maybe we should start over," I suggested. "If you're

multitasking this evening, how long do we have before your next meeting?"

I'd meant it as a joke, but when she glanced at her watch, I huffed out an incredulous laugh.

Greer cleared her throat, a crisp, pointed sound. "Parker didn't give me many details, just that it was a little girl's bedroom. How can I help you, Beckett…" Her voice trailed off. "I didn't catch your last name."

"Coleman," I supplied.

Again, she bit down on her bottom lip, a smile blossoming on her lips.

"Something funny?"

She closed her eyes. "No."

"Mm-hmm."

Greer blew out a slow breath, and when she opened her eyes, she was more composed. "I'm not laughing at you, I promise," she said.

I arched an eyebrow, my gaze unyielding. I usually didn't sit across from a beautiful woman and use the same facial expression as when I stared down a defensive end who was trying to knock my ass over.

It had been a long time since I'd sat across from a beautiful woman, in general, and from the looks of how this was going, I wasn't quite sure how to handle it anymore.

She cleared her throat, settling her clasped hands on the table.

"Our meeting tonight is just for me to get a sense of which direction you'd like to go for the room, then I'll work on putting together some inspiration boards for your approval." She reached over and pulled out an iPad from a bag tucked onto the bench, swiping the screen to life. "Something like this."

When she flipped it around, I saw an image of some furniture, a lamp, a ceiling light fixture, and some paint color swatches arranged on a crisp white background.

"What do you need from me?"

Her frame was more relaxed now, and in place of the subdued laughter was a brisk professionalism that I appreciated. "This is for your daughter, right?"

I nodded.

Whenever I thought about this room for Olive and what it represented, my chest felt tight with pressure. And excitement.

For six years, all I'd had was snippets of time that were never long enough. An afternoon here or there during the regular season. Every other week and every other holiday during the off-season.

And finally, I'd have my chance to be a full-time dad to the person who was the anchor of my world.

Greer traded the tablet for a small notebook. "How old is she?"

"Six. Almost seven."

Greer smiled. "I love that age. My sister Poppy was an absolute terror when she was that old. If I'd designed a room for her back then, it would've needed a climbing wall, a mattress on the floor, and unbreakable glass."

People said things like that often. About the craziness of that age. It was hard for me to wrap my brain around anything of the sort, knowing Olive.

I managed a nod. "Olive is a pretty quiet kid. No need for any of that."

Greer wrote something down. Her hair—dark and long—fell over her shoulder as she focused on her notebook.

I took another sip of water.

"Quiet," she said. "Likes to read? Draw? That sort of thing?"

I nodded.

"So maybe an area where she can do arts and crafts?"

"She'd like that," I said.

"What's her favorite color?"

"I, uh, I'm not sure." I tugged at the collar of my shirt. Greer's eyes flicked up to the movement and back down to the paper.

Her pen slowed. Her face was composed when she looked back up again. "What color clothes does she pick the most?"

What a kind way of redirecting a question that every dad should know.

Her mom picked all her clothes, mainly because I wasn't sure Olive had ever expressed an opinion about it. "She wears a lot of pink and red." I thought about the dress that she was wearing the previous weekend. "White, too."

"That helps." She smiled.

Her hands were elegant, her fingers long and graceful as her hand flew across the page, free of any jewelry or adornment. Her nails were bare, filed into perfect round edges. But despite all that refinement, she had terrible handwriting.

"What?" She'd noticed my staring.

My chin lifted in a slight nod. "You can read that?"

She laughed. Her smile transformed her face—bright eyes and pretty lips that I shouldn't have noticed. "Shocking, I know." Greer set down the pen. "Someone offered to analyze my handwriting once, but I said no because I was so afraid he'd say I had hidden psychopath tendencies because of how I swooped my y's."

I wanted to smile, but I didn't. Greer's shoulders rolled with obvious tension.

"Do you have a picture of her room now?" she asked.

"Uh, it's not…it's not set up for her, per se." I pulled my phone from my pocket and opened my email. The guest room still looked exactly the way it had been staged for the real estate photos. "I just moved in a few weeks ago, and she doesn't stay with me much during the season. She lives with her mom most of the time."

Greer's eyes tracked over my face as I handed her the phone. The guest room of my new house was devoid of any personality. A queen bed with a solid color comforter sat in the middle of the large room, a beige armchair tucked into the corner by a tall nondescript lamp.

It was generic and bare, and I'd hardly noticed until I decided to make the room something special for Olive.

Greer tried to hide her wince.

"This is in Portland?"

I shook my head. "It's east of Salem. That's where her school is, and we want to keep her routine as consistent as possible, so I commute the hour or so to the team facilities when necessary."

Greer bit down on her bottom lip, worrying it with her teeth. "Okay."

Was she judging me? Wondering why I was just now moving closer to my daughter?

Most of my teammates knew about Olive, but only a couple knew any deeper than the obvious. Parker Wilder was one of them. Clearly, he hadn't shared any details with his sister.

"Is she…" Greer paused, shaking her head as she reconsidered her question. "Can I see a picture of her?"

I nodded. I didn't have many pictures on my camera roll. Ninety percent of them were Olive. When I found the last one I'd snapped, my heart ached in a sudden, fierce sort of way. It was rare that she'd smile for anyone, let alone for a picture by herself. Usually, she'd tuck her face against the side of my neck and peek out at the camera when I took a picture of the two of us.

But I'd caught her crouched in the grass of my new backyard, patiently waiting for a small yellow and white butterfly to land on her finger. When it did, she looked over at me—eyes bright and smile wide.

Greer made a soft, happy sound when she looked at the picture.

"She's beautiful," she said quietly. "Those big, dark eyes." She stared for a few more moments, then pulled her gaze up to mine. "Do you mind if I text myself this picture?"

"What for?"

"This is the inspiration for her room," she said, eyes back on the photo. "Anything that makes her that happy should be worked in."

"Yeah," I said roughly. "Go ahead."

The amount of time I was apart from Olive never felt larger, had never loomed so ominously over my head as it did in moments like that. When a stranger picked up on something about her that I hadn't.

And I was her father.

As Greer's fingers tapped efficiently on my phone screen, I studied her.

She was very, very beautiful.

The slight curl of attraction I felt beneath my ribs was wholly unwelcome, given what was going on in my life and the bigness of how it was about to change. But I could hardly make it disappear.

It triggered something edgy and uncomfortable in my brain. I should be able to make it disappear, if for no other reason than I didn't have time in my life to be attracted to a new woman.

"Is that all you need from me?" I asked.

My tone was harsher than I anticipated, and Greer's face showed it. She carefully set the phone down on the table and slid it in my direction. My hands were fisted under the table, and I made a conscious effort to relax them before I even contemplated pulling them into view.

"What's my budget?" she asked.

I shook my head. "Spend whatever you need. I want it to be perfect."

Greer licked lightly at her bottom lip as she studied my face. "I don't usually get carte blanche. What if I show up with gold-threaded sheets and a diamond chandelier?"

I arched an eyebrow, and she smiled.

"If you need to leave, I think I have enough to start my preliminary design, yes." Her eyes were speculative. "I'll need room dimensions, though. And if you have any other spaces for her—a bathroom or playroom—I can tack those on too." She smiled. "No extra charge. We'll give her something amazing, I promise."

I nodded.

"Parker didn't"—she paused—"he didn't give me much information about you. Or why you need a space for her now."

"Probably because I didn't tell him."

She pursed her lips as she studied me. Crossing her arms, she unabashedly flicked her gaze around my face, then down my chest to my hands, where they still rested on the table.

"What's your story then, Beckett Coleman?"

The answer to that question stayed buried somewhere deep, caught long before I was able to drag it up my throat. It wasn't a story I shared often, and I wouldn't be sharing it with her if I could avoid it.

The crux of it, of course, was that this was my one shot to be the dad I'd always wanted to be. Transforming a space that would make her happy, make her feel welcome and safe, I'd do whatever necessary to have that for her.

Sharing my story with Greer Wilder wasn't necessary.

"I thought you had another meeting after ours."

The evasion was clear, and she narrowed her eyes. I found myself holding my breath to see if she'd push, but Greer took another darting look at her watch and exhaled slowly.

"I do." She smiled lightly. "Lucky you."

"I'll email you the dimensions," I told her.

"Perfect. I'll get to work on the mood board, and we can go from there." She stood as I did. "What's your timeline on this?"

"I've got a bit over a month before Olive moves in full time," I told her.

Greer emitted a low whistle. "Okay then. I've always loved a challenge." She held out her hand again. "Pleasure to meet you, Beckett."

This time, I was taking her hand with a different sort of awareness. I didn't like it. Awareness meant noticing things—like soft skin and strong fingers and direct, unflinching eye contact. My hand tingled when I pulled it away from hers. I wanted to flex my fingers, shake the sensation free from my skin.

Her eyes were heavy on my back as I walked away.

As I approached the door, a tall guy around my age, with blond hair and a wide jaw, held the door open for me.

In his hand was a single red rose.

"Go ahead," he said.

"Thanks," I told him.

When I cleared the door, I turned briefly and watched the hostess walk him back to Greer's booth. Something uncomfortable flickered behind my chest.

I blew out my breath and walked with long strides toward where I'd parked my SUV. It wasn't until I'd gotten in, turned it on, started pulling out of the parking garage, and went to call Josie that I realized my phone was still sitting on the table at the restaurant.

The line of traffic stretched out in front of me, and I closed my eyes, pulling from whatever well of patience I might have left to drive back around the few blocks between me and the restaurant.

The twenty minutes it took me to loop around to the restaurant and drive the street until I found an open spot felt about four times longer than that.

Once I'd found an empty spot and walked back to the restaurant with quick, impatient strides, I pulled the door open with a bit more vigor than I should have. The hostess's head snapped up, her eyes wide.

"Umm," she said, eyes flicking back to Greer's table. "She's… busy?"

"I forgot my phone," I said. "She didn't happen to bring it up here, did she?"

She smiled, but it was tight and nervous. "No."

"It's fine. I'll get it."

"Sir," she called to my retreating back.

I approached the booth and saw the blond guy with the jaw sitting in the space I'd occupied. The rose was laying on the table. Her spot was empty, and my phone wasn't on the table where I'd left it. He was staring at his own screen, and I glanced at the back of the restaurant toward the restrooms. There was no sign of Greer, but she had to be somewhere.

As I neared the hallway that led to the restrooms, I heard the sound of her voice, followed by male laughter. I paused.

"Thoughts?" she said.

I tucked my hand in my pocket and leaned forward enough to steal a look at who she was speaking to.

It was the server.

"Cute." He was holding a plate of food, and Greer shoveled a bite into her mouth. "Not as cute as the guy before him, but definitely the best of all the options you've had."

My eyes narrowed.

"No one is as cute as the guy before this one." She sighed. "He was…" Then Greer shivered.

My stomach tightened at the realization she was talking about me. My face felt warm, and I glanced around to make sure no one was paying attention.

She kept talking. "But he was a business meeting, not a…*you know* candidate."

*What* was going on?

"More dates tomorrow night?"

"I don't know if I can handle another night of this. They were all so awful, Rocco."

"I know, girl. I saw." He cleared his throat. "I'll do it as long as you don't need me moving across the state. I don't think I could explain my income to my mom very well."

Because of the dark color of his skin, I couldn't tell if Rocco was blushing, but the way he glanced at her—shy and a little bit smitten—I wouldn't have been surprised if he was.

She laughed. "You are so sweet, but you're about a decade too young for this. My parents would never believe I'm robbing the cradle, but if I thought they would"—she set a hand on his arm—"I'd take you up on it in a heartbeat." The sound of a fork scraped against the plate. "Can you wrap that up for me? I want to eat an entire casserole dish of that before I pass out."

"You got it, boss." His attention turned toward the end of the hallway, and I ducked out of sight. "Are you gonna ask this guy then? He kinda looks like Lord Farquaad from *Shrek*."

If I hadn't felt the sharp edge of alarm at everything I was hearing, I might have laughed. What the hell was she getting herself into?

"Rocco," she said on a laugh.

"He *does*."

"If I'd figured out how to ask this without sounding crazy, I might ask him. He's good enough, right? He's cute. He's tall. One year older than me. He said he's between jobs at the moment, so the money might entice him. I think my family would believe it. But I still have to figure out the whole *I'm offering you money to pretend to be married to me* thing." My eyebrows shot up to my hairline. "You know," she continued, "without sounding completely desperate."

The server hummed knowingly.

"I know," she wailed. "It's insane, I know."

I glanced back at the booth, my heart twisting in rapid beats as I surveyed her companion in the booth again. He was holding up his phone for a selfie, the rose next to his face. He pursed his lips and tilted his chin at an arrogant angle.

What a tool.

I thought about Parker, one of my only close friends on the

team. If his sister was into something, I'd never be able to look him in the eye if I didn't speak up.

I cleared my throat and walked around the corner. The server's eyes widened to a comical degree. Greer choked on the bite of pasta.

"Have a minute?" I said smoothly.

She swallowed, eyes darting to Rocco.

"Up to you," he said quietly.

Greer's eyes fell shut, then she nodded.

"Can you tell him I got a phone call and I'll be right there?" she asked.

Rocco gave her a friendly pat on her shoulder and left us alone.

"What are you doing?" I asked her. "Because I know this is not normal date behavior."

Her eyes wouldn't meet mine.

All my instincts were screaming that something was off.

"What the hell is going on?" I asked.

Greer slicked her tongue over her teeth, a mighty internal battle waging on her face. I'd heard what she told Rocco, but I needed to hear it from her.

"I'm just…" She paused, glancing down at the ground as she shook her head. When her head lifted, determination was stamped all over her face. "I'm looking for someone to do something for me, but it can't be anyone I know."

I gaped at her. "That is wildly unhelpful."

She huffed. "Listen, you didn't want to tell me your story either."

My jaw ticked. "You're not in trouble, though?"

Greer rolled her shoulders. "No."

"Is it illegal?"

"No?"

The way she said it had me staring her down.

"It's not." She swallowed hard. "I don't think," she finished in a slightly more tentative voice.

I glanced back at the living Ken doll sitting in the booth. "He looks like an asshole."

"I don't need him to be—" She stopped abruptly. "I don't need to explain this to you. I've known you for five minutes."

"I'll be able to face down your brother with a clear conscience when I see him next week? I'm not walking away while you're about to get trafficked or something, am I?"

"Please," she said. "I have a taser in my purse, and I'm wearing five-inch heels. He wouldn't get very far if he tried."

"Greer. This isn't a joke."

She faced me square on. "I need a husband, okay?" she hissed. "And I'm trying to...find one," she finished miserably.

I wiped a hand over my mouth as I tried very, very hard to process what she'd just told me.

"A husband," I said.

Her cheeks blushed furiously.

"Not a real one." She rolled her shoulders again. "I just... It's a long story, okay?"

"I bet it is."

She blew out a short breath, then tucked her hair behind her ears.

"So your brother doesn't know about this."

"No." Her eyes held mine, intense and unwavering. "*Please* don't tell him."

I swore under my breath and stared down at the ground. Holding that dark-eyed gaze of hers for too long felt like I was making a promise, and I didn't know her quite well enough to keep her secrets.

Greer stepped forward and set her hand on my arm. "Please," she said again.

I glanced up, teeth clenched together and a voice in the back of my head screaming that agreeing to *anything* she was asking was the worst fucking idea I'd ever had.

"You seeing him tomorrow?" I asked. "Because if he asks me anything, I won't lie."

She blinked. "Tomorrow," she said slowly.

"The family event at the team facilities. I assumed that's why you were in town."

Greer sucked in a breath. "Yes. Right. I…forgot."

"Interviewing husbands will do that to you," I said dryly.

Her eyes flattened in annoyance. "I don't have time for this. I need to get back to interview this guy because he might just be perfect. But I won't know that if I'm standing here talking to you."

She brushed past me, and without thinking, I shot my hand out, wrapping my fingers around her wrist in a firm grip. Her jaw dropped open; her eyes locked where I held her in place.

Not because I wanted to hurt her. Not because it was any

of my business. Because something in my gut screamed that I shouldn't be walking away right now.

Underneath my fingers, her pulse was *wild*.

"Be careful," I said urgently. "I don't know what you're trying to pull off, but no matter what it is, it's not worth you trusting a stranger with something like this."

Greer's eyes were unwavering on mine, and the longer we stood there, my fingers around her wrist, the faster my heart started pounding. It was so loud, hammering against the cage of my ribs, I was sure she could hear it.

I didn't know her.

I certainly didn't know her well enough to be worried, but as I uncurled my fingers, I tried to breathe through the sudden pressure on my chest at what she'd said.

Greer swallowed, then walked back to the booth and took her seat with a pretty smile on her face.

The server joined me in the hallway. "You all right, man?"

"I have no idea," I said.

"She seems to have that effect on everyone who's sat in that booth with her tonight, if that helps."

I gave him a dry look. "It doesn't."

## CHAPTER 3

# Beckett

**Most days, it felt like my life could be separated into four** distinct categories.

Prepare for playing football.

Play football.

Wait for Olive.

Time with Olive that goes far too fast.

Even though it was the off-season and months before training camp started, I was still at the team facilities multiple days a week.

And days like that one, as I waited in the parking lot for Josie to drop off Olive, I realized just how much the waiting for her overshadowed everything else—even my job.

I loved football. But I'd never been able to deny that the all-consuming nature of the sport I played had always given Josie the edge in maintaining primary custody of our daughter.

Which is why I tried, as often as possible, to include her in that world. Allow for some overlap in those two pieces of my life when I could.

Leaning against the hood of my SUV, I watched her pull up to the security gate and get waved through. In the back seat of Josie's car, Olive was wearing pink, heart-shaped sunglasses—her favorite accessory—and when I waved, her lips split in a smile so sweet that my heart cracked open into a messy burst.

It did every single time she smiled.

Every time she laughed.

Every time she hugged my neck and wouldn't let go.

It made the waiting, all the hours I wished I was with her, completely bearable.

Josie pulled her car next to mine and looked over her shoulder to say something to our daughter. The pink suitcase that went between our houses was on the back seat next to Olive, and she patted it reassuringly with her little hand. Josie nodded, and then Olive unhooked her seat belt and yanked on the car door handle. I crouched in front of the door once it was open.

Because of the sunglasses, I couldn't see her eyes, but she climbed from the car straight into my arms.

"Hi, Daddy," she whispered. No one was around to hear us, but she always whispered, just in case there was.

"How's my favorite girl?"

She burrowed her face into my neck, squeezing me tight, and the way my ribs expanded just from the weight of her against my chest almost felt supernatural.

Forty pounds, and she could crush me if she wanted to.

Hardly a blip of what my muscles could handle, yet nothing else in the world impacted me the way holding my daughter did.

"Back open?" Josie asked.

I nodded.

"Ready to go play some football?" I asked Olive.

She pulled her face away, studying the team facilities rising on the horizon. Despite how reserved she was with…everyone, she had a few places she clearly enjoyed.

This was one of them.

Her lips curved up in a smile, and she gave a tiny nod.

I settled my hand on her back. "Good. I think Parker is in there warming up for you. He said he'd play catch with you."

Her smile grew a little bit bigger. More than anyone else on the team, Parker was her favorite. In fact, she was about the only person I saw him soften for anymore.

As I said it, I noticed a tall brunette get out of a vehicle a few rows over and slide some sunglasses down over her face as she walked toward the building. She was wearing a T-shirt in Portland colors.

Something in the set of her jaw and the way she held herself as she walked was familiar.

Greer.

My stomach tightened, and I wasn't sure why. I turned my attention back to Olive, kissing her temple.

Olive's arms tightened around my neck.

Josie joined us by the side of her car, and she held out her arms for a hug.

Olive motioned to get down, and once her feet were on the ground, she ran to her mom to say goodbye.

Josie closed her eyes as she hugged our daughter, and I looked away.

It was hard, knowing that my excitement of having primary custody of Olive for an entire year was because Josie was making a choice of her own. And it was one I understood. Saying goodbye to the tiny person who owned our hearts was the hardest thing I knew how to do.

We'd both had to do it in different ways. Splitting the time never really got easier, even if the routine was well-established. We did it, though, because there was comfort in knowing that she was loved in both places, and she was the priority in all our choices.

Josie's eyes were glossy with tears when I glanced back down, but she blinked them away when she pulled her face from Olive's. "Barry is still in the back seat," she told Olive. "Why don't you find him a safe spot in Daddy's car before you go in."

Olive nodded, clambering into Josie's car and pulling her fluffy white stuffed animal from the back seat floor.

Josie stood with a sigh.

"You okay?" I asked her.

She swallowed, watching our daughter as she walked over to my SUV and started buckling the stuffed animal into the back seat. "No."

"She'll be all right." I glanced sideways, and Josie had rolled her lips together, clearly trying to keep her emotions in check. "Your first visit will come quickly."

Her hand was shaking as she swiped underneath her eye. "I don't know if I can do this," she whispered. "What if she needs me? Or you get sick? Or she gets scared? Or you have to work a long day?"

My stomach tightened uncomfortably. "If any of those things happen, we will handle it, okay? She's gotten scared before at my place, and it's been fine. I've had to work, and we figure that out too. All your reasons for going with Micah are still there."

At the mention of her soon-to-be husband, she visibly relaxed. "I know. I just… I didn't expect it to keep getting harder the closer we get to leaving." She pressed a hand to her stomach. "And I don't know, maybe I stay back and we keep the custody the same, or…maybe Olive would do okay if she was with us there half the time."

My head snapped up. "What?"

Josie gave me an apologetic look, opening her mouth to say something, when Olive slammed my car door shut, Barry safely tucked away in the seat next to hers.

My heart thundered uncomfortably in my chest.

"Josie," I said under my breath, "we talked about this. Leaving her school, her friends, going across the world, it's exactly what her pediatrician said we should avoid if we want to help her come out of her shell. *Consistency* is what she needs."

Josie gave a quick look at Olive, who was skipping over the parking lot lines next to my car, completely oblivious to what we were discussing.

The two of us argued so rarely, but if one thing would trigger a fight of epic proportions, it would be this.

We'd picked apart this topic for the last year—and not just me but her and Micah too. Olive's pediatrician. The child therapist that our daughter had been seeing for months leading up to this change. We'd covered every angle. Again and again and again.

And as a group, we decided this was best. It's why I bought my big, boringly decorated house less than ten minutes from Josie's…because it was in Olive's school district.

"I know," Josie said on an exhale. "I'm sorry to do this now. To have second thoughts at this point. Micah is frustrated too, if that helps."

I gave her an incredulous look. "No, it doesn't help. I don't want that for you."

Olive skipped over to us, gripped my hand in hers, and tugged impatiently. Unwittingly, I smiled.

"I know, sweet pea, we're going."

Josie blew out a hard breath. "I think having Micah living in the house with us for the past year has made me realize how much harder it was when I was doing it by myself."

Somehow, I managed a nod.

"And I know we don't ever talk about your personal life…" Her voice trailed off. "But you'll need nannies, and…you'll be alone."

Now it wasn't just my heart and my stomach reacting to this conversation. My lungs could hardly pull in a full breath. A train could've run over my chest, and I wouldn't have been able to tell. That's how hard it was not to react to what she was saying to me.

Now. Less than a month before I finally got my chance to be a full-time dad to Olive, and she was doing this now.

"*Daddy*," Olive said, tugging on my hand again.

"We can't do this right now," I told Josie.

"I know." She pinched her eyes shut. "I'm sorry, Beckett."

I swallowed. I didn't want to say anything. I didn't want to let unchecked frustration color my mood or Olive's. Josie and I had come so far in six years of co-parenting, and I wouldn't let one moment of irritation undo how hard we'd worked to do this in a healthy, balanced way for the sake of our daughter.

"I know you are," I told her. I exhaled slowly, then ducked my chin so my gaze met hers. "We'll talk later, okay? I can call you and Micah after she goes to bed."

Her shoulders slumped in relief. "Okay. That sounds nice."

Olive was pulling on my hand again, so I reached down and swung her up into my arms. She giggled breathlessly when I caught her after a brief, weightless moment in the air. Her arms locked around my neck, her legs tight around my waist.

"Ready?" I asked, tickling her side. She squirmed, smiling wide and nodding excitedly.

Josie rubbed Olive's back. "See you in a few days, baby."

As Olive and I walked toward the stadium, she blew Josie a kiss. Normally, there were a few tears anytime she moved from one house to the other. In the off-season, when she could spend longer stretches of time with me, she had a harder time leaving.

For her, settling into a routine had relaxed her.

That's why we'd made the decision for her to stay with me.

And I mulled over Josie's words, trying to pick apart what she'd said, what she could've meant by them, and how on earth I was supposed to convince her that Olive was still better off staying here if she was already at the point that she and Micah were arguing about it.

I pulled open the doors of the facilities, and the hallway leading down to the primary practice field was decked out with deep-green and aqua-blue balloon arches.

Olive wiggled to get down, and we walked the hallway slowly so she could lightly touch her fingers to all the balloons as we passed.

It was good to see life like this in the halls where I'd spent most of my ten-year career because it hadn't always been like this.

The Portland Voyagers were the youngest team in the league, a six-year-old expansion effort that meant taking a risk for every single one of us who'd been on the roster since that inaugural season.

No one tells you how hard it will be to gain a foothold among teams that have decades of history and culture behind it.

To gain respect in a league where the fans identify themselves by which team they root for, no matter how that team performs year in and year out.

We'd had more losing seasons than winning ones, especially the first four years, but our owner—a man with more financial acumen than football savvy—was dedicated to making the Voyagers a powerhouse in the NFL.

He hired a cutthroat GM and went after the best coaches—the ones who couldn't resist the challenge of being at the helm of a team as it started making waves.

They were small at first. But with each smart decision, the waves grew.

We added strong players with trades and draft picks.

It was season four when things started to change. The general sense at the team facilities went from a cloud of frustration and helplessness to cautious hope. A spark of optimism that matched our passion for the game.

That year, we got the first pick in the draft after a dismal two-win season. With that pick came Christian Reyes—a Heisman-winning quarterback with the ability to drop his shoulder and run for a first down and a natural ability to lead. We won six games his first season as QB, and the stadium in Portland slowly started filling its seats for the first time.

Once we had Christian, it became easier to start adding weapons to our offense and build a team around his arm.

Parker Wilder was one of those players when he got an offer he couldn't refuse and an opportunity to play closer to his family.

Like me, he was a tight end. We clicked easily when he was traded from Ft. Lauderdale in season five, and it didn't take long for Coach to see that we were a lethal combination with Christian in the pocket. He revamped our offense to a two-tight-end lineup on offense, and once we racked nine wins under our belt because the defenses in our division couldn't keep up, the walls of the team facilities could hardly hold the trembling anticipation as we headed into our sixth season.

Events like this one—friends and family gathering for some informal games and food—became integral to forming the strong foundation at Portland. I'd always taken Olive because it was a way to keep her involved at the place I spent so much of my time.

She didn't like going to games—they were too loud with too many people—but this was something she could handle.

*Not just handle*, I thought with a rueful smile as she caught sight of Parker by the doors leading to the field. *She loved it.*

She froze, bouncing on her toes and pointing at my teammate.

I took her hand and squeezed it. "Give him a second, sweet pea."

Olive looked up at me with a pleading expression. "Please," she said.

I laughed under my breath. "I think he's talking to someone. We don't want to be rude, okay?"

She sighed heavily.

Parker was tall—taller than me by a couple of inches, and I couldn't really see who was standing by him, but I found myself undeniably curious if it was his sister, and what she might be telling him about her previous night of activities.

Parker shifted, turning his head so I saw his profile. His hands were on his hips, and there was a surprisingly angry set to his jaw as I caught sight of Greer standing in front of him. She didn't look much happier with her arms crossed over her chest.

When she set her hand on his arm, his frame relaxed, but he shook his head at whatever she was saying.

"*Daddy.*"

I glanced down, eyebrows high. It was about as forceful as my quiet, reserved daughter ever sounded.

"Okay," I conceded. "Go ahead."

She tugged off her sunglasses and handed them to me, tiptoeing lightly along the lines in the floor as she approached Greer and Parker.

Greer saw her first, her eyes narrowing, then her mouth falling open in recognition.

Her gaze snapped over to me, and she sucked in a quick breath.

For as polished and professional as she looked at the restaurant, this was a more casual version of the woman I'd met.

There were no five-inch heels today, but jeans with holes in the thighs and knees and crisp white-and-gold sneakers on her feet. Her hair was braided off her face, and around her neck was one of the Portland VIP badges that would grant someone access to just about any event the team held.

Parker noticed her attention shift behind him, and he turned. The stormy expression on his face cleared immediately when he saw Olive.

He held his hands out to my daughter, who ran straight up to him, laughing when he tossed her up into the air and caught her easily.

"Olly-pop, I haven't seen you in way too long," he said. "You keeping your dad in line?"

She smiled, tugging on the ends of his shaggy golden-brown hair.

"I know, I know, everyone keeps telling me I need a haircut." He notched his chin up. "Shoulders?"

Olive nodded excitedly.

Parker swung her up with ease, and I smiled when she gripped his hair in both hands. He winced, tapping on her knuckles so she would loosen her grip. "You teach her how to do that, Coleman?"

"Worked on it on the way in." I slapped him on the shoulder. "I'm hoping she helps you go bald before you turn forty."

He scratched his nose with his middle finger.

When I laughed, Greer's eyes were bouncing between me and her brother. She looked…confused? Relieved? I couldn't tell.

Something about our exchange had her eyes wide and her mouth hanging open.

She cleared her throat when she realized I was staring. "Beckett," she said, with a small smile.

Parker looked in her direction. "Oh, right. You two met recently."

"Thanks again for connecting us," I told him.

"That's why you're here," Parker said to his sister. It sounded accusatory.

"One of the reasons," she answered.

I blew out a slow breath, and she gave me a long, steady look.

*Keep your mouth shut,* that look proclaimed.

"I'm glad Beckett mentioned this event today," Greer continued. "I would hate to miss an opportunity to see my brother."

When Parker's jaw tightened, the subtext of her statement had me staring down at the floor.

"I didn't think anyone would drive over to Portland for this," Parker said.

"Well, maybe you can let us decide that for ourselves next time."

I knew Parker had a large family—a couple of brothers and at least as many sisters, but he'd been quiet about them the last few months.

Olive patted Parker's head. Hard.

I smothered a smile.

"Sorry, Olly-pop, is the adult conversation boring you?" He squeezed her leg, and she giggled. "Ready to go play catch?"

She nodded, even though he couldn't see her. My daughter's eyes settled on Greer and the curiosity was clear, even though she'd never instigate conversation with an adult she didn't know.

I tapped Olive's leg. "That's Miss Greer," I told her. "She's Parker's sister."

Greer somehow knew not to push for a handshake or high five, something most people did upon meeting my daughter. "I love your dress," she said. "It's perfect for playing football."

Olive's cheeks blushed pink, but without anywhere to hide, she simply dropped her gaze from Greer's and tugged again on Parker's head to get him to move.

This was always the point when I watched the people's reactions carefully.

My daughter—for whatever reason—was painfully shy. Had been from birth, it seemed like. Meeting new people was difficult for her. And Josie and I had worked very hard, with more than one professional, to make sure we wouldn't push her further into her shell by forcing her to interact before she was ready.

We never shamed her for not wanting to talk, and we gently corrected any adult who attempted to do that when they met her for the first time.

My gaze moved to Greer, the breath catching in my lungs while I waited to see how she'd react.

Olive's eyes darted back over to Greer, who simply smiled. "If you need a third person to play catch with, you just wave me over, okay?" She leaned in. "I'm *really* good at making Parker miss."

Parker scoffed. "Yeah, because you can't aim for crap."

When Olive smiled back at Greer—only the slightest curl to her lips, but a smile nonetheless—my heart stuttered over a few beats.

Parker walked into the practice field, where families and friends gathered in large groups. Music was playing, and they'd set up lawn games all over the field. The front office staff mingled, handing out balloons and gift bags full of Voyager gear to the kids running around, and the sound of chatting and laughter faded when the door swung shut behind Parker.

"So," I said, "Parker had no idea you were coming, did he?"

Greer grinned. "Nope. I do love surprising my brothers, even when there's a very healthy chance it'll piss them off."

"You have a big family."

She nodded. "The biggest."

"He told me a little bit about them."

"Sort of a Brady Bunch situation," Greer said absently. "My mom had three—me, Erik, and Adaline. Tim had three—Cameron, Parker, and Ian. They added Poppy into the mix after they got married, and now it's just chaos all the time."

It was impossible for me to imagine. I was an only child, and now I also had an only child.

Quiet ruled our days, and I couldn't wrap my head around the concept of chaos in a house.

Through the glass, I watched Parker deposit Olive onto the turf and snag a football from one of the racks next to the edge of the field. He knew her well enough to stay a bit removed from the crowds of people. She took the football out of his outstretched hands and waited until he jogged about ten yards away.

She cocked her arm back and tossed the ball, an ugly, wobbling throw that he caught with ease, rolling onto the turf as he did and pulling a delighted laugh from my daughter.

When I glanced over at Greer, she looked…sad.

I didn't want to ask. And maybe I shouldn't have, but the words came out all the same.

"Why didn't he want you here?"

She blinked, then swallowed hard. "He's a bit upset with our dad right now. Well, Tim is my stepdad," she corrected. "But he's Parker's dad."

I nodded because I'd known that too.

"Why's he mad? I thought your whole family was really close."

"We are," she said quietly. Her eyes held mine. "He hasn't told you anything about Tim's health?"

I shook my head.

"He's sick." She paused, her eyes glossing over while she waited to speak again. "Really sick. It's not the first time. It's not even the second," she added quietly. "But he doesn't want treatment for this round. He wants to enjoy what's left of his life, and even though that's really hard for us"—she paused, clearing her throat—"Parker is struggling with that decision more than the rest of us."

Parker's mood—darker, grumpier than normal for the past few months—made a lot more sense.

"I'm sorry," I told her. "That's gotta be hard for all of you."

Greer managed a nod, and when she swiped a finger under her eye, I looked back out on the field.

My brow furrowed.

"Is that why...?" My voice trailed off because it wasn't any of my business. "Never mind."

She exhaled a laugh. "Is that why I was trying to hire a husband?" she finished lightly.

My gaze darted to hers. "Yeah."

Greer inhaled slowly, then blew it out with puffed-out cheeks. "Yeah."

"Because of Tim," I said.

"I can't believe I'm telling you this," she muttered. Her eyes were intense, her mouth firm. "And I *wouldn't* be, if you hadn't walked back in last night. This goes nowhere, do you understand?"

I nodded.

She turned back toward the field, watching her brother play with Olive. "Last week, I was about to walk in the house and heard Tim talking to my mom." She swallowed. "Believe me, we've had a lot of hard conversations as a family since he made this decision, but I think there are some things he just doesn't want us to know. And I get why. I really do."

"What did he say?"

Greer didn't speak for a solid minute, and I caught the slightest quiver to her chin before she did. "That one of his biggest regrets is that he won't be able to walk one of us girls down the aisle. See us get married." A tear slid down her cheek, and she immediately brushed it away. Like if she rid her face of the evidence, it never existed. "He started crying. Then my mom started crying," she ended on a whisper. "He's going to miss *so* much. There will be years of events and moments—big and small—when we talk about him. What he'd say if he was there. How he'd feel. How much we miss him. And if this is my chance to give him even one of the moments off that list, I'm going to do it."

It was insane.

I looked out at Olive on that field and thought about how far I'd go for her. The constant stretch of love that just kept going and going, no end in sight of what I'd do to make her happy and feel loved.

It was easy to get caught up in the love on my end, but for just a moment, I thought about how I'd feel if I knew I'd be missing out on the opportunity to see her fall in love, get married, and maybe have kids. My ribs clenched—a tight, aching vise, something impossible to breathe through, and then the moment passed. But it wouldn't pass easily for Tim Wilder. He simply had to make peace with it.

And it told me exactly how much Greer Wilder must love her family if she was willing to do something like that, simply to allow a dying man a moment he didn't want to miss out on.

She sniffed, blowing out a quick breath. "I know it's nuts. But I don't know what else to do."

"Besides not fake a marriage?"

Greer gave me a dry look.

"Sorry."

She shook her head. "I feel so helpless. And I don't like when that happens. I need to *do* something. So maybe it's crazy, but his happiness is worth that to me." Briefly, her face turned toward mine, a pleading sort of look in her eyes, like she desperately wanted someone to understand what she was doing. "Haven't you ever had someone you love so much that you'd risk *anything* to bring them happiness?"

I closed my eyes and breathed out through my nose. "Yes."

Behind my closed eyes, it was Olive's face I saw.

It was always her.

I tucked my hands into my pockets while I processed her words—how they stacked up against my own family history. Nothing about my relationship with my parents would ever have registered that kind of blind devotion.

It was too ambivalent.

And it was why I did everything I could for Olive.

When Olive whispered something to Parker, I had that familiar tightening in my chest whenever I saw her happy, saw her comfortable. Parker nodded encouragingly, and she turned toward where Greer and I were standing. My daughter wasn't looking at me. She was looking at the beautiful woman at my side.

And she waved.

Greer exhaled a soft, wondering laugh. "Looks like I'm being summoned," she said lightly.

I stayed where I was as she walked into the field and approached my daughter and Parker. Greer crouched next to Olive, somehow knowing not to get too close, to not touch her when it was clear how reserved she was. Greer held out her hand, and after a solemn, appraising look, Olive carefully set the football in her grasp.

Greer smiled and stood, using an exaggerated motion with her arm to explain something to my daughter. Olive nodded.

Greer stepped back, waited for Parker to take off running, and then did a little hopping step back, stepped forward, and threw a perfect spiral, which Parker pulled in with one arm.

Olive bounced on her toes and smiled.

Wide. Happy.

Parker back-flipped onto the field and, once he'd found his feet, tossed Olive the ball underhand. She tried to catch it, but it bounced right out of her arms.

Greer scooped up the ball and sat cross-legged on the turf next to my daughter. My chest warmed at how easily Olive seemed to take to her, taking a careful seat next to the woman with the pretty eyes and even prettier smile.

My phone buzzed, and I pulled it out of my pocket.

> **JOSIE**
> I'm sorry I ambushed you like that. It wasn't the right way or the right time.
>
> Micah told me I needed to be honest with you, and I couldn't hold it in anymore.

With clumsy thumbs, I tapped out a reply.

> **ME**
> It's fine. We can talk about it later.
>
> **JOSIE**
> Trust me, I want to feel perfectly okay leaving her. I just don't know how to do that right now.
>
> I'm sorry.

She'd have every right to want Olive to go with her to London, even if the process to get there would be messy. Short of taking her to court—which I didn't want to do—I'd have no choice but to deal with it. Or she'd stay, and I'd still lose my chance to be a full-time dad to Olive. I didn't want that either. My mind raced—tumbling thoughts and snippets of conversations vying for the top spot.

Greer.

Josie.

Me.

Olive.

Greer's dad.

Absently, I rubbed at my chest because something was growing underneath my sternum.

An idea.

Something taking root that should be yanked out and ignored.

If I thought on it too long, I'd probably come to regret it.

I knew exactly how I could help Greer with her insane—albeit noble—cause.

And how she could help me with my problem in return.

# CHAPTER 4

# Greer

"Remember when we were little and Mom and Dad used to make us hug it out and say something nice about each other?"

Parker gave me a brief side-eye, snapping up the ball again to toss it underhand to Olive. "Yeah."

"I found something I can add to your list someday."

Olive dropped the ball, twirling in a small circle while her dad picked it up and handed it back to her. Parker set his hands on his hips, determinedly quiet.

I hated when my brothers didn't take my bait.

"You're not going to ask what it is?"

"Wasn't planning to."

Olive tucked her tongue between her teeth and heaved it back to Parker. With an exaggerated stretch, he caught it, securing it against his stomach and aiming a killer smile in her direction. "Nice throw, Miss Coleman."

I sighed. It was impossible to be mad at him when he pulled shit like this.

Everyone around us played and laughed and talked and mingled. Had been for a couple of hours. And I hadn't gotten a single minute of decent conversation with my stepbrother. "Well, I'm going to tell you anyway," I said. He muttered something under his breath, which I ignored. "You are *so* very good at using an innocent young girl as a buffer from being alone with your sister when you don't want to hear what she has to say."

His eyes snapped up to mine, and the angry fire was so bright in them, I almost took a step back. But if there was any rule of survival to being in a big family, it was do not show fear to the sibling you're currently trying to engage. Parker might've been six inches taller than me, but dammit, I was older and definitely wiser and that had to count for something.

"Ooh, he doesn't like that one," I said. "I wonder why."

Parker leaned in. "Maybe I don't like you joking about it when you know this isn't easy for me, Greer."

Behind the anger, behind the distance he'd put between us and him, was a scared boy who didn't want to lose his dad. The big sister in me wanted to drag him by his ear back home, wanted to smack him upside the head for acting this way.

But I wasn't stupid. And I didn't want to make anything worse.

Parker was trying to assert control in a situation where he felt like he had very little.

Something uncomfortable tugged underneath my ribs. Wasn't I trying to do the same thing?

"It's not easy for any of us, Parker," I said quietly. "That's the point. Just give me ten minutes, and I'll go."

Olive skipped over to us, and I immediately softened my expression. She only gave me the briefest of smiles, but I could already tell that those were hard-earned.

Very much, I mused, like her dad. He kept his distance from where Parker and I stood, watching his daughter as she approached. When she tugged on my brother's hand, he crouched and leaned in closer. Olive cupped her hand over his ear and whispered something, only allowing the briefest glimpses in my direction.

"I'd love to play bean bag toss, Olly-pop," Parker said. He gave me a smug smile. "Since there's no conversation here that needs to be had."

I narrowed my eyes and gave him my best *I'm flipping you off in my head* expression.

Judging by the look he gave me in return, he was giving me one right back.

My shoulders sank when he scooped Olive into his arms and strode to the opposite side of the field to play whatever game awaited them next.

Kids ran in screaming, laughing packs, players and front office staff mingled with families of all sizes, and suddenly, I felt very alone on that big field.

*You can't fix everything, Greer.*

Oh, I hated hearing that voice whisper in the back of my head because yes, I fucking could.

Determination had me gritting my teeth, and as I tried to figure out my next move when it came to the big tall dummy currently ignoring me, a quiet figure joined me.

I didn't feel dwarfed by many men—the perks of being tall—but Beckett Coleman's broad shoulders and big arms brushing against mine did the trick quite easily.

When he left the restaurant the night before, I tried to imagine how I would've felt if he'd sat down as a husband candidate.

Besides the immediate and obvious *holy shit, the heavens have opened up and smiled upon my quest.*

"Do you have a minute?" he asked, breaking up the pointless path of my thoughts. "There's something I want to talk to you about."

I let out a slow breath, tearing my eyes away from Parker. "Yeah, what's up?"

He held out a hand, gesturing toward the doors. "Privately, if that's okay."

My gaze moved to his face, but I couldn't read anything on it.

The man had a really good poker face.

I nodded.

"There's a conference room right across the hall. I'm going to tell Parker to stay with Olive, but I'll meet you in there."

How very mysterious.

He didn't wait for me to agree; he didn't give me a smile or a hint as to why this couldn't take place right there. Our little foursome had stayed removed from most of the crowd the entire time I was there.

Instead of leaving the field for the conference room, I turned by the doors and waited for Beckett to join me. He crouched by Olive, his big hand spread over her back. She nodded as he spoke to her, right by her ear.

Watching him with her was like poking a particularly nasty bruise, for multiple reasons.

I was younger than Olive when my mom married Tim. He was the only father I remembered.

My older brother Erik remembered our dad, just bits and pieces before he left Mom. But my sister Adaline and I were lucky in that way. I had no recollection of the sperm donor.

The only thing I knew was the man who cleaned our scraped knees and helped pull our hair back for ballet recitals and who taught us how to shoot a .22 and throw a punch.

I tore my eyes away from Beckett as he straightened, faced me, and made easy, long-legged strides in my direction. He had the same long-limbed strength as Parker—tall and broad-shouldered, big hands and strong arms.

And still, I couldn't get a read on his face as he neared where I stood. The only thing I could see was caution.

That, in and of itself, was interesting.

Beckett pulled open the door and motioned for me to go first.

The hallway was empty, the sound muted when the doors swung shut to the field.

"This one is fine," he said, stopping by the first conference room. When I walked in, there was a whiteboard covered in Xs and Os, the bent arrows scrawled messily around them to denote a play.

I tapped the surface with the tip of my finger. "I'm trying to decide whether this need for secrecy is intriguing or nerve-racking."

When I glanced over my shoulder, his brows were furrowed, his mouth bent in a slight frown.

"Why would you be nervous?" he asked.

I shrugged. "Just trying to figure out why we couldn't talk out there."

Beckett's eyes never wavered from mine. "I don't want Olive around, and I'm pretty sure your brother would go for my head if he heard what I'm about to say to you."

At that, I turned, settling one hip on a stool in front of the whiteboard and crossing my arms over my stomach. "Really?"

Beckett's chest expanded on a deep inhale. "Mostly, it's so Olive doesn't hear, though."

"She's sweet. I'm glad I could meet her before I start working on her room."

His eyes stayed steady on my face, and I tried to decipher why that sent the slightest of tremors through my body—fingertips to toes.

It was his quiet that had me feeling edgy with nerves.

When he spoke, his voice had warmed slightly. "You were good with her. Not everyone knows how to deal with a shy child."

"Oh." I shrugged self-consciously. "I know what it's like

when I don't want to talk to people. The last thing I want is someone getting in my face and telling me I have to be friendly and smile more. That usually just makes me want to punch them in the throat."

His gaze sharpened. "That's what her therapist said in our first meeting. To imagine how we'd feel if someone tried to force us into something we weren't ready for."

"Has Olive always been shy?"

He nodded, settling against the edge of the long conference table. "She didn't talk until she was almost three. We started her in speech therapy when we realized we couldn't will her into it. When she picked it up so quickly, Josie—Olive's mom—and I realized that maybe her shyness was why she didn't talk, not because of any actual speech delay."

"Is Josie your…?" I let my voice trail off.

"We were never married." He braced his elbows on the tops of his thighs and let his clasped hands dangle between his legs. "We were…friends, I guess, before she got pregnant with Olive. I'd just moved here, and so had she." He smiled, but it was self-deprecating. "When she found out she was pregnant, we tried. But it didn't take long to realize we were better off as friends."

"And she lives here too?"

He nodded. "About ten minutes away from my new place. She's getting married next month."

My eyebrows popped up. "Oh. And that's a good thing?"

He nodded again, slower this time. "Micah is a nice guy. They've been dating for a couple of years."

I tilted my head. "You mentioned in our meeting last night that Olive will be moving in with you full time. That's not because Josie's getting married, is it?"

His chest expanded with a deep breath. "Sort of. Not the marriage, per se. But Micah has to relocate to the UK for a year to help set up an office for his company. They're going global, and because he's the chief operating officer, they want someone there to help get the new location up and running."

"Wow." I exhaled slowly. "And she's going with him?"

"Yeah. And after meeting with Olive's pediatrician and therapist, a lawyer to help us work through the legalities, we all decided that it made the most sense for Olive to stay here with me. She needs consistency. Uprooting her for a year in another country wouldn't be good for her." He held his hands out. "Buying my house is to make things easier for her when Josie is gone."

I nodded. "That's why you want the perfect room for her."

The edge of his mouth ticked up in a tiny smile. "Yeah. I want her to love it. It won't be easy, but anything I can do to help, I'll do it."

Well shit.

Forget poking at a bruise, Beckett was about to melt my heart into a gooey soft puddle.

I cleared my throat, straightened my backbone, and tried to keep my face professional. "Why did you need to meet with me? I don't think it's because of Olive's bedroom."

Beckett didn't speak at first, he simply stared.

His jaw clenched, and so did the hands hanging between his legs.

"Beckett?"

He blew out a slow breath. "Josie is having second thoughts about leaving. She texted me a bit ago and told me she may stay back. Let Micah go to the UK, and she'll just visit him a few times."

I wasn't sure what he was expecting to hear from me, but I kinda felt for Josie in all this too.

"It's gotta be hard to think about leaving Olive," I said slowly.

"It is." He closed his eyes and took a long inhale. A steady exhale. "She's planning to visit a few times. But I know she loves Micah and doesn't want to start their marriage with a year of being apart. That would be hard on any newlyweds."

My brows lowered as I tried—quite unsuccessfully—to figure out why he was telling me all this.

He must have seen the confusion on my face because his eyes sharpened.

"That's why I asked you here," he said.

I shifted on the seat. "Why?"

"I think we can help each other." His eyes held mine meaningfully. "I can help you with your dad. You can help me convince Josie that she doesn't need to stay back because I won't be doing it alone."

Oh.

*Oh.*

I covered my mouth with my hand as my mind fucking raced.

This was *not* what I expected.

"You want to…?"

When my voice trailed off, he nodded slowly. "Be your fake husband. If you'll be my fake wife."

"Holy shit," I whispered. "Are you *serious*?"

He rubbed the back of his neck. "I think so. I've never had the chance to be her full-time dad, not like I've always wanted. And Josie is a good mom. She's a great mom. But she deserves a chance to start her marriage off in the right way too, you know?"

Did I nod?

Was I still *conscious*?

"You look a little…"

"Like I'm gonna pass out? Yes."

His jaw clenched. "Look, I know this isn't ideal. I hardly know you."

I laughed incredulously.

"But how is this different from you asking the douche with the rose to marry you for money?"

Honestly, I wanted to be annoyed. I wanted to say that the guy from last night wasn't a douche, but he really kinda was.

"I would've asked him if Rocco hadn't planted the *Shrek* image in my head."

Beckett's gaze sharpened immediately. "So you didn't approach anyone else?"

"No," I said begrudgingly. I rubbed my forehead. "I didn't… I don't know how to say it. It sounds—"

"Insane?" His voice was dry, but his face was quite serious.

I managed a nod.

"Because it is," he said easily. "Only someone desperate would ever think about marrying a stranger for something like this."

My heart raced. He was serious.

There were a million things to consider.

Two million things we needed to discuss.

"And you're desperate enough to do this for me?" I asked quietly.

"That's the thing, Greer. I have enough reason of my own. You won't find anyone else who can say that." His eyes blazed with intensity, something visceral that I felt all the way down to my toes. "I will do anything for my daughter, and if this is my chance to have the kind of time with her I've only ever dreamed of, then I'm going to take it."

A father's love for his daughter. What a powerful, unique thing.

They watched us grow and wanted to protect us. They wanted to make us strong and confident and brave, and be by our side when it mattered.

I thought about Tim, and how the only time I heard him break down about his cancer was because of this specific moment he'd miss.

To be the man who held his daughter's arm as she began a new life with her husband. The symbolic giving away of a woman he helped to raise, whom he loved and cherished.

He had that kind of love for me, and Adaline and Poppy. It didn't matter that Adaline and I didn't share his blood, he loved us all the same.

He'd do something desperate and reckless for us, just like Beckett was willing to do for Olive.

And just like I was willing to do for Tim.

I stood from the stool, approached him with even steps and a growing sense of determination.

Maybe I couldn't fix everything. Maybe I could only fix one thing for each of us.

Beckett unfolded his body when I got within arm's reach, and the tendons in his jaw rippled underneath his skin as he took in my expression.

Because I was in flats, I tilted my chin up to meet his eyes. "I was going to talk myself out of the plan before you pulled me into this room," I admitted.

"You make it sound like I kidnapped you," he said, totally affronted.

A smile threatened when I patted the side of my purse. "Nah. You know what I keep in here."

Beckett did not smile. "I've always wanted to start a relationship off with threats."

That somehow made me want to smile more. "All the best ones do, I hear."

"We have a long way to go before we actually pull this off," he told me.

"I know."

He took a step closer. "Any addictions I should be aware of?"

I nodded gravely. "A weakness for baked goods and the never-ending quest to find the perfect dry shampoo."

"Greer," he said, tone full of warning.

Slowly, I exhaled, attempting an apologetic smile. "And a horrible tendency to tell a joke when I'm uncomfortable and want a reaction because I don't know how to break up the rampant tension in the room?"

He swiped a hand over his mouth, eyeing me carefully.

We were standing so close.

He smelled so good.

My tongue itched with the impulse to say something about it, that I never imagined a fake husband smelling so good, but I swallowed it down.

"What about you?" I asked. "You were awfully judgy about one of my best husband options last night, but you could be a total psycho for all I know."

"He was taking a selfie with the *flower*."

Laughter bubbled up dangerously in my chest. But it ebbed away when his face went heartbreakingly earnest.

Beckett.

"The biggest problem you will find with me is that very few people in my life have ever seen me do a single impulsive thing. This, by its nature, is so out of character for me that even I can't believe I suggested it."

I tilted my head, sifting through his words.

Objectively, I knew it was meant as a warning.

"That sounds very thorough. And slow. You'll have to teach me how that works."

"Yes, I'd imagine it's a foreign concept for you." His eyes

flickered over my face. "And you... That's another hurdle we'll have to cover."

"*Excuse* me?"

He licked at his bottom lip. "You, Greer Wilder, are not my type."

My jaw dropped, an affronted noise slipping out of my mouth. "You're not my type either, Mr. Quiet and Judgy."

Beckett arched an eyebrow. "So you see why we have a problem."

"You worry they won't buy it," I offered.

Beckett looked away, then managed a tight nod. His eyes tracked back to mine after a moment. "Don't you worry the same?"

I shrugged lightly. "My parents got engaged three weeks after they met," I told him softly. "They just *knew*. So will they ask? Maybe. But that's not enough to stop me."

"You sound really certain that we can pull this off."

I smiled. "It's one of my most annoying traits. Ask my siblings."

His face was serious. "If I lose her because we don't do this the right way..." His voice trailed off.

Well shit.

I had to go and find a husband who was my opposite. He probably thought ten steps ahead at any given time, choosing careful placement before he made a single move forward.

It was so responsible.

So levelheaded.

It was such an inconvenient time to weigh how he stacked up against any of my exes.

Maybe this is why I'd often ended up with a bruised heart and a battered ego. I went for guys who were impulsive and adventurous and *romantic* in all the ways they kept me on my toes.

Read between the lines on this—the sarcasm was heavy when I said they were romantic.

"We can do this," I told him. I infused every ounce of my blind, reckless optimism into my voice. And when his eyes locked steady on mine, I made another blind, reckless promise in my heart.

We'd pull this off if it was the last thing I did.

"We can do this," I repeated. And then I held out my hand.

Beckett let out a shaky exhale, sliding his big, warm palm against my own. His fingers were firm and strong. They curled around mine, and chills slid down the back of my neck.

"You really think they'll believe us?" he asked.

It was the biggest question of all, wasn't it?

"We won't know until we try."

Beckett's eyes flickered, maybe because he didn't expect my honesty. I could practically feel the massive cloud of his thoughts, churning and restless, filling the room with an ever-growing list of ways he could talk himself out of this.

We stood with his hand wrapped around mine, hovering over a massive, life-altering decision.

Then he tugged my hand up toward his mouth, brushing a feather-light kiss along my knuckles.

The moment his lips touched my skin, heat bloomed over my face.

Oh. Okay then. My heart catapulted somewhere over the building. My fingers itched to stretch over the stubble on his face and see how it felt against my skin. I took an unwitting step forward, and he exhaled against my skin.

That's when the door opened into the conference room. I tried to step back, but Beckett held firm onto my hand.

Parker stood in the doorway, Olive perched on his hip, with a glare on his face when he saw my hand against Beckett's mouth.

"Oh for fuck's sake," he muttered. "Really?"

Olive's eyes widened, and Beckett cleared his throat, dropping my hand.

"Language, Parker," he said in a dry tone.

My brother set Beckett's daughter down, and she ran over to her dad. When he scooped her up, Beckett's eyes met mine over her head.

Had he done that on purpose? I hadn't heard anyone approaching, but with my hand tingling at my side, I couldn't help but wonder if he'd known.

"First Adaline, and now you," he said, referencing our sister who was happily with one of his former teammates. "I am never introducing my sisters to anyone ever again," he mumbled, walking out of the room with a scoff.

I exhaled a laugh.

Beckett's hand was so big over Olive's back, and he pressed

a small kiss to the top of her head. My heart churned with the absolute bigness of what we'd just stepped into.

"They'll believe us," he said. His voice was so smooth and sure, his face so confident, that I felt an unwilling fluttering sensation underneath my chest. "They'll believe us, Greer."

I sucked in a deep breath. "Then let's do it."

# CHAPTER 5

# Greer

"I already told you, that's not how I want it to look."

My brother—not the football-playing one but just as stubborn—crossed his arms over his chest and stared me down. "Greer, you have to make up your mind."

"I did make up my mind. You just don't want to do it my way."

"Your way is wrong," Cameron said.

The crew behind my brother was completely unfazed by our bickering. They'd worked with us long enough to know that at Wilder Homes, there was a very specific process to the completion of each gorgeous custom house we worked on.

Cameron was the general contractor. He was the level head and organizer of the chaos that would bring us from start to finish.

But I was the imagination. I oversaw the construction plans with the architect. I was in charge of the design of each square inch and pulled together our client's vision through many, many conversations and calls and texts and Pinterest boards.

"My way isn't wrong," I said through gritted teeth. "You just have the creativity of a potato, Cameron."

He sighed, rubbing at the back of his neck. "Fine. Explain it to me again."

While the work continued around us, I unrolled the plans, and we stood side by side at the makeshift table in the middle of what would eventually be a kitchen. We'd been working with Marcia and Bill for over a year already on one of the biggest homes we'd ever built.

Because we were still in rough-in stage—wires and plumbing and HVAC getting filled into the frame before drywall would start—the house was still a skeleton of what it would end up being.

And most importantly, it was when plans could still shift and change on a dime.

Like when Marcia found something on Pinterest and called me the night before asking if we could add hidden shelving with built-in electric around her massive fireplace.

I pointed at the plans. "If you wire here and here, we can still leave the ductwork for the fireplace where it is. We just need to bump this out about four inches on either side to accommodate the adjustable shelves." I nudged his shoulder. "But it's doable. I'll find some flat hardware that will tuck along the top, and they can affix the paneling with those invisible hinges we used on the Marcos's job last year."

Cameron sighed. "Fine." He shoved a pencil behind his ear and hollered for the foreman on this site. "Wade, Greer has something fancy to add."

Wade ambled over, his beat-up hat pulled down over his face and an unlit cigarette hanging from his lips. I could never quite tell how old Wade was. He could've been forty-five, could've been sixty, but he did damn good work, and without fail, he bitched like a mule when I sprang last-minute design changes on him.

"Of fucking course she does," he grumbled. "What now?"

I laughed, setting a hand on his arm. "I'll bring cookies tomorrow to make it up to you."

He grunted. "Hopefully, you're not the one baking them because the last time you tried, they tasted like tire rubber."

Cameron snickered, and I leveled him with a glare.

While my brother started explaining the changes, my phone buzzed in the back pocket of my jeans. I pulled it out, stomach fluttering briefly when *Beckett calling* appeared on the screen. The room was loud with the sound of nail guns and saws and cursing workers, so I stepped around a sawhorse and hopped over an air compressor next to the front door.

"Hey."

"Do you have a minute?"

Directly behind me, someone shouted about needing an extra set of hands, and I leveled the kid with a glare.

He winced. "Sorry, Greer. Didn't see you there."

I sighed, returning to the phone. "Yeah, I have a minute, just very little privacy, depending on the nature of what needs discussing."

"You're on a jobsite?" he asked.

"Yeah, we've got a home on Detroit Lake that we've been

working on for months. I've been out here most of the week." I walked farther out from the house, exhaling slowly as the noise and chaos receded the closer I got to the water.

Beckett went quiet. "You'll be there all day? Or do you have to go back to Sisters?"

"I planned to be here all day, why?"

"Detroit is only about forty-five minutes from my house," he said. "I'm east of Salem."

I swallowed hard. The logistics of how we planned to pull this off was very high on my list of things we needed to discuss. "I noticed, when you sent me your address."

Beckett pulled in an audible breath. "Josie plans to come out here tonight after Olive is in bed. I think she wants to discuss some options, considering she's having second thoughts."

With the toe of my work boots, I kicked at a loose stone on the ground in front of me. What would be a good wifely thing to say?

"Do you want to talk about it?" I asked.

"No," he said immediately. "I was wondering if you could… come."

My head snapped up. "What?"

"I know it's last minute. But I was thinking about what you said. That we won't know unless we try. And maybe if Josie sees us, sees that I'm not alone." His voice halted. "And more importantly, if she sees how you are with Olive, I think she'll stick with her plan to go with Micah."

I glanced back at the house, blowing out some air through

puffed cheeks. I chewed on my thumbnail for a second while my thoughts raced at breakneck speed.

"When will she be there?" I asked.

"Around eight. I know it's late, and it's asking a lot, but…" Beckett paused. "I think this is the best place to start. If she doesn't buy it, or tonight fails, then we have no reason to involve your family at all."

"Oh, she'll believe us," I said. "I refuse to consider any other option."

We'd convince the baby mama. We'd convince my family. We'd convince everyone.

"Okay. But…if we don't, then the fallout is minimal at this point."

My almost husband was not going to get away with this half-ass belief in us.

Everyone would believe us because dammit, I said so.

"If that's the kind of pep talk you give your team, I'd hate to be in that locker room at halftime," I told him.

He muttered something, but I couldn't understand it. But the grumbly, annoyed tone had me grinning nonetheless.

"I'll be there before eight," I said. "And Beckett, you better get your game face on because I'm not failing anything."

I glanced down because ripped-knee work site jeans, my steel-toed boots, and a black-and-red-plaid shirt over a plain white tank wasn't exactly what I would've chosen to wear when meeting my fake husband's friendly ex of a baby mama, but I was nothing if not flexible.

If my arms hadn't been loaded down with samples in a big cardboard box, I would've taken a few more minutes to admire Beckett's place upon arrival. His porch was big—incredible space for chairs and a swing, some big planters. And the land was beautiful—mature trees tucked next to the house, lush green grass and big flowering bushes.

But the weight of the box was clumsy, and it sort of felt like my shoulders were about to fall out of the socket, so my only option to announce my arrival at Beckett's door was a good swift kick to the solid wood surface with my steel-toed boots.

He swung the door open, appraising me with wide eyes. "You look…"

"A mess, I know." I let him take the box from my grip, and I blew out a quick breath as I studied the room in front of me. "But give me ten minutes and a brush, and I promise I won't scare Josie away."

He cleared his throat. "I was going to say different. Every time I see you, it's like a new version of Greer Wilder."

That had me grinning. "Yes, there are a few of those, depending on which hat I'm wearing for the day."

"And today's hat?" he asked, setting the box on the floor by the front door.

"Jobsite dictator," I said absently, studying the bones of the room. "Making changes and breaking the hearts of every man in the room who thought the plans were finalized."

There was a large open kitchen, a massive island with a sink in the center. Wooden beams stained in a warm brown stretched along the peaked roof. The cabinets were slightly outdated, as were the floors, but everything was clean and light and comfortable. The furniture was big and solid, everything in a dark, soft-looking leather.

"Nice," I told him.

The fireplace in the middle of the room was made from large rocks with jagged edges in varying shades of gray.

He needed some rugs and throw blankets, maybe some artwork on the wall to soften it up, but it wasn't terrible. It simply looked—for better or worse—like a man who didn't care much for decorating put it all together.

I hummed. "Would you ever consider painting your trim?"

He blinked. "What's wrong with how it is now?"

"Nothing," I said honestly. "But once I'm done with Olive's room, believe me, the rest of this place will need a freshening up." I patted his arm. "Trust me. I'm very good at my job."

"Speaking of Olive's room." He ran a hand through his hair. "She's upstairs getting pajamas on after her bath. Do you want to see the space?"

Hands on my hips, I turned to study him. "Not yet. First, I need to..." I gestured vaguely to my face and hair.

"Right." He showed me down a hallway past the kitchen. "My bedroom is in there. There's a brush in the drawer below the sink."

His bedroom was immaculate. The bed, large and centered in

the room, was covered in crisp white linens, made with military precision. On his nightstand was a charging cord, a lamp, and a picture of Olive—the only personal touch in the entire space.

It didn't escape my notice that he was doing a lot for Olive to have a space that she loved, but Beckett didn't seem to put the same thought process into his own bedroom.

Our bedroom? I wondered.

Was that where I'd sleep?

My stomach went weightless at the thought—me and him and beds and how this would all work—but like every other unanswered question, I slotted it somewhere in the middle of the ever-growing list.

His bathroom was much of the same. A big glass-enclosed shower that could use some updated hardware and a double vanity that desperately needed some new light fixtures. But the floors were fine and so were the counters and cabinets.

I brushed my hand over the edge of the countertop, trying to imagine us dancing around each other in the mornings. The clear glass shower doors were so very, very clear, and I had to blink away. My eyes landed on the mirror.

I studied my reflection with a grimace.

"This," I said, plucking sawdust out of my ponytail, "will not do."

Five minutes later, I'd washed the jobsite grime off my face, slipped on a fresh coat of mascara, my hair was brushed back into a low bun, and my plaid shirt was tied around my waist to hide the smears of dirt on my ass.

Beckett didn't comment on my appearance when I joined him in the kitchen, but his eyes tracked over me in a way that left a trail of warmth over my skin.

That is why I was early.

Without giving him any warning of what I was going to do, I let my eyes wander in the same way. He was casual today too, wearing dark track pants and a soft-looking gray T-shirt that hugged his biceps and broad chest.

"What?" he asked.

"Were you affectionate with Josie?" I asked, eyes lingering on his arms. He shifted them over his chest, clearly uncomfortable with my pointed perusal.

"I...no. Not really." He cleared his throat, and I let my gaze snag there too. What a nice throat he had. "Greer, what are you doing?"

"Favorite food?"

He blew out a harsh breath. "Grilled cheese."

I smiled. "Fancy grilled cheese or regular?"

Beckett was so off-kilter. He blinked a few times. "Both."

"How long did you and Josie try?" I paused. "After she got pregnant with Olive."

He scrubbed a hand over his jaw. "I don't know. A month. Maybe two."

My eyes moved over his lips. The shadow of stubble on his jaw.

"Greer," he practically growled.

"Siblings?"

Completely bewildered, he shook his head.

"I have a lot. You know that, though. Four brothers, two sisters, one sister-in-law." I walked a bit closer, trailing my hand over the edge of the counter. "Biggest pet peeve?"

"People assuming my daughter is stupid because she doesn't talk much. And drivers who don't use their blinker."

Goodness. I fought the smile threatening to grow, not because what he said was funny, but he was so earnest, so damn serious, I could already imagine him taking on every person standing in Olive's way.

"You and Josie went on dates? Things like that?"

He dipped his chin to his chest. "I suppose."

"Favorite color?"

Beckett didn't hesitate this time, looking a bit more comfortable with the constant barrage of questions. "Blue." He paused. "Should I be asking you the same stuff?"

"No." I took another step closer, studying his chest and arms. "Josie won't worry about whether you know this stuff about me," I said. "But if she's even slightly protective, she'll want to trust that I know you."

That seemed to trip him up. "I don't know if she will be or not. I've never… I haven't dated anyone since her."

My eyebrows popped up in surprise. "Really?"

"I only cared about Olive. And my job."

I nodded slowly. The picture was coming together. Men like Beckett—conscientious and steady and solemn—were often the guys who flew under the radar. I'd never sought them out, and maybe that was where I always got it wrong in my past relationships.

Maybe I was about to find a whole new specimen that had gone previously undetected.

*The good guy.*

"And it just…didn't work between the two of you."

His eyes held steady to mine. "No."

Just that.

No.

He gave me no other explanation. No further information.

Curiosity curled under my ribs, and I tamped it down ruthlessly. Now was not the time to indulge it. I'd have plenty of time for that.

Time ran down, bringing Josie's arrival closer and closer, and there was only one other thing I truly worried about.

Slowly, I nodded. "Okay."

With a deep breath, I walked straight up to him. He dropped his arms just before I buried my face into his chest and wrapped my arms tight around his waist. Beckett froze, arms out wide.

Oh. Oh yes. Okay then.

He smelled *so* good. And he felt even better than that.

He was warm, so very solid, what with all the muscles and skin and muscles.

Maybe I could still get butterflies from a nice body, despite what I'd always thought.

"Greer?" He'd yet to drop his arms, and when I imagined what we must look like, I smiled.

"Put your hands on my body, Beckett," I said calmly. "Because if you do that while she's here, or if you look like I electrocuted you when I'm just trying to get a hug from the man I'm supposedly madly in love with, we are in a world of trouble."

I had to fight the instinct to melt into his body because we had *perfect* height proportions. Without heels, I could set my head comfortably against his shoulder, my mouth only slightly lower than his.

If we were to kiss.

Eventually, we would, of course. There was no getting fake married without a little kissing, but we weren't ready for that now.

There was a moment when I worried he wouldn't do it, but then in the next breath, Beckett's hands splayed wide along my back, smoothing along the length of my spine.

One palm came to rest along the back of my neck, and I blew out a slow breath to steady my racing heart. His fingers brushed the skin just under my hairline, and I could feel the hammering of his pulse where my forehead rested on his neck.

"Good," I managed unsteadily.

I pulled my face back to look up, and Beckett's face was serious. Full of questions. Full of intent.

"I didn't think about this," he admitted. His thumb brushed along the edge of my jaw. The movement surprised me, unprompted as it was. Like he simply wanted to know what my skin felt like. "And I should have."

"Daddy?"

Her voice was hardly above a whisper, but it was loud enough in the quiet room that we both heard.

Slowly, I extricated myself from Beckett's embrace, turning with a sheepish smile for Olive. She had a red brush gripped in her hand and a wide-eyed curiosity stamped all over her face.

"Hi, Olive," I said.

Beckett's eyes caught mine, color high in his cheeks. "Ready for your hair?" he asked.

She nodded, skipping over to a stool at the island. She handed him the brush, and Beckett handled it with ease, pulling it in careful strokes through her wet hair.

"Braids tonight, sweet pea?" he asked.

Olive nodded, closing her eyes, and I was absolutely destroyed watching his big hands maneuver her hair into two plaits on either side of her head. He pulled two small hair ties out of his front pocket and wrapped them deftly on the ends of her braids.

I had to roll my lips together because this was about the hottest thing I'd ever seen any man do, and I saw a Magic Mike live show in Vegas once upon a time, so that was saying something.

"Is that a butterfly on your pajamas?" I asked.

Olive's eyes shyly darted up to mine, her fingers playing with the small white, gauzy wings that decorated her soft pink pajama dress.

"Have you ever seen a swallowtail butterfly?" I asked. "It's got big wings with black on the edges and pretty yellow markings."

Her eyes brightened, but she didn't answer.

I pulled my phone out of my back pocket and started scrolling through my camera roll. Beckett watched me with careful eyes as he finished up her second braid.

Turning the screen toward Olive, I made sure to give her plenty of space. "I took this picture today when I was at work. It landed on my car while I was eating lunch."

She fought a smile as she stared at the picture, eyes darting up to mine and back to the photo.

"Maybe we could try to find one," I told her.

Olive set the phone on the counter, and without holding eye contact, she allowed the tiniest nod.

Beckett's gaze snapped to mine, and I grinned.

That's when the knock sounded at the door, about ten minutes earlier than expected.

Through the glass, I could see a pretty, petite brunette and a tall redheaded man. She was staring at me with a polite, curious smile on her face, and I straightened, letting out a slow exhale as I did.

Olive hopped off her stool and ran to greet her mom.

"We're a little early," Josie said apologetically, picking up Olive as she wrapped her arms around her mom's neck. "I wanted to say good night to her first."

Beckett smiled easily. "No problem."

He joined me by the island, his shoulder brushing mine. Our eyes met and held.

Here goes nothing.

Josie gave me a cautious smile. "I'm sorry, I didn't know

anyone else would be here. I'm Josie, and this is my fiancé, Micah."

The man next to her gave me a friendly smile, and I returned it.

"Greer Wilder," I said.

Before Beckett could say anything further, Olive lifted her head and whispered something to her mom, just loudly enough that everyone could hear.

"Miss Greer and Daddy were hugging in the kitchen," she said.

Josie's eyes widened.

Beckett exhaled a quiet laugh, his eyes darting over to mine incredulously.

Micah smothered a grin. "Well… I guess someone let the cat out of the bag first."

"Really?" Josie asked Beckett. "Are you two…?"

Beckett slid his arm around my waist. "I was going to tell you tonight."

Her smile was immediate and relieved. "Oh Beckett, it's about time," she said with a laugh. "How did you two meet?"

"My brother," I told her. "He plays with Beckett." Then I nudged Beckett in the stomach. "He hired me to help fix the most boring little girl's room I've ever seen in my life, and we just…clicked."

Beckett's hand tightened on my waist as Josie watched us with undisguised glee. "Oh thank goodness, that room is horrible. You're an interior designer?"

I nodded. "I brought some samples if you want to give me

any input based on what Olive likes." Then I winked at the little girl. "I might have some butterflies in there if you'd like to help too, Olive."

Olive nodded against her mom's neck. Josie's eyes actually filled with tears. She slapped a hand over her mouth. "I'm sorry," she said behind her fingers. "I didn't expect to get so emotional about this."

Beckett dropped his chin to his chest, and only I was close enough to hear his relieved sigh. "Thank you," he breathed.

Taking a chance, I tilted up and placed a featherlight kiss against his cheek.

I didn't look at his face as I walked toward Josie and Olive, or as I picked up the box of samples and took a seat on the couch to show them some of my ideas.

But I felt him staring at me the entire time.

# CHAPTER 6

# Beckett

"Why is Parker looking at you like that?" Reyes asked, leaning in close but saying it loudly enough that everyone in the immediate vicinity could hear him.

The man in question, sitting in front of his locker as we all showered after running some drills, was glaring mightily in my direction.

I sighed. "Because he's trying to provoke me."

"My *sister*," Parker said. "I haven't seen you show any interest in any woman since I've met you, and you have to go for my sister."

Reyes whistled under his breath. "Got it."

I scratched the side of my jaw. "Feeling overly protective, Parker?"

He huffed a laugh. "Not for you. I think Greer is going to eat you up and spit you out, and then I'm going to have to deal with your mopey ass. You'll stop working as hard, and you won't catch for shit, and we'll lose all our games, all because my sister broke your heart."

There'd be no breaking of anyone's heart, not that I could explain that to Parker. I gave him a hard look. "Do I look like the kind of guy who'd stop doing my job if that happens?"

Reyes snapped a towel at Parker's thigh, and he yelped. "Leave him alone. Maybe Coleman needed to get laid, and now he won't be so serious all the time."

"My *sister*," Parker reiterated, snatching at the towel. Our QB laughed, snapping at him again.

Roberts, one of the offensive linemen, ambled up, a towel around his waist and another over his neck. "Your sister is hot, Wilder. You know I got a girl, but"—he shook his head—"she's got those legs and the dark eyes and those perfect—"

"Enough," I growled. Something under my chest roared at the way he was talking about her. I'd never been one of those guys—who enjoyed the picking apart of a woman like her only good attributes were the physical ones—but hearing him talk about Greer that way had me clenching my fists.

Parker noticed.

He grinned, the first crack I'd seen in him since we'd met at the facility that morning. When the grin faded, he turned to Roberts. "Better watch out, Robbo, Beckett might not like you as much if you talk about his girl like that."

She wasn't my girl. Not really.

I was just…borrowing her for a while.

"Who says I liked him before this?" I asked.

Roberts laughed, shoving at my shoulder as he walked past. I smiled because I liked him just fine.

Reyes and Roberts started talking, and I felt Parker's eyes on me. He tugged a shirt over his head, raking a hand through his shower-damp hair, and then pinned me with another unreadable look.

"You got something to say, then say it," I said easily.

He shrugged, settling back into his seat so he could keep studying me. "Just trying to picture you two together," he answered.

Something uncomfortable spiked in my stomach because this was exactly my fear.

Josie and Micah had warmed to her immediately, spending a couple of hours at my place the night before while we talked through Josie's reservations—and how long she'd struggled with the idea of me doing this alone when I'd never not had her and Micah around for backup.

Neither of us wanted to bring a judge into the situation, and that's what would need to happen if she decided to take Olive to London.

And it was clear that Micah would respect Josie's decision to stay, even if he'd miss his wife for the year he was gone.

But I couldn't deny the power of Josie being able to see Greer there in the house with me. It made a difference.

They talked at length about Olive's bedroom, and Greer asked a lot of questions about my daughter that clearly pleased Josie. She caught my eye numerous times, just to give me a relieved smile.

But they were so focused on Olive in this equation, not necessarily how Greer and I were together.

Parker, however, did not have that issue.

"I know I'm not her usual type," I told him.

He snorted. "No."

I chose my words carefully—I hated lying. It was the worst part about this entire thing.

"Sometimes that doesn't matter, though," I told him. I pulled my clean shirt on, tossing the towel from my shower into the laundry container just past the bench where he was sitting. "You ever met someone who's just…a game changer?"

Parker sat back a little at the gravity of my words. "Game changer," he repeated slowly.

"Yeah." I pushed my dirty clothes into my duffel and shook my head. "I never have before. And I don't think it has to make sense, or fit into whatever definition of right I held prior to meeting her." I set my hands on my hips and faced him fully. "I think that's your sister for me, Parker. She's a game changer in my life."

"You're serious."

I nodded slowly. "Yeah, I am."

Reyes and Roberts had quieted, shamelessly eavesdropping on our conversation.

"Didn't you meet up with her, like, once?" he asked.

"More than once," I told him. Enough of the truth that I could let the words out without feeling like I might choke on them. "And"—I glanced at my watch—"if I don't leave here in the next five minutes, I'll be late meeting her for lunch."

Parker swiped a hand over his face, shaking his head slightly. "When's she taking you to meet the family? Because I know she'll do that soon, if she views you the same way."

I smiled a little. "Soon. In the next couple of days, I believe."

"Shit," he muttered. "This is actually happening."

I exhaled a laugh. "Any words of wisdom before I head in there?"

Parker swallowed heavily, not answering right away, and I thought about what Greer told me, about why he was avoiding home—a scared boy who didn't want to lose his dad.

"Tell them I said hi," he managed. His jaw was tight when he glanced up at me, but I could tell he meant it. Then he grinned. "And don't let Poppy scare you off."

"Which one is Poppy again?"

He smiled softly. "My youngest, pain-in-the-ass sister."

"She hot too?" Roberts asked in a dramatic whisper.

Parker was off the bench, shoving at him with a laugh, and the two tussled good-naturedly.

I blew out a slow breath. It felt a lot like crossing over our second big hurdle.

There was only one left. And to prep for that required a picnic lunch halfway between my work and hers.

―――

Greer was waiting when I pulled up, head down, rifling through a giant takeout bag that was sitting on the picnic table next to her. Instead of sitting on the bench, she was on the surface of the table, her sneaker clad feet on the bench.

At the sound of my vehicle, she lifted her head, smiling widely as she pushed her aviator sunglasses up into all her dark hair. We picked this spot because it was quiet, set off the road, and neither of us would have to spend too much time in the car.

These were the kinds of logistics we had to figure out, now that Josie was on board.

"Nice spot," I told her.

She glanced around the park, humming appreciatively. "It is. It would probably be a nice easy hike too, if you ever wanted to take Olive."

I took a seat next to her on the table, pulling my ball cap a bit lower over my forehead when a young family passed us, the dad giving me a wide-eyed look of excitement. He whispered something to his wife as they passed, and she quickly aimed her phone in my direction to snap a picture. They put their heads together and chatted excitedly.

Greer breathed out a laugh. "You're lucky I'm used to this part because of my brothers," she said lightly.

"Would it make you back out if you weren't?"

"Nah," she said easily. She pulled plates, two water bottles, and a covered bowl of cut-up fruit out of the never-ending bag. "Besides, I know firsthand that it doesn't really happen as much as people would assume."

I nodded. "I usually get something along the lines of, *do I know you?*"

She laughed. "Exactly."

While Greer turned, getting two more containers out of the bag, I settled my hands between my knees. "Parker asked when I was gonna meet the family."

"Did he now?"

"He said if you were serious about me, you wouldn't wait long for that to happen." I glanced sideways. Her face was still hidden while she got our lunch settled. She handed me a takeout container. The top was clear, and when I saw what was inside, I laughed. "Really?"

Greer grinned. "Seemed appropriate."

I opened the top, peering at the contents. "Looks pretty good."

She picked out the first half of her grilled cheese—identical to mine—and took a big bite. She hummed, the sound lifting the hairs on the back of my neck.

"It's amazing," she said, after she swallowed her first bite. "And believe me, if you'd driven over to my apartment, a chef I am not, so you still would have gotten takeout."

At the first taste, I closed my eyes, sighing happily. It was delicious.

When I opened my eyes, she was watching me with an amused smile on her face. "Does that mean it passes the Beckett Coleman grilled cheese test?"

"Yes." The sandwich was gone in about five bites, and I moved on to the fruit. "Speaking of your apartment," I said.

"My lease is up in about a month," she said. "There's no way for me to keep it and not raise suspicion, so I'll move the furniture into storage—my parents have plenty of outbuildings. But sometimes I will stay with them on the weekends, especially if Tim is…" Her voice trailed off. "If they need my help," she amended.

"Of course." I poked at a grape with the tines of my fork. "I don't expect you to be a full-time caretaker for Olive. I have a nanny who helps out during the season. Josie knows and likes her."

Greer nodded. "So…what do we do when Josie comes back?" she asked lightly. "Big dramatic breakup where I storm out and you're finally free of me."

The words were meant in jest. And there was a smile on her face when she said them.

But the smile faded the longer I sat there and studied her.

"I didn't mean it like that," she said in a quiet voice. "I guess this is the part that I can't really envision, you know? We're going to spend all this time making people believe that we got swept up in something romantic and huge, and then…"

"Then it's over," I added. I rubbed my forehead. "I know. Olive will…" I paused. "It'll be hard for her. It always is when something big changes, especially because she likes you."

Greer's cheeks flushed a pretty pink. "We'll figure it out. I don't think we need all the answers right now."

I exhaled a quiet laugh. That was the difference between myself and my blushing bride. I needed to know everything—because how else could you be certain you were making the right decision? That you were taking the correct path?

"I won't abandon her," Greer added. "I hope you know that."

"Thank you." I set down the bowl of fruit. She'd hardly eaten any of her lunch since we started talking. "Not hungry?"

She shrugged one shoulder. "Not really. I think I just want to get this night at my parents' over with, you know? It went great with Josie and Micah, but they don't know me." She smiled. "It's a whole different ball game when you're trying to convince the people who know you best."

I tried to imagine a house full of people like that and couldn't.

"Can't really say I know what that's like," I admitted.

Her eyes were soft, her words tentative. "No family?"

I shook my head. "Parents have been gone a long time. No siblings." I glanced at her. "Just me and Olive."

"And me now," she added.

My chest warmed at the easy way she inserted herself into our family picture. "And you."

Greer gently nudged my shoulder against hers. "I hope you're ready for the rest of the Wilder family, Beckett. They're gonna love you."

CHAPTER 7

# Beckett

**Nothing was going right.**

I was late, and I hated being late.

Olive spilled all over her dress, and that set off a tantrum that I hadn't seen from her in months. It took close to an hour to calm her down and get her settled into the car so I could return her to Josie's.

The domino effect of that was that I couldn't pick up Greer the way we'd planned, and I'd be showing up at her parents' house alone.

She'd been understanding when I texted her. I didn't even have the emotional bandwidth to call after I dropped Olive off at Josie's because all the unexpected stress of my afternoon and the expected stress of my meeting the Wilders was compounding into one epically bad mood for my drive east to the small town of Sisters.

I'd been there once before—for a charity event with Parker

and a few other teammates. But his parents hadn't been able to come, so I'd never met them.

Now I was going to walk into a house full of people by myself—Greer's warnings of how loud and chaotic it always was meant I wouldn't be taking Olive—and pretend that I was head over heels in love with someone I hardly knew.

"Fuck," I muttered darkly, a glance at my dashboard clock showing a time that had my knuckles tightening on the steering wheel. Sisters was a two-hour drive from my house, and even though Greer assured me it was fine that she temporarily relocated from her apartment downtown, the distance didn't make events like this very convenient.

The sun was still in the sky as I turned onto their tree-lined driveway, which wound back through acres of wooded property. Set out of sight from the road and in the middle of a massive clearing in the fir trees was a sprawling two-story wood cabin.

From a stone chimney in the middle of the roof was a friendly curl of smoke even though it was a mild spring day. The open porch wrapped all the way around the house, bikes lined up against the logs, and chairs grouped for conversation between the tall windows.

It was a well-loved home, that much was obvious. Pulling my car next to Greer's, I let out a deep breath, trying to get a handle on why this felt so much different from when Greer bulldozed into my house two nights earlier and had Josie eating out of her hand in less than ten minutes.

Maybe it was because I was supposed to arrive with her,

allowing some of her contagious energy to pull the focus off me. Now, there was no distraction.

Just me walking into their home, ready to tell the biggest lie of my life.

Yes, I love your daughter, and yes, I want to marry her.

My hands tightened on the wheel before I pushed the door open, and I had to pull Olive's face into my mind.

It was the only thing that could get me through this.

She was the only thing that could get me to do this in the first place.

I thought of her as she wailed under the covers, unable to calm herself enough to let me see her.

Lifting my chin, I exited the car and breathed a short sigh of relief when Greer slipped from the front door to meet me on the porch.

"You found it," she said. Her smile—bright and fierce—was like a punch to my chest. She genuinely looked happy to see me, and I couldn't figure out if it was just easier for her to manage this entire thing, or if my soon-to-be wife actually enjoyed my company.

"I'm so sorry I'm late." I scrubbed a hand over my face and exhaled heavily. "I hope you didn't wait to eat until I got here."

With a quick glance over her shoulder, Greer sidled closer. From the inside of the house, it might look like we were kissing, and my stomach tightened at the thought of Greer's lips.

"You look like you're gonna puke," she said quietly, straightening the collar on my shirt. "We run a very casual household here. If someone's hungry, they eat; if they're not, we pile onto the couch and wait. My mom and Poppy are playing a card game, and Tim is watching *SportsCenter* and pretending like he's not falling asleep."

Her hair smelled like something citrusy and sharp and clean. "Poppy is your youngest sister, right? Parker warned me about her."

Greer laughed. "She's the only child they had together after they got married. She's spoiled rotten by every single member of this family, and even though us older siblings complain about it, we'd all stand down a moving train if it meant protecting her." Greer's eyes went a little sad. "She's home a lot these days. Tim's sickness is hardest on her."

"Isn't it hard on all of you?"

Her gaze moved across my face, but eventually, she nodded. "Yeah. I suppose it is. Sometimes I get so caught up in making it easier for everyone else that I forget how much it hurts."

My nerves blew away with just that little touch of honesty between us.

I didn't have to picture Olive or her tears or all the battles she faced that I couldn't take away. With a quick glance into the house, I saw a thin, balding man dozing in a big brown recliner, and it was enough of a reminder that my reason for doing this wasn't the only one that mattered.

The truth, I thought with a sudden blinding thought. "What if we…" My voice trailed off. "What if we tell them the truth?"

Her face went slack with shock. "What?"

I shook my head. "Not the full truth. What if we tell your parents about Olive?" I asked. The thought grew and grew until it was full and solid and right.

Greer's eyes went speculative, the gears in her mind shifting right along with my own. "That's not a horrible idea," she said slowly. "And Josie?"

I sucked in a quick breath. "We tell Josie about your dad. They both get some truth. If it's the one thing we do, the only thing we do, we stick to the truth as much as possible. With each other, too. We need honesty wherever we can get it, Greer."

Her pulse fluttered wildly at the base of her throat. Then she nodded slowly. "Okay. Let's do it."

"What's your favorite food?" I asked her.

Even though the question came out rough, my voice ragged and tired and not at all how I wanted it to be, Greer exhaled a short burst of laughter. "Apple pie," she said.

"That's a dessert."

"So?" Her eyes were shining. "Who says dessert can't be your favorite food?"

"But…" I scratched the side of my jaw. "Your favorite food is something you'd have for a meal."

"You've clearly never had leftover pie for breakfast, and it shows." She patted me on the stomach. "I found you just in time, Beckett Coleman."

"In time for what?" I asked, undeniably intrigued by her, unable to resist the pull of her energy.

"To teach you everything I know." There was a glimmer in

her eye as she said it, and she tugged my hand between hers and pulled me into the house.

---

"You're sure I can't get you any more, Beckett?" Sheila Wilder asked.

"No, thank you, ma'am." I settled a hand over my stomach. "If I eat any more, I'll be hurtin'."

She smiled. "Ma'am? I don't hear that very often from men your age."

I nodded. "I'm a Southern boy at heart. My parents lived in Tennessee until I was ten, then they needed the dry climate of Arizona for my dad's health. I've lost a bit over the years, but it still comes out every now and then."

Tim stretched his arm out behind Poppy's chair. "They still live down there?"

"No, sir. My parents passed away a few years ago. They were older when they had me, so they still lived a good long life."

Greer took a slow sip of her water, eyeing me over the rim of the glass. The whole dinner had gone amazingly. Tim and Sheila were gracious and friendly, Poppy was funny and energetic, much like her brother and sister, and conversation flowed easily through our meal.

But the shift in topic, and the truthful answer behind my quiet branch of my family tree, settled a cloud over the table.

"I'm sorry to hear that," he said. Tim had the slightly gaunt look of a man not in full health, but he still walked just fine on his own, he ate a full meal, and he proved to be exactly the kind of dad I'd always wanted to be to Olive.

Poppy set her drink down and pinned me with a guileless look. "So you and Greer met because of Parker, right?"

"That's right." I set my arm along the back of Greer's chair. "I can't say he's too happy about this development, but…"

Sheila smiled, as did Tim.

"And how long have you two been together?" Poppy asked.

Greer slid her leg forward, and I felt the snap of impact when she kicked her sister underneath the table. Poppy rolled her lips together, narrowing her eyes at Greer.

"Leg slipped, sorry," Greer said, smiling sweetly. "You okay, Pops?"

Her sister's gaze narrowed. "Oh, I'm great."

I swallowed hard.

"We haven't been together long," Greer said, a smooth, quick recovery from the under-the-table violence. Then she looked at me with a soft smile and a happy glow in her eyes that looked so damn real that I had to remind myself it wasn't. "Sometimes you just know."

"Know *what*?" Poppy asked.

Sheila simply rolled her eyes. "Beckett, I convinced myself that my kids would stop fighting when they became adults, but here we are, and I still feel like a referee half the damn time."

"You ever think about having more kids?" Poppy asked. "I'm sure men have a biological clock too, right? I mean, you're… thirty-two? Thirty-three?"

Tim sighed. "Ignore her, Beckett. We all do."

Greer snapped her foot forward again.

"Ouch," Poppy cried.

"Stop asking rude questions," Greer hissed.

Sheila came from the kitchen with a large plate in her hands. Greer gasped when she saw the blue ceramic pie plate.

"Is that…?"

Sheila set it down with a wink. "Apple pie."

"I love eating at home." She sighed.

I smiled. The ends of her hair tickled my arm since she was wearing it down tonight. I leaned in toward her ear. "You can have my piece if you want," I whispered.

She smiled. "If you don't try this, you'll regret it for the rest of your life. Trust me."

"It's true," Tim said. He patted his nonexistent belly. "My wife makes the best Dutch apple pie in the entire Pacific Northwest, Beckett."

Sheila served me the first piece.

"So it's your fault Greer likes to eat pie for breakfast," I said.

At my smooth delivery, Greer gave me a secretive smile.

Poppy watched us with a speculative gleam in her eye. Maybe it should've made me nervous, but I was enjoying myself too much to care.

Sheila laughed. "Guilty as charged. I'm afraid she learned that from me. I start the day after Thanksgiving every year with a piece of leftover pie."

I waited until she'd served everyone and sat down with her

own piece before using my fork to scoop off a large bite. When the flavors exploded on my tongue, I moaned appreciatively. "I take it back," I told Greer. "I'm not sharing."

They all laughed, Greer leaning into my shoulder as she covered her mouth.

When the table was cleared and Poppy helped Sheila with the dishes in the kitchen, Greer and I sat out on the front porch with Tim. His eyes were closed as he rocked back and forth in the big wooden chair, and I studied Greer's face as she watched her dad.

The love was clear. It didn't matter that he wasn't her biological dad.

Greer looked at him like I looked at Olive.

She'd do anything—moral implications be damned. Quietly, I slid my hand over hers, gripping her fingers. Greer's eyes were glossy with tears, and I watched her force them back by sheer force of will.

"I like you, Beckett," Tim said quietly. His eyes slowly opened, locked unerringly on the place where my hand held hers. "And I like seeing you happy, my sweet Greer."

"You're the only person who calls me sweet," she said, voice light and teasing.

"Maybe." He sighed. "Maybe. But that's because I know you. Do you think she's sweet, Beckett?"

I turned, giving her a frank appraisal, which she met head-on.

"No," I said quietly. "I wouldn't call her sweet."

Her cheeks blushed a pretty pink, but she kept her gaze on mine. "What would you say, then?" she asked.

"She's fearless," I said. "Some people are too afraid to love that way, undaunted by whatever might come next, which might look like sweetness to some. But I just see a big, brave heart."

I blinked away, shocked by what I'd said. Based on how Greer's hands fidgeted under mine, she felt the same way.

When I glanced back at Tim, he was watching us with a small, satisfied smile on his face.

"I like that answer," he murmured. The front door opened, Sheila joining us while Poppy continued to dry dishes in the kitchen.

I squeezed Greer's hand, and when she gave me a questioning look, I nodded.

We'd never find a better time to do it or better circumstances.

"Sir, ma'am," I said to Tim and Sheila, "I know this is going to seem awfully sudden. I'm never a man who does something without thinking it through or without being sure of my next step." I sucked in a deep breath. "Your daughter has spun my world around since I met her. And I think she feels the same way about me."

Greer gave me a soft smile. My heart thundered in my chest when Tim and Sheila exchanged a look.

My voice was strong and steady when I spoke next. "I'd like to marry Greer, if we could have your and your wife's blessing."

Tim's mouth fell open, his brows shooting up on his forehead. Sheila sank down into the chair next to him, like her legs slowly gave out. "You…" He exhaled a shocked burst of air, meeting his wife's eyes briefly. "Holy shit, really?"

"Greer," Sheila breathed.

Greer laughed quietly. "I know how this sounds." She turned her hand over, winding her fingers through mine. "And we know how fast we're moving."

The woman beside me squeezed my hand, passing the proverbial baton.

"I need you both to know something," I said. "About my daughter, and how she plays into this."

And they listened without interruption, their expression varying between sympathy, and understanding, and blatant concern. Weaving that kernel of truth into the conversation helped me look them in the eye.

When I finished, Sheila was covering her mouth with one hand. Tim let out a slow breath.

"You're a good father, Beckett," he said. "No one would ever doubt that. And I know a little about how much a loving parent will sacrifice for their kids." He cleared his throat. "I've got seven adults walking around this earth, and they all have pieces of my heart. I can't get them back, and I wouldn't want to, even if I could."

Sheila wiped away a quiet tear, settling her hand on her husband's back.

"But I don't want my daughter used as a pawn, either," he said quietly.

"I'm not," Greer said. "I promise." She paused, catching my eye for a moment. "It's just speeding up what we already know," she said quietly. "I can't think of any good reason to wait, when I already know I want to marry him."

It was Tim's turn to blink away tears, but his gaze never moved from his daughter's face. One tear slid down his grizzled cheek. "Greer, are you sure?"

She turned and looked at me, nodding slowly. "Sometimes you just know when it's the right thing to do."

It would have been a perfect time to kiss her. In the soft dusk light on her parents' front porch. While I imagined it, my eyes locked onto her mouth. She exhaled shakily, and I tore my gaze from her face.

Tim's hands were folded over his middle, and he shook his head in stunned disbelief. "I did not see tonight ending up this way." Then he smiled. "You'll take care of my girl?" he asked.

One side of my lips ticked up in a lopsided smile. *If it's the one thing we do, the only thing we do, we stick to the truth as much as possible.*

The words came easily when I thought of it like that. "I don't know that Greer needs me to take care of her, but I do know that I need her in my life. That she makes everything just a bit easier when she's around." I cleared my throat. "She gives the best hugs. And her mind is the most terrifyingly incredible thing I've ever seen."

Greer grinned. "Is that your way of saying I scare you?"

"Only a little," I admitted.

Tim let out a happy sort of sound, a hum, a sigh of relief. Slowly, and with only the slightest wince, he pushed himself to standing, extending his hand as he did.

I stood as well, gripping his hand firmly as we shook.

Tim's voice was rough with emotion. "Welcome to the family, Beckett."

CHAPTER 8

# Greer

With the family dinner behind us, we were able to fully pivot into wedding planning mode. But I still had to keep my guard up as I navigated a hundred different conversations. Because the way I imagined it, there would be three family members who'd be the hardest to convince.

Cameron—because I spent the most time with him, and he'd have no problem taking a sledgehammer to any logic that he found flawed (a side effect of being a really good builder meant he had a bloodhound's nose for seeking out the weak spots in any ideas).

Adaline—she was the sister I was closest to, and because we were so close in age, she'd always had the uncanny ability to read my mind. My saving grace in this situation was that her boyfriend, Emmett, had kept her so preoccupied with their shiny new disgustingly perfect romance that I could skimp on some details and she might not call bullshit.

My mom.

The woman who gave birth to me.

Who could take one look at my face and know when I needed a hug or a drink or chocolate or to just cry it out over a good movie.

The same mother who was currently sketching out chair and aisle layouts for a backyard wedding.

"If we line up the chairs this way, you and Dad can come from inside the house and Beckett won't have to see you before the wedding."

Poppy tilted her head. "Are we doing that old-fashioned stuff?"

"No."

"Yes," my mom said at the same time.

She and I traded a look.

When I saw the mom-glint buried deep in the depths of her blue eyes, I held up my hands. That was not a battle worth fighting.

I'd lose, judging by the look in her eye. I'd lose painfully, too.

"Fine," I said. "No looky beforehand." I paused. "Even though it ruins the ability to take pictures before the wedding so the reception can start right away, but whatever," I muttered under my breath.

Mom ignored me, a satisfied smile covering her face as she tapped her finger on the paper in front of us. "Yup. This is it. Your brothers can string patio lights from the trees and use those poles your dad has out in the barn to anchor them behind the chairs. I'll rent a couple of long tables for the reception."

Poppy snatched a piece of blueberry muffin off the plate in front of her. "You know what's weird? Adaline has been in Florida with Emmett for a couple of weeks, and she missed, like, your entire relationship."

I narrowed my eyes. Maybe I should have added Poppy to my list.

"Do you have a point?"

She grinned. "Nope. Just that she's gonna die when she comes back, and I can't wait to hold it over her head that I knew something first. That never happens."

Mom sighed.

Poppy finished the muffin. "So why can't you wait to get married until after the baby mama leaves? That's what I don't understand. Aren't you kind of stealing her thunder by going down the aisle first?"

Was it over the top to keep kicking Poppy under the table? Maybe I'd always keep her within reach of my leg so I could nail the shit out of her calf every time she asked an annoyingly rational question.

"We're not stealing her thunder," I said, the very picture of patient big sister who was not at all feeling the urge to muzzle their little sister. "Josie is only coming to the ceremony for Olive, and then they'll head back home. It's not like Beckett and I are inviting all the same guests that Josie and Micah will have at their ceremony. It's basically our family, and that's it."

"And she doesn't find it weird that you're just popping out of the woodwork?"

The fact that Poppy didn't register the absolutely lethal glare I leveled in her direction was staggering. I kept my tone even, though. "Josie and Beckett never really talked about his personal life, so she wasn't surprised that she didn't know about me. They had healthy boundaries in their relationship, and he's…private."

"He's so serious," Poppy said. "I always pictured you with someone outgoing like you."

"He's a gentleman," Mom interjected. "And some of the best relationships come from finding balance between the personalities."

The truth of that snagged on something in the back of my brain, how I'd never felt that balance before, always seeking out men who'd match my energy.

Tim shuffled into the room, snagging a muffin as he passed. "Like me and your mom. I'm the sane one."

My mom clucked her tongue as Poppy and I laughed.

All three of us watched Tim make his way outside.

"He's having a really good week," I commented.

Mom smiled, but I could see the tiredness around her eyes. "He is. I find myself bracing for a bad one after this. I felt like he was exhausted for a solid month over the winter. But he just… finds a way to keep surprising me."

Our family was no stranger to Tim's health problems. His first two bouts with cancer were met with stubborn treatment as soon as his tests came back abnormal. Each one rocked our family in a different way, and each sibling had a different emotional reaction to it.

My stepbrothers lost their mom to cancer when they were young, and the thought of losing their dad too sent shock waves through the foundations of the entire household.

Me and Adaline, along with our oldest brother Erik—who didn't live far from Adaline in Seattle—loved Tim like he was our real dad, but we hadn't already lost one parent to the disease, so it settled differently inside us. Our pain was wrapped up in something else. Just as significant, just as hard to process.

I patted my mom's hand. "I'm sure he'll have a good week for the wedding too," I told her.

Her eyes misted over, and I wished I could will them back for her. That was part of this whole deal. Everything, every conversation, every moment, felt like the last.

Round three of cancer was advanced enough, in enough places in his body, that Tim had made a quick decision to enjoy what was left of his life without harsh treatments sucking out all of his energy.

On the good weeks, like we'd just had, it was easy to forget just how sick he was. That eventually, the bad days would outnumber the good, the tired days would eat away at the rest of them, and the cancer would spread.

Eventually, he wouldn't have any more good days.

Poppy cleared her throat, ready to change the subject at the sudden veer into the heavy emotions. "Who will be able to make it to the ceremony?"

I pulled a notebook in front of me and started counting names.

"Erik and Lydia will be here," I said, referencing my oldest brother and his wife. Then I went down the list by age. "Ian can't swing it with his work schedule, and last-minute flights from London are astronomical. Cameron is a yes. Adaline and Emmett will be here. Parker is coming, thank God." Then I added under my breath, "Because I'd kick his ass if he didn't."

"He's doing his best, Greer," Mom admonished.

I raised an eyebrow, and she wisely dropped it.

"Mom and Dad, obviously. You," I said to Poppy.

"What about family friends?" my sister asked. "Guys from work."

I blew out a harsh breath. "I hadn't thought about it, to be honest. I don't say this to be rude, but most of them probably don't, you know, care."

My mom laughed. Poppy fought a smile. "They care. They've worked with you for years."

In my head, I imagined Wade rolling up to the ceremony in his dirty ball cap and an unlit cigarette hanging from his lips. "I really don't think they do."

"Even Jax?"

She asked it *so* innocently, doodling on the edge of the notebook, eyes firmly planted on the paper.

Mom slid me a look. I rolled my lips together.

"Jax does work with us from time to time," I said slowly. "But he's Cameron's friend. Not mine."

Mom wiped down the counter. "Jax is also…" She paused, searching for the right word.

"Feral?" I added.

"He is not feral," Poppy said. "He just doesn't get out much."

"Or talk," I said. "Or…people."

Mom chuckled.

Poppy's crush on Cameron's best friend was well-known within our family. Jax, however, had no freaking clue because considering the fact that he was rounding past thirty-five and Poppy had just turned twenty-two, he'd rather chop his arm off than give her the wrong impression.

"Jax will not be there," I told her gently. "This is pretty much immediate family only."

Poppy deflated a little but gave me a tiny nod as she kept doodling.

"What about flowers?" Mom asked. "We haven't talked about what you want, honey."

"Anything that's in season is good with me," I told her. "We can grab some bouquets from the farmers' market the morning of. I have a white dress in my closet that will work just fine anyway. I'm keeping it pretty simple."

My mom's eyes tracked over my face, and my chest clenched at the questions I saw buried there.

"What?" I asked. I was incapable of not asking.

"I know you care about your wedding, Greer," she said softly. "And if this is happening too quickly because of whatever Beckett has going on, maybe you feel like you're not able to be as opinionated as you normally would."

Poppy snorted. "Greer's always opinionated. The only way she keeps her mouth shut is if someone has duct tape over it."

I scratched my nose with my middle finger, and she simply smiled.

The front door to the house opened, Cameron stomping his boots to rid them of mud from the backyard. "Hey, Ma. Anything to eat?"

I rolled my eyes. "Is that all you guys think about?"

"That and how to survive working with you every day, yes." He ruffled Poppy's hair. "Still not sure on the second one, if you were wondering."

"I wasn't," I muttered.

He kissed Mom on the cheek, snagging a blueberry muffin and wolfing it down in two bites. "What's this?" he asked with a full mouth.

"Greer's wedding layout," Poppy answered. "I told her we should invite Jax, but she said immediate family only."

Cameron laughed. "Jax would rather pluck his eyeballs out than get dressed up for a wedding." His face got serious, his eyes locked on mine. "Speaking of which, you got a minute? I was going to ask you about your schedule for the next couple of weeks in light of…" He motioned over the papers.

I followed him outside, stretching my arms over my head as the sun hit my face. "It's nice out here."

Cameron stared out at the front yard, then pulled the hat off his head. "Talk to me."

"Well, I'll need a couple of days off around the wedding,

but we're not taking a honeymoon or anything, so I don't think you'll even notice I'm gone."

"Uh-huh. Just a couple of days off?"

"Yeah. The intern is good. And she knows the clients, so she can communicate with them if I'm unreachable, which is highly unlikely." Under his intense eye contact, I shifted uncomfortably. "We'll get married on Saturday, and I'll be back to work on Monday."

"A week from now," he said. "Your wedding."

"Yes."

His eyes were unflinching, and I started getting the distinct feeling that Cameron wasn't actually asking me about taking time off.

It was bound to happen.

And I'd known. I'd known there would be one person who tried to call BS.

Unfortunately for Cameron, someone calling me out on my really good, really well-thought-out plan was like waving a red flag in front of a really pissy bull.

"You got something to say, Cameron?" I asked. "Say it."

"What the actual *fuck* is going on, Greer?" He set his hands on his hips. "Maybe they're caught up in flowers and wedding shit and the fact that your fiancé has a chiseled jaw and big muscles, but I am with you every *single day*, and you never said a word."

I swallowed hard because okay, that was a little bit more aggressive than I'd imagined.

Thank goodness I wasn't intimidated by men who thought they could drop a simple f-bomb and make me back down. I'd worked on construction sites way too long to be swayed by that.

"You don't give our family much credit," I said. "They're not simple, and they aren't impressed by stupid things. They like Beckett. They met him. Saw us together. Which is more than I can say for you. You're just stomping into the room and making really big accusations when you haven't even given him a chance."

Cameron's eyebrows arched slowly. "I haven't accused you of anything, so that's an interesting turn of phrase."

Fuck.

My hands went a little cold, and my heart somersaulted in my chest.

He jabbed a finger in the air. "That. I know that face."

I turned away, blinking rapidly before he got the upper hand in the conversation. "Maybe it's my I'm annoyed that my brother is yelling at me face."

He huffed a laugh. "Please. When you get annoyed that I'm yelling, all you do is yell right back. Threaten to kick me in the nuts. Something like that."

His face softened, and somehow that made things so much worse. My brother was big and strong and gruff, and he was one of my best friends. I spent more time with him than anyone else in my family. And together—with Adaline—we'd promised years ago to stay close to take care of this family that our parents had built.

I wished Beckett was with me. It seemed so much easier to face down the reality of what we were doing when it was the two of us.

But right now, I had my brother looking me in the eye demanding the truth.

No matter what plan we had, what justification we'd managed to come up with, I wasn't sure I could lie when someone was bringing me their naked disbelief.

The longer I stayed quiet, staring out at the trees, the more I proved Cameron's suspicions right.

He ran a hand through his golden-brown hair, then muttered a curse. "Greer," he bit out. "You keep standing there, and I'm only going to assume the worst."

I pinched my eyes shut. "You cannot tell anyone what I'm about to tell you," I whispered.

His frame went still as stone.

I turned to Cameron with pleading eyes. "Cameron, you swear to me that you won't say anything."

Cameron slicked his tongue over his teeth, weighing the massive thing I'd just asked of him. He nodded. "On my mother's grave."

My shoulders slumped in relief. "Okay. Come on, let's go for a walk. We need a little bit of privacy for this one."

## CHAPTER 9

# Beckett

**GREER**
Are you home?

**ME**
Yeah. What's up?

**She didn't answer right away, and because I had to get** Olive's bags ready for Josie to pick her up, I set my phone down on the kitchen counter and didn't think much of it.

The knock on the front door came less than five minutes later.

Greer breezed into the house when I pulled open the door. "You're…here," I said.

She was pacing the kitchen, one hand tore at the bright red tie holding her hair together, and Greer shoved a hand through the tangled mess that fell around her shoulders. "I know I should have called or something."

I glanced toward the back deck, verifying that Olive was still coloring at the outside table. "What happened?"

"My brother Cameron knows," she said. She stopped, rolled her lips together and widened her eyes to an almost comically apologetic degree.

"What do you mean?"

"He *knows*. While my mom and sister and I were doing some planning for the ceremony, he pulled me outside and did not hesitate to call me out on what we were doing." She crossed her arms tightly over her chest, and I swore I could see her entire frame vibrate from the energy pulsing into the room. "He was swearing, and then I didn't back down because I hate it when he swears at me."

"What did he say to you?" I asked, voice quiet and dangerous.

Greer stopped, eyebrows popping high on her forehead when she registered my tone. A smile, slow and sweet, broke open across her face, and she took a step closer. "Nothing I don't hear on the jobsite every single day I'm at work," she said. "He was just…thrown. And he knew something else was going on."

My jaw clenched. "So you told him."

"I'm sorry. I know this isn't what we decided, but Cameron knows me so well. Maybe even better than any of my other siblings." She deflated, slumping against the island, rubbing a weary hand over her forehead. "When it came down to it, I couldn't lie to him. He's the first person to look me in the eye and say something wasn't adding up."

The ramifications had my stomach tight with nerves.

If Cameron told anyone else in the family, they'd step in. They'd stop the ceremony.

And I'd be back at square one.

Greer wouldn't be able to give her dad the thing he wanted.

Suddenly, both of those felt like equally horrible options. I'd met him now. Looked him in the eye as I shook his hand, so I didn't particularly want to let Tim down either.

On the back deck, I could see Olive's legs swinging happily as she hunched over her new coloring book.

"Now what?" I asked.

Greer pulled one of the stools away from the island and perched on the edge, fixing her hair with a few simple swoops of the hair tie.

"He promised me he wouldn't tell," she said next.

"And you believe him?"

"Yes." There was no hesitation. "I told him everything. It felt…easier, I guess."

I swiped a hand over my mouth as I studied her.

"What about your other siblings?"

"Adaline called me the other day," Greer said. "She was shocked, of course. But when I told her about you and Olive, she…" Greer paused, giving a slight shake of her head. "She won't question it."

"This is the sister who lives in Seattle?"

Greer nodded. "She's engaged, but she and Emmett decided on a long engagement while they build their house." She laughed. "Isn't that the biggest irony of all? My parents have a daughter with a ring on her finger, but she's in no rush to go down the aisle."

"I'm gonna need a flow chart to memorize your family tree," I told her.

"I know," Greer groaned. "It's nuts. We're not normal in any way. And what's even weirder is how normal it feels to us to have so many kids and so many stories of why we're like this. Why we get in each other's business and worry ourselves sick over what's going on in each other's lives."

Every time she talked about her family, love and affection coloring every single syllable of every single word, I felt the oddest sense of disquiet under my skin. Something that itched in a place where I couldn't scratch.

I wanted to understand her, understand her world and why all of this made sense to her, but the truth was that I couldn't.

"If you trust your brother with this, then I do too," I told her.

I had no other choice.

"Thank you," she said on a relieved exhale. "Maybe it'll help to have someone on our side."

"Our side?" I asked. "It's not a competition."

She conceded that with a nod. "Wrong choice of words." Greer leaned forward like she wanted to take my hand or lay her hands on my arm.

She didn't, though, and settled back in her seated position without doing anything.

Those simple touches felt different underneath the watchful eyes of her family than they did now in my quiet, empty kitchen.

We'd have to navigate this, and so many other things, in only a week.

"Dealing with a big family is..." I paused. "It's not something I'm familiar with. So I'm going to have to take your lead."

Greer scrubbed her hands over her face. "I think this'll be the biggest hurdle. Erik has been away long enough. He won't bat an eye that I'm jumping into something a little..." She waved her hands by her face, and I wasn't entirely sure what it was supposed to mean. "Ian has been gone in London even longer than that, but he can't come home for the wedding. He might be an issue because he's the biggest dick in our entire family." At my incredulous expression, she laughed. "You know what I mean. He has no filter. And he challenges anyone who tries to come into our family." She shrugged. "His total distrust of anyone new is his love language, I suppose."

It was slowly becoming clear to me why Greer was almost impossible to intimidate.

I'd never thought of that as a trait I'd find attractive in a woman, but there was something about her, knowing that no matter who came up against her, she'd never back down easily.

It made me wonder, just for a moment, what she was like in submission.

My hands tightened into fists, and I ruthlessly shoved that thought to the back of my head.

"You have a lot of brothers. Is it too late to back out?"

I didn't mean it as a joke, but she took it as one, laughing delightedly.

"Yes." She tilted her head. "You're not really intimidated by my brothers, are you? You face down linebackers who want to rip your arms off if it would stop you from catching the ball."

I chose my answer carefully. "I'm worried that Cameron knowing would affect you," I said honestly. "Might affect your choice to move forward."

Greer watched me, her eyes taking on a soft, understanding glow that had my skin itching uncomfortably.

"Cameron and I went on a walk today," she said. "I told him the whole story. He's always been a good listener. Cameron and Adaline and I were so close in age when Tim married our mom, less than eighteen months between all three of us." From the counter, she picked up a small fidget toy that Olive used at school, small metal loops in a rainbow pattern. Greer kept it in her hand, mindlessly pushing at the loops while she spoke. "And he's really good at hearing the stuff people don't say. What's underneath their words."

"What did he hear underneath yours?" I asked.

"He asked if I needed help calling everything off." Her gaze was unflinching. "That he'd deal with any fallout with our family if I just needed to…go."

I released a breath through my nose, trying to picture the big strapping builder walking through the woods with my fake fiancée, a concerned brother who immediately knew something was off. He was probably spending that entire walk imagining a circular saw on my balls.

I didn't ask Greer what she said because despite how little I knew her, I trusted her.

With this massive, important thing, I trusted her.

So I didn't do her the disservice of asking her. And when her lips, soft and pink, edged up in a tiny smile, I knew she understood what I was doing.

"He also asked me one other thing," she said absently. "If I'd found someone who was willing to do this for a paycheck, who had no other motivation outside of financial gain, would I have backed out by now?"

My chest clenched.

"He asked me if I was still staying in this because of you." I couldn't read anything in her eyes. It was the first time since I'd met her that her face was completely unreadable. "Because of what you want to do for your daughter."

An invisible vise locked in tight around my ribs, squeezing and squeezing until I fought to take a full breath.

This time, I couldn't stay quiet. "What did you say?"

The question sounded raw and ragged when it came out, a voice that didn't quite sound like my own.

Instead of answering, she nudged her chin up and flipped another question back at me.

"Why is it so important for you?" she asked. "I know you love her. I know that you want more time with her, but most men would not go this far to have primary custody of their daughter when they have a good relationship with their ex."

Before I sat down, I glanced at Olive one more time. She was still absorbed in her coloring. Greer turned, making room for me to sit on the seat next to hers.

Her legs had widened to accommodate mine, and when I set my forearm on the counter, my fingers brushed the edge of her elbow. Naturally, we'd turned in toward each other, creating a small space where she could ask me to be honest about why we were doing this. And she'd earned that.

"Your dad asked me about my parents the other night," I started. "And I told you they'd passed away."

She nodded. "I'm sorry they're gone."

My eyes dropped to where she still held the fidget. Her fingers rolled it around and rolled it around in an unthinking motion that didn't create a sound.

"My parents were older when they had me. My mom was forty-two. My dad forty-five. They'd long given up hope that they'd ever have kids, so they'd created the life they wanted by that point. Quiet. Simple. Easy. I learned to be the same because they couldn't really handle anything upsetting the life they'd built." I eased my hand toward her, sliding the fidget out from her grasp and into my own. "The only place I experienced a family, the kind you're used to, was on the football field. It was easy to make that into my life. They were tired by the time I finished high school. Exhausted by the time I graduated from college. My dad's health made it so they never came to games, but I don't think they would have even if he was fine."

"Did they ever see you play in the pros?" she asked.

I shook my head. "I always offered. Tickets to a suite and a wheelchair for my dad, but it was just too much for them."

*Oh, we'll just watch on TV. You know we can't be bothered with all that fuss.*

You can give a kid everything they need—food and shelter and clothes, drive them to practices and sign them up for clubs—and you still have every chance not to show them that they're your world. You can go through the motions, do all the things you're supposed to, and no one would ever be able to convince me that their little brains can't tell the difference between that and a parent who'd light the world on fire to take care of them.

I would burn everything down for Olive. And I had to believe she could feel that.

"Josie is a good mom. A *great* mom," I told her. "But this year might well be the only chance I ever have at uninterrupted time with my daughter. I can't let that opportunity pass without fighting for it, no matter what I have to do."

Greer's attention never wavered, and I could see the way she tucked every word of my answer somewhere important. I wanted to know where she kept it. Where she locked it away. What question it answered in her mind. This answer, the biggest piece of who I was, *mattered* to her.

And that, in turn, mattered to me.

I let out a quiet sigh, my gaze locked onto hers. Something warm buzzed in the air between us, the slightest energy that I couldn't quite name.

I snagged her finger in mine, and with a crooked smile, I pushed the rainbow-colored metal fidget past her first knuckle.

It was horribly ugly as a ring. Too big for the graceful length of her finger.

"Will you still marry me next week, Greer Wilder?"

The breath caught audibly in her throat at the sincerity of my words.

I didn't qualify it. I didn't amend the wording or call it fake. We still hadn't figured out how we were going to slip the marriage license from the minister, so there was a very true possibility that I'd end up with a real wife, and she'd have a real husband.

Instead of answering, I heard her suck in a fortifying breath, and then she cupped my face in her hands and leaned forward to press a sweet, close-lipped kiss to my mouth.

The quick jolt of electricity over my skin at the press of her lips had me cupping the back of her head in one hand, the silk of her hair luscious and smooth between my fingers.

But before I could deepen the kiss, before I could weigh the wisdom of pushing off my stool to bring my body closer to hers, she pulled away and let her forehead rest against mine.

Her nose brushed against mine.

"Nothing will keep me from walking down that aisle, Beckett," she whispered. "I promise."

## CHAPTER 10

# Greer

**My wedding day was beautiful.**

Sunny, warm—not hot, and a perfect, gentle breeze to whisk away the terrifying whiff of mind-numbing guilt that I felt every freaking time I caught a glimpse of myself in my pretty white dress.

"You look amazing," my sister Adaline said as she adjusted one of the soft curls that cascaded down my back. She was on hair duty, and even though she was sad I wouldn't allow her to do anything fancy, I was just glad she'd hopped on board the wedding train without much suspicion.

"Thank you," I told her. I kept my gaze on her face while she curled a few more pieces, gently pulling a brush through to soften them.

"I still can't believe you're not going on a honeymoon," she said.

"We have time for that later," I told her. "You know this isn't the way either one of us would've planned it under normal circumstances."

That had my sister eyeing me for a moment. "I know. The thing with his daughter makes it…unique."

I managed a tight swallow. "She'll be with Josie now until their wedding, and then we'll have her that weekend. They're not doing a honeymoon either since they leave for London shortly after getting married."

Adaline stepped back to survey her touch-ups. "Perfect."

"When do you move into his place?" Poppy asked.

"Technically today," I answered. "We went over a lot of stuff when I stopped by the other day. But I'll still be moving things from my apartment over the next couple of weeks."

She gestured for me to pucker up, and I did, pursing my lips so she could slick a new coat of tinted lip balm over my lips.

After much debate and pouting by my younger sister, I won the battle of not wearing sticky lip gloss or a deep, rich color for the ceremony. I was already nervous enough kissing the guy in front of my family when we'd hardly traded more than a sweet kiss in private.

There was promise in that sweet kiss, and that was somehow even more alarming.

A gentle press of lips, just to take the edge off today's performance, and it set off a terrifying, trembling swarm of nerves under my skin.

Because all I'd wanted to do was lean in. No part of me wanted to pull back. I wanted to tilt my head, open my lips, and see if he'd slick his tongue over mine.

But I did pull back.

Beckett pulled back too. His eyes were intense and full of surprise, but because there was no leaning, no deepening, no furthering of whatever had been started there, I wasn't quite sure where he stood on the idea of kissing his wife.

Poppy gave me a restrained smile. "Everyone's moving away. Now it's just Cameron and me. One, he's not nearly as fun, and two, I can't raid his wardrobe."

Adaline and I traded looks. Leaving our family was never easy, and it was made even harder by harmless comments from our youngest sister. Poppy still lived at home, and if it were up to her, all of the older siblings would live within walking distance of our big family cabin.

Mom and Tim bought it when they got married all those years ago, fifteen acres outside of Sisters, with enough bedrooms and land and space for the seven of us to roam.

"I'll be home every week, Pops," I promised her. "You may not be able to steal my clothes as easily, but... I'm not abandoning anyone."

"I know," she conceded. Poppy swept a brush over my cheeks, then declared me ready. "You look amazing, Greer."

The door to Mom and Dad's bathroom opened, and my mom was already misting up when she saw the three of us in there. "Oh honey," she said. She swiped underneath her eye. "You look beautiful. Beckett is gonna lose it."

A panicked laugh almost broke loose from my chest because hopefully no one was expecting my oh-so-serious groom to burst into emotional tears at the sight of me. More than likely, he'd be standing up there mentally calculating all the ways this could go wrong.

If someone grabbed their phone to record Beckett's reaction for some sweet viral video, they'd be sorely disappointed. He already texted me four times that morning asking how I planned to take care of the minister not filing the marriage license.

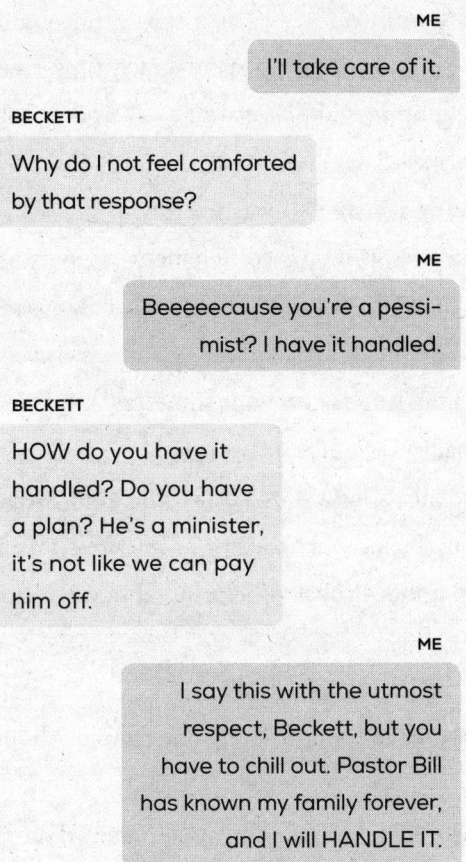

**ME**

I'll take care of it.

**BECKETT**

Why do I not feel comforted by that response?

**ME**

Beeeeecause you're a pessimist? I have it handled.

**BECKETT**

HOW do you have it handled? Do you have a plan? He's a minister, it's not like we can pay him off.

**ME**

I say this with the utmost respect, Beckett, but you have to chill out. Pastor Bill has known my family forever, and I will HANDLE IT.

Those were the sweet, romantic last words that my future

husband and I shared before I met his overthinking ass at the end of the aisle. My chest trembled in anticipation because this one day was the whole reason I was doing this.

Letting my sisters help me with my hair and makeup. Allowing Mom to zip up the back of the beautiful white dress that I'd had hanging in my closet. It was simple and sleek with a clean silhouette and a softly draping neckline that made me feel beautiful and elegant.

Truth be told, I'd never spent much time thinking about what kind of bride I'd be. It was one day, and one day did not a marriage make.

The thing I imagined was the guy at my side, my partner in life. The person who'd complement my personality, in the same ways that Tim balanced out Mom's. I always imagined that man would be gregarious and funny and excessively charming. He'd have a big laugh and a wide smile, and we'd be so charming together that it was almost nauseating.

The details of how I got down the aisle, what flowers I'd clutch in my hand, what the cut of my dress was—they never crossed my mind. Probably because I'd never met that faceless man.

Now I had a partner, all right.

My partner in lying to both our families about this entire charade.

My partner in deciding how much time I'd stay at his house, and how much time I'd be at my parents' during the week if they needed me.

It was the guy who was sweet and quiet and thought through all the millions of details that I hadn't.

The guy texting me at six o'clock stressing about how we'd dupe the eighty-year-old minister from the church down the road from my parents'.

The guy who checked if I had any food allergies before he went grocery shopping because he didn't want to stock anything in his house that I couldn't eat.

I know.

The thoughtfulness was out of control.

So when my mom said things like *Beckett is going to lose it*? She was probably right. I had no doubt his overworked head was throbbing with all the things he was trying to keep balanced.

Instead of commenting, I simply smiled at her in the mirror. "Did Josie get here with Olive?" I asked.

She nodded, picking up the small bouquet of wildflowers from the bathroom counter. "She's so happy for you two. And Olive is adorable. So shy, though. Once she saw Beckett, she hardly popped her head out to look at anyone else," she added. "It would've been nice if she could have been your flower girl or something."

Protectiveness roared hot and quick in my belly, but I tamped it down.

"Quiet kids are kind of a foreign concept in this family," I said.

Adaline laughed.

Poppy slung her arm around Mom's shoulders as she grinned. "Speak for yourself. I was an angel."

I burst out laughing. "Oh please. You were more savage than the rest of us combined, and we were beastly in our own right. It's a miracle this house didn't burn down when we were kids."

All four of us laughed at that, my mom wiping happy tears as her shoulders shook.

The bedroom door opened again, and Tim poked his head in. His face softened immediately at the happy atmosphere he walked into. He was having a good day, and even though his walk was a bit slower, his frame a bit thinner underneath his suit, there was a brightness to his eyes and a spring in his step as he walked toward us.

I stood from the stool and turned to face him.

Immediately, his eyes welled with tears. "My God, Greer, look at you," he said, voice snagging on the words, emotion thick in his voice. "You are the most beautiful bride I've ever seen."

Adaline wound her hand through mine, and I gripped it tight, allowing that anchor to help me keep the makeup on my face and my emotions in check.

Tim pulled a handkerchief from his pocket to dab at his eyes. My mom joined him, wrapping her hand around his arm, probably as much of a show of support as a way to make sure he was steady on his feet.

I heard Poppy sniff behind me, but I kept my eyes on my dad.

"You're not gonna make me cry, are you?" I said quietly. I approached him when he tucked the handkerchief back into his pocket, and he emitted a choked laugh.

"I don't know. I'll try." He exhaled, long and slow, an

obvious effort to get his own emotions in check. "Your groom is down there charming the pants off everyone. He even has Erik smiling."

My oldest brother hardly smiled at anyone except his wife.

My eyebrows popped up. "Really?"

Mom laughed. "That surprises you?"

"A little," I hedged. "Beckett is usually pretty…reserved."

"Yet he's marrying you," Adaline mused. "I hope he's buckled in to have a wife who's not."

I shot her a dark look.

Tim chuckled, walking forward to pull me into a tight embrace. "Be nice to your sister on her wedding day," he told Adaline. "And when it's your turn, Greer has to be nice to you too."

Adaline grinned. On her ring finger was the obnoxiously beautiful ring her fiancé, Emmett, gave her. They were so perfect together that I'd want to puke if I didn't love them both so much. And in truth, I was happy to let them plan the wedding of their dreams if it meant this casual backyard wedding would allow Tim the moment he wanted.

As I stood in the room with them, I couldn't deny that this was giving me something I'd miss too. I'd have this moment with Tim—real or fake or whatever anyone wanted to call it—where he proudly walked me down the aisle. I'd always have this with him. No matter what the next year of our life brought.

Before I could burst into tears, he pulled back and settled a hand on Adaline's cheek. "I hope I get to be there for your day too, sweetheart."

The tone shifted immediately, Mom dropping her chin to her chest with a quiet sniff. Poppy pulled a tissue from a box on the counter and wiped under her eyes. Adaline pressed a quick kiss to Tim's cheek.

"Now, now," Mom said, her voice only trembling slightly. "None of that. We have a wedding to start."

Tim winked at me. "I'm always the one causing trouble."

When eyes were sufficiently dry, makeup touched up, and bouquets in hand, we walked downstairs. Even though Adaline and Poppy would be proceeding me down the aisle, Beckett and I decided to stand by ourselves underneath the gentle arches of the lights strung from the tree.

From the kitchen window, I smiled at how pretty everything looked. It was a small crowd, just my immediate family and Josie, Micah, and Olive. Olive had her hair braided back off her face and was wearing an adorable light-green dress with floating ruffles along the skirt. In her hair was a small sprig of white flowers.

My heart clenched at the way she looked up at her dad, standing solemnly next to the pastor, waiting for me to appear.

Beckett looked…good.

Handsome and tall and strong in his dark-gray suit and his pale-colored tie. His face was solemn, but I caught no hint of reticence, and that had me breathing a little faster, my ribs tightening in anticipation.

*We were actually doing this,* I thought.

Tim caught me staring and squeezed my arm with his hand.

"You ready, cupcake?"

I nodded jerkily. "Holy *shit*, Dad, I'm getting married," I whispered. The words tumbled out before I could stop them.

He grinned, so wide and happy, that all those deep wrinkles by his eyes and mouth appeared. Gently, I reached up and traced those smile lines with my thumb.

"You've smiled a lot in your life to get those," I told him.

He caught my hand in his and pressed a sweet kiss to my knuckles.

He leaned in. "And they're gonna get a workout today, my beautiful daughter. Because being here with you on a day like this, I am the happiest father in the entire world."

*Don't cry.*

*Don't cry.*

*Don't cry.*

One tear slipped out, the sneaky little fucker.

Tim snagged it with his thumb, his smile gentling. "Only happy tears today, you hear me?"

I nodded again. Stronger this time.

"I love you," I told him.

It was Tim's turn to have his eyes gloss over. "You and your sister and your brother are some of the best gifts I've ever been given. It's always been my honor to step in as your dad where you'd let me."

Another tear threatened, but I willed it back. "There is no one else I'd rather have walk me down that aisle."

Tim pulled me into a quick embrace, and I felt the shaky way he exhaled before he pulled back. "Come on now, your mother will have my head if we make them wait too long."

With my hand tight around his elbow, and my other gripping the flowers, we walked out of the house as my family stood from their seats.

My sisters wept openly, as did my mom. Parker stood stoically next to Mom, his jaw tight and his eyes red as they locked onto his dad. I saw her reach over and grip his hand with hers.

My oldest brother Erik cleared his throat, reaching up to swipe quickly under his eye, and his petite blond wife smiled up at him, their daughter sound asleep in her arms.

There was a song playing, but I could hardly hear it, my mind and heart were so full with all the feelings fighting for top spot.

And when I fought the spinning sensation of which would win—grief and sadness and sheer overwhelm of both—my eyes locked onto Beckett.

It was enough to hook me straight into the moment, quiet all those thoughts, and allow me something firmly planted to hold.

His chest expanded on a deep breath, and the side of his mouth tugged up on a crooked grin. His eyes were dark, holding mine steadily, and it was that steadiness that anchored each step, making each one surer than the last.

Tim and I took the slow walk down the aisle, and when I broke the connection with Beckett, it was only to allow myself a moment to memorize the face of the man who stood at my side.

Any battle against my tears was lost.

Because he looked so happy and so wonderfully proud to be taking that walk with me.

We got to the end of the aisle and paused, and behind me, I heard my mom's quiet sobs. Tears streamed down my face as Tim gripped my hands in his own. He shook his head, so much love in his gaze that it took everything in me not to collapse into his embrace.

"This is it, cupcake," he whispered. "You're officially someone else's problem now."

I laughed through my tears, and when my brothers laughed too, I knew they'd all heard him.

The pastor cleared his throat. "We are gathered here today to celebrate Greer and Beckett as they proclaim their love and commitment to each other. And we are gathered to rejoice, with them and for them, in the new life that they undertake with each other."

Tim's hands squeezed mine.

"Who gives this woman to be married to this man?" the pastor asked.

"Her mother and I do," Tim said, voice clear and sure.

My ribs were too tight, my heart overflowing with love and gratitude and so much fucking sadness that he wouldn't be with us forever that I could hardly stand straight.

But I pulled strength from his face and allowed him to hand me off to Beckett, whose eyes were suspiciously red as his palm slid under mine.

My tears ebbed, faced with this handsome stranger who I hardly knew. His hand was tight on mine, a necessary anchor in the midst of all the whirling chaos in my head.

We listened, eyes on each other as the pastor said a few words about love and commitment.

We repeated our vows, the words hardly even registering as they passed my lips.

And when we slid rings on each other's fingers, mine trembled slightly.

Maybe it wasn't going to be legal, but as Beckett pushed a simple gold band past my knuckle, holy hell did it feel real.

"By the power of the state of Oregon, I now pronounce you husband and wife." He smiled. "You may kiss your bride."

Right.

Beckett gave me a small, secret smile, and I exhaled a quiet laugh. Like I was something precious and rare, he cupped my face in both hands, eyes unbearably earnest, and then he leaned forward to slide his lips over mine.

My free hand curled around his forearm, and I found myself leaning forward when he pulled back.

He didn't retreat, though. He searched my eyes, then kissed me again, sucking my lower lip between his, yanking a surprised whimper from underneath my ribs.

Someone whistled, and I pulled away, resting my forehead against his while my family clapped and yelled.

"We did it," he whispered.

"Almost," I said, and grinned. "Just gotta get that marriage license," I whispered against the shell of his ear.

Beckett tipped his head back and laughed, and I imagined how we must look.

The blushing bride and the happy groom.

Even I was almost convinced it was real.

Almost.

# CHAPTER 11

# Beckett

**The marriage license hung over my head like a guillotine,** but Greer assured me throughout the day that she had it handled—after the ceremony when we posed for some pictures, during the simple, hearty lunch her mom had prepared for the family, and afterward when the dessert was being passed out.

There was no tall, ornate wedding cake because neither of us particularly liked cake, but I couldn't help but watch Greer eye the apple pies on the long dining tables outside. There were donuts too, but instead of getting myself either of those, I asked Sheila if I was allowed to serve up the first slice of pie.

She cut a healthy piece, handing me the plate with a gleam in her eye. "If you take a bite of that before she gets it, you may not survive your first night as a newlywed."

"I wouldn't dare," I told her seriously.

Greer was seated at the end of the table, chatting amiably with Josie while Micah pushed Olive on the swing set just behind the house. It was odd to see these two women—so incredibly different and filling two massive roles in my life—connecting with such ease.

Josie had always been on the reserved side, and between the two of us, there was no doubt that Olive came by her withdrawn personality honestly.

When I approached with the apple pie, Greer said something that made Josie laugh, the type of laughter I'd never heard from her—unrestrained and loud.

Josie caught my eye and laid a hand over Greer's. "I love her," she proclaimed.

There was no easy response because I could hardly say, *I love her too.* I was saved from conjuring something when my brand-new wife saw the apple pie.

"Oh, you are the best husband ever," she gushed.

I set the plate down in front of her, sliding my hand over her back as I took a seat. She leaned into the touch, and because it felt like the right thing to do, I dropped a kiss against the top of her head.

Josie watched the entire exchange with a softness in her eyes. "It's so good to see you with someone, Beckett." She tilted her head toward the swing set. "I think she'll be good for Olive too."

Greer covered her mouth as she tried to swallow the bite of pie, her eyes wide at the easy compliment.

"Thank you," she said, voice muffled through her food.

I chuckled under my breath.

Josie shared a look with Micah and nodded. "I think we're

gonna head out soon, but I can't thank you enough for inviting us. Your family is amazing," she gushed. She let out a slow breath, leaning in to speak quietly. "I know everything with your dad may have had this happening sooner than you planned, but it really has helped me feel better about leaving with Micah."

Greer and I traded a look, and underneath the table, she slid her hand over my leg. The gentle touch had the hair on the back of my neck standing up because it was nothing anyone could see, and that quiet show of support in light of how many heavy emotions had gone into this day was almost more than I could handle.

"I want you to be happy, Josie," I told her. "You and Micah are going to have an incredible year in London, and you know we'll take great care of Olive while you're gone."

"I know," she admitted. "And I know you could've done it on your own." She paused, shaking her head. "It's still hard to leave her, but I feel that way even when I drop her off for the weekend."

"It's hard for me too," I told her.

Josie and I shared a smile.

Greer took another bite of her pie, her eyes widening when the pastor shuffled up to our table. The man looked close to ninety, and at one point in the ceremony, I wasn't sure he even remembered my name. But he'd known the Wilder family for thirty years, and Greer insisted that he perform the ceremony.

"Greer, Beckett," he said. "I must be off soon. Shall we take care of the signing of the license?"

My stomach dropped into my feet, but Greer nodded, an easy smile spreading over her face. "Sure. I'll grab Cameron to witness. We'll meet you inside the house in five minutes?"

His bushy gray eyebrows popped up. "Oh, you don't want to take care of it right here?"

She shook her head. "I'd hate to get food or have someone spill on it. Let's go inside where it's quiet."

She was good. Not a flinch on her face.

It was equal parts terrifying and impressive.

He walked toward the house, the folder holding the license in his wrinkled hand. Greer held my gaze for a loaded moment, then broke the connection. "Shall we?" she asked.

I nodded, still fighting that wildly out-of-balance sensation I'd felt any time the license subject came up. For both of us, it was important that the marriage wasn't legal. That we could simply not file it with the state, and there was no need to go through a divorce or an annulment after Josie returned from London.

We'd tell our families it didn't work out, but we wished each other the best of luck, and they'd never be the wiser.

As long as we could get the damn thing from Pastor Bill.

I hung back while Greer interrupted a game of horseshoes between the Wilder men. Erik and Parker shouted over rules and cheating and giving correct points—not surprisingly, given they were the two professional athletes in the group—and Cameron laughed with his dad where Tim sat in a chair.

Greer touched Cameron's arm and said something in his ear.

He gave me a brief unreadable look, and then nodded at his sister.

The brother who knew the truth, I thought, as he walked toward me with his hand outstretched.

Cameron reminded me a lot of Parker—the tall, muscled frame, the shaggy golden-brown hair and stern features.

"Congratulations," he said, gripping my hand as tightly as possible without breaking any bones.

He might not be the defensive lineman I went up against on the field, but the nature of manual labor his whole life meant that Cameron Wilder was still an absolute beast.

"Thank you for helping out," I told him.

He merely arched his eyebrows and followed Greer as she led us toward the house. When one of her younger cousins raced by us, she snagged his shirtsleeve, yanking him to a halt in front of our group.

She whispered something in his ear—the kid couldn't have been more than eighteen, but his eyes widened almost comically as he nodded, then ran away.

"What was that?" Cameron asked.

Greer straightened, smoothing her hands over the front of her dress. "Insurance."

"Good Lord," I muttered under my breath.

Cameron slicked his tongue over his teeth, staring his sister down with a look that I could only describe as horrified incredulity. There was a minor comfort that I was not the only one a little wary of whatever it is Greer was about to do.

She didn't seem quite as bothered, gliding up the steps like a queen about to step into court, only pausing once at the front door to take a deep breath.

"Am I about to commit fraud to protect your asses?" Cameron whispered.

She glanced over her shoulder, one dark eyebrow raised. "It's not fraud, Cameron. You're signing your name that you witnessed our ceremony. Nothing untrue about that."

He narrowed his eyes. "Remember when you convinced Poppy that if she dyed her hair pink that it would keep growing in that way?"

She sniffed. "I was sixteen and she was driving me nuts. What's your point?"

"I caught Poppy just as she was about to permanently dye her hair *by herself* and never told Mom."

"Cameron," she sighed. "I know, *I know*, okay. What else am I supposed to do right now?"

I crossed my arms over my chest, watching the sibling interplay with unabashed curiosity. I couldn't really tell what Cameron's angle was either, but for all I knew, this was a well-established pattern of him looking out for his younger sister.

Along with the addition of Greer in my life, bold and fearless and resolute, I was gaining what seemed like an endless list of in-laws, with a lifetime of history that I'd probably never understand.

The pastor glanced through the window, catching my eye with a friendly smile and a tap of his watch.

"We have to go in," I said to them. "He's watching."

Greer nodded, her eyes catching on mine. "Ready?"

She didn't aim the question at her brother, who was still shaking his head.

She asked me.

Because at the end of the day, this was about me and Greer. The whys and hows and justifications were ours. No one else could own them for us. And we weren't really asking them to.

With a polite nod toward Cameron, I moved behind Greer to hold the door open and settled my other hand low on her back. Her dress was smooth and soft, silky under my palm. And underneath that, her skin was warm and firm.

The pastor greeted us with a kind smile. "Here we are. Let's get this signed, and I'll make sure it gets taken care of."

Greer took the pen he extended toward her over the length of the island. He tapped a finger where her signature was needed, and I watched her rib cage expand on a deep breath before she scrawled the pen along the line—a dramatic swooping signature that somehow matched her well.

"Ah, there now." His eyes twinkled as he handed another pen to me. "Your turn, Beckett."

A knot of nerves wedged tight in my throat, and I worked to swallow around it. The tip of the pen hovered over the paper, the blank space over the thick black line getting larger and larger in my head. Greer sensed my hesitation, and she smoothed a hand over my back.

My breathing evened out. My heart rate calmed.

The pen skated over the paper, the neat tidy lines of my own signature looking small and compact next to hers.

"Oddly nerve-racking, isn't it?" the pastor asked. "Almost all my couples find this part a little daunting, even though the ceremony is over."

She exhaled a laugh, the color high in her cheeks when I glanced over at her. "A bit," she admitted. "I'm not sure why."

"This is what makes it official, my dear. Without this paper, it's just a nice party."

The words dropped into the room like a bomb, and Cameron cleared his throat. "Where do I sign?"

"Right here." He tapped the paper again. "Oh, but we need one more witness, Greer."

She sighed. "Of course, sorry."

Right as she said it, the front door to the house opened, and the young cousin popped his head in. "Am I interrupting?" he asked.

Cameron and I shared a look.

"Perfect timing, Jay," Greer said silkily. "Can you sign as a witness real quick?"

The pastor's eyebrows popped up in surprise. "You don't want your sister to do it?"

She smacked the cousin's back, a little too hard to be considered polite. "Nah. He's just fine."

The kid finished signing his name. "Uhh, Pastor Bill, someone out there started asking questions about performing exorcisms."

He said the words in such a nervous rush that we all paused, no one moved, not a single sound could be heard in the entire house.

"What now?" Pastor Bill asked, his head tilting to the side.

"Is that like, a thing people do? I don't know if they meant now or for future reference or if there's an actual"—he swallowed, his face getting red and blotchy—"demonic possession happening. Maybe you should take some holy water out there just in case."

Cameron swiped a hand over his face. Greer rolled her lips together, fighting a laugh.

I, on the other hand, was feeling mildly nauseous.

Paster Bill blinked. A few times. "Well... I'm not that kind of pastor, I'm from a nondenominational church, son, but I think maybe I should see what's going on."

Jay nodded wildly. "Right now, I think."

He ushered Pastor Bill toward the door, and Greer snuck her hand over the marriage license, sliding it toward her as the two vanished into the front yard.

"What the *fuck*," Cameron breathed. "That's what you told him to do?"

Greer wheezed in shocked laughter. "*No*. I just told him to make something up to get Pastor Bill outside for like, two minutes. I told him I'd pay him a hundred bucks if he could manage it."

I sank down onto one of the kitchen stools. "This is a nightmare."

"Holy water," she said around her breathless laughter. "Oh, Pastor Bill's face. He's never going to come back here again."

"Now what?" Cameron asked.

Greer straightened. "Now Beckett and I are going to hide in my bedroom until he leaves."

I leaned forward. "We're…what?"

With precision, she folded the marriage license in half and tucked it into a purse that was sitting next to the fridge. "My new husband and I are going upstairs. Cameron will tell Pastor Bill that we're going to take care of the marriage license and that he's free to leave once all wedding guests are safe from the fictional exorcism."

Cameron's jaw ticked ominously. "And why would I do that?"

Greer heard something in his voice, and I saw the first flicker of nerves in her otherwise undaunted facade.

"Because it's important to your sister," I said. My voice was quiet and steady, and I stayed seated.

Cameron's eyes locked unerringly onto mine, and I didn't so much as blink, straightening in the stool. It was easy enough for another man to recognize a challenge when he heard one.

And make no mistake about it, I would stand, meet him toe-to-toe if I thought it would help. But it wouldn't. All it would serve was to add tension into an already stressful situation.

"I'm not foolish enough to ask you to do any favors for me," I continued. "But it's important to Greer that we keep this out of the realm of actual fraud. So unless you want to set us both into a legally binding marriage—recognized by the state of Oregon, and something we'll have to undo someday—then I suggest you do as she asks and not make her feel worse."

Cameron broke the stare first, glancing down at his feet. He exhaled heavily, fingers rapidly drumming against the side of his leg, until finally, he nodded.

Greer moved toward him, wrapping her arms around his middle. Cameron returned the hug immediately, pressing an absentminded kiss to the top of her dark hair.

"Thank you," she breathed. "I know how much we're asking."

"You owe me," he told her. "I'm about to go lie to the pastor that you and your fake husband are upstairs having *sex* so you can steal the paperwork in order not to legalize your marriage. I will burn for this, make no mistake about it."

Greer fought a smile.

But he softened. "But I'd only do something this insane for one of my sisters," he added.

"Not your brothers?" I asked, impossibly curious.

"Hell no. Those assholes are on their own."

Greer grinned, a dimple popping out in her left cheek.

As Cameron left us alone, I couldn't help but stare at the woman who I'd just spoken vows to.

She was beautiful—the kind of beautiful I'd probably never quite get used to. And all the energy trapped under her skin, the way she seemed to make the air around her vibrate, it was terrifying.

Greer held out her hand. "Shall we go hide from the minister?"

"Do I have a choice?"

And it was to the sound of Greer's laughter that she led us from the room, my mind looping over one single thing: what the hell did I just do?

## CHAPTER 12

# Greer

**I tried to imagine explaining all of this to the teenage** version of myself. The girl who hung posters on her walls of grungy musicians and sweaty, muscle-bound athletes, and sexy pop stars. That version of Greer would lose her absolute mind that I was married to a professional football player. She'd have stars in her eyes if I told her that the guy who said I do and slipped a ring on our finger was six-five—because when you were taller than all the boys in your class, that was on par with winning the lottery.

She'd swoon if I told her he made a good strong pot of coffee and did quiet thoughtful things like leave a mug out for me the first day I was there, even though he was up a couple of hours before I liked to start the day.

She'd squeal at inhuman decibel levels if I told her that he had dark hair and dark eyes, a nice smile, and was in possession of those deep muscles cutting down in a V on either side of his neatly stacked abs.

Not that he walked around the house shirtless, but he tended only to wear athletic shorts when he did yard work, and the house had a lot of windows, and I was only human, *okay*.

And if I tried to explain to teenage Greer that I'd spent the first two nights of our married life to this prime specimen of a man in a guest room with a *beige* comforter—very much by myself—she'd wonder what the absolute hell I'd done wrong.

I couldn't help but wonder the same thing.

We'd coexisted quite nicely the first couple of nights. My new roommate kept himself very busy in Olive's absence, so busy that I couldn't help but wonder if that was intentional, given my new presence in his home.

It was necessary, though.

Josie lived so close, if she stopped by with Olive, or came earlier, or they needed to pick something up from his house, it needed to be obvious that I was staying there. The lease was up on my apartment next month, so even though I wasn't in a huge rush to pack up my entire life, a sleepover at the Coleman house was a requirement of my new gig.

With a stretch, I winced when the ache in my shoulders and arms screamed at me.

Because no one expected me back at work for a couple of days, and my honeymoon held very little in the way of bedroom activities to keep me busy, I decided to get to work on Olive's room. Beckett and Micah had cleared out the furniture before the ceremony, on my request because I knew that her space was the first on my list in that house.

The first coat of paint was up—a soft dreamy pink on three of the walls—and I'd finish the second coat after breakfast, followed by a hot ass shower and a lot more ibuprofen than was probably recommended, but my body *hurt* from all that rolling.

My wallpaper guy was coming over the next day, installing a gorgeous floral pattern on the wall where I'd be moving the queen bed. Everything after that was a matter of staging all the fun stuff.

Beckett only offered a minor protestation when I told him he wasn't allowed to help, but I really wanted him to be just as surprised as Olive when I was ready to unveil the finished product.

Josie loved everything I'd chosen, tearing up at one point when I showed her the mood board of my ideas. And because Beckett was not sparing any expense on his daughter's room, my shopping finger got a workout purchasing absolutely everything for this dreamy little space.

The first of the boxes arrived the day before our wedding, and by my second day in the house, he gave me a long, wordless look as he added box after box after box to the stack growing out in the three stall garage.

He may not have realized it yet, but I'd happily spend my year and some change in this house transforming it into a magical place for him and Olive, something welcoming and warm and full of life.

Instead of simply a house, it would be a home. A place they'd love to be, instead of four walls and a roof that served only the most basic of functions.

It was already a little strange to be in the house when Olive wasn't there, and it served as a stark reminder why he was doing all this.

The home he'd bought was big—a place meant to be grown into, plenty of land for exploring and adventuring, and 80 percent of the time, he was here by himself.

Or he was, before I'd slotted myself into the mix.

Tying my short cotton robe around my waist, I shuffled downstairs with bleary eyes, only to find a quiet house.

There was a note on the counter, tucked underneath the edge of my favorite blue coffee mug, in Beckett's tidy handwriting.

> *Went to train at the facilities, I should be back around dinner. Text me if you want me to pick something up in town.*

There was no flowery inscription. No XOXO before his name.

But there was something about that little note, tucked underneath the corner of a large coffee mug, next to the coffee pot holding more than enough of the fragrant brew that had a little seed sprouting in my chest.

Maybe it was the understated attentiveness that had me feeling the first inklings of something inconvenient. But instead of squashing it out before it could grow, or manically yanking it out like a weed, I simply let the seedling stay where it was and filled the mug with coffee, taking an appreciative whiff.

After coffee, I searched the pantry, grinning when I found a new box of oatmeal next to his very healthy, very boring options. It hadn't been there the day before.

I pulled it out and laughed.

Apples and cinnamon.

On it was another note.

*Now you can have apple pie for breakfast.*

The smile stayed on my face through breakfast, through painting the second coat of the room. As I showered and washed my hair, ridding it of the flecks of pink, then readied myself for a jobsite visit on the lake, I knew teenage Greer would never believe this, even if I tried my hardest to explain it.

———

The Detroit Lake house was buzzing with activity—work trucks jockeying for spots on the edge of the property—so I had a little bit of a walk to the work trailer.

Cameron was standing at the desk with Wade and his best friend Jax, studying the house plans.

I got a few grunts and one nod of greeting, and as I unloaded my samples onto the table where I worked, I noticed Wade giving me a thoughtful look. The ever-present unlit cigarette hung from the edge of his mouth.

"Out with it," I told him.

"You got married."

There was no question in the gruffly spoken sentence, which

didn't surprise me from our foreman. Cameron and his friend Jax traded a silent look, and I shifted my weight to one leg, arms crossed over my stomach. "Good news travels fast, I see. Did you get me a present?"

"Nope." He scratched the side of his face. "I coulda done it."

My eyebrows arched.

Cameron narrowed his gaze at Wade. "Done what?" he asked.

"Married you," he said.

Jax choked on his coffee. Cameron dropped the measuring tape in his hand. My stomach bottomed out because if my big brother told our foreman what we'd done, I would punch him in the throat.

"I..." My voice trailed off. Words escaped me, at least polite ones, because Wade was old enough to be my father and had never been even the slightest bit inappropriate with me.

He huffed, exasperation heavy in the sound. "I mean, I could've done the ceremony for you. If you were in a hurry."

My head tilted to the side. "What?"

He shifted his weight between his feet, clearly uncomfortable. "I'm one of those internet pastors."

My jaw hinged open.

"You are *not*," Cameron said.

Jax might have been smiling, but his face was hidden behind his mug, and I wasn't actually sure I'd ever seen him smile anyway.

Wade puffed his chest out. "Am so. My cousin got married in her backyard and asked if I'd officiate. Paid forty bucks and filled out something on her computer." His face actually blushed the slightest shade of pink, and I fought to keep my laughter at bay. "I coulda done it for you. As a friend."

Moving slowly, so as not to scare him off, I laid my hand on his forearm and leaned in to kiss him on his grizzled cheek. "Thank you, Wade," I said. "I'm sure you would have been great."

He could hardly make eye contact, clearing his throat and mumbling a congratulations as he practically sprinted out of the trailer.

"Oh my," I breathed. "These guys just never cease to surprise me."

"Just think," Cameron said, "if Wade had done it, you wouldn't have had to steal the license from an actual man of God, and you could've just told him what you were doing and why."

I rolled my eyes. "Glad to know your promise to keep this a secret doesn't extend to Jax."

The man in question gave me an inscrutable look.

"I know," I said. "You don't care, and you won't tell anyone."

"Nope."

That was all he said. Cameron smiled at the tersely spoken reply.

"You know how when someone tells you a secret, you get an unspoken pass to tell your spouse?" Cameron said.

"Is that how it works?" I asked.

He ignored me. "Jax is the spouse I get to tell."

"Thanks," Jax said dryly.

I nodded sagely. "Considering the complete lack of a woman in your life, I will concede that point."

Cameron sighed. "I don't have time for a woman. I work too much."

"I have been telling you for the last two years that we need an office manager. Maybe if we had someone else besides my intern helping with the admin stuff, you'd have time to date."

"I know, I know." He gestured back toward the plans. "Speaking of work, we need to get this figured out, if you don't mind."

I left them alone, tuning out their conversation while I pulled open my laptop and got to work. I answered a few calls, spent about an hour on emails, tweaked a few design renders for potential clients, and then walked through the site when Cameron had a question on light placement.

The three of us stood in the middle of the large room and measured out some options for placement of the dining room table in relation to where we'd hang the massive light fixture.

"If you face it this way, it might obstruct the natural flow of the room," I said.

"But the light placement will make more sense with the pendants we have over the island," Cameron pointed out.

"What do you think, Jax?" I asked.

He'd remained quiet during our discussions, as he often did, but he backed up to view the room from farther back, eyes narrowed as he imagined the space.

His back was to the front door, and because he was so big, I couldn't see who walked in when the door swung open behind him.

"Oh!"

At the sound of Poppy's exclamation, Jax turned. Her eyes were wide, clearly surprised at the sight of him, and in that surprise, she didn't watch where she put her next step. Her toe hooked on a coil of tubing that was connected to the nearest air compressor, and she pitched forward.

Jax's hand shot forward, snatching her underneath the arm before she fell face-first into the unfinished house.

Her face was bright red, his was furrowed in a furious grimace, and I sighed at the painfully obvious crush my little sister had on Cameron's best friend.

"Oh boy," I breathed.

Cameron made a noise of assent. "I know. I told her to get over it because he's more than a decade older than her and...kind of a dick."

I glanced over at him. "He's your best friend."

"My best friend who's occasionally kind of a dick and thankfully has no interest in younger women because *then* it would be a problem."

I smothered a smile.

Jax pulled his hand away when Poppy was back on two feet, and she gave him a stilted smile in thanks. He walked away from her without a backward glance.

"Pops," I said, glad to interrupt the heavy cloud of awkward hanging over the entire thing, "didn't know you were coming by today."

I eyed Jax meaningfully once he'd passed, and she gave me

a hard look in return. "I didn't expect to see you either, brand-new Mrs. Coleman."

The name was jarring because for a moment, I had to think about who she was addressing.

I exhaled a weak laugh. "Right."

"I figured you'd be in bed for *days*," she said.

"Poppy," Cameron groaned.

I stifled a laugh, imagining my beige comforter in the beige guest room. "Too much to be done for that, my darling little sister. Beckett is at the team facilities today, and I was hoping to pick out a few last things for Olive's room."

"I'm surprised you're not at the team facilities," she said, glancing absently around the room. "Oh wait, that thing is tomorrow."

I blinked. "What thing?"

Poppy's forehead creased. "He didn't tell you? It's all over their social media this week. How have you not seen it?"

"Uh, I was a little busy getting married. What are you talking about?"

"The charity thing, where the wives and girlfriends come play against their significant other."

My eyebrows popped up because I did actually know what she was talking about. I'd seen it the year before, just after Parker transferred to Portland. It looked fun and raised huge amounts of money for some of the players' foundations.

"*That* thing," I said under my breath. "It's tomorrow?"

She nodded.

I gave Cameron a pleading look. "How do you feel about me playing hooky?"

"Don't you need to check with your husband about this first? Things are going about as I expected when I heard about this whole marriage thing."

I smiled, so very politely. "Imagine what finger I'm holding up right now, Cameron."

He snorted, turning back to the light fixture issue. "We can put it the way you want it," he said. "And yes, you can play hooky."

"Excellent. Now... I have to get some more stuff for Olive's room."

Her eyes brightened. "Ooh, can I help?"

I slung an arm over her shoulder as we left the house. "Yup. No budget on the project, which is always more fun. I finished painting the room earlier."

She sighed. "So you really didn't spend the weekend in bed? That's so disappointing."

"Cheer up, Poppy. There was hot coffee for me when I came downstairs, and he bought me a box of apple pie oatmeal so I didn't have to eat his healthy shit."

"Is that supposed to make me feel better?" she asked.

"I don't really know."

"Can I come to your place and help you set up Olive's room? I really want to see his place." She gave me a pleading look. "He *is* my new brother-in-law. And that makes her my step-niece, right?"

Hysterical laughter got lodged somewhere at the base of my throat, and I somehow managed a nod as I attempted to swallow it down.

"Uh-huh," I hedged. "I'm not sure when I'm doing all that, but we'll figure out a time for you to come over, I promise."

"She was so cute," Poppy gushed. "And if he doesn't have any family, then I am a shoo-in for the favorite aunt."

My stomach went a little cold, and my heart churned restlessly.

Act first, think later didn't seem quite as funny as it had when I sat down in that Italian restaurant for all my stupid dates.

At every new turn, I was getting tangible, weighty reminders of what we were doing and the possible fallout. I couldn't fight the tremble of nerves at the thought that this would all blow up in my face someday.

And who'd get caught in the crossfire as a result.

CHAPTER 13

# Beckett

"Coleman's wife is already done with him." The sound of a clucking tongue hit my ears, and I exhaled quietly.

"I asked for her phone number," someone else said. I ignored them, stretching out my legs, making sure I was warmed up for the game. "He told me she was *busy*."

She said the word like it was dripping with acid, and I looked up at Reyes and his wife, both of whom laughed at the expression on my face.

"Greer has a job, Melinda," I said patiently. "Just because we're married now doesn't mean she can drop everything to be here for every single event."

All around us, players and their significant others warmed up for the charity game. We'd started the traditional flag football game about four years earlier, and it was a hit with fans and families alike. We opened the training facilities to a few ticket holders, filling the sidelines with a few hundred fans and sports journalists who loved watching the players go up against their spouses or girlfriends.

And my quarterback's wife had been relentless all week, wanting Greer's contact information. Even Parker lifted his hands and said he was staying out of it when I wouldn't pass along her phone number.

Christian shook his head. "Did you do the thing I told you to do?"

My face felt warm, so I angled away from him to stretch out my back. "Yeah."

"What thing?" Melinda asked.

"The coffee," he said.

She sighed, melting into her husband almost instantaneously. "I love it when you make the coffee for me."

He slung an arm around her shoulder, kissing the top of her head. "I know you do. That's why I do it."

What a simple thing.

When Christian heard in the weight room that she was moving in after our quickie wedding, it was his number one piece of marriage advice.

*Set up the coffee she likes before you go to bed. Put out her favorite mug. It'll be waiting for her when she wakes up.*

"Seriously?" I asked him. "That's the advice?"

"Yes." His face was shockingly earnest. "Every single day, she wakes up knowing you're thinking about her. That shit matters when you do a job like this one. They don't get the time they want with us during the season, but you better believe my wife knows I go to bed and wake up with her on my mind."

So that's what I did.

Even though we'd been nothing more than polite roommates those first couple of days, only passing glimpses of each other while she worked on Olive's room, the awareness of Greer moving around my house was a weighty thing.

In truth, I hadn't even considered telling her about the charity event. She wasn't really my wife, and it would only serve to complicate things if she became a fixture in this part of my life too.

And despite all the cameras around the room, most professional players didn't live with their life on display, regularly consumed for gossip and celebrity chatter. Even if my single status had been commented on, I never would have known it.

"I asked for her number because I want her on our starting lineup, though," Melinda said again. She tightened the ponytail on top of her head, on her cheeks were small temporary tattoos with the Voyagers logo. "She's got brothers who play, and she's tall, so she'd help us win."

"If you win." Christian snorted.

At their easy banter, I smiled, but it was impossible not to imagine what it would be like to have Greer there with me.

I pulled my gaze from Christian and Melinda, glancing around at the general chaos, the happy buzz of noise. A few kids on the sidelines caught my eye—one of them was wearing my jersey. I turned my ball cap backward and walked over to where they were waiting.

"You guys ready for a good game today?" I asked.

They all spoke at once, telling me about their favorite plays and their favorite games and asked if I'd sign jerseys and programs. I laughed, scrawling my signature over everything they held out in my direction.

We took a few pictures, and when Parker ambled up out of the corner of my eye, their excitement ratcheted up about ten more degrees.

I smiled. "They like you better than me, Wilder."

The kids laughed, shoving all the same items at him to sign.

"Of course they do," he answered smoothly. "They're really smart."

As he signed, he tilted his head back toward the entrance to the field. "Figured you'd need to go anyway."

"Why?"

His eyebrows popped up slowly. "Your *wife* just arrived."

My head snapped over to the doors, and there she was.

Greer was ready to *play*.

She was in black leggings, a Voyagers tank top that hugged her chest, her hair braided back off her face, a blue-ish green ribbon threaded through the ends of the braid, and a gleam in her eye as she looked around that should have terrified anyone meant to line up against her.

Me.

It terrified *me*.

"I didn't tell her about it," I said under my breath. "I figured she had to work."

Parker sighed. "Yeah, my sisters have an annoying habit of finding out about everything, whether I want them to or not."

I thought about the family event that started this entire thing, and I couldn't help but laugh.

With a nudge to Parker's back, I walked over to where she waited with a serene, infinitely patient smile on her face. Her hands were tucked behind her back, and I scratched the side of my face when I was in front of her.

"Didn't expect to see you here," I said.

Her eyes did that gleaming thing again. It wasn't so scary this time. "Apparently not."

I winced, looking out at all the other wives and girlfriends running warm-ups on a different side of the field. "I'm not really used to…having people in my life who can join me for this stuff. I guess I didn't think about it."

Greer smiled. "I think we can cut each other some slack," she said easily. "Less than a week with a spouse means we both have some things to get used to."

I exhaled heavily. "Indeed we do."

Her eyes lingered over mine. "You did manage to think about setting up the coffee for me, though. I appreciate you making enough for both of us."

I cleared my throat, glancing down at my shoes. "Yeah, no problem."

There was no way I was admitting it now.

Greer leaned in, and when I caught a whiff of something clean and fresh and soft, my stomach tightened. "So...what's the setup here? Do I get to pick my team?"

I shook my head, trying not to breathe in too deeply. "Offensive SO's play with the defensive players. Defensive SO's line up with the offense."

"SO's?" she asked.

"Significant others," I told her.

"Ahh." She stretched her arm out over her head and groaned. "Perfect. That means we get to start our marriage with me kicking your ass."

My eyebrows arched slowly. "You think so?"

Greer waltzed past, her shoulder brushing mine as she did, and she gave me a searing look over her shoulder. "I don't think so, Coleman. I know it."

I blew out a harsh breath and tried very hard not to stare at my wife's ass as I followed her over to line up.

# CHAPTER 14
# Beckett

"Please let me help you," I said, my eyes covered because that's what she'd asked of me.

"Nope." She grunted. The sound of something sliding up the stairs at a glacial pace had me clenching my jaw. "I don't want to ruin the surprise." Another grunt. "Ahh, there. Got it," she said through gritted teeth.

It didn't take long for me to realize that Greer Wilder did not know how to sit still. The moment she walked through my front doors and deposited her stuff into the guest room, she got to work.

For five days, other than when she *did* kick my ass in a flag football game, she'd worked almost nonstop. On Olive's room. Organizing my pantry. Cleaning out the fridge. There were bins in there now. Bins and circular trays that spun around, and I didn't really understand any of it, but she certainly looked pleased with the results when she finished.

Even if she did sit long enough to turn the TV on, she had her laptop out, construction plans next to her on the couch, or stacks of samples on the coffee table in front of her that she referenced when sketching mysterious little things on her iPad.

And now that Olive's room was almost complete, she'd spent the entire day staging it for Olive's return that evening. Josie—thinking that she was giving the newlyweds privacy—insisted on bringing her over later than normal for the Friday night drop-off.

With that impending return, Greer was frantically trying to get all the finishing touches in place. My last glimpse of my brand-new roommate had been a surprising one. She still had pink paint speckles in the ends of her hair and all over her white muscle tank. Her short denim shorts carried more than their fair share of the wall color, and when I'd glibly asked if any of the paint had ended up on the wall, I got a very dirty look in response.

"I was doing a little touch-up after we got the bed in there," she'd answered primly, "and I dropped the brush and then forgot I had some paint on my hands, okay?"

When I asked how the bed frame and mattress got into the room without my help, she told me that her wallpaper guy helped her move it in after he finished.

I'd narrowed my eyes slightly at the mention of wallpaper, but she held up a hand. "You told me I had free rein once Josie saw my mood board. No backing out now, mister."

And she was right. There was no backing out now.

With my hand still covering my eyes, I listened helplessly as she issued one more grunt, followed by a victorious whooping sound.

"Oh good, you didn't throw your back out moving the nightstand by yourself?" I asked.

"I told you I could do it," she called from the top of the stairs. "Give me thirty minutes, and it'll be ready for her. Just need to make the bed and stage the nightstand."

The stack of boxes in the garage could build an entire house, if I felt so moved.

And even though I hated sitting around while she was working so hard, I couldn't deny the small curl of pleasure I felt at the clear and obvious effort she put into creating a special space for my daughter.

I'd chosen right, I thought for the hundredth time.

She was stubborn.

She crackled with energy, even when she was sitting.

The only time she was still, I learned, was when she was sleeping. I'd caught a glimpse of her once when I walked quietly past the guest room to get something from the upstairs bathroom. She slept curled up on her side, hair piled on top of her head with some sort of pink velvety-looking scrunch thing, and her face smooth and peaceful.

Even though I'd been very busy all week, not allowing much downtime with Greer, it still felt a bit like someone had unleashed a dark-haired tornado inside my house.

There was evidence of her everywhere.

Not destructive or unwelcome, but there was absolutely

no chance that I could ignore her presence when Olive wasn't around as a distraction.

A new blanket draped over the arm of the couch, something soft and fuzzy that I'd never touch outside of a very cold, winter night. A few throw pillows angled into the end seats, muted textures and colors that worked with the furniture I already owned. And a lamp she'd tucked next to the armchair where I liked to read.

From Olive's room, I heard a muffled, *oh fuck*, and fought a smile.

"You okay?" I called.

"Yup. You stay right where you are. Just…" She made a strangled sort of noise. "Fighting with the fitted sheet."

Earlier that day, I sat in a meeting with our offensive coordinator, discussing plans for the future. How we put in the work now for something we can't predict down the road.

We didn't know how our games would play out.

We didn't know what injuries might plague our team or whatever circumstances would shift between now and kickoff of any single game in the season.

But we made choices that helped us be the best version of whatever we wanted to be.

Strangely enough, his pep talk made me think about Greer. Made me think about our unconventional situation.

We'd made choices, had conversations that laid the ground work, and now we had to trust we'd done our best to weather whatever came our way.

With her dad.

With Olive.

It was the kind of work that I enjoyed, the effort that put my mind at ease when it was tempting to overthink how everything could go wrong.

Greer hopped down the steps, flopping onto the couch with a dramatic sigh. "Done," she breathed, eyes closed in obvious relief.

"You still have paint in your hair," I pointed out.

She pulled at the end of her ponytail. "Ugh, I know. I'll get it eventually." Her eyes were bright, her cheeks flushed. "When is Olive gonna be here? Do you want to see it now or wait until she arrives?"

I was weighing my answer when she stretched her legs out, bending forward from her seat on the couch to wrap her hands around her toes.

"Oh my gosh, my legs are so sore," she groaned.

My eyes got stuck on the impossibly long, toned stretch of bare skin under her denim shorts. "I'll…" My voice trailed off.

Greer lifted her head. From that angle, I could see straight down her tank top.

Her bra was white. Cut low on her chest.

I blinked.

"I'll, uh, I'll wait," I managed, pinching the bridge of my nose.

"You okay?" she asked, a smile clear in her voice.

"Yup."

How you got used to the lack of something in your life was amazing.

Since Josie, I'd only had a handful of nights with a woman who sparked my interest. But those sparks always faded fast.

Nothing, and no one, had held my interest past an evening. And I wasn't a one-night stand guy.

I never had been.

Sex, without commitment, without loyalty or trust, had never appealed to me. I wanted to be in love with someone again, but no one had lit up that part of my brain.

The part that studied curves under shirts and wondered how they might feel in my hands.

That part where I couldn't help but study long legs; I wonder how they'd wrap around my waist.

And as I watched her roll her head to the side, stretching out her muscles as the silky fall of her hair moved over the back of her neck, oblivious to my study, I knew that Greer was managing exactly that.

Instead of a light, it was a warning siren.

*Danger. Approach with caution.*

*Do not touch the wild creature if it comes near you.*

Greer stood, gently arching her back with another groan, ambling into the kitchen, her hips swaying unconsciously as she pulled a drink from the fridge.

I pinched my eyes shut.

Because fuck, this was not good.

She'd told me, clearly and repeatedly, that I was not her type. I'd told her the exact same in return.

Yet there I sat, wondering what my fake wife would do if I

walked up behind her and slid my hands underneath those short shorts.

Wondered if she'd make a different sort of noise, with a different arch of her back.

There was a knock on the door, and I blew out a hard puff of air. With a slight glance down at my lap, I made a brief concerted effort to think about algebra before I stood to greet Josie and Olive.

The door opened, Josie's smiling face popping through. "Can we come in?"

My brow furrowed. "Of course."

She aimed a loaded look at Greer. "Just checking."

Greer cleared her throat delicately, cheeks flushed a pretty pink. "You're safe," she said.

Olive skipped into the house, and I crouched down to greet her, my heart melting when she jumped straight into my arms. "Hey, sweet pea," I said, dropping a kiss onto her hair. "You have a good week with Mommy and Micah?"

She nodded, pointing to a new headband covered in sparkles and tiny little printed butterflies. "Look what I got," she whispered.

"It's beautiful," I told her.

Olive beamed. Her eyes slid over to Greer, and I held my breath a little to see how this would go.

"Wanna go show her?" I asked quietly.

Olive's gaze locked with mine, and she managed a shy nod.

Josie and I watched quietly as Olive tiptoed toward the

kitchen, light little steps on the balls of her feet. Greer kept her expression neutral, setting her drink down as Olive approached. Then she crouched down in the same way I did.

Olive stopped a couple of feet away, spinning back and forth, then tapping her headband with a tiny smile.

"Did your mom pick that out for you?" Greer asked, keeping her hands tucked between her knees. Her eyes were warm and steady on my daughter's face.

Olive nodded.

"Can I see it?" she asked.

Olive nodded again, coming a few steps closer and tilting her head down.

"I *love* it," Greer said. "I wish they made one that could fit me too."

Olive smiled, shyly reaching out her hand to touch the ends of Greer's hair, right where the pink paint stained the tips.

Greer's eyes met mine, and she grinned.

"Do you like pink?" she asked Olive.

My daughter nodded again, a bit more forcefully.

"I'm very glad to hear that," Greer continued. "Is it okay if I put a little bit of that color in your bedroom upstairs?" she asked quietly, tapping a light finger to her hair, where Olive's fingers still rubbed against the dried paint.

Olive's eyes widened, and a quick gasp left her mouth. "Yes," she breathed. "Can I go look?"

"Go ahead," I told her. "But don't open the door until we're up there with you."

Olive raced up the stairs, hair streaming behind her, and the three of us laughed.

"I can't wait to see it," Josie said to Greer.

"Me too," I added.

Josie's eyebrows arched in surprise. "You didn't help?"

I tilted my head toward Greer. "She wouldn't let me."

Greer smiled. "I'm a little bit stubborn."

Josie wound her arm through Greer's as they preceded me up the stairs. "I think you'd have to be if you're married to him," she said.

Greer burst out laughing.

At the top of the steps, Olive practically bounced in place, her hand on the doorknob as she waited for us.

"Go ahead," Greer told her.

Olive sucked in a deep breath and pushed open the door.

Josie gasped, hand covering her mouth immediately. "Greer," she exhaled quietly.

Olive walked slowly into the room, her eyes as wide as I'd ever seen them, her mouth hanging open.

Three of the walls were a soft pink color, and covering the wall behind the bed was a bold pattern of pink and white and coral flowers.

Fluffy white bedding and some fuzzy pastel pink pillows in a lighter shade than the wall covered the bed. There was a big scoop-shaped reading chair with a small circular table and a tall gold lamp next to it.

On the opposite wall from the bed was a long sleek white

desk, neatly organized clear bins filled with colored pencils and crayons and markers. And like it was growing out of the wall was a graceful arch of big white, lace-winged butterflies flying toward the windows overlooking the backyard. Right in the middle of the flight path of all the white wings was a canvas print of the picture I showed Greer, so it looked like all the delicate flying creatures surrounded Olive.

My eyes darted to Greer, who was wringing her hands in the wake of our collective stunned silence.

"It's incredible," I told her, voice hoarse with emotion.

She breathed a quiet sigh of relief but then moved her gaze back to my daughter, who still spun in a slow circle like she could hardly take everything in.

"How did you *do* all this?" Josie asked.

Greer looked around the room with a pleased smile. "Some great vendors who owed me favors and a lot of priority shipping."

"This is mine?" Olive said. Her voice trembled, and her eyes were glossy with tears.

"Yeah, sweet pea," I told her. My chest was tight, heavy from the unexpected wall of emotion. "Greer did this for you. She's been working on it all week."

Josie wrapped her arm around mine, and I heard her emit a quiet sniffle.

Greer crouched next to Olive, and I could tell in the twitch of her hands that she wanted to set her hand on my daughter's back, but she didn't.

"Do you like it?" she asked.

Olive didn't answer. She let out a shaky exhale, then turned to Greer, throwing her arms around her neck in a tight hug. Then she nodded into Greer's neck.

"You gave me butterflies," Olive said.

My eyes burned when a tear slid down Greer's face unchecked. She carefully returned the embrace and let out a huge, shoulder-dropping exhale. "I did."

A new sort of awareness slid underneath the space in my chest, unfurling warm and slow.

It was so much more dangerous than lust.

Far more explosive than thoughts about legs and arching backs and short shorts.

I'd chosen right, I reminded myself.

But one wrong step, with this new awareness, these new thoughts, and everything we were building would come crashing down.

# CHAPTER 15

# Greer

**There was a problem with Olive's new room. It took me** three hours after Josie left to figure it out.

I sat downstairs on the couch sketching on my iPad, playing with some renders for a client, when the light bulb went off.

It happened with occasional sounds filtering down the steps—usually Beckett's low, rumbling voice, punctuated with warm bursts of his laugh.

My pencil slowed whenever I heard it because I didn't often get to see him laugh, and I wondered what Olive said that made it happen.

The problem in that room, as I'd discovered over the lonely three hours I'd spent on the couch, was that neither of them wanted to leave it.

It shouldn't have seemed so complicated, whether or not I was welcome, but I sifted through all the reasons I shouldn't go in there with them over and over and over.

In theory, I was her stepmom. Someone to act as a partner to her dad, but I wasn't invited into Beckett's life to mother her.

She had a mother, and a really good one from what I could tell.

In reality, I was her dad's roommate. A backup if something went wrong, and an extra adult in the house for emergencies.

That roommate label was uncomfortable to slip into. I didn't really like how it fit now that I was separate from them.

It was different when Olive had been gone. Easier to maintain boundaries between how we spent our time in the house.

I'd kept myself so busy in that room all week because it was something tangible I could do, but now that it was done, my role in the house felt incredibly uncertain.

Beckett laughed again, and I tapped a pencil against the side of my leg.

My phone buzzed next to me, and I smiled when I saw a message from Josie.

> **JOSIE**
> I just want to thank you again for her bedroom. I keep thinking about how much she'll love it over the next year, and I'm so grateful that Beckett found someone so thoughtful.

Guilt tore through any happy feelings that the text might

have brought, shredding at the edges of my already tenuous mood.

I hated being alone when the feels got too big. These were the moments when I'd go home, let the noise and chaos of my parents' house stabilize my heart, and replenish whatever felt lacking. My chest felt tight and achy, and I carefully tapped out a reply.

**ME**

> You're very welcome. She's been up there drawing and coloring since you left. We may never get her out of there!

**JOSIE**

> Lol! I'm not shocked at all. Oh, but that reminds me, I forgot to tell Beckett that she's been having some nightmares this week. I think it's our departure around the corner. But don't be surprised if she crawls in bed with you guys tonight!

"Oh shit," I whispered.

I glanced over at the main bedroom, just at the bottom of the stairs. The bedroom where I had definitely not been sleeping since the wedding.

After sending a quick reply to Josie that I'd let Beckett know, I tucked my phone in my pocket and ascended the stairs.

Olive was chattering happily to her dad, and I waited just out of sight to listen, unbearably curious to hear her when she was fully relaxed, felt fully safe to be herself.

"There are fifteen small butterflies and six big butterflies," she said. "I counted them all. And all the flowers behind the bed are like my own garden."

"Please don't water the wall. It would make an awful mess."

She giggled. "You don't water walls, Daddy."

"Oh you don't?" he said. "I've never been very good at gardening, sweet pea."

Olive was quiet. "You don't draw very good, either."

He laughed, warm and rich, and my toes curled up inside my fuzzy slippers. "I do great with a football, though, don't I?"

"Mm-hmm."

I leaned against the wall, listening to the scratch of pencil on paper, closing my eyes as I imagined the sweet scene. But once I popped my head around the corner, I'd interrupt it.

This is why we'd done this.

He'd get hundreds and hundreds of nights with her, instead of every other weekend, scrambling to catch up for lost time.

"I'm really good at drawing," she said in that sweet little voice.

"You get that from your momma," Beckett answered. "She's always been artistic."

It was so unbearably attractive that he and Josie had such a healthy relationship. That he spoke well of her and respected her. And that at moments when only his daughter could hear him, he said complimentary things.

Not my type.

*Not my type,* I reminded myself.

It was shockingly hard to remember sometimes.

Watching him sign autographs for little kids.

Falling onto the ground, laughing deep from his big chest when I tore his flags off in the charity game.

When he relaxed, when he felt comfortable to be himself and not hold everything so tightly bound, he was impossible to look away from.

Moving slowly, I peeked beyond the doorframe. Olive was lying with her stomach on the carpet, one elbow on the floor as she colored on a big piece of paper on top of a thick book. Her feet were crossed at the ankle, shifting back and forth as she concentrated on the paper.

Beckett sat on the floor, too, his back braced against the bed and his long legs stretched out next to Olive.

"Greer is good at drawing too," Beckett added. He was watching his own paper so closely that he hadn't noticed me yet.

Olive's colored pencil slowed, and she twisted her lips in thought. "Maybe she wants to color with us."

Beckett glanced at her, studying her face. "Would you like that?"

She nodded immediately. "I like Greer. She has nice eyes."

Beckett smiled. "I think she has pretty eyes too."

My cheeks flushed warm, and I was just about to back away from the door when Olive shook her head, selecting a different shade of the color pencil. "No. Not pretty. I can see her nice through her eyes."

My heart lurched, like some great big pulse of joy couldn't quite push through my veins.

Beckett slowly lowered his pencil and stared incredulously at his daughter. "You mean you can tell she's a good person from her eyes?"

Olive nodded. "That's why I like Parker too. I can see his nice too."

The bridge of my nose tingled ominously, a telltale burn pressing at the back of my eyes, and I willed that shit back. I'd already cried once that night because she hugged me and was not trying to keep that streak alive.

The hug was worth it, though, because nothing I'd ever done had felt so hard won as her skinny little arms tight around my neck.

I shifted my weight to my other foot, and Beckett caught the movement out of the corner of his eye.

I smiled, walking into the room like I hadn't just been shamelessly eavesdropping. "You two have been hard at work up here." Carefully perching on the end of her mattress, I made sure my legs didn't brush against Beckett's arm. "Can I see?"

Olive gave me a shy smile and slid her paper closer.

"Are those dahlias?" I asked, eyebrows climbing on my forehead because I was impressed.

She nodded.

"Those are really good, Olive," I told her. "I hope your daddy plans to put you in art lessons because you are very talented."

Olive slid a questioning look toward the man in question, and when I caught a glimpse of how he was looking at her, my whole body went butter soft and squishy.

Beckett nodded. "I think that's a good idea, sweet pea. I'll ask your mom and see if we can do that this summer."

Her pleased smile was slightly hidden because she tucked right back to work on her garden.

"Can I show you a trick?" I asked her.

When she nodded, I moved to the ground, crossing my legs and reaching for the container of thin-tipped markers. Glancing at Beckett, I tilted my chin at his paper. "Got some extras over there?"

He pulled from a small stack on the other side of his legs, offering me the large hardcover picture book he was using as his drawing surface.

Olive scooched closer.

"Your petals are beautiful," I told her. "But I can show you a really easy way to make the leaves." I arched the spring green marker along the paper for a stem and with a few quick flicks, I added some leaves. "If you make little marks like this, see? You make your shape of the leaf, and then you can connect them once you've got it. It's easier than trying to draw them the other way."

The look on Olive's face when she glanced back up at me was nothing short of pure adoration and awe.

"You're so good," she breathed.

I exhaled a laugh. "I have to draw a lot for work," I told her, voice low and conspiratorial. "I'm usually doing bedrooms and kitchens and stuff, but every once in a while, I get to draw some outdoor pictures for what the house will look like when it's done." Gently, I capped the marker and handed it back to her. "Including flowers. Why don't you give it a try?"

As she tucked her tongue between her teeth and attempted what I'd shown her, the big, quiet man next to me slowly shifted forward to watch. His shoulder brushed against mine, and I registered the smell of his body soap.

It was clean and crisp and I fought the instinct to close my eyes and lean into him.

When Olive showed me her first attempt, I beamed. "Love it."

She rolled her lips between her teeth, then sat up to mimic my posture. "Can you show me some more?" she asked.

Beckett and I traded a loaded look.

I was officially in the Olive Coleman circle of trust.

*Be cool.*

I managed a small nod. "I'd love to."

She exhaled in relief, her shoulders dropping.

It was that little glimpse that had my heart cracking straight down the middle because even as an almost-thirty something, I knew that shoulder slumping relief. And she was way too young to be feeling the kind of tense anticipation that held her body so tight.

Beckett gave her an apologetic smile. "Not tonight, Olive. We're getting close to bedtime, but maybe tomorrow?"

Her eyes lit up. "I'll practice really hard," she promised.

Beckett laughed under his breath.

I held his gaze. "Can I talk to you for a second?" And I tilted my head toward the hallway.

He nodded. "Ten more minutes, then we get pajamas on, okay?" he said to Olive, ruffling her baby-fine hair with his big, big hand.

"That's it?" Her face was so heartbroken.

"Ten," he repeated. "You can draw tomorrow."

She sighed, obviously disgruntled, and I managed to stifle my laugh.

Beckett's eyes were warm and happy when they met mine. He stood first, holding out a hand to help me up. I didn't realize I was holding my breath until his fingers curled around mine and I stood, the oxygen pressing from my lungs in a fast, hard whoosh.

Because before he let go, he gave my fingers a slight squeeze, his thumb brushing just once along the inside of my wrist.

I didn't dare search his face to see if it was intentional.

Some friendly little sign like, *hey, thanks for being a good enough human that my daughter likes you*. Maybe that was it.

Or maybe he had a thing for wrists.

I clenched my teeth and willed the thoughts away. Violently and ruthlessly shoved them back.

This…might be a problem.

Hand holding, in general, did not make me feel light-headed, heart-racing, overthinking type things. Hell, my last boyfriend, six months of my life that I would not get back, never held my hand at all.

He liked touching my ass.

And he had an unfortunate penchant for staring at *other* women's asses, in the end, but there was no casual gesture like that.

I found myself rubbing the spot where his thumb had brushed as we left the bedroom. He pulled the door shut behind him. "What's up?" he asked.

"I had a text from Josie when I was downstairs."

His eyebrows furrowed.

"She forgot to tell us earlier that she thinks her impending move to London is causing some nightmares for Olive. Apparently, she had a few this week."

He sighed, glancing back at the room. "She's done this before," he said. "Before she started school for the first time. She was terrified. Woke up almost every night."

I sucked in a breath, blowing it out through puffed cheeks. "Umm, Josie also said that Olive would likely just climb into bed with us if she woke up with one of those nightmares."

Beckett's entire frame went almost comically still.

His eyes locked onto mine.

After a moment, I nodded meaningfully. "Might be hard to explain if she tells Josie that I sleep in a different bedroom."

His throat moved on a hard swallow.

"So," I said. "That's the update."

Beckett's jaw ticked.

His silence made me edgy, so naturally, I couldn't shut up. "It'll be fine. It's a big bed."

At his side, his hand clenched in a fist.

I exhaled in a huff. "I know, I know, it's not ideal. You hate change and surprises, and now you have to share your bed with your wife who you do not find even remotely attractive."

"Don't put words into my mouth, Greer," he cut in. "That's not what I said."

His voice, so low and rough and charged, had my mouth going dry.

He was right. In my nerve-laden babbling, I'd said the words without thinking.

"What did you say then?" I asked evenly.

He gave me a long, unreadable look. "Not that," he finally answered.

Before he could say anything else, before I could say—or do—anything else, like launch myself at his face and see what happened, Olive opened her bedroom door. "My flowers are done. Pajama time?" she asked.

Beckett snapped the gaze, and with his eyes off mine, I let out a quiet, slow exhale at the easing of whatever had been pulled so tight between us.

"Yeah, sweet pea."

She hopped back into her room, the tuneless humming lightening whatever mood had settled over the two of us.

Mood.

Temporary insanity, whatever.

But he still looked very thrown-off by this new development.

And oh, it made me want to tease him mercilessly. "Do I have to get pajamas on now too?" I asked lightly.

His eyes churned with something I couldn't quite define.

Beckett brushed past me and down the stairs with light steps, and with a hand over my suddenly weightless stomach, I turned into the guest room to grab my clothes and move them into his bedroom.

Olive's bedtime routine was a well-oiled machine, and as I moved my things from the second bedroom upstairs down to Beckett's, I watched them navigate it with ease.

There was a snack at the kitchen counter. A graham cracker and a small glass of milk. She methodically dunked the cracker into the milk until it all but fell apart.

She brushed her teeth, standing on a step stool in her bathroom, for the full recommended two minutes, I was informed. No cavities for Miss Olive.

Beckett brushed out her hair, and the sight of *that* did things to me at an almost biological level.

Have you ever seen a six-five guy with huge biceps brush out his daughter's hair to make sure it wasn't tangled when she went to bed?

It would do things to you too, no matter *what* your type was.

In an effort to cool said things down to a manageable level, I closed myself into the main bedroom, finding an empty drawer or two in the bathroom to unpack my cosmetics after moving them from the guest bathroom and a section of the walk-in closet where I could hang the shirts I had with me.

The room was so clean and tidy, he didn't keep clutter anywhere, and even his clothes were mixed in among each other—dress shirts hung next to T-shirts and jeans folded in by athletic pants.

I ran my hand down the sleeve of a worn Portland Voyagers shirt, and before I could stop myself, I pulled it up to my nose to take a deep inhale.

Maybe Beckett wasn't my type, but fucking A he smelled addictive.

He found me there, just after the sleeve fell out of my hand.

"I've got some work to do in the back garage," he said. "I told Olive I'd build her a gardening bed, and I want to get started on it while it's still light."

I nodded, cheeks warm because five seconds earlier and he would have caught me sniffing his clothes.

"Need any help?"

He shook his head. "Just doing some measuring and cutting tonight. I may need a second set of hands tomorrow."

I found myself wringing my hands, standing in that closet with him, and he noticed, quirking one eyebrow when I stretched them out in an effort to stop.

"Umm, what side of the bed do you sleep on?" I asked. "I'm pretty beat, so I think I'll turn in early."

Beckett glanced at the bed, staring hard for a beat. "I like to sleep closest to the door," he said.

He held my gaze for a long moment, and I finally nodded. "You got it. You can be my body shield if someone breaks in."

"That's the idea," he murmured. "Though knowing you, you'd probably have your taser out before I even wake up."

I laughed, and his eyes snagged on my mouth for just a fraction too long.

He cleared his throat. "Well. I'll see you in the morning then. I uh, I hope I don't snore."

My smile threatened to overtake my face. "I guess I'll let you know tomorrow. Tell as much of the truth as possible, even if it's the only thing we do."

Beckett took one long look at my face, and then left the room just as quietly as he'd entered it.

My halfway husband—champion brusher of hair, horrible artist, and secret room-sneaking ninja skills.

An hour later, face washed, clad in my most appropriate pajamas—cotton shorts and a baggy T-shirt—I climbed between clean fresh sheets that smelled incredible. I pushed my face into the pillow and sighed happily.

"Oh I could get used to this," I moaned.

I fell asleep thinking about Beckett and wondered just how things might change when the sun came up.

## CHAPTER 16

# Beckett

**It could have been any number of things that woke me in** the middle of the night because I often found myself trying to get settled back into sleep when the skies were still dark.

The first fact that solidified was that the house was quiet.

There were no cries from Olive's room.

There was no small body creeping up onto the mattress with us.

And it was that thought—*with us*—when the second fact crept in.

Greer was in bed with me, and she was pressed tight against my back.

In her sleep, she'd moved against my body, her arm slung over my waist.

I hardly dared to breathe while I took stock of how we'd ended up in the handful of hours since I'd slipped as quietly as possible into bed next to her.

If Greer hadn't been in bed with me, I would have only been in boxer briefs, but out of deference, I'd kept on athletic shorts and that was it.

Her arm, a slim, warm anchor curled around the front of my body, her fingers twitching lightly in her sleep, brushing over my stomach.

I pinched my eyes shut.

*That's* what had woken me.

Her knees were tucked behind my legs, and because I couldn't help it, I took a deep breath, cataloging the soft press of her breasts against my back.

Every inch where we touched, Greer was warm and soft, the gentle lull of her even breathing was soothing enough that if I hadn't been so impossibly turned on, I might have been able to slide right back into sleep.

I pinched the bridge of my nose and counted to five, willing my body into submission.

This was better than the alternative, though, where I woke to my body draped around hers, my hand over her stomach, and my chest curved around her back, my hand sliding over her skin while she slept.

That wasn't helping, I realized quickly, when the image in my head roared hot and bright so quickly that it practically caused me pain.

Greer shifted in her sleep, emitting a soft, breathy noise.

I clenched my jaw, beginning the slow, incremental movement out from underneath her arm without waking her. Rolling to my stomach felt like it took an hour, but it was probably closer to a couple of minutes. Even though she didn't wake, she didn't roll with me either, her hand still sat on my back.

She twitched again, and when the edge of her fingernail scraped delicately over my skin, I pressed my hips into the mattress to seek any sort of relief from the building pressure.

The pillow under my face muffled the tortured groan, and only a few moments passed before Greer inhaled, then turned onto her back, her hand sliding off my body without inflicting further damage.

I exhaled in relief.

And when she rolled again, her back facing me now, I could finally relax.

It took reciting multiplication tables until my body was under control, and just as I started succumbing to sleep, I heard the quick patter of Olive's feet coming down the steps.

I sat up, rubbing my face.

"Daddy?" she whispered.

Olive had never liked the bottom of the stairs—the darkness always scared her—so we'd started keeping a night-light plugged in just beyond the last step.

It wasn't normal for her to wake up in the middle of the night, but we'd done it just enough times that I knew she wouldn't leave the stairs on her own.

"I'm up," I said. Greer stirred, murmuring something unintelligible as I found Olive on the bottom step, trying to peer around the corner.

When I swung her up in my arms, she buried her face into the side of my neck, sniffling quietly and taking sharp, shuddering breaths.

"Deep breaths for me, okay, sweet pea?" I said, smoothing my hand on her back in circles. "I'm right here."

Greer was sitting up in bed, watching us with bleary eyes.

With Olive clinging tightly to my chest, I sat against the headboard and rubbed her back while her breathing slowed incrementally, the tension seeping out of her body.

"Do you want to talk about your bad dream?" I asked her.

Sometimes she did, and other times she didn't.

"Not yet." She sniffled.

Greer mimicked my posture, positioning her pillow on her lap while she braced her back against the headboard and watched us quietly. She gave me a sleepy smile, and the sight of it triggered a reaction somewhere deep under my ribs.

It was different from earlier, with her hand on my skin. This was warm and slow, something that lingered and took its time to roll through my body.

Even with my daughter in the bed with us, sharing this kind of moment with her was strangely intimate. A different kind than coloring the night before. Or having her study our bedtime routine and eat with us for dinner.

After a few minutes, Olive's breathing slowed, and her body went lax.

She had fallen back asleep.

I didn't ease her onto the mattress immediately. I took a

moment to breathe in her sweet scent and memorize her slight weight in my arms. Every year she got older, these moments felt increasingly fleeting.

But we all needed sleep. I kissed the top of her head, then met Greer's gaze in the darkened room. "Can you grab an extra pillow?" I said quietly.

She nodded, climbing out of bed to snag one from the pile on the floor. Her legs were bare again, the hem of her dark-colored sleep shorts disappearing underneath the edge of her long shirt, and I tore my gaze away when she sat on her knees to shift her pillow to the side and make room for another.

Turning onto one hip, I was able to move Olive onto the bed without waking her, and she immediately curled onto her side, tucking her face into the pillow.

I blew out a slow breath.

"Poor thing," Greer murmured. Gently, she pushed some stray hairs out of Olive's sleeping face. "I used to get nightmares at this age too. I always wanted to climb in bed with my mom and Tim."

"Did they let you?"

She nodded. "Tim moved us back to our beds after we fell asleep. When you've got six kids in the house—seven after Poppy was born—there's only so much room for scared kids in the middle of the night."

There were so many questions I wanted to ask, but my eyes were heavy, and after only a moment, Greer slid back down onto her side of the bed, careful not to jostle Olive.

Her eyes found mine in the dark. "No snoring that I heard," she said lightly. "Did I hog the blankets?"

My lips edged up in a smile. "No."

"Good," she answered, voice drowsy and quiet. "G'night, Beckett."

I didn't answer right away. I simply watched the rise and fall of her frame as she slipped back into a deep slumber. Olive was facing her, their hands only inches away from each other.

Intimacy, I thought again.

Most people I knew confused the idea of it with sex. With the physical release of one body with another. And maybe that was a big part of it, the willingness and desire to cross those lines too. To let your pleasure loose alongside someone else's.

But to me, intimacy was trust.

When I tried to apply the lens of logic to what Greer and I were doing, I came up short every single time. It wasn't logical.

But despite that, I trusted her.

I trusted her with this part of me, the overwhelming desire to be the best father that I could, to prove that I was capable of loving Olive in a far more tangible way than I'd ever been shown growing up.

Even more, I trusted her with Olive.

We'd had such a short amount of time since I met her: less than a month since I'd walked through the doors of that restaurant.

Logic had no place in this.

But already I couldn't help but wonder how quiet and empty this house would seem when she wasn't part of it anymore.

With that thought lingering in the back of my head, it took a long time for me to get back to sleep. But I must have slept hard once I was there because when I pried my eyes open the next morning—the sun was already up, and the bed was empty of the two females who'd previously occupied half the king-size mattress.

Normally, when Olive climbed in with me, I woke with a foot somewhere under my ribs, but I took a moment to stretch out with a groan, slinging my hand over my face.

Saturdays when Olive was home usually started with pancakes or waffles or some scrambled eggs, and I wondered if she'd roped Greer into making her breakfast.

I tugged on a T-shirt, scratching my stomach underneath it when I walked out of the room.

I stopped short.

Something had happened in the kitchen, but I couldn't quite say for sure what it was.

Bowls were on the counter, pancake mix was dripping off the corner, powder dusting areas of the floor between the island and the sink. I ran a hand through my hair, blowing out a harsh breath.

There was a skillet sitting untouched on the stovetop.

No pancakes had been made, of that I was sure.

A burst of sound came from the back deck, and I turned to find the source.

They were both in their pajamas, standing over a giant piece of paper that had come from a roll of paper easily four feet tall.

Olive had a paintbrush in her hand and a smudge of red on her face.

Greer was no better. There was some yellow on her arm, which she must have swiped over her forehead.

I approached the slider with a strange mix of trepidation and sweet, warm curiosity.

Olive's eyes brightened when she saw me. "We're painting a garden," she said, bouncing lightly on her toes. "A big one."

"I see that." I scooped her up in my arms and kissed her cheek. "What on earth happened in the kitchen?"

Olive looked back at Greer, who offered only a sheepish smile.

"Greer isn't very good at cooking," Olive whispered, cupping her hand over my ear. "But we don't want to make her feel bad about it."

Greer suppressed a grin. "I put a bit too much water, then overcompensated with the mix, it was a whole thing. Then we decided to paint instead." She walked closer. "I'll clean it up, I promise."

"Please tell me you're not going to be responsible for the pancakes, though," I said.

She laughed. "I will happily cede that to you."

Olive wiggled to get down, hopping over the paper and dipping her paintbrush into a bowl to clean it off. "Watch what she taught me," she said, then swooped her brush over the paper, a proud grin on her face when she'd completed her stem.

"Amazing," I told her. My chest was warm, heavy with happiness, and something else that I couldn't quite name.

Greer lightly touched my arm and pulled me away from the painting. "I kinda stressed her out with the mess in the kitchen," she said quietly. "When I remembered the rosin paper in my trunk, I figured this was the best distraction I could think of."

I nodded. "Yeah, she doesn't love a big mess."

Greer studied my face. "She's exactly like you."

My eyes locked with hers.

She swallowed but didn't pull her gaze away. "Olive—she's exactly like you. No one's ever really said it, but she's quiet. Serious. A bit reserved when you meet her," she continued, like she wasn't yanking on some raw, exposed part of me that I'd never heard anyone verbalize before. "She doesn't like a loud, crazy environment if she's not expecting it. Makes it easier to think about how to fit in here," she said. Then she smiled. "I've got two peas in a pod as my brand-new roommates, so it helps that she's exactly like you, as long as you guys can make room for me while I'm here."

Then she patted my arm and walked back toward Olive, leaving me in stunned silence, wondering what the hell Greer Wilder was going to do to my life—and my heart—while she was in it.

# CHAPTER 17

# Greer

**Until I moved into the Coleman house, I was a very deep** sleeper.

My brothers used to joke that it would take a thundering hoard of angry men stomping into my bedroom to jar me awake. They tested that theory a few times too.

But upon sharing a bed with Beckett Coleman, I learned that I could be pried into consciousness with something far softer, far quieter, and far, far more complicated.

Namely, Beckett's hand on my tits.

Because eight days after I started sharing a bed with my fake husband, I woke up to his hand sliding under my shirt, over my rib cage and his big, hot hand spread wide over my skin.

I woke with a shocked gust of air, awareness was foggy and muddled, and my back arched instinctively. My thighs pressed together, and I registered the skipping rhythm to my heart at the intimacy of our position, and how very, very badly I wanted it to continue.

Normally, the biggest hint to his presence in the mornings when we both worked was the waiting pot of coffee—hot and strong—to let me know that he'd been there at all.

But now the hot was him—his palm skating over my bare skin and his broad chest at my back. The strong was him too because the ropes of muscles in his arms banded tight around my waist.

I knew he was still sleeping because his movements were slow, like there was no thought or intention behind them. His breaths ruffled the hair on the back of my neck, deep and even and strong.

Goose bumps pulled up along my arms, and I breathed quietly through my nose, trying to stay still, stay calm.

The sun was just starting to peek through the sky, so I knew it was early.

What was a girl to do?

I had been sharing a bed with the hottest man I'd ever met in my life, who I'd traded vows with, and I'd kept my hands off.

What would happen if I *didn't* keep my hands off?

As I was filtering through all the pros and cons of this particular situation, his thumb moved.

Just his thumb.

There was a slight callus to the edge of his finger, and when it brushed over the bottom curve of my breast, the air hitched in my lungs.

Beckett's arm tightened, his hips pushing closer to my backside.

My lips rolled between my teeth because a whimper threatened to escape my mouth.

He was hard.

And big.

And hard.

And right fucking *there*.

I pinched my eyes shut and wondered how the absolute hell I was going to navigate out of this, or if I even wanted to. There were options, of course.

Arch the ass back, just a little.

Cover his hand with my own, ease him just a few inches higher because I may not have a large chest, but I desperately wanted to know how much of my skin he'd be able to fit into his big palm or what he'd be able to manage with that calloused thumb if he pushed his hand down underneath the elastic band around my shorts.

The thought of it had my thighs pressing together again, slightly harder than the last time, seeking relief where there was none.

I could turn gently and see what would happen if I woke him up with my mouth against his. My body started melting as I played that one out in my head for just a few selfish moments.

He'd roll me to my back, press me hard into the mattress, yank my thighs open so he could fit his hips between mine.

Gawd. It had been so long since I'd had a good

over-the-clothes make out session, and let me tell you, the men of my generation did not appreciate it far enough. They went straight for the Promised Land, and sometimes, you wanted to torture yourself a bit with the feel of him rocking against you.

Because it *was* a promise.

And judging by what Beckett was pressing up against my ass, he could make really, really big promises.

My whole body melted like butter the longer I lay there, and in the moment I finally relaxed into his embrace, I felt him freeze.

His arm went stiff.

His hips moved back just an inch.

And *dammit all*, his thumb stopped moving.

I kept breathing even because if he made one move forward, I'd turn.

I'd turn and see what happened.

But Beckett eased his arm off my waist, and in only a few seconds, rolled gently onto his back and exhaled.

"Fuck," he whispered.

Even as I kept my body motionless, my mind raced.

Was that a good fuck? Or a bad fuck?

Because there was a wide range between the options.

All I knew was that he did his best to ease out of bed, creeping across the room as silently as possible.

It took Beckett less than five minutes from first realization to getting the hell out of Dodge, and I had no clue what that meant.

And listen, I was no chickenshit, okay? But I didn't exactly feel like chasing him out into the kitchen to ask if he liked the idea of his thumb on my nipples.

I did.

I wanted that thumb right back where I'd found it upon waking.

I wanted both thumbs, actually.

Maybe his tongue. And some teeth.

With the room free of his confusing presence, I rolled to my back and speared a hand through my hair.

Olive hadn't climbed into bed with us for the last handful of nights.

With no one to wake us, no one to interrupt our sleep patterns, maybe it was inevitable that this would happen.

I pinched my eyes shut, rolling back onto my side.

That muttered curse of his, low and rough and ragged, echoed in my brain as I tried to dissect what it meant.

It stayed on repeat, just that one murmured word, as I fell back into a fitful sleep for another hour or so.

When I woke, it was to the sound of the kitchen door slamming shut. With a glance at the bedside clock, I knew it was Beckett leaving to take Olive to school.

I stretched and yawned, tugging my hair into a ponytail as I shuffled out to the kitchen to find the coffee—hot and strong and waiting for me as usual.

I glared at the steaming liquid as I poured it into a generous-sized mug. Not that it was the coffee's fault.

It wasn't anyone's fault, really.

But the problem lay in just how unclear all this was. What I wanted to do was call Adaline and dissect this with her. Ask for her advice.

Obviously not an option, given she thought this was very, very real.

And when I thought about calling Cameron to ask him, I almost snorted coffee up my nose at the look of abject horror that would cross his face.

"That might be worth it actually," I said to the empty house.

I tried to push it from my head, showering and getting ready for a day of computer work and phone meetings with a few of our clients. The intern and I hopped on the phone so I could give her a list of things to follow up on, and after two quick calls from Cameron about Detroit Lake, I spent an hour updating some of the budget projections for upcoming builds. By the time I got to lunch, I heated some leftovers and called my mom, setting the phone on the counter with the speaker on so I could eat.

"How was Dad's appointment with the palliative care doctor this morning?"

She hummed. "Fine. We're adjusting some of his meds, see if they can help with the breathing issue we noticed this week."

During my visit a few days earlier, I'd noticed the slightly labored quality to his breathing.

That was the hardest part of all this. We didn't know exactly how the next few months would go. How the cancer might spread and how fast it would move.

Everything about it felt precarious. Each good day still held a slightly unsteady quality, like it could all come crashing down without warning.

"I'll come out this weekend," I said. "Maybe Saturday?"

"Bring Beckett and that sweet little girl if they can make it too," she said. "I'd love to spend some more time with them. Your dad would too."

I pinched my eyes shut. "I'll ask him when he gets home from the facilities later."

"It's nice to have a bonus grandbaby," she said quietly. "Erik and Lydia live too far away, so I've only gotten my hands on Isla a couple of times since she was born. And I know Olive is still getting to know all of us, but…it's nice to think about having her over here." My heart tore in two at the sound of her voice. "Maybe she could help me bake some cookies or something, if she likes doing that."

I pressed the heels of my hands against my eyes and fought a wave of cold, prickling tension as it crawled up my body. Somehow I managed to keep my tone light. "I don't know if she likes baking. I certainly won't be any help there if she does."

My mom laughed. "That's the truth, my darling daughter. That is the truth."

We chatted for a few more minutes, and when I disconnected the call, I decided to work out, channel some of the uncomfortable energy left lingering at my mom's innocent excitement.

*You idiot,* I thought, a vicious edge to my internal voice.

This is the shit Cameron warned me about, and I just didn't want to listen, so focused on the why, so focused on the good that it would bring. And all those things were still true, but there was a fallout that we'd have to talk about. Boundaries that we'd need to discuss.

I eyed the clock while I changed into leggings and a tank top. Beckett told me he'd pick up Olive from school on his way home, so I had some time to kill until I could talk to him about all this…extra.

Maybe I'd talk to him about the morning too.

As I wandered across the backyard to where he had his gym equipment set up in the heated barn, I thought about all the various ways that might play out.

I stretched, thinking about the way he'd uttered that single solitary *fuck*.

I warmed up with a slow jog on the treadmill, thinking about the heat of him at my back, the size of his body compared to mine.

I moved to the rower, a sleek machine angled so that I could stare out at the gorgeous land surrounding his house, and as my body hummed, my blood pumping and the sweat beading along my back and chest, I found myself thinking about his thumb.

I pushed harder, thinking about the roughness of the skin and the gentle touch he'd given me when he wasn't thinking.

The air sawed in and out of my lungs, and I thought about the way his hips pressed against my backside.

I snapped my eyes shut and refused to go any further in my head.

Because I had a feeling that the very quiet, very serious man who I shared a bed with every night could unleash holy hell on me.

The really, really good kind.

I climbed off the rower, my legs shaky and my lungs screaming for air, when a call interrupted the music playing in my earbuds.

"'Lo," I said through my labored breathing.

"Oh my gosh, were you having sex?" my sister Adaline asked.

"Do you think I would have answered if I was?"

She paused. "No."

I laughed. "He's at the team facilities. I was feeling jittery and decided to get some energy out after I ate lunch."

"You've been married for a couple of weeks and you still have enough energy to work out voluntarily during the day?" She hummed obnoxiously. "Anything you'd like to share with the class?"

My face—already hot from the workout—felt bright red. "Nothing juicy, calm down. Olive has been having nightmares, so there are a lot of…interruptions at night," I answered carefully.

She made a sympathetic noise. "Stepmom life, eh?"

Gawd, my family. Maybe they had a meeting that morning and decided to shove all the complexities of my situation right into my face.

"Yup," I said lightly. "She's a great kid. It's hard to complain."

"When our house is done, you'll have to bring her up to Bellevue. Maybe we could do a girls' weekend, have Lydia and the baby come. Poppy too, if her schedule allows it."

"Don't you have, like, six to eight months of construction left?"

She sighed. "Yes. If everything stays on schedule."

"And what a mighty big if that is." I smiled. "What are they working on now?"

Adaline launched into her construction stories, something I loved hearing about because nothing was better than watching her build a beautiful, happy life with the man she loved.

By the time we hung up, I was done with my workout, and I took a quick shower before sitting back down with my laptop.

I was neck-deep in studying some plans from our architect when my phone buzzed with a text.

**BECKETT**

> I know this is last minute, but are you okay with Olive for a few hours if Josie picks her up from school? The guys kind of forced a bachelor party on me because I didn't tell anyone I was getting married unless they found out from Parker. And I can't really...not do it.

I grinned, imagining how this might play out in a team's weight room. No, there wasn't much he could do about it if he didn't want to raise suspicions.

**ME**

I'd love to hang out with her tonight. But are you and Josie okay with me watching her for a few hours? Because I'd understand if Josie wanted to keep her until you got home. I'm still new.

**BECKETT**

I trust you.

**ME**

Okay, then yes, I'm in. Would it be easier if I pick her up from school?

**BECKETT**

You're not on the approved list yet, but we'll take care of that before Josie leaves.

Josie said she'll be there in about an hour. I told the guys I'd hang out, but I had to be home to put Olive to bed.

The simplicity of that trust was an even greater weight than any of the things my family had said to me throughout the day. They were viewing our situation through the lens I'd handed them. It was almost right. Sort of clear. But at the end of the day, incomplete.

Beckett was the only one truly in this with me, and the fact that he was trusting me with the person he treasured most in the world...

It was a lot to process.

> **ME**
> Then a girls' night it is. Have fun and be safe.

He responded with a simple, *I will*, and I was able to get most of my work done before Josie's car pulled up to the house a bit over an hour later. I blew out a quick breath, opening the door for them when they arrived.

"It's the art phenom," I said. "How was your day?"

She grinned, flipping a folder around so I could see a brightly colored watercolor painting on crinkled paper.

"Whoa, that is very cool."

Josie smiled. "She told me all about the flower trick you taught her." She leaned in, dropping her voice low. "I think you have a fan for life now."

My cheeks flushed warm. "Well, so does she. She's a great kid, Josie."

Josie eyed me as she set Olive's backpack down on the floor. "It's a big deal that I'm willing to leave her here with you," she said carefully. "I don't take this lightly. I hope you know that."

I nodded. "I do. I don't take it lightly either."

"Good," she said. "Now, what junk food did you bring into

the house for an after-school snack because I know Beckett never has anything good."

I laughed, ushering her toward the cookies my mom sent home with me on my last visit, and the three of us sat at the island. Josie told me stories about Micah when they first started dating, how hard it was for Olive to warm up to him.

"Drawing flowers is the way to go," I said with a shrug. When I sent a tiny wink to Olive, she giggled around a mouthful of chocolate chip cookie.

Josie smiled. "Apparently." She stood from the stool with a glance at her watch. "I should go. Micah will be home from work soon, and I promised him we'd do some wedding stuff tonight." She kissed Olive on the top of the head. "I'll talk to you soon, okay?"

"Love you," Olive said.

They hugged, and Josie dropped a few more quick kisses onto Olive's cheeks, pulling some more laughs from the little girl.

Olive dashed away from the island, hopping up the stairs to go put her things away in her room.

Josie watched her go with a sad smile, pulling her purse over her shoulder. "It never gets easier," she said. "I always think it will."

I hated those moments when I damn well knew there was nothing I could say to make it better. It butted up against that side of my personality that wanted to *do something*, take away the hard if I could manage it.

Instead, I offered her a sad smile in return and a small bit of truth. "I can't even imagine."

"It helps a lot that she's happy here," Josie said. Just before she opened the door to leave, she turned. "Oh," she said. "When I got her from school today, I added you to the approved pickup list in the office. Just in case something happens while I'm gone, I wanted to make sure you were cleared to get her."

"Thank you," I said feelingly. "That's really nice of you to take care of that for Beckett."

She opened her mouth to answer when her phone buzzed. She glanced at the screen with a wince. "Ooh, I lost track of time. Thanks for the cookies and the conversation."

"Anytime."

Based on the smile she gave me in return, she knew I meant it.

I exhaled slowly because the entire day was a whole lot of a *whole lot*. We'd basically hit every loop on the roller coaster of a blended family, and it showed no signs of stopping any time soon.

But now was the fun part.

I dug into my bag and found my paper sketch pad, deciding to ditch the iPad for my evening with Olive.

When I found her, she was sitting at her desk, tongue tucked between her teeth and a mess of crayons and markers around her paper.

"All right, my little Monet. Want to go outside and find some flowers to sketch?"

Her eyes lit up. "Really?"

I tilted my head toward her window. "The rain stopped a bit ago, and that rhododendron bush back by the barn is very pretty right now. I think we have to."

We decided to keep things simple, just a basic lead pencil and some paper, and before I knew it, her stomach rumbled loud and furious as we both worked on a patch of wildflowers we found a ways beyond the house.

Olive and I both sat cross-legged in the grass, even though it was still a bit damp from the morning rain, and when her stomach rumbled again, she slapped a hand over it in shock.

"That was you?" I teased. "That was as loud as Parker's stomach when he's hungry."

She peeked at my paper, eyes wide when she saw my various sketches. "Yours is better," she said softly.

"I've had a lot of years of practice. And I went to school to learn how to draw the way I do now," I reminded her. "And when I was your age, I definitely wasn't as good as you."

Some of the sadness cleared from her big eyes, and she hopped onto her feet, swiping the grass and dirt from the back of her pink leggings.

"What should we have for dinner?" I asked as we walked back.

She didn't answer right away. "Is Daddy gonna eat with us?"

I shrugged. "I'm not sure. He just said he'd be back to put you to bed."

"Maybe pizza?" she asked, glancing up at me. "He never eats that."

Judging by the state of his abs, this did not surprise me. When I thought about his shirtless chest against my back again, I cleared my throat.

"Pizza it is," I declared.

We called the closest restaurant that delivered, sharing an apple and some grapes while we waited for it to arrive. Olive asked if we could watch TV—her favorite show featured an animated horse—so we watched an episode while we polished off a respectable half of a medium pizza.

She had one piece.

So…the respectable polishing was really just me.

The clock neared seven, and Olive told me she was going to read in her room for a little bit. While I cleaned up our dinner mess, I decided that the sort of stepmom gig wasn't all that bad.

When the counters were sparkling and clean, I stood back and surveyed the family room. Maybe he'd let me do a little painting in here too. I eyed the rock fireplace. It needed a big mantel to add some visual interest. I made a note to ask Cameron if he'd be able to build something that could be mounted on the large stones.

In my head, I imagined ways to frame some of Olive's artwork when an unfamiliar vehicle pulled into the driveway. A few guys were in the car when I saw Beckett climb out of the passenger seat. Someone tossed a gym bag out at him, and it fell on the ground. He stared at it for a beat, slowly bending down to pick it up, and I realized with a grin that he looked a little tipsy.

I covered my mouth with one hand, emitting a shocked laugh when he stumbled on the first step of the porch, and whoever was driving the car stuck his head out and hollered at Beckett. I didn't know every player on the roster, but I was fairly certain he was one of the offensive linemen.

Beckett couldn't see me where I was standing, and I watched him try to sober up right before my eyes. He blinked, very hard. He blew out a long, slow breath and then opened the door with great intention.

Because he'd gone from the weight room to…wherever they'd brought him, he still had that slightly rumpled look after a good workout. His hair was slightly disheveled, and it should not look as good on him as it did.

Probably because he was hardly ever this out of sorts.

I crossed my arms and watched as he let himself in the house. His eyes landed on me and his mouth curved in an adorably crooked grin.

"Wife," he said in greeting.

My eyebrows arched slowly. "Husband."

"Where's Olive?" he asked.

I pointed upstairs. "Reading. We had a fun night."

"Good." Beckett swallowed, his gaze tracking down the entire length of my body.

I felt that look.

Like a hand over my ribs.

Like a thumb on the curve of my breast.

"How much did you have to drink?" I asked.

"Not much," he admitted. "But… I never drink, so it doesn't take much either."

"Ahh." I walked over and held my hand out for his bag. "I'll take that. There's some pizza in the fridge if you want to put something in that stomach."

He hummed. "That sounds good. I never eat pizza."

"I can tell," I mused.

"How?" He swayed a little in place.

I plucked at the front of his T-shirt. "How do you think?" I asked. "Guys with stomachs like yours never eat the good stuff."

Beckett's eyes seared into mine, surprisingly lucid for a guy who wasn't sober.

"What?" I asked.

His eyes burned when he answered. "The guys told me I should come in and take you straight to bed."

My cheeks heated, but I refused to look away. "That so? I dearly hope my brother wasn't in the car because I'm about to feel really awkward."

He laughed, a dimple popping in the dark stubble on his face, and my stomach clenched at the sight of it.

"What'd you tell them?" I asked lightly. "When they made that helpful little suggestion."

Beckett didn't answer right away, but his gaze locked on my mouth. "I told them the truth."

I sucked in a sharp breath. "Which truth would that be?"

He was still staring at my lips when he answered. "That when I woke up this morning, I had my hand up your shirt, but I couldn't do anything about it because I knew I had to leave. That's when they told me to go finish what we started."

My mouth fell open, a shocked burst of air pushing from my lungs.

He pinched his eyes shut. "Shit, I shouldn't have said that, you slept through the whole thing and I felt like such an asshole. This is why I never drink."

I swallowed, dredging up a moment of vulnerability because this could go sideways so very, very fast.

"I didn't," I managed to push out.

His gaze snapped to mine. "Didn't what?"

"I didn't sleep through the whole thing." I took a step closer, and his face went wary. "I...was awake when you left the bed."

Beckett breathed hard, his eyes dark. "I'm drunk."

I nodded.

"We shouldn't talk about this right now."

"Right."

"You weren't asleep?" he asked, voice low and demanding.

I shook my head.

Beckett clenched his jaw. "Why didn't you pull away?"

My heart rattled urgently, and it was really hard to keep the honest answer crammed down somewhere safe, but we were about to revisit this whole 'you're not my type' thing, and I wasn't sure this was the right time.

Because I had a feeling—something I couldn't ignore even if I wanted to anymore—that my husband was very much my type, and I had no idea what to do about it.

"I thought you didn't want to talk about this right now," I reminded him gently.

He sighed, rubbing his face, suddenly looking very tired and a touch more sober than he had when he first walked in. "I know."

"Maybe tomorrow?"

The sounds of Olive up in her bedroom pulled his attention away. "Yeah." He managed another slight smile. "And maybe some of that pizza to start?"

I patted him on the shoulder. "And a big glass of water."

## CHAPTER 18

# Greer

**When I was younger, I had a major obsession with Julia** Roberts. The entire Roberts catalog is locked so deeply into my brain that I can recall any line of dialogue from one of her movies.

And the very first thing that I thought of when I got a call from Olive's school—the absolute first thing—was Julia Roberts in *Stepmom*.

She swooped in, so cool and levelheaded and helped her stepdaughter lay the smackdown on some bullies.

It was totally going to be me, I thought, as I marched into the elementary school office ten minutes down the road. The woman at the front desk greeted me with a smile. "Can I help you?"

Before I could tell her why I was there, Olive was already running around from behind her desk, hurtling at my legs, emitting the tiniest, most pathetic little sniffles I'd ever heard.

I crouched down and rubbed my hand down her back as she hugged me tight. "What happened?" I asked.

Olive didn't answer. She just tightened her arms around my neck. Her whole body was trembling.

The school secretary came around from her desk. She spoke quietly, an understanding smile on her face. "We had a little exchange on the playground, and she wanted to go home. Let me get the elementary school dean. She can tell you a little bit more about what happened."

Once Olive had calmed down a little, I asked if she'd go wait back behind the desk while I spoke to the dean. I crossed my arms as a serious-looking woman in wire-rimmed glasses explained to me that it involved an upper elementary school boy.

"One of Olive's friends found her crying underneath the slide. She told the friend the boy pushed her, but we couldn't find anyone who actually witnessed the…incident."

"What did the boy say when you talked to him?" I asked.

The dean offered a small grimace. "He said nothing happened."

"Yeah fucking right," I muttered.

She gave me a reproachful look but didn't correct me.

"Olive won't tell us much of anything, and we're not going to force it," she said. "We know she's a shy kid, and we also know she's not prone to lying. Unfortunately, without any witnesses, the best we can do is let him know he can't…" She paused.

"Push little girls on the playground," I finished helpfully.

"Yes." She shrugged. "I'm sorry. These are tricky situations, and we never want our kids to feel unsafe. If Beckett and Josie would like to come back in to meet with me, I'm happy to schedule something."

I nodded. "Josie was at the dentist today, and I think Beckett just didn't hear his phone ring. But I'll tell them what you said."

She handed me her card. "Thanks for coming so quickly. Normally we'd try to get her to stay at school, but we know Olive is really sensitive to changes in her environment."

I managed a smile. "I'd be sensitive to someone shoving me over too."

At my terse reply, she didn't get defensive, simply smiled in understanding. "I have a daughter. I get it. Tell Olive we hope to see her back tomorrow, okay?"

When I rounded the front desk, I held my hand out. "Ready to go?"

She nodded, eyes still red and her cheeks splotchy from crying.

"Bye, sweetie," the secretary said as she left.

Olive gave her a tiny smile.

The playground was a buzz of activity when we walked through the parking lot to my car, and I made sure she was buckled into one of the booster seats I'd snagged from the garage on my way out the door. Olive stared out the window at the kids playing, sniffing loudly as I set her backpack onto the seat next to her.

"Want to tell me what happened?" I asked quietly.

She didn't answer at first. Then she blinked up at my face,

and my heart turned slow and smooth in my chest. There was so much trust there, after just a couple of weeks.

"He ripped my picture," she said. "I was going to show my friend, and he pushed me down and took it and ripped it and told me it was ugly."

"Oh that little fucker," I breathed.

Her eyes got huge in her face.

"Sorry." I winced. I stared at the playground. "Do you see him over there?"

She turned in her seat and stared for a few minutes, then nodded. "He's the tall boy with red hair and the gray shirt."

He looked like an asshole. Beady eyes. Sharp nose. And easily four to five years older than Olive. He was far bigger than most kids on the playground, and I narrowed my eyes when I saw him knock over another little girl when he ran past. He laughed too.

I wanted to kick the shit out of him.

"You all right in there for a minute?" I asked her.

She nodded.

I closed the door and pulled my phone out, pulling up Cameron's contact info. He answered on the second ring.

"What's up?"

"How do we feel about threatening children?"

"Bad?" he answered immediately.

I rolled my eyes. "I mean, like a bully. I'm at Olive's school, and some little a-hole kid pushed her down and ripped her picture. I'm probably supposed to walk away and be an adult, but this kid is big, and he's mean, and they can't do anything about it because no one saw it happen."

Cameron whistled.

"I know," I huffed. "And I just saw him knock over another little girl. He's a *menace*."

"Greer." He sighed. "You've already decided what you want to do. I've got a hundred things waiting for me right now, so if you don't mind, I need to get back to work."

"So I can go threaten him? Think about what you'd do if it was your kid."

"Olive isn't your kid," he reminded me quietly. "You're in her life for a short time, and yes, you can make a positive impact, but you're not her mom."

My eyes burned as I stared at her little face through the window. With the back of her hand, she swiped underneath her nose.

My ribs squeezed.

"I know she's not," I said. But I couldn't do nothing either. If it was a niece or nephew or one of my cousins, I'd feel this same hot flare of protectiveness.

"Don't do anything crazy, Greer," Cameron warned. "I've gotta get back to work."

He hung up, and I kept staring at that playground.

There was something uncomfortable about how far I'd go to take this feeling away from Olive. And wonderful. Because I'd never quite felt it before.

Only for my family, I realized. And they'd never been *helpless*.

Not like this. Not the kind of helpless that a little girl felt when a larger, scary boy set her in his sights.

I opened the door. "I'll be right back, okay?" I told her.

"Where are you going?" she asked. Her eyes were big and scared.

I leaned in so she could see my face. "Just right there by the fence. Your teachers can't do much about this because they didn't see it happen, and they have a lot of rules they need to follow. Which is good. Teachers need rules to keep order, right?" I tapped her nose. "I don't."

When she gave me a tentative smile, I smiled back. She unhooked her seat belt and scrambled around onto her knees so she could see out the back window of my car.

By the time I approached the fence, the kid was dragging a huge stick along the metal edge.

"Hey, kid," I said.

He glanced over. "What?"

"Can I ask you a question?"

"It's a free country, lady, you can do whatever you want."

What a *peach*. I took a deep breath.

"What a true statement that is," I murmured. "You the one who pushed my stepdaughter and tore her picture?"

His face pulled into a slight sneer. "I'm not stupid. If I say yes, you can get me in trouble."

I crossed my arms. "Also true. You ever seen what a nail gun can do to someone's balls?"

His eyes widened, his face leeching of color. "You're crazy."

I smiled, leaning in closer to the fence. Then I tapped my temple. "I'd remember that if I were you."

He reared back. "I'm telling my teacher."

I shrugged. "Go for it. No one heard me say anything. That's how it works, right? You push her when no one's watching so you can't get in trouble for it?"

His face bent in a frown.

"Someday, you're gonna bully someone who's ready to fight back, and I can't *wait* to hear about it."

He sucked in a breath and took off running.

I didn't feel smug, though. And I didn't quite feel as victorious as Julia Roberts in *Stepmom*.

I felt helpless.

When I got back in the car, Olive was eyeing me with a mix of curiosity and caution. "What did you tell him?"

"Nothing you need to worry about," I told her.

And probably something I'd get in trouble for, once Beckett and Josie were apprised of the situation.

I knew him well enough now, he would have been the pragmatic level head. He would have approached everything with calm deliberation.

As I buckled myself in, a hysterical laugh fought to break free at how very much the opposite I was.

"I think I might get in trouble with your dad for that," I told her.

She met my gaze in the rearview mirror. "I'll stick up for you, Greer."

Well shit.

My throat went all tight and achy. "Thanks, Olive." Before we left the school, I sent Josie and Beckett a text that I had her from school and that I could tell them about what happened later, then I glanced at my watch. "We've got a couple of hours until your dad is home. Want to stop at the art supply store and pick out some new stuff?"

"Can we get some new markers?" she asked, eyes bright and the tears long gone.

I'd probably drop thousands without hesitation if it kept her in that kind of mood, but I decided not to tell her that. "You got it, lady. Let's go do some damage."

---

As it turned out, the damage was already done. We pulled up to the house about two hours later with two big bags from the art supply store and our bellies full of ice cream from the place we'd found just next door.

Even with her newfound trust in me, Olive was a quiet companion for running errands, but the girl did know how to spend someone else's money just fine.

All it took was a few big-eyed looks, and the expensive markers magically found their way into our cart, along with some nice spiral-bound drawing notebooks and some new pencils I'd been eyeing for myself.

I felt good.

I felt like I was totally nailing the stepmom thing.

Until I put my car in park and caught sight of Beckett waiting for us on the front porch. Through the windshield of my car, his eyes snagged heavy and loaded on mine. My stomach churned uncomfortably, and it felt like someone was pressing with all their might against my chest.

"I'll get the bags, okay?" I told Olive. "You go say hi to your dad. I'm sure he wants to hear about your day."

She gave me a quick, nervous look. "Do I have to tell him about the boy?"

I paused. "I think you should, yeah. He'll want to know that someone was hurting you."

Olive sighed but gave me a tiny nod.

She hopped out of the car, and I purposely took my time. As I cleaned up the ice cream bowls and walked them to the garbage bin next to the garage, I glanced at Beckett and Olive. Where he sat on the front porch, she was standing between his legs, her hands resting on his forearms, which had looped around her back. He listened intently, occasionally interjecting something but speaking too low for me to hear. After a few minutes, he wrapped his arms around Olive in a tight hug.

The fact that I paid attention to his face first, then Olive next, was my first sign that I was getting in just a touch over my head. Because the way the muscles in his arms flexed hardly registered as a distant third.

His face was bent in pain and frustration, and I knew Beckett was feeling that same type of helplessness that I had. Probably worse because it was actually his kid.

I hung back, the art bags in my hands, and he nudged Olive's chin with his thumb, then gestured for her to go into the house. She gave me a little smile over her shoulder but did as her dad asked.

When he turned his focus back onto me, I swallowed hard.

Oh yeah.

I was in trouble.

"So I guess he went into the office after I left, huh?" I asked weakly.

Beckett's eyes never wavered. "The dean called me about fifteen minutes before you got home, just after school got out. His parents are furious."

Swallowing back any sort of defensive reflection, I fought to keep my face steady.

"You threatened a little kid?" he asked, voice low and disbelieving.

I tilted my head back and forth. "Not technically, I just asked him a hypothetical question that could've been…misconstrued as a threat in the right circumstance." But my voice tapered off because *okay fine*, it sounded way worse now that I was standing in front of him.

Beckett's jaw clenched. "Tell me what happened."

He was still sitting on the top step of the front porch, and because I was awkwardly standing in front of him with the bags in my hands, I felt a bit like I was in front of the Spanish Inquisition. All I was missing was the giant spotlight aimed at my face to really send this thing home.

"Can I join you?" I asked.

He sighed, scooting over to make room. I set the bags down on the porch and took my seat next to Beckett. He was close enough that I could feel the heat from his body but far enough away that we weren't touching.

It felt very symbolic, and I tried not to read into it too deeply.

I told him everything that happened in the office, about my conversation with the dean, and then what I saw on the playground when we were leaving.

He listened quietly.

"I saw him knock over that other little girl, and I saw Olive's face, and I just... I couldn't *stand* it." I glanced over at him. "She's crying in my back seat, and she looked so sad, and she hugged me so tight when I got there. The dean knew what that little punk did, and she can't do anything about it, which I get, okay? I get it. The school's hands are tied. But my brothers got in trouble more than once because they'd take on some bully who picked on me or Adaline or Poppy, and they didn't care about the consequences."

"But *you*"—he interrupted—"are an adult. You're not another kid." His eyes seared into mine. "You think it doesn't kill me to hear her say she was scared? That she hid under a slide because she didn't want anyone to see her cry? Of course I want to get in that kid's face, but I *can't*."

His hands were tight and tense as he spoke, and I had the feeling that he was holding his entire body rigid. That all that anger, all that helpless frustration had nowhere to go.

"You're not her parent," he added quietly. "No matter how any of this feels, no matter what role we're playing every day, you are not her stepmom, Greer, and it's not your responsibility."

My eyes stung, and embarrassment prickled like ice all over my arms and hands.

The breath tangled in my lungs, unable to come out clean or easy or smooth.

It wasn't anger or defensiveness; it was humiliation.

But underneath it, I couldn't help but pry open a truth that he didn't want to admit.

"It's a role you asked me to play," I said, quiet but firm.

Beckett exhaled a puff of air, turning slightly toward me to fully meet my gaze. His eyes were hot and his face stern, but he didn't argue.

I kept going. "And it's a responsibility that you and Josie have given me of your own free will, more than once. When you had your bachelor party, and when she called the school of her own volition to add me to the pickup list." An urgent, undeniable knot of emotion was climbing up my throat, and I ruthlessly shoved it down. "Two days ago, I wouldn't have even been able to pick her up, let alone walk her out of that school and be in a position where I'm the first adult she can confide in. And she did."

The heat in Beckett's eyes shifted a little with each word. It didn't fade, and it didn't disappear. It changed. And I wasn't sure what it meant.

"She *trusts* me, which I don't take lightly. And I know you don't either."

He groaned, covering his face with his hands so I couldn't see his expression while he processed that little gem.

"I know she's not my daughter." My throat tightened at the words. "And I've never had to deal with school politics before, so I hear you. I shouldn't have said what I said. I will apologize to Josie. I will happily call the little shithead's parents and apologize for crossing the line, but I can't apologize for protecting her in the same way I'd protect anyone else in my family." I paused, my voice threatening to crack on the last word. "I had to do *something*," I whispered.

Beckett was pressing the heels of his palms against his eyes, and I tried to figure out if this was making it even worse or if I was making some invisible headway.

The corded muscles in his forearms flexed, and it was no longer the third thing I noticed. With his elbows braced on the tops of his thighs and his hands covering his face, he was the very picture of a conflicted man.

I could only imagine the thoughts going through his head. There were so many to choose from, but they all pretty much rotated around one theme.

*What the ever-loving fuck did I do marrying this woman?*

Something urgent chased through my brain because last night had felt so different when he came home—sweet and flirty and a new sort of comfortable. This was not sweet. Or flirty. And it sure as shit wasn't comfortable.

"Please don't ask me to do nothing if she's in my care," I continued. "I know that part of your job as her dad is teaching her how to fight her own battles. That's what my parents did too. But I can't do nothing if I see her like that."

Beckett speared his hands through his hair and stared down at the ground. Then he pushed off the porch and paced forward a few steps.

Oh gawd, he couldn't even look at me.

This was really, really bad.

Finally, Beckett dropped his hands and took a deep breath. But still, he didn't face me.

"I'm sorry I did that," I whispered. "And I hope you can forgive me."

He held up a hand, turning slightly. "I'm not mad." The sound of his voice was husky, curling around the words like he couldn't believe he was saying them.

I blinked.

"Not mad is a good start," I ventured. "I mean, you'd have every right to be if you wanted. I did ask a kid if he knew what happened when you took a nail gun to someone's balls."

"You said what?" Beckett's voice was a low hush, something I felt all the way down my spine.

I winced. "It wasn't my finest moment, I know. I was just so...*angry*. And it really is okay if you're upset. I overstepped."

The muscle in his jaw flexed.

"I'm not mad," he said again. His eyes were on fire. "I'm trying very hard not to kiss you right now."

# CHAPTER 19

# Beckett

**The words dropped between us, detonating with the** grace of a nuclear bomb. And for once—finally—I was the one delivering the blow.

It was always her—the head-whirling storm that had descended into our lives, who didn't think before she spoke or acted or pushed forward.

But for once, the truth burst out of me without a single attempt to stop it. Because if I hadn't said the words, I would've simply grabbed her, simply would've taken her face into both hands so I could stamp my mouth over hers.

For once, it was me.

And Greer, who'd stood from the step after I strode away, looked like she was about to fall over.

"You…" She shook her head. "You what?"

My blood thrummed fast and furious, I could hardly think from the rush of it through my ears.

The way it screamed her name as it raced through my veins.

I took one step closer. "You heard me," I managed, doing my best to speak through gritted teeth. That tight lock of tension the most flimsy of leashes. The only thing holding me back.

Her chest heaved, her eyes wide and shockingly vulnerable. "Really?" she whispered. "You want to kiss me right now?"

More than that.

So much more than that.

My hands tightened into fists at my side, and she noticed, her big brown eyes snagging on the motion immediately. Her mouth fell open, a gentle O of surprise.

Then her gaze sought mine again. "Beckett," she said, a slight pleading in her voice.

From what she'd told me last night, that she'd been awake when we both woke with my hands on her body, I damn well knew that I could smash through whatever line we'd erected. With greedy hands, I could snatch her close to me, be selfish with this feeling when it roared hot in my chest.

I closed my eyes.

She wouldn't just *let me*. There'd be no mild, meek allowance. No lukewarm permission.

She'd meet me there, jumping headfirst.

She'd toss kindling onto the flames, tipping over a full can of gasoline, and see how much damage we could do to each other.

And I knew that with every violent drumming of my pulse while we stood facing each other.

It was all so blurry in my head. Ever since I climbed into

bed with her already there, soft and warm and sweet in sleep, the lines had faded into something insubstantial. And I didn't do well without clarity, without knowing what was going to happen and feeling steady in that path.

So I took a step back and sucked in a great, cleansing breath.

"Greer," I said, rubbing a hand over my forehead. "I have to... I have to bring Olive to Josie's."

Her shoulders slumped. "Now?"

I nodded.

Disappointment filled her eyes. There was no hiding it.

It should have had a cooling effect on how much I wanted her. But it didn't. The desire was still there, sizzling under the surface and angry about being pushed aside. The strength of it, though it was still contained inside my own body, had the ability to knock my breath from my lungs.

Before this exact moment, anything I'd felt for another woman was so tepid, half the force of what had me wanting to cross those last few feet between us and slide my tongue against hers, test the way our bodies would feel wrapped tight around each other.

The sheer force of it was staggering—maybe because I hadn't seen it coming.

Maybe because she was so fearless in the way she loved and did it without thinking. A natural protectiveness for the person who meant the most to me in the entire world. That she'd risk my anger, risk Josie's, risk trouble with the school simply because Olive was sad—it was like a battering ram to whatever guard I'd been able to hold up with her.

And it was in that stunning level of surprise that I found a foothold of caution.

Because it couldn't be the right way to do anything like this, no healthy foundation for any sort of relationship. We were already on shaky ground—lying to the people in our life as the bedrock of what we'd started.

I took a step back and exhaled heavily.

Her face smoothed out, the disappointment hidden, but the color still high in her cheeks.

"Josie asked if I'd bring her over a day early," I told her. My voice had lost that ragged edge to it, steadier now that I'd been able to wedge some distance between us. "I think she just needs to see for herself she's okay."

Greer nodded. "Should I come with? I'd like to apologize to Josie too."

I held her gaze but shook my head. "That's okay. If you want to call her while I'm driving over, that's fine. I don't plan on staying long."

A gust of wind kicked up in the yard, and a few stray pieces of dark hair flew into her face. She tucked them behind her ear, eyeing me warily.

I didn't blame her.

I was all over the place, and that wasn't like me.

It was unsettling, something I couldn't quite trust.

Greer must have been able to read that in my face, must have been able to see something in my eyes that betrayed how conflicted I was. Because she gave a slight nod of concession.

"I'll bring our stuff in and say goodbye to Olive," she said. "She won't be back with us until after Josie's wedding, right?"

A solid week of just the two of us.

No interruptions.

But no reason for her to stay in my bed either.

My chest clenched as I nodded.

"I'll go say goodbye to her then." Her lips hooked into a crooked grin. "She has a lot more to pack now," she said, pointing at the art bags.

I watched Greer walk into the house with a growing emptiness under my ribs, an unsettled gnawing sensation in the pit of my stomach.

Dropping off Olive only took about ten minutes—mainly because Josie and Micah were waiting out in the front yard, shifting some boxes from the inside of their house to the moving pod they had in the driveway.

Greer had called Josie while I drove Olive over to the house, and Micah laughed when he heard what she said.

Josie gave him a chastising look, but even she was fighting a smile. "Not funny," she said.

"It's a little funny," Micah replied.

"I'll see if the dean needs us to do anything else," Josie said. "I told Greer I wasn't mad, but remind her when you go back home. There are worse things in the world than you marrying someone who's really protective of our daughter."

Too many things were knocking around inside my head. The rage I'd felt at the idea anyone had dared hurt Olive. The helplessness at not being able to do anything about it. The wildly inconvenient timing of my attraction to Greer. And now, Josie's absolute trust. That one had an immediate sinking effect on my stomach, like she'd dropped an anchor down my throat.

All of it left me exhausted.

Weary down to the bone.

I gave Olive another hug, told her I loved her, and I reminded Josie and Micah to call if they needed any help leading up to the wedding.

As I drove back to the house, knowing that it was just me and Greer for the next stretch of days, I tried to make sense of how we'd gotten here.

How I was supposed to move forward. And I had no one to talk to.

Except my wife who wasn't my wife.

And her brother, I realized. When I was at a red light, I tugged my phone out of my pocket and scrolled through my contacts to see if I'd saved his number. I sighed heavily when I found it.

*Cameron Wilder.*

"Here goes nothing," I mumbled.

He picked up on the second ring. "This is Cameron."

"Cameron, it's Beckett."

He was quiet on the other end.

"Beckett Coleman," I said. "I'm Greer's…"

He interrupted me before I had to attempt a label that wasn't completely fraudulent. "I know who you are, Beckett." I could tell he was smiling. "Everything okay? Didn't expect a call from my new brother-in-law," he said lightly.

I blew out a hard breath. "I'm not sure what to do with your sister, and I have no one to talk to about it."

If I thought he was quiet when he answered, it was a whole different kind of quiet now.

"I'm going to regret answering this phone call, aren't I?" he said.

"Most likely."

He sighed. "What happened? Because I got a really weird call from her earlier about threatening some kid—"

I interrupted him. "She told you about that?"

"Greer does this thing where she tells someone when she's about to do something crazy because then it makes her feel like she's been given permission, but really, she just wants someone to know so she can feel better about it."

I pinched the bridge of my nose. "That sounds about right."

"She get in trouble?"

"Not with me and Olive's mom," I told him.

"So...what's the problem then?"

I was so glad I couldn't see his face. "I told your sister the day we agreed to this crazy plan that she wasn't my type. Not even a little bit."

It sounded a lot like Cameron choked on a drink of something. "You did not."

"She said it back to me if that makes a difference." I flipped on my turn signal. "And I think... I think maybe she's more my type than I thought. But we started this entire thing on the premise of lying to the people we love because it felt justified in our heads."

He made a quiet humming sound.

I kept talking. "None of that feels like the right way to start a relationship. It feels confusing. And like we're set up for nothing but failure if we...let ourselves do what we want to do."

"I will not talk about you having sex with my sister," he interjected. "I have personal boundaries, and that is one of them."

I exhaled a laugh. "That's fair."

"I don't know how much help I'll be, Beckett." He sighed. "I love all my sisters. They drive me up a fucking wall on the regular, but I would move heaven and earth for every one of them. That said, I know how impulsive Greer can be. And how hardheaded she is when she wants something. And I'm no relationship expert, either. But if you feel like you're starting a relationship on shaky ground, adding...physical stuff," he said carefully, "on top of all the *other* complications..." His voice trailed off. "You've just gotta be honest with her. You'll be fine if you just talk it through. She's good at that."

Everything he said rang true. And even if it didn't help me to know exactly what I wanted to say when I got back home, I knew he was right.

All I could do was talk to her.

Be as honest as possible without causing harm.

I thanked him for his time and tried to sift through my thoughts when I pulled the car up to the house.

The barn doors were open, and I caught sight of her on the

rower, white earbuds in her ears, some confusing configuration of straps wrapped around her chest and high-waisted black leggings over her long legs.

Because of the mirrors on one side of the wall, she caught sight of me walking in, slowing her pulls. The muscles in her upper arms flexed as she pulled, and I gently tapped the skin of her upper back.

"Sit up higher," I told her. "Like you're trying to squeeze a tennis ball between your shoulder blades."

She nodded, chest heaving on great gulping breaths of air. Greer straightened her back on her next few pulls, and I nodded. The warmth of her skin still lingered on my fingertip, and I realized just how much of this confusion had started when I woke up with the feel of her body against mine.

It wasn't that I didn't want to indulge, that I didn't want to see what it would feel like with her.

I wanted to very badly.

So badly that it clouded all my rational thoughts. And that was the problem.

If I pushed her against the wall behind us, slid my hand to anchor behind her neck, if I devoured her mouth, swallowed all the sounds she'd make with my hands on her sweat-warmed body, I knew it would feel good.

It would feel amazing.

With very little effort, I'd be able to justify this one indulgence, just so we could know. So we could have an outlet for all this bound energy coiled tight between us.

And it just might wreck everything else around us.

As Greer came to a stop, I snagged her water bottle from the edge of the wall and handed it to her. She took a big gulp, and when a drop of water slid down the edge of her neck, I fought the urge to lick it off her skin.

"You okay?" she asked, still slightly out of breath.

She'd sound like that, sprawled out on the bed. She'd be flushed in the same way, if I let myself peel off her clothes and unleash all this foreign energy in the way I wanted. The way she wanted to, I could tell.

It would be so fucking good.

I closed my eyes for a moment and let out a slow, controlled breath.

"Olive won't be back now until after the wedding," I said.

She nodded. "I know."

"And when she's here, everything is…a little bit unclear." My eyes traced her face. The strands of hair stuck to the graceful line of her neck. She was so beautiful. And every time I thought about touching her, those thoughts got louder and louder, eclipsing everything else in their path. "The role we're playing feels a bit more real, doesn't it?"

She exhaled a quiet laugh. "Yeah."

I took a step closer and allowed my thumb to catch a drop of water where it clung to the edge of her jaw. Greer inhaled shakily.

"And when I touch you," I told her, "or think about touching you, I forget that it's a role. That it's not real."

Her brow furrowed.

"That's what we need to remember. What I need to remember."

"Can't we allow things to change?" she asked. Of course she wouldn't easily back down. I thought about what Cameron said. How stubborn she was when she wanted something. And I saw it in her eyes. She wanted me. She wanted me in the exact same way I wanted her. "Things don't stay the same simply because we want them to. That's not how life works, Beckett."

"I know." I dropped my hand. "But I can't afford to get distracted right now. I have too much on the line."

Greer smiled, just a little. "So you're admitting you want me," she said.

My laugh was nothing more than a shocked gust of air.

She was so fucking fearless.

"Yeah," I told her. "I am."

"And you're not going to do anything about it because this is all fake. Because we lied to protect these certain pieces of our life," she said quietly. Her eyes glowed though, like she could read through every line, every piece of subtext, every tangled thought in my head. "So even if it feels real. And the attraction between us is real. You're deciding to leave it the same because it's easier in your head if it stays that way. The risk of acting on it is too much for you. Am I getting that right?"

My jaw clenched. I managed a nod, unable to tear my gaze away from hers.

The way she looked at me was hypnotic. I'd fall into her so easily if I let myself.

Greer licked her lips and exhaled slowly. "Okay."

I blinked. "What?"

She searched my face. "I hope you change your mind, Beckett."

Just that.

How many people simply said what they wanted without battering through the wishes of the other person in the equation?

How many people could do what she'd just done? She wasn't toying with me. Wasn't tempting me—beyond the temptation she already was just by being herself. She wasn't playing games or teasing me for struggling with this.

Somehow, it made me want her even more.

And then she walked past me, her arm brushing against mine as she passed. I closed my eyes at that one single touch.

"I'm gonna take a shower," she called over her shoulder. "In case you're wondering."

I muttered something foul under my breath. "I'm gonna go…hit something for a while."

As she walked away, she laughed, and I used that sound as fuel while I worked every ounce of frustration clear from my body.

# CHAPTER 20

# Greer

**"You haven't worn it in at least five years. It has to go."**

"I *might* still wear it."

"When's the last time you thought about that shirt?"

Poppy sighed, tossing the shirt into the donate pile. "Last year when we did this, and I told you I'd absolutely wear it again someday."

"Exactly."

Every year when she finished her last spring class, we did a big purge of her bedroom.

Clothes.

Shoes.

The crap that had accumulated on her dresser and the entire spare room she used as her study since she was the only one left at home.

She was close to being done with her master's program—maintaining her dean's list status every single semester—and worked part time at a diner in downtown Sisters. And when she was home, she helped our parents as much as she possibly could.

None of this left much room for her to clean out all the shit in her closet.

That was what big sisters were for.

Especially big sisters who were avoiding being home because their hot husbands were driving them out of their mind doing yard work without a shirt on, and he wouldn't allow fun things like…showering together. Or kitchen make-out sessions. Or sex in the giant tub in the master bathroom. Or cuddling on the couch while watching *SportsCenter*.

I cleared my throat, sharp and pointed. Poppy gave me a curious look, which I ignored.

"When are your grades posted?" I asked.

She sighed, folding some old T-shirts into a neat pile. "A few days. I'm almost done, and I still have no idea what I want to do with my life." She paused, her motions slowing. "How did you know you wanted to be an interior designer?"

I laughed. "When I failed a math test in middle school because I was too busy sketching in the margins to actually answer any of the questions."

"You didn't."

"I did. Got zero percent. And Mom and Dad never disciplined me for it." With a shake of my head, I pulled a sweatshirt from a pile, tossing it into the box when she grimaced. "I watched Dad build all these amazing houses growing up. See them from start to finish, beg him to take me to jobsites so I could imagine where the furniture would go and what paint colors they'd choose. I've always wanted to be a part of that—helping people create the spaces where they'll live their life. Cameron did too, so we just…never thought about doing anything else with our lives but keeping that legacy of Wilder Homes going."

My little sister stared down at her hands. "I wish it was that clear for me."

I didn't try to talk her out of the way she was feeling. At her age, just twenty-two, I was already neck-deep in running Wilder Homes with Cameron and loving every single second. Our whole family was like that—a bone-deep certainty of what we were meant to do. Erik played football. Ian made fancy-pants custom wood furniture for a company in London. Adaline had a successful event planning business in Seattle. Cameron always knew he'd be a builder. Parker followed in Erik's footsteps, his own football legacy gaining steam even though he'd only played professionally for a few years.

And lagging just a little bit behind, just as she had in her arrival to the family, was Poppy.

Maybe because we'd all doted on her so much, she'd spent so many years following us around in our various pursuits, her own wasn't quite as clear.

"You'll figure it out," I told her. "I think you should just enjoy this part of your life while you're in it."

She gave me a look. "The part where I'm single, twenty-two, and still sleeping in my childhood bedroom."

"Hell yeah," I said. "No rent. No maintenance. Mom's baking. You're winning by any definition."

Poppy smiled. "I feel like everything in my life is just…on pause."

I pulled another batch of hangers out. Her voice had taken on that sad tone. Like everyone's did when Dad's health came up. "I know."

She pointed at the donate box when I held up a bright-pink button-down shirt. "Dad keeps having more bad days than good," she said quietly. "And I know I can't just sit around here and wait for…" Her voice trailed off. "For something to change. But I can't help it. I want to be here if he needs me."

"You know Dad doesn't want any of us not living our life because of this," I told her. "Especially you, Pops. You're right about to step into all the good stuff." I folded a shirt in half. "A career, maybe love," I said with a grin. "There's a lot of time for that, though. You're just a baby," I teased, ruffling the top of her hair.

She snorted. "Of course you'd say that. You run off and get married and leave me with just the boys to commiserate with about being single. They're worthless."

I thought about our brothers with a shake of my head. "They truly are. Cameron needs a woman with more patience than a saint because he's such a know-it-all. Parker needs someone who will knock him on his ass. *Hard*."

Poppy nodded. "Gawd, that would be so gratifying."

"Right?" I shivered. "Hopefully, someone gets it on camera, and we can watch it on a loop when we're having a bad day."

Our eyes met, and we burst into laughter.

"Ian is…" My eyebrows rose slowly.

She laughed. "Impossible? Mom said he's thinking about moving back home from London, though."

"That's good."

Poppy chewed on her bottom lip. "Speaking of married life…"

"Were we?" I mumbled, turning to face into her closet so she couldn't see my wince. "What about it?"

"Adaline doesn't tell me anything," she groaned. "I just want to know—"

When her voice cut off, I glanced at her over my shoulder. Her cheeks were bright pink.

"Poppy, are you trying to ask sex questions?" I teased.

"Fuck you, okay?" she said without heat. "I had one shitty, boring, entirely forgettable experience with that idiot kid from my study group my sophomore year of college, and I know there's more out there than shitty, boring, and entirely forgettable."

I laughed. "Yes, there is. The right person will be the exact opposite of those things."

"And Beckett is the right person for you?" she asked quietly. "He's so…serious. I never pictured you with someone like him."

I kept my face even—internally *weeping* that I couldn't turn around, plop on the bed with my little sister, and have a juicy sex talk about my hot AF husband.

I was the one who told Poppy how to make sure her first kiss didn't suck.

I was the one who had the real sex talk with her after my mom gave her the sanitized version.

I was the one who gave her the dirty books to learn all the best things.

And now I had to add this onto the heaping mountain of bullshit we kept peddling to the people in our lives.

Damn Beckett and his unwavering moral compass—Mr. We Can't Act On It Because Lies Are Bad.

They were bad.

And with my little sister asking me perfectly reasonable questions, continuing those lies felt an awful lot like sucking on a rancid lemon.

"*Greer*," Poppy repeated. "Are you even listening to me?"

"I'm listening. Just…thinking." I blew out a sharp breath. "If it helps, I never pictured myself with someone like him either. Opposites attract and all that," I answered, keeping my tone airy.

"But what's he *like*? How did you guys even… I mean, I know about Olive. It's admirable. But you must have had some magic juju happening between the two of you to get a guy like that to marry you so fast."

"Thanks," I said dryly.

"Oh come on, you have to admit it's insane. You have always needed…" She stopped, searching for the right word. I found myself holding my breath until she did. "Fireworks. You've always needed fireworks."

It was hard to swallow because she was right.

I had always needed those. Which is probably why my

relationships tended to end with messy explosions that left a lot of collateral damage. Usually to me.

Now it was my turn to choose my words carefully. "There weren't fireworks the night I met Beckett," I told her. I glanced up at the ceiling, refusing to label the truth of what I was about to say for what it was. "But there was recognition. It was almost like"—I shook my head slightly—"like I knew something was very different about him. Even if I wasn't sure what that thing was."

My answer still left her wanting. "So you moved from recognition to insane chemistry to I could see us together but let's speed this up for the sake of my child. In just a couple of weeks?"

I rubbed the back of my neck. "Yes?"

"Greer."

"What do you want me to say, Poppy? I know how it sounds, trust me. But he's just... He's so earnest. He says what he means, and he's not afraid of my crazy ideas, and he doesn't try to make me be anything other than what I am." I shrugged helplessly. "I don't know what else you want me to tell you."

That was also a lie.

Poppy wanted to know if my serious, quiet, earnest husband had a hidden dirty side. She wanted to know what feminine power I held in order to unlock it, and I *knew* that because I knew exactly what ran through her mind at all times.

But fucking A, I wanted to know if my husband had a dirty side too, and there was no way I could tell her that.

Her eyes were wide in her face. Pleading eyes. Begging eyes. Little sister 'tell me all the things' eyes. "If you've got magic moves, then you better share tips because someday I will have someone I want to use them on." She paused. "Especially if they're experienced, and I only know shitty and boring and forgettable."

The light bulb went off over my head. Oh did that bitch go off in a major way. Warning sirens accompanied it, blaring and harsh.

I gave her a stern look. "Poppy, is this about Jax?"

"No." But her face was bright red. "Or not exactly about him. I know he only looks at me like I'm an annoying little sister type, but he does…" She paused, searching for the right words. "Represent the dream."

I studied her face. "What dream?" I asked softly.

Before she answered, Poppy took a long moment to stare down at her lap. When she glanced up, she focused on one of the framed pictures on her wall. Our parents, not long after they got married.

They looked so young. So happy. Surrounded by the six of us kids—and all the chaos it entailed. I was mid-wallop on Parker, who was tugging my hair. Ian had his face covered. Erik was frowning. Cameron was eating a piece of cake with his bare hands, and Adaline sat in the middle, smiling perfectly without a single hair out of place.

I didn't even need to hear her say it. She wanted a love like theirs.

We all did.

Carefully, I sat on the edge of her mattress and wrapped my arm around her.

Any advice I gave her suddenly felt cheap and brittle. Easily broken because I could hardly form the words without feeling like I might choke on them.

I didn't have a love like our parents' either.

But just like Poppy, I'd always wanted it. Had always dreamed of finding my own version of it.

"They built something incredible," I said quietly. "They found something beautiful and pure and amazing out of some really horrible parts of life. And they'd like nothing more than if all seven of us end up with exactly the same kind of love."

She nodded. "They're off to a good start. Erik did with Lydia. Adaline did with Emmett." Poppy sniffled. "And you did with Beckett."

My ribs squeezed painfully, like someone tightened a wrench over my midsection.

"I just wanted to know more about yours," she admitted. "You're the sibling who tells me everything. It's weird to feel like I'm on the outside of this big part of your life when I can't even imagine it."

It was enough to break me in two.

She wasn't trying to catch me in a lie. She wasn't digging with malicious intent.

And somehow, that made it even worse.

"I'm not trying to keep you on the outside, Poppy." I kissed the top of her head. "We're still kind of getting to know each other. So we've been…protecting that space a little, I guess."

She leaned into my embrace. "But the sex is good, right? I bet it's really good."

I pinched my eyes shut, dredging up the truth where I could manage it. "There are no words, Poppy. I couldn't describe it even if I wanted to."

CHAPTER 21

# Greer

Adaline squinted, pulling her face toward the phone screen, so close that I snorted.

"You look so cute," I told her. "Another inch and I can count your pores."

She centered her middle finger into the screen.

"Go closer to the mirror," she instructed.

I did as she asked, and she nodded. "The neckline is pretty. I couldn't see the beading detail from far away. And I like the lilac color. Very springy."

I turned so she could see how the halter crisscrossed in the back. "You don't think it's too fancy for a wedding?"

She made a slight humming noise. "Depends on the wedding. If it was short, you wouldn't have to worry, but because it's floor length, it might be. You said Micah's family is pretty wealthy, though, right?"

I nodded. "And he's in a bigwig corporate job, so I think they're going pretty high end on the ceremony and stuff."

"Beckett wearing a tux?" she asked.

It was probably weird that I didn't know that, but I managed a very casual shrug. "I don't think he's decided yet either. But I doubt it. A suit at most, if I had to guess."

"What's your other option?" she asked.

"Hang on," I told her. "I'm going to set the phone down and grab it. Unless you want to watch me change," I said.

As I set the phone down on the long dresser against the wall, propped so that she could see the area by the foot of the bed, she smiled. "Not particularly. I'm gonna go pee a second while you change." Her face disappeared, then came back. "Unless you want to listen."

"Not particularly," I called out.

In the closet, I pushed a couple of hangers aside until I found the other dress. The lilac was a safer choice, no doubt about it. It was elegant and demure, with a high, halter neckline and a flowing skirt that brushed the floor.

My second option was not any of those things. The cut was classic—fitted along the bodice and through my hips, a straight, streamlined hem that fell just past my knees, and I'd bought it on a whim a couple of years earlier.

It was vivid red—with a square neckline that made my cleavage look absolutely incredible (if I did say so myself). On the left strap was a small diamond cutout, the only detail on an otherwise deceptively simple dress.

Carefully, I pulled it up over my hips and slid my arms through the straps. I was still attempting to pull the straps into place with one hand when I walked out of the closet, carefully laying the lilac dress over the edge of the bed. Adaline wasn't back on the video call yet, so I stepped back to study my reflection in the mirror across the room.

I exhaled a relieved laugh when it still fit just as well as it had the day I bought it. I turned, smiling at what I saw.

The bedroom door opened just as I did.

We both froze. His eyes tracked down the entire length of my body, his mouth falling open as they did.

In the wake of his admission of how hard it was for him to have blurred lines, we'd danced around each other for days. I'd worked long hours, and so had he.

When we were both home, we kept a safe distance. He kept busy outside. I kept busy inside.

And at the end of the day, we went our separate ways.

But it seemed, as his eyes traced the simple square neckline, that the dance had come to an abrupt stop.

I slid my hands down the front of the red dress, an uncharacteristic flurry of nerves dancing through my belly.

"Just trying to figure out what to wear for the wedding," I told him. I gestured to the other dress on the bed. "It's this or the purple."

Beckett didn't say a thing. And he didn't move his eyes away from me, not for a single second, to look at the other dress.

The silence in the room was sharp and heavy, so loaded down with the things he was thinking but not saying, and I could *feel* it.

It wasn't uncomfortable.

And it wasn't unpleasant.

What it did was set off an ache, something deep and throbbing and persistent.

I settled a hand over my stomach and gave him a tiny grin. "I've never had a place to wear it before." I paused. "It might be too much for a wedding, though, so I know the purple might be a better—"

"The red," he interjected, his voice gruff, his eyes searing. "Wear the red."

I took an unthinking step closer, and his jaw flexed.

My sister's voice came from the phone. "Should I hang up now?" she whispered. "I have my eyes covered, I swear."

Beckett's head swiveled to the phone, and he swiped a hand over his face. For just a moment, his gaze moved back to mine, held for a prolonged beat, and then he left the room.

I exhaled, my whole body slumping over. "Shit," I muttered.

Adaline laughed. "I don't know whether that was awesome or horrifying for me. Do you need to go?"

I gave her a dry look. "I think the moment is over, thank you."

She grinned. "I think if you go track him down, you could get it back on track *pretty* easily, based on how that man was looking at you." Adaline waved a hand in front of her face. "At least you know what dress you're gonna wear."

With another look at my reflection, I shook my head. "You've got that right."

"I'm glad he likes it because it gets my vote too."

"Thank you." I picked up the phone and blew her a kiss. "Love you. I'm gonna go."

She waggled her eyebrows. "I bet you are."

I hung up with a laugh, turning the phone screen down on the dresser so I couldn't see anything else she might say because my sister's sudden obsession with my nonexistent sex life was very inconvenient. If it had been Poppy on that FaceTime, she would have kept her mouth shut and her eyes wide open to see how all that played out.

By the time the dresses were hung and put away, and I tugged my regular clothes back on, Beckett had fled the house.

It was quiet in the kitchen, and I glanced through the windows into the backyard when I heard some noises from the barn. The sun was hanging low enough in the sky that everything looked soft and pink and warm, the beginnings of what would be an incredible sunset.

All week, I'd hardly spoken to him. Not more than a few sentences each day. Small talk. Safe topics. Like we were roommates who didn't think about banging the bejeezus out of each other.

It was easy to respect what he'd told me when he wasn't looking at me like he wanted to tear that pretty red dress off my body.

What would have happened if Adaline hadn't been on the other end of that phone?

The question plagued me as I tidied up my piles of work papers on the table.

That same persistent sound came from the barn, and I let out a deep breath, sliding on my flip-flops so I could walk out to see what he was doing.

I didn't want to ignore this.

*Bam.*

*Bam.*

*Bam.*

The sound intensified as I got closer, and just before I turned the corner, I recognized it as the sound of gloves hitting the heavy bag he had hanging in the corner. My brothers had one in our gym too.

Beckett was in profile, the dark navy shirt clinging to his chest as he moved around the bag. He wasn't doing this for speed or perfect form.

The heavy smack of his fists on the bag were for power.

For the release of pent-up energy.

*Bam. Bam.*

Two hits in rapid succession, and the bag swung from the force of it.

He slowed when I walked into the barn but didn't take his eyes off the bag in front of him.

His biceps were glistening with sweat, and the roll of his muscles underneath his skin had the blood humming in my veins. Instead of walking closer to him, I moved to the side of the barn, taking a seat on a stack of two plyometric boxes—the kind I'd seen him use when he was doing that jump type of training that looked like hell on earth.

From where I sat, I could see his face. And he could see mine.

He paused, studying my expression before he hit the bag a few more times.

*Bam. Bam.*

"I think we need to clear something up," I said.

His eyes locked on mine for a moment, then moved away.

*Bam.*

"I can respect the no sleeping together, cuddling, hand up the shirt rule for general day-to-day coexistence." I made sure he was listening before I continued. "I'm not saying I wouldn't be open to adjusting that rule, but I can respect it."

He stopped, hands on his hips as his chest heaved.

"I already know all this," he said.

"We're about to go to your ex's wedding. In that pretty dress you just told me to wear. You'll be in a suit, I'm assuming. There will be moments of hand holding. Dancing." When I said it, his eyes darkened. "Touching. And I need just a little bit more clarity on why two consenting adults who are clearly attracted to each other can't just…" I fought a shiver at the way he was looking at me. "Explore what that looks like together," I finished quietly.

When he answered, it sounded like someone ran his vocal cords through a wood chipper. "I already explained this to you."

"Not fully," I said. I refused to drop my stare. "If there's one thing we do," I reminded him. "If there's only one thing…we tell each other the truth."

"The truth," he said quietly.

Slowly, I nodded.

Beckett held my gaze, tearing off his gloves while he did. My heart tumbled over itself, unevenly thumping in my chest.

*Please oh please oh please*, I thought.

With the gloves tossed onto the ground, he walked toward me, and I notched my chin up as he got closer.

*Kiss me,* I begged him with my eyes.

*Touch me.*

He set his hands on either side of my hips, inches away from my thighs. My legs slowly unfolded, so that if he chose, he could slot himself right in the space between them.

He didn't move even a single inch closer.

My skin was on fire with how close he stood. I wanted to lick up the column of his neck and suck at his jawline. I wanted to fist my hands in his shirt and reel him in the last few inches of space between us.

But I didn't.

"Once," he said, low and urgent. "Once in my adult life, I acted without thinking through the consequences. I allowed my own loneliness to eclipse anything rational. Josie and I should never have slept together that night. There was no world in which the two of us were right for each other or could've built the kind of family we both wanted. My daughter is the best thing I've done, but I have not been able to give her the kind of life I wanted to."

I sucked in a slow breath.

"I have only ever wanted to build a family when the time in my life was right for it. When they could be my very first priority. Know that nothing came before them. And instead, I have a daughter who—even though she's loved beyond words—has a split life. Never fully in one place, never fully settled anywhere. And I hate that she suffers the consequence of my choices because I can't give her the thing I want. The only thing I've ever wanted for her."

My heart wasn't racing anymore. It wasn't thundering beneath my ribs.

It ached. Something full of anguish, poking viciously at a buried bruise that I'd rather stayed hidden.

"Once," he repeated. "I let myself be selfish. And I won't do that with you."

I couldn't tear my gaze from his.

"I won't risk you being another consequence, I won't risk the fallout of allowing myself free rein to touch you in the way I'm thinking about right now."

I let out a shaky breath, and even though I didn't want them to, the words escaped on a low, hushed whisper.

"I wish you would."

"Greer," he breathed. He dropped his head, and for just a moment, his forehead rested on mine.

For a long time, I didn't think men like this existed in my generation.

That there was someone with a big heart, who'd tear down the world for the people they loved. Who was selfless and giving and kind.

I'd never really even started looking because someone like this felt like a figment of my imagination.

The dream, Poppy said.

And somehow, with every odd stacked against us, I'd married someone who was all those things. And all I had to show for it was a useless piece of paper that I'd shoved into his jacket and a devastating, earth-shattering, staggering kind of want for something that I couldn't have.

This was all black and white to him.

There was the right thing to do.

There was a wrong path to follow. Clearly delineated.

My brain buzzed ineffectually around what I was supposed to do with all this when the sound of a car door punctuated the silence.

I sagged, allowing my forehead to press back against his.

"Always something," I said lightly.

"Hello!" Poppy called. "I saw you when I drove up."

As she entered the barn, she grinned wide when she caught sight of our position, and Beckett stepped back with a loaded exhale.

I gave Poppy a long look. "Honestly, is there a bat signal going out to my sisters today?"

"Not that I know of. I was in the area, and since I keep telling you I might stop by..." She paused, studying the workout equipment. "I figured I might as well do it."

"In the area," I said dryly.

She smiled sunnily. "Imagine that."

Beckett gave me a look. "I'm gonna go shower. Poppy, you're welcome to stay for dinner if you'd like," he said.

"Is she?" I muttered.

Poppy shoved at my shoulder. I shoved back.

"Come on," I told her. "Let me show you around, you nosy little jerk."

# CHAPTER 22

# Beckett

**The fact that I'd already seen her in the dress once was** my saving grace because when she came down the stairs—lashes long and fully lined with something dark and smudged and unbearably sexy, her lips slicked with some sort of shiny gloss, and her hair hanging in a smooth, straight line behind her back—any restraint I had left when it came to Greer would have been brutally eviscerated.

But I was prepared.

I knew how dangerous she was, her body covered in that deceptively simple red dress.

And so I braced myself like she was an incoming blow to the chest when the door to the guest room opened, and she came down the stairs.

I managed a swallow and held her eyes as she approached. Her lips quirked while she studied the cut of my dark-gray suit. I'd ditched the tie and left the top button of my dress shirt undone.

It was a good thing, too, because it was hard enough to breathe when I saw her.

"You look nice," she told me.

For a second, I didn't say anything because I was terrified to tell her any of the things running through my head.

But there were so many things I couldn't give her, that I didn't feel capable of. So I managed to pull the words out and take the risk that I might say too much.

"Nice isn't even close to describing you right now, Greer," I said. "It's far too tame."

She stopped close to me, but we didn't touch. We both knew that would happen at the wedding, where we'd be on display, and my hands itched to reach forward.

"Dare I ask how you would describe me?" she asked.

Most women wouldn't have pressed. And I liked that she did. It was an unfortunate realization, that I seemed to like everything about Greer Wilder.

"Relentless," I answered immediately. "There is no escaping how beautiful you are, Greer."

Her cheeks blushed pink, eyes softening when I uttered that inconvenient truth.

Her lips curled in a pleased little smile. "For a man of few words, you sure do pick the right ones, Beckett Coleman."

It shouldn't have felt so good, to make her happy in this way.

I blew out a slow breath as we walked toward the car. "Not always," I admitted. "But maybe today I will."

She laughed, and I tucked the sound of it away, so I could think about it later.

The drive to the church was short, and we arrived early, parking in one of the front rows because Olive asked if she could see us before her big walk down the aisle.

"How nervous is she?" Greer asked.

I waited for her by the front of the car, holding out my arm when she met me there. With a happy gleam in her eyes, she tucked her hand into the crook of my elbow.

"Josie sent me a text this morning, said it's been a little rough while the bridal party was getting ready. She doesn't want to walk down the aisle anymore. We thought she'd be okay with Micah's nieces walking with her, but she said everyone would be watching her in case she messed up with the flowers."

Greer glanced up at me. "Is there anything I can do to help?" she asked.

I shook my head. "We just try to encourage her as much as possible and don't let her back out of things like this unless she really starts panicking, just so she can see she's capable of doing it."

Entering the church with Greer on my arm was a fairly surreal experience. We'd existed in our little bubble for a bit over a month, and to have our relationship on display in such a public place had me feeling a strange sort of weight tugging on the center of my chest.

We made small talk with Micah's parents, and his dad nudged my elbow before we walked away, raising his eyebrows meaningfully at Greer. Then he whistled under his breath. His wife shook her head but smiled.

Greer didn't see the exchange, turning to wait for me to catch up. Beyond her was a small group of guys that looked like they'd climbed straight out of their fancy corporate offices. Two of them eyed Greer unashamedly, a telling gleam in their eye as they murmured quietly to each other. One of them stared at her ass, and I wondered briefly what would happen if I broke someone's nose in the lobby of a church.

I cleared my throat pointedly, sliding my hand around the curve of her waist until it rested on her hip. They straightened, averting their gazes immediately.

Greer turned, mouth gently hanging in shock. "Did you just…mark your territory?" she whispered, a gleeful smile curving her lips.

I clenched my jaw. "No."

She laughed, turning toward me, her hand smoothing down the lapel of my jacket. "Don't worry, I'm sure I'll have to before the night is over too," she said. The feel of her hand on my chest had my head spinning. "Some tipsy bridesmaid is going to get one look at you across the room." She sighed. "And that'll be it."

"What will?" With her flush against my chest, it was so easy to study every inch of her face.

She gently toyed with the button on the top of my shirt, her finger dangerously close to making contact with the skin at the base of my throat. Everything about our pose screamed of intimacy, an ease that took me by surprise.

It didn't feel fake.

It didn't feel like a lie.

Didn't feel like we were performing for any one of the number of people who could have been watching.

Greer looked up, her gaze locking unerringly on mine. "I'll have to throw down if they try anything with my husband," she said lightly. "Because if there's only one shot to be had with you tonight, then it's fucking mine."

I tipped my head back and laughed. My skin felt warm and relaxed, my blood hummed effortlessly as we stood that way. I could hardly imagine a world where relationships felt like this all the time. I'd certainly never experienced it.

Micah approached, and I shook his hand. "Big day," I told him. "You ready?"

He nodded, eyes bright and excited. "As ready as I'll ever be. I was told to come fetch you. I think Olive was hoping to see you before the ceremony." He pointed down a hallway to our right. "Third door on the left is where the girls are getting ready."

"Do you want me to come?" Greer asked. "I can wait here if you'd rather see her alone."

I held out my hand in answer, and she slid her fingers through mine with a relieved smile.

"Good," she whispered. "I didn't really want to stay, but I thought it was the polite thing to do to offer."

I was still smiling when the door opened up a crack. Josie's friend answered the door, making sure the bride was out of view before she let us in.

"Hey, Beckett. They'll be right out," she told me and Greer.

I squeezed her hand.

Josie and Olive came around the corner, and my chest cracked open in a big, messy burst.

Releasing Greer's hand, I crouched down as Olive approached. "Sweet pea, you look so beautiful," I said. Her dress was a pale yellow replica of Josie's, with little cap sleeves instead of thin straps, but the same lace along the skirt. In her hair was a delicate crown of white flowers. She walked into my arms for a hug, and I smiled up at Josie, whose eyes were glossy with tears.

"Did you see my flowers?" Olive asked. Gently, she touched the wreath in her hair.

"I love them." I tapped the end of her nose.

"Josie, you look incredible," Greer told her. "I love the lace on your dress."

Josie smiled, but then gestured at Greer to spin. "Umm, I'm sorry, I'm too busy checking you out right now." She shook her head. "You are *hot* in that dress."

Greer laughed, her cheeks going pink again. "I wondered if it was too much," she said, then she glanced down at me. "But he insisted."

Behind us, one of the bridesmaids snorted. "I bet he did."

Her tone wasn't outright mean, but there was enough of an edge to it that I stood and wound my fingers through Greer's again.

Josie pinned her bridesmaid with a sharp look, then smiled at Greer. "I'm glad he did. You look amazing."

Olive did a spin of her own, smiling when the skirt swooshed out around her. "You ready to walk down the aisle?" Greer asked her.

Olive stopped, briefly shrugging one shoulder. "I told Mom that I probably didn't have to. No one will notice if I don't do it."

Josie and I traded a look.

This was always Olive's struggle. She didn't want eyes on her, in case she messed up. But she almost always hinted that no one would notice her absence.

Greer made a small humming noise, pulling up slightly on the edge of her skirt so she could crouch down by Olive. I wasn't sure how she managed it with her feet encased in dangerous-looking heels. But she balanced effortlessly, gently taking one of Olive's hands.

"You know, I was a flower girl in my second cousin's wedding," she said. "I had a huge basket of pink rose petals."

Olive held her own basket out. "Mine are yellow and white."

Josie and I traded another look. Normally, this is where I'd step in if Josie wasn't making headway. It was an odd comfort, having someone else who seemed to know how to handle her.

"Do you know what I did when I walked out there?" Greer asked.

Olive shook her head.

"I hung onto that basket for dear life and didn't drop a single petal because I was so focused on getting to the end of the aisle," Greer said. Then she shrugged. "And even though I didn't do it perfectly, I was so glad I did it when I got to the front of the church because only a super special group of people get to stand at the front of a wedding." She leaned in. "It's the Very Important People group. The people who love the bride and groom the most."

Her eyes went wide, and she glanced up at Josie, who winked.

"You're definitely in the group," Josie said easily. "You probably love me the most, don't you?"

Olive nodded, her eyes earnest and her face serious. "And Micah. He can be up there too."

We all laughed, and when Greer straightened by my side, I set my hand on the lower part of her back. I leaned in to whisper next to her ear. "Thank you."

The flower pep talk complete, we said our goodbyes and found a place to sit right next to the aisle, so that Olive would see some friendly faces on her way toward the front.

The rows filled, the music slowly changing into something more grand as the bridesmaids made their way toward where Micah waited nervously. He tugged on the edges of his jacket, smile spreading when the flower girls started their journey.

True to what Greer said, Olive gripped her basket like it was the sole thing keeping her tethered to the ground, and she did not drop a single solitary petal, but she did it—eyes at the front of the church, marching in a straight line without a single moment of being distracted by what was going on around her, and when she turned at the front of the aisle, she gave us a huge, beaming smile.

Sighing in relief, I stretched my arm out along the back of the bench, and Greer took a deep, quiet breath when the tips of my fingers brushed her shoulder.

The ceremony was so different from ours—longer, for one, and far more formal. The front of the church was blooming with white flowers. They stood under an impressive arch covered in vines and lights.

It felt like a real wedding.

And I couldn't help but wonder what the woman by my side had conceded by doing what we'd done.

If she'd dreamed of a wedding like this someday.

When they said their vows, Greer tangled her hands together in her lap, tightening her fingers until the skin on her knuckles went white.

The simple gold band around her ring finger seemed so loud. So bright.

Most days, I didn't even really notice it. But with the warmth of her pressed against my side, and the red of her dress pulling my attention back again and again, it was those details that I couldn't seem to ignore.

After thirty-something days of coexisting with Greer, today was the first time she truly felt like my wife. Today was the first time I felt like I had the right to touch her. Like I was justified in how proud I was to have her by my side.

And I couldn't even put to words what had changed in my head. I still knew the risk incurred every time I had my hands on her. Every time I allowed myself the luxury to feel the things

I wanted, keeping the right and wrong and ever-growing list of consequences firmly planted outside the realm of what this day was.

When the minister pronounced them husband and wife and Micah leaned in to give Josie a lingering kiss, I moved my arm from the back of the bench to clap along with the rest of the crowd. The side of my arm felt cold without her body pressed against it. Greer inhaled slowly, holding it for a few beats before releasing it in a rush.

The reception made it easier to clear my head, and maybe hers too.

We were at a table with one of Josie's cousins, his wife, and some college friends of Micah's. The conversation was pleasant, even if Josie's cousin Connor kept me occupied a bit more than I would've liked, given his love of football.

"I think Portland will win their division this year," Connor said after a fifteen-minute dissection of our offensive line changes over the past two years. "You came within two games last year, so it's doable."

I offered a vague smile. "I certainly hope you're right."

Greer leaned in closer. "As long as the veteran tight end doesn't lose any speed this year." She patted my arm. "He *is* the senior member on the roster."

The couple laughed, and I turned to give her an incredulous look.

She laughed, setting her hand on top of my leg under the table. My whole body tensed at the casual touch. But with the way her arm was angled to the side, it was obvious she was touching me, and I reminded myself for the hundredth time that this wedding was the biggest show we'd put on for the entirety of our marriage.

Connor's wife smiled at Greer. "It must be hard to be married to a football player, though," she said. "Doesn't everything come second when the season starts? And all the attention. I can't even imagine what that must be like."

My eyes cut over to hers, and I waited patiently to see how she'd answer.

Greer's fingers tightened slightly on my thigh, and I fought the urge to slide my fingers over hers. Instead, I draped my arm over the back of her chair, sitting like we had been inside the church.

"Beckett works a strange job," she conceded. "But their families don't come second, just because they're gone a lot. It may seem like a strange thing to say, but it's true. For most of them, at least. But because my brothers played, not much about this life is a hard transition for me."

"Who are your brothers?" Connor asked, eyes bright with interest.

"Erik and Parker Wilder."

"No shit," he breathed. "Erik was amazing at Washington. He was one of my favorite defensive players."

Greer smiled. "Mine too, but I can't tell my brothers stuff like that too often, or it goes to their heads."

I exhaled a laugh.

While we finished dinner, I was able to angle a little closer to her, keeping my voice quiet enough that no one could hear.

"How long do you want to stay after dinner is done?"

She finished her bite of chicken. "Is Olive coming back home with us?"

I pushed my plate away. "I have to check with Josie's sister. She doesn't get to see Olive very often, so she and her kids might sleep at Josie's place if Olive wants to hang out with her cousins while they're in town."

Greer nodded. "Makes sense. So we'd just have to pick her up in the morning if she stays? My mom actually asked if we would come out to their place." She studied my expression, her smile tentative as she said it. "I think they're chomping at the bit to get to know you two more."

Her tone was apologetic, and I fought the churning sensation in the pit of my stomach.

Sitting in that big room, tastefully decorated and filled with soft, warm lights, I hated thinking about all the things she'd given up to help me with this.

"Yeah, we can go out there," I told her.

She beamed. "Really? I know you hate…faking. But they'd love it. And we'll have to do some of that when Josie is gone anyway. You know they're going to want to do birthdays and holidays and school plays…all of it." She scrunched her nose. "Honestly, they will want to show up at an almost obnoxious level, and I don't actually know how we'll be able to stop them."

I managed a nod.

It was the stuff Olive and I had never had. The stuff we'd never been able to give her.

The big loud Christmases.

A chorus of people singing "Happy Birthday" while she waited to blow out the candles on the strawberry cake she always asked for.

People to fill the rows at school functions.

It suddenly felt like Greer was giving so much more to this situation we found ourselves in.

She was bringing life and warmth into our house.

She made my daughter laugh; she made *me* laugh.

And she was bringing us an army of people who wanted nothing more than to embrace me and my daughter, make us feel loved and welcome.

What was I giving to her in return?

I'd given a day. I'd given her a performance that brought joy to her family.

That was it.

"I'll be right back," I told her, my voice ragged.

Her eyes filled with concern, and I didn't wait to see how she responded.

I cut through the room, managing a few smiles to familiar faces as I passed, but no one stopped me. In the corner of the room, Josie and Micah had their heads bent at a private table, and he said something to make her laugh. Olive had her own seat there with them, and she was scribbling something on her napkin.

By the time I walked into the hallway outside the reception hall, the quiet was deafening. I took a slow breath, fighting the build of helpless anger that I'd somehow thought this would be easy. That it would be clear cut and neatly defined.

*This is the problem we both have. And here's the best solution.*

Simple as that.

Music swelled in the reception hall, filtering through the doors, and I sank against the wall, head resting against the hard surface.

The doors pushed open.

"I need a smoke, man," one of the men said. The other one was already pulling a pack of cigarettes out of his pants pocket. They didn't look down the hall to where I stood.

They were the same guys from the church, who'd ogled Greer so shamelessly, and I took a slow deep breath, hoping they'd move outside quickly.

One of them nodded toward the doors, tilting his head so he could see through the small windows that looked into the reception hall. "Red dress incoming," he murmured. "Fuckin' A, she's hot."

I clenched my jaw.

"She's with Josie's ex," the other one said. "Micah seems to like him."

The other guy snorted. "Like that matters. I bet if you got a couple of drinks in her, she'd be open to some fun."

I pushed off the wall, fire in my chest roaring hot and quick when the door pushed open into the hallway. Greer stopped short when she saw them, offering a tight-lipped smile.

"Excuse me," she said, eyes moving down the hallway until she saw me.

One guy held out his hand. "Don't be in a rush. We didn't get to introduce ourselves earlier—"

She interrupted him before he could continue, hand raised. "I'm *so* not interested. You can save it for someone else."

He made an affronted noise. I approached behind them, but neither noticed.

"I'm just being friendly," he said.

"No, you're not," I spoke from behind them.

Greer smiled, slipping between them to approach me. "There you are," she said quietly. "I was looking for you."

The dickhead stared at her ass, even after his friend nudged him with his elbow. "*Dude*," the friend whispered.

"What? She's just…there. I can't help it."

I opened my mouth to… I wasn't sure what, but Greer settled a soft hand on my chest, then wheeled slowly, a serene smile on her face.

"Pro tip," she said silkily, "don't be a giant greasy douchebag, and you'll have a much higher chance of getting laid in any given situation."

"Not with you, though," he said. "Which is a damn shame because you are the hottest woman in that room."

I started to push past Greer, and she snagged my arm. Her grip was shockingly strong.

"No, sweet child, not with me." At her tone, I bit back a smile. It was the verbal equivalent of a condescending pat on the head. She curled her hand around my bicep and started walking backward, pulling me with her. "My *husband*, however, is about to get very lucky. I truly hope you don't stick around, but if you do, you might want to take notes because I have a feeling you need them."

Greer pulled open the closest door and tugged me inside.

It was an empty conference room, the lights from outside making it glow a dim blue-ish color. She sagged against the door with a wide grin on her face. Her chest heaved on a short burst of laughter, and my hands curled into fists at my side.

My heart banged against my ribs, and something hot kindled low in my stomach.

"What," I whispered, "was that?"

She had no idea what she did to me. Absolutely none.

Her smile merely spread further, her eyes glowing in the low light of the room. We were so very alone, and I was feeling so very out of control.

"Sorry," she said. "I can't help myself when guys act like that. He wouldn't know what to do with a woman, even if she came with a color-coded map to the clit."

I refused to smile even though I desperately wanted to. She was incredible.

I took a step toward her. "Why would you need to apologize?"

She lifted one shoulder in a delicate shrug. "I probably should've let you do the protective man thing."

I took another step closer. She eyed me carefully.

"What thing is that?" I asked.

Her chin rose a notch. "You know...*get away from my girl. She's mine, asshole*. Those things, which are very fun to hear every now and then."

I took another step, bracing my hand on the door next to her head. She sucked in a breath, her chest rising dangerously against the neckline of her dress.

"You forgot one," I told her.

"Did I?" she asked, voice as quiet as mine.

I pulled in a slow breath, nodding slightly.

"Which one?"

I ducked my chin, my lips brushing against her temple. "Touch her and I'll break every fucking bone in your hand," I murmured. The words came out with soft brushes against her skin, belying the absolute savagery of how much I meant them.

Because it's what I'd wanted to say.

It's what I'd wanted to *do*.

If I didn't get to touch her—this wild, fearless creature that was almost, but not quite, mine—then I couldn't imagine anyone else doing it either.

Greer inhaled, shaky and unsteady, and her eyes locked unerringly on my mouth.

There were no sudden movements between us, like we knew exactly what line we were tiptoeing against. I promised myself one thing, and one thing only, before I made my next move.

I could give her the truth of how much I wanted her.

My thumb moved to the doorknob. Greer licked her lips, throat moving in a nervous swallow. I pressed down, and the decisive click of the lock echoed in the room.

# CHAPTER 23

# Greer

**In front of me—so unbearably, painfully handsome—was** the most conflicted man I'd ever seen in my life.

It was etched on every part of him, head to toe. In the perfectly still way he held back, the way his brow furrowed, a slight wrinkling that made me want to smooth it out with my fingers, and the absolutely brutal look in his eyes when he looked down at my mouth.

I'd been wanted before.

I'd experienced lust and attraction and the head-spinning ache of desire.

But I'd never experienced this.

Every inch of me ached.

This was yearning.

It wasn't violent or loud. It wasn't fast and furious and frantic. It was delicate and perfect. Like he'd knotted something fragile to the base of my spine, curling through my belly, and had the ability to tug me into him, pull me closer simply by breathing.

My entire life, I'd never really known what to do with those kinds of feelings. With the tender and quiet and soft that came with the right kind of love. Maybe because I'd never experienced it.

If I leaned forward, if I fisted my hands in his jacket and tugged his body against mine, it would become all those things… the fast and furious and frantic.

And the absolutely awful part of the entire thing was I knew how much it would cost him if he touched me in the way he clearly wanted.

If there was any place in my life where I couldn't be selfish, couldn't dive headfirst into the thing I wanted, it was with him.

Because I cared.

I cared about him too much.

It wasn't fake, and it wasn't forced.

And if I dared think it, I knew I was falling in love with him, maybe just a little too much.

The brush of his mouth at my temple sent a shiver down my spine, and I pushed him back with just the tips of my fingers. His forehead creased in confusion.

"Sit," I told him, lifting my chin toward a chair that was just a few feet away from us.

Beckett swallowed, the line of his throat moving in a way that had my mouth watering. With a searing look, he shifted back, pulling the chair so that he was less than a foot away from me, settling his big, long body into the chair, sprawling his legs open while he watched me against the door with hooded eyes.

I straightened against the door. I'd never felt more naked in front of a man, had never wanted anyone in my entire life like I wanted him, and even if this could backfire spectacularly, I took a deep breath.

"Tell me," I said.

His brows furrowed. He sat up, fisting his hands on the tops of his thighs.

"If you can't think straight when you touch me," I said. "Then tell me." I traced the edge of my pinkie along the neckline of my dress. "Tell me what you want me to do."

He sucked in a breath through gritted teeth, his eyes lit with something dark and dangerous. "Greer."

Just the sound of my name on his lips while we both straddled this most exquisite line had me pressing my thighs together. I brushed my fingers underneath the edge of the strap of my dress, and it slipped off my shoulder.

"I understand why you can't," I told him. I speared my hands through my hair, a slight tug as I tightened my fingers. My blowout would be wrecked, but I had a feeling it would be a worthy sacrifice. "This is as much for me as it is for you."

His chest expanded on a deep breath, his eyes hadn't moved a single inch off my face. And underneath those tailored darkgray pants, I saw exactly how much he wanted me.

I bit down on my bottom lip while I studied that bulge in his pants, and he made a dark, growling noise from deep in his throat.

"I'd kiss you first," he ground out.

"How?" I asked. I touched the pads of my fingers to my lips. "Hard? Or soft?"

"What do you think?"

I pinched my eyes shut and imagined it. He'd grip the sides of my face. Seal his mouth over mine, suck the air from my lungs like a punch, and I'd fucking love it.

He'd devour me whole.

"Hard," I answered immediately. Dazedly, I opened my eyes again. Leave it to him—the man who I thought wasn't my type—to give me the most visceral sexual experience I'd ever have in my life without laying so much as a finger on me. "Especially right now. You look…angry about how much you want me."

His jaw clenched tight.

"You'd have your hands in my hair," I continued. "It would hurt a little."

His hands shook. He was fisting them so tightly.

"But you wouldn't *only* kiss me for very long," I said.

Slowly, he shook his head. "No. I wouldn't."

"You'd touch me." I gently pulled down the other strap of my dress until both sides hung over my shoulders.

"There," he said, voice full of agony and tight with desperation.

I nodded. Despite the tight fit of the dress, the material had just enough stretch, and when I pulled down the bodice, he let out a short, pained sound, something ripped from his chest.

"All night," he said. "You've been walking around with nothing under there all night?"

Again, I nodded.

Beckett stared, his eyes greedy as he memorized the sight of my breasts. I traced them delicately, small circles with the tip of my finger, and he hissed out a slow breath.

"You're so beautiful," he said, voice low and rough. He pinched his eyes shut and tipped his head back. "Fuck, this is not helping."

"Do you want me to stop?" I asked, head tilted.

His gaze locked on mine. "Not a chance."

I smiled.

He didn't. "Lift your dress," he said.

Oh yes. The bossy tone did things to me. Beckett could see it in my eyes too, and he leaned forward.

"Anything under that skirt, Greer?" he asked.

Slowly, I shook my head.

He dropped his chin and muttered a string of curse words. A hot burst of delight sprang from my chest, bleeding warmth I could feel all the way down to my toes.

As I inched the dress up, I paused when it was around my upper thighs. "Here?" I asked.

His eyes narrowed in on the hollow between my legs, where he couldn't quite see. The place I wanted him, and by the looks of it, where he wanted to be too.

"There." The word was sharp and harsh, and it caused the first flutter of pleasure in the base of my spine. "You lift that dress another inch, and I'll stop playing this little game, Greer."

He meant it too. My fingers curled in the hem, and I wondered what he'd do first if I ignored him, if I rucked it up around my waist and damned the consequences.

"It won't feel the same," he said.

"It would be better if it was you," I agreed easily, sliding my hand between my thighs.

His leg was bouncing ceaselessly, and I tossed my head back against the door when I imagined that it was him.

My hips rocked, seeking the kind of friction I just couldn't get without him.

Without his big hands, without his longer fingers, and without the press of his big hard body against mine.

"Tell me," he commanded. His eyes were so dark. His face so stern and severe.

So I did.

My voice came out breathy, choppy on the words, while I tried to tell him how it felt.

When I said things like *wet* and *hot* and *tight*, his whole body locked with tension. When I rolled my hips and bit down on my bottom lip, a swirling ball of heat crawling up my back, his nostrils flared dangerously.

When I moaned my way through the beginning spark, he watched my face like I was something precious and rare.

"Show me," he said. "Show me now, Greer."

The build was slow, achingly, painfully slow, and when it crested, the pleasure was a sweet, sharp spike that had me arching my back, chanting a chorus of *yes, oh yes*, warmth unspooling down my body in a wave.

While my breath heaved, I hardly registered that he'd moved closer. That his hands were locked tight between his legs.

And then he laid his forehead against my trembling stomach.

"You are incredible," he whispered.

My fingers threaded through his hair, soft and smooth and cool. I held him to me while we both breathed heavily.

Me from spent relief. And him, from an impossible wall that he didn't quite know how to climb.

Oh how I wanted to do it for him. To tear down whatever he'd put between us.

But for the first time in my life, I couldn't.

After a few more moments, he lifted his head. I traced my thumb along his brow, and he closed his eyes at my impossibly light touch.

As I came down, Beckett slowly stood, towering over me as he glanced down the front of my body with unreadable eyes.

Carefully, without touching my skin, he tugged one strap up into place. Then the other.

While he did, I slid my skirt back into place.

I let out a loaded exhale as he stepped back. It wasn't awkward, per se. But a good make-out session would have been a little bit nicer way to ease back into reality.

Still… I couldn't regret it.

When had a man ever looked at me like he wanted me that

badly? Where his body shook from the force it took to hold himself back?

Never.

"I'll meet you in there in a couple of minutes," he said quietly.

I arched an eyebrow in question.

He gave me a level look. "I need to recite the Gettysburg Address or something," he said wryly.

I exhaled a laugh. "Ahh. Right." I cleared my throat, pulling at the knot in my hair, even though it was halfway sliding back down my neck. "I'm assuming you don't need help with that."

It was his turn to raise an eyebrow. "I don't."

I was still smiling when I let myself out into the quiet hallway. And a small knot of disquiet formed at the base of my throat the moment the door closed behind me.

Because I knew at some point, he'd either have to choose to break down that wall between us, or I'd have to make peace with the fact that he'd live behind it forever.

What I'd said to Beckett was still true—this was a way to allow an outlet for some of these feelings, the ones building and building with no place to go. Maybe the consequences were unseen and wouldn't affect an entire life, but it would take time before we knew that.

Walking out of that room, I still felt sexy and desired. But even more than that, I felt adored. By someone so guarded that he couldn't even bring himself to touch me without fear of what it might unleash in him. In his carefully constructed life.

By the time he joined me in the reception hall, his cheeks

were slightly flushed, and Micah gave us a knowing look, laughing behind the rim of his champagne.

We didn't dance, and there was no more under the table touching, no more arms draped behind my back. But every time our eyes met and held, there was a new buzzing sort of awareness. A distinct hum that hadn't been there before.

Olive visited our table and informed her dad she was doing a cousin sleepover at Josie's house, and I felt a visceral thud of disappointment.

He looked at me over her head, his face unreadable.

No reason to share a bed tonight.

No reason to tempt fate beyond how we'd already tempted it.

When Beckett broke the gaze, I wondered if he felt relief. Or if the same edge of dissatisfaction knifed through him as it did me.

And for the first time since this whole thing started, I wasn't sure that I'd come out of this without a broken heart.

# CHAPTER 24

# Beckett

**The steady dripping of the coffee maker was strangely** hypnotic. Or maybe I couldn't tear my eyes away from it because I'd hardly slept the night before.

There'd been no movement from the guest room, and I would've known if Greer had experienced the same restlessness that plagued me.

Lying in the middle of that big empty bed, I stared at the ceiling and tried desperately to banish the image of her from my racing thoughts.

Tried desperately to convince myself that I could make it through the year without blurring the lines between us any further.

We'd simply have to come up with a plausible reason for why she slept in the guest room.

Because if I had Greer in that bed with me—knowing what she sounded like, knowing what she looked like when she came—I'd give in.

The coffee stopped its brewing, and I carefully pulled down the mug she favored and set it down next to the machine.

Give in, I thought helplessly.

That was the wrong phrase.

It was passive. Hinted at submission, or a concession that needed to be made.

And when I allowed myself to think about what might happen if she was there with me, nothing was passive about it.

My body reacted immediately, standing in that quiet kitchen. I'd tear through clothes, and I'd use my teeth and tongue like weapons. My hands would take. They'd ravage and mark because I knew exactly how she'd react.

She'd devour me right back.

And when that first taste was done, when our lust had been temporarily satisfied, I knew that Greer would bend—pliable and warm and soft. She'd let me take. She'd submit.

I swallowed hard, moving away from the coffee maker while I pulled an apple and a protein shake from the fridge.

There was a text on my phone from Josie's sister. Olive was awake and having breakfast with her cousins. She attached a picture that had me smiling.

"Good morning."

I turned at the sound of Greer's soft, sleepy voice. Her hair was a tangled mess around her shoulders, her mascara slightly smudged around her eyes, and the sleep pants low around her hips were worn so thin that they looked ready to disintegrate at the slightest hint of pressure.

"Morning," I told her.

She yawned as she grabbed the bright blue coffee mug, and as she filled it, she gave me a grateful smile. "I had no idea how spoiled I'd feel with someone else making the coffee first. I'm not sure I can ever go back."

It didn't require much of an answer, so I didn't give her one. But something about it, the one small, simple thing I'd done for her had my heart tumbling behind my ribs.

"What were you smiling at?" she asked.

Because the island was between us, I quietly slid my phone toward her. She angled the picture so she could see it better, and she grinned.

"Cute. How often does she get to see her cousins?"

"Not often," I admitted. "They live in Upstate New York, so they don't get out here very often. I think the only reason she was comfortable with the sleepover is because they came out over Christmas last year, so she saw them recently."

Greer nodded, taking another sip of her coffee. Over the rim of the mug, she studied me with a serious expression in her big eyes.

A million questions hovered over this brand-new day.

We couldn't un-know the things we knew now, and it was clear we were both aware of it.

"I told her we'd pick up Olive in about an hour, if that works for you. We can get her on the way to your parents'."

Greer's expression brightened. "You're still willing to come?"

"Why wouldn't I?"

She exhaled a laugh. "Well, last night was a little…" Her voice trailed off.

"Intense," I supplied.

Greer nodded. "I wasn't sure if you needed some space."

The truth.

It was the thing between us that helped as much as it caused pain. We were telling lies to so many people, that I somehow couldn't bring myself to tell them to her.

"I don't know what I need," I admitted.

Greer took such a long moment to consider my answer, her eyes so thoughtful and quiet, that I shifted in place.

"Okay." She took another sip of coffee. "Then the distraction of my parents' house is good. No one can get any good thinking done there."

"Easy as that, huh?"

She carefully set the mug down and walked around the island. I braced myself when she came closer, but she didn't touch.

"Maybe not *easy*. It goes against my nature to be patient," she told me. "But I think you already know that."

"I might have an idea," I answered wryly.

Her lips curved into a smile so self-deprecating, so sly, that it took every ounce of my willpower not to grab her and kiss that smile right off her face.

Every shred of restraint not to boost her onto the island and fuck her through every reservation beating through the back of my skull.

She was shorter without her shoes on, and when she tilted

her chin up to look into my face, I set my jaw, hands clasped loosely at my side. Her sleep shirt was loose, and she wore no bra underneath.

I didn't close my eyes, didn't fight the image of her breasts pushed up by the neckline of her dress when she pulled it down.

"I have to tell you though, I might have to revise the definition of what my type is after last night," she said, eyes glowing. "I never thought that a man who's strong enough not to touch me could ever make me feel that good."

Her words set off such a strong wave of longing. I didn't feel strong. I felt weak.

She made me feel weak.

Powerless because of how much I wanted her and what I might be willing to concede if I could have her, even for a while.

"I'm not worried about whether you're my type, Greer," I told her.

"No?"

I shook my head, taking a calculated step back. She watched with curiosity.

"You'd ruin me, if this goes wrong," I admitted. Her face went slack with shock. "And I can't afford to be ruined right now. No matter how badly I want to try."

I didn't wait to see what my words did to her. I couldn't.

There was no way to chase the threads I'd just pulled open. Not quickly or easily.

Because if they made her sad, I'd do just about anything to erase that feeling for her. If they frustrated her, I'd let her tell me why, simply to undo a little bit of the burden we were both carrying. If they angered her, well…we'd probably end up naked on the floor within three minutes, her thighs tight against my side, my hands gripped tight in her hair, and none of those options seemed especially prudent.

"I'm gonna shower," I told her. "I'll be ready to leave in about thirty minutes."

The drive to pick up Olive was quiet.

Painfully.

Uncomfortably.

I'd seen Greer a lot of different ways since she barreled into my life, and I'd never seen her quiet.

And once my daughter was strapped safely into the back seat of my car, the quiet continued. Olive told us about her sleepover, and Greer asked her some questions about her cousins, but the two of us didn't have much in the way of interaction.

Suddenly, the distraction of being at her family's house wasn't quite so simple.

Because we couldn't distract ourselves forever, and the one time our eyes caught and held before I turned down their driveway, I could tell she was thinking the exact same thing.

Showing up this time, more than the first or even the second, I felt like a fraud.

It crawled up on me slowly, throughout the drive. Like a delayed ramification of the purely need-driven moment we'd shared at the reception.

It was all wrong.

It shouldn't be this way.

And the only reason it was this way was because of me. Because I'd convinced myself that it would work, I'd convinced myself that it had to work so that I could have this chance to be the parent I'd never had. Be the parents I needed and hadn't got.

My lungs felt brittle and cold. My brain raced in choppy pulses that I couldn't stop.

Olive gripped my hand tightly as we left the car, still holding the slightest of nerves at showing up to this big, welcoming place where everyone was so thrilled to see us.

Poppy greeted us first, a tight hug for Greer and a more reserved polite smile for me. And for Olive, she crouched down and told her that their barn cat had some kittens, if she wanted to go for a visit.

Olive glanced up at me with excited eyes, and I nodded. Poppy held her hand out, and Olive took it tentatively. Standing quietly by my side, Greer glanced up at me with questioning eyes.

"You look like you're freaking out a little," she said evenly. Her parents hadn't come outside yet, neither had Cameron.

I managed a nod. "A little."

But there was nothing to be done. We just had to get through this day of pretend.

Sheila opened the door first, smile wide and eyes happy. "Come in, come in, I've got some bread right out of the oven."

Greer sighed. "I love coming here."

"I *have* offered to teach you," her mom said gently.

Greer slung an arm over her mom's shoulders. "I can't help it if it tastes better when you make it."

Tim gave his daughter a hug, and I couldn't help but notice that he'd lost weight, even in the couple of weeks since I'd seen him. But he was still walking on his own, and when he shook my hand, his grip was strong.

"How was the wedding?" he asked.

Greer choked on her piece of bread.

"Good," I told him, very much not thinking about how his daughter slid her hands between her legs for me with a room full of people on the other side of the wall. "Josie deserves to be happy. She and Micah just took last night by way of a honeymoon, but they'll be picking up Olive tonight so they can spend their last week with her before they leave for London."

He hummed. "Makes sense. Well, I'm glad Greer dragged you back here for the day. I'm sure y'all have had a lot on your plates getting ready for this."

"Yeah, we've been…busy," I answered.

Cameron wandered out of the kitchen with a huge slice of bread in his hand. He cocked a brow at my answer, and I fought an uncomfortable roiling sensation in my stomach.

"He's good at the guilt trips," Cameron said easily. "If it were up to Mom and Dad, we'd all still live under their roof."

Sheila snorted. "You wish. I'm down to one adult child, which is plenty. And I still somehow have to feed you half the time."

The conversation stayed easy and warm while we ate some

lunch. Poppy sent Greer a picture from the barn, and she slid her phone over to me on the table.

Olive had a small orange-and-white kitten cuddled up on her chest. Her smile was as big as I'd ever seen it, and I got that same feeling in my chest whenever I saw her happy—like I'd burn down the whole world just to keep that smile on her face.

"She's gonna want that cat, isn't she?" I asked.

Greer laughed.

Sheila nodded sagely. "Might as well give up now, Beckett. I have a feeling Tim and I could part with her for a pretty fair price of some more time with that darling girl of yours."

Greer's eyes caught mine, and I swallowed past a knot of emotion lodged in my chest.

"I'll think about it," I promised.

She patted my hand. "They'll be ready to leave momma in about three weeks."

Another car rolled in front of the house, and Greer popped up out of her seat with a gasp. "Is that Erik and Lydia?"

Tim nodded. "Lydia had to be in Portland for an event, so they tacked a couple of extra nights on so we could see the baby."

Greer shoved Cameron out of her way as she sped toward the door. He braced his feet on the floor and blocked her path.

"Move," she said, grunting from the effort of pushing him out of the way. "I want to get the baby before Poppy gets back."

Sheila laughed. "Oh, I have a feeling she and Olive will be playing with those kittens for a while. They're still slow to run around."

Erik, tall and dark-haired, with the same eyes as Greer, was the first in the house. In his grip was an expensive-looking diaper bag. He opened his arm to get a hug from Greer, and she ducked underneath to race out of the front door.

He blinked. "Okay then."

Sheila patted him on the shoulder. "This is what happens when you have a baby. Get used to it."

He gave me a nod in greeting. "Beckett. Did Tim rope you into some manual labor yet?"

"No?" I glanced back at the man in question, who was helping himself to some of the bread.

He merely smiled at his eldest son.

Cameron smacked me on the back. "There's time yet. You'll learn that he has a list for us every time you step foot on this property."

"Oh, it's not that bad," Tim said. "Just a few of those dead trees need clearing out by the gym. You boys are strong enough to move them."

Erik nodded. "I knew it. Should I change now, or do I have time to eat?"

Tim paused, Cameron and I trading a look. "Might want to change now."

I exhaled a laugh when Cameron rolled his eyes. Erik shook his head, elbowing his brother as he passed through the kitchen.

The door into the house opened again, this time by Erik's wife—she was telling Greer a story with big movements of her hands. The sound of Greer's laughter preceded her, and when she walked through the door, Erik and Lydia's daughter in her arms, I felt like someone had punctured my lung with a steel beam.

Even though Lydia was talking to her, Greer's focus was entirely on the baby. She held her small body up against her chest, her shock of dark hair against her face. She placed soft kisses along the baby's forehead, only stopping to inhale greedily.

"She smells so good," Greer said. "Why does she smell so good?"

Lydia laughed. "Well, she got a bath at the hotel this morning because she had a blowout, so…"

Greer made a nose-scrunching face, then blew in the baby's neck, which drew a sweet gurgling sound from the child. "You wouldn't do that to Auntie Greer, would you?"

The sight of Greer holding that baby would haunt me for another sleepless night.

It was too much.

Because it was far too late to realize that maybe she'd already ruined me, even without knowing how she felt. How her skin would be under mine, or what noises she made when we kissed.

The room was getting hot around me, the sounds of so much laughter and ease and love.

Erik approached his wife, stealing a lingering kiss while Greer nuzzled their daughter. Cameron reached behind his mom to swipe a piece of bread. Tim said he was going to go down to the barn so he could see Olive with the kittens.

All of it was too much.

Something I'd lied to get.

Something I'd done nothing to deserve. Not for myself or for Olive.

I'd let all of this get too far. Stupidly thinking that by drawing some arbitrary line in the sand when it came to Greer that we could all escape unscathed.

But none of us would be.

Not Olive.

Not Greer or her family.

And not me.

Through the windows, I saw Olive and Poppy returning to the house.

Tim met them in the front yard, and when he gestured to the large play set around the back of the house, Olive nodded.

And she skipped as she went, one of her sure signs that she was happy.

Because of this place. And these people.

"Excuse me," I said to Cameron. Greer gave me a questioning look when I let myself out the front door.

I braced my hands on the front porch, staring out into the endless acres of fir trees that lined the Wilder's property.

I tried to imagine what it would have been like to be raised in such a place, with people like this.

The door opened quietly, and instead of Greer, it was Sheila Wilder. She had an understanding look in her eyes.

"You all right, Beckett?"

I straightened. "Didn't mean to make a scene. Just needed some fresh air."

She glanced back into the house, her eyes landing on her daughter, who was watching us while she rocked the baby gently.

"You didn't," she assured me. "I just know that look when someone isn't quite sure what to do with all of us. You're not the first who's been overwhelmed by this family."

I nodded.

"Sit," she said, gesturing to the chairs on the front porch. It was the same place we'd sat when I asked their permission to marry Greer. My stomach was in a thousand knots when I sat in them again.

"Thank you for having us out today," I told her. "Olive and I didn't get much of this before Greer."

"Your daughter is a precious little thing. I hope you don't mind everyone doting on her. We can't help ourselves."

I smiled. "She likes it here. That's a big deal."

"Good parents will do just about anything for their kids, won't they?" she asked.

If only she knew.

She smiled knowingly. "Greer's told you about how Tim and I met, right?"

I nodded. "A little. Parker did too, when he first transferred to Portland."

Sheila hummed. "We managed to create a lot of good out of the pain that comes with life. I've had more than my share, and so has Tim." She glanced back at the house. "Despite his health, we're in a sweet phase of life right now. It's nice."

"Tim lost his first wife, didn't he?" I asked.

Her smile was soft as she nodded. "Cancer. Quick and mean and there wasn't much they could do to stop it by the time she saw her doctor." She sighed. "He had three boys under the age of ten who'd just lost their mom, all looking at him on how to navigate this big ugly thing."

I didn't ask Sheila about Greer's father because I knew she didn't have the same type of sad story. Her spouse left voluntarily.

He had the beautiful wife. He had the son and two daughters, and when Greer wasn't all that far from Olive's age, he walked out.

Sheila must have understood the clear evasion of the next natural question because she smiled. "He was always better at handling these things than I was."

"Tim?"

She nodded. "The grief. The loss. How their little brains hardly knew what to do with it for so many years. He always managed to talk through things when I was still stuck in feeling them. Even now, we have to help them through it when they don't handle it well." Her eyes misted over. "I don't want to lose my husband, any more than I want my kids to lose their father. But he's always better at just listening to what's behind their hurt, what's behind the things they do because of it."

I thought about Parker's avoidance. And I thought about Greer's frantic need to act.

"He'll come around," I said quietly. "Parker."

She nodded. "Oh, I know he will. He loves his dad too much not to. The wedding was a start," she said pointedly. "For a lot of things."

There was some meaning hidden in her words, and I studied her face as she said them.

"But I'm not too worried about Parker right now if you can believe it." She shook her head. "Nothing about our life—then or now—was perfect or convenient. And definitely not like we planned it. And some of that is watching how our children have to move through the hard. The things they'll do, the lengths they'll go to avoid feeling it."

After a pointed glance at my wedding ring, her eyes met mine knowingly, and I felt a quick jolt of realization.

She knew.

"Sheila," I said quietly, "I don't know what to say—"

But she held up a hand. "You don't owe me any explanations, Beckett. I know your own reasons for doing this. And I think they're noble. I had my suspicions, even if I didn't find it necessary to voice them to my daughter."

I sat forward, my elbows braced on my thighs, and I hung my head down while I processed through what this might mean.

"I'm so sorry," I said quietly. "I feel terrible lying to you and Tim."

She didn't reply for a long moment.

"I know you do," she said finally. Her voice was slightly unsteady. "Greer has always been my fierce heart. She jumps in—headfirst and eyes blazing, especially when it comes to her family. I had a feeling she heard Tim say what he did that day, just because of how she was acting."

"Why didn't you say anything?"

Her smile was secretive. "I had my reasons, and I'm old enough and wise enough not to share them."

I sat up. "What sealed it for you? Why we'd done it?"

"Pastor Bill," she said with a wry smile. "I ran into him last week, and he just couldn't stop rambling about that marriage license and how he's been losing sleep wanting to know that Greer sent it in."

I huffed a humorless laugh. "I told her that wouldn't work."

"So you're not actually married," she said quietly.

I stared down at the simple gold ring on my hand, gently spinning it. "No."

Why did it hurt to say it out loud, after all the weeks agonizing over it?

One simple word felt like it was cutting my throat open, exposing a raw nerve that hadn't existed before. It was the hardest truth I'd admitted yet.

"It felt like the right thing to do, at the time," I said. "We had, I don't know, sixty days to file it with the state, thought we could at least avoid committing fraud."

She inhaled slowly. "And you said your vows…"

"Forty-five days ago," I finished. I'd counted the night before while I stared up at the ceiling.

Sheila raised her eyebrows slowly.

"I don't know what the right thing is anymore," I admitted. "If a lie is ever worth the cost of telling it."

"I wish I could answer that for you," she said. "But I'm afraid it's not my place."

I gave her a curious look. "But you still told me you know."

"I did. Because I could see it eating you up, and I don't want it to do that either." She smiled gently. "You both have good hearts, you made a decision rooted in the love of someone else, and that matters to me. It should matter to you too, as you think about what you do moving forward."

I weighed her words before answering.

There was a choice to be made, and she was leaving it up to me. To me and Greer.

"You're not planning on telling anyone," I said quietly.

After a long moment, she shook her head.

"Not even Tim?"

She let out a slow breath, and as she did, a tear slid down her cheek. She made no move to brush it away. "It's not my story to tell, Beckett. It's yours and Greer's. My husband was as happy as I've seen him in months that day, and no matter where it came from, you and Greer gave him something he's always wanted to experience." Her voice trembled. "He's the best man I've ever known. Stepped up in a million ways for kids that weren't his and loved them through all the hard. So no, I'm not going to take that moment from him."

There was nothing for me to say, all I could do was sit and listen. Absorb all the different shades of gray in this situation that I'd ignored.

All I could do was weigh the truth, how it stacked up for the people affected by this. What it would cost by telling it.

She stood, settling a hand on my shoulder.

"You're a good man, Beckett. And a good man for my daughter, which I realize is a separate issue from what you're facing. But I just need you to know that so you can stop beating yourself up."

I stayed out there after she went back in the house.

I thought about everything she'd said. What it meant in the context of the last couple of months, and how they'd parented their kids, how they'd modeled a healthy kind of love that I'd never known myself.

Maybe that was why Greer always seemed to know how to handle Olive so well because she was raised with love and support, by parents who accepted that all their kids came with different struggles and different ways of handling things.

Why she loved without reservation.

And then I couldn't help but wonder who I'd want Olive to learn from as she grew up. What kinds of lessons she'd learn from me if I kept on this path.

I wasn't sure how much time passed, but eventually the door opened, and Greer joined me.

Just her presence alone set off a reaction inside me.

When she walked past to take the seat her mom had vacated, I thought about Sheila's words. Her fierce-hearted daughter who jumped in without thought, eyes blazing.

I glanced over at that woman and wondered how I'd been so blind when she slowly infiltrated herself into every facet of my life.

How was I ever so stupid to think I could resist?

It wasn't stupidity, I realized, as I cataloged her face. It was arrogance. And now I had to dismantle that, brick by brick by brick.

"Olive named the cat," she said.

I exhaled a quiet laugh.

"Of course she did." I sighed. "What'd she pick?"

Greer's lips curved into an irresistible smile. "Clarence."

"What? Why?"

She laughed. "No clue. She told my dad he looks like an old man, so she picked an old man's name."

I didn't laugh like she might have expected. All it did was heap another weight onto the pile weighing down my chest.

Greer sighed before she spoke again.

"You and my mom were having a pretty serious discussion out here," she said.

Slowly, I nodded.

"Want to talk about it?"

I took a deep breath, then locked eyes with Greer. Her smile faded when she caught sight of my face.

"I have to tell Josie."

## CHAPTER 25

# Greer

I thought Olive might fall asleep on the drive home, but she was way too busy making plans for Clarence the Cat to do something as boring as sleep.

"Can we get him a cat tower for my room? He needs his exercise to stay strong."

Beckett nodded. "I'm sure we can, sweet pea. We've got a few weeks until he's big enough to leave his mom, though, so we'll take our time and find all the best stuff for him."

"And toys," she added. "He'll need toys."

"Yup," he said easily, his eyes locked on her in the rearview mirror.

"Can we get a cat bed too?" she asked.

Beckett made a noise of agreement. "You don't think Clarence will be sleeping in your bed?"

"I hope he does." She made a soft happy sound that had my

chest clenching tight. "But he should have a bed for naps too. Or when I'm at school and he wants to feel safe."

My eyes closed, and I fought the desperate urge to burst into tears.

The energy under my skin had nowhere to go, and during the entire drive back to Salem, I could feel it clawing desperately under the surface.

Somehow, I'd kept my shit together during the remaining time at my parents'. My mom studied me a few different times—that Mom look that had the power to reduce me to a blubbering mess—so I refused to make eye contact.

After pushing Olive on the swings for a while, Tim had fallen asleep on the couch.

Poppy was too distracted by the baby to notice my internal freak-out gauge had reached code red levels, and my brothers were about as observant as a Pop-Tart, so…

Here I sat.

Alone in my feelings, casually waiting for them to burst out of my mere mortal flesh that had never done a very good job at keeping me calm and steady when shit like this happened.

Cameron used to joke that I was like a ticking time bomb when I didn't have something to do.

And this was the worst possible thing to remember at the given moment.

Stuck in the car with the man I was likely falling in love with, his daughter who I was definitely in love with, knowing that everything he'd sacrificed for Olive was about to explode in his face, and I couldn't do a fucking thing about it.

My hands trembled in my lap, and I linked my fingers together to keep them steady.

Underneath my ribs, my heart was a knotted mess.

Beckett kept the conversation going with Olive because it was the chattiest I'd ever heard her, and when I managed a sidelong glance, the warmth in his eyes just about undid me, as she talked about the kittens and the swings and the trees and Cameron's big truck.

"I'm glad you had fun, sweet pea."

I stared at his hands, the way he held the steering wheel. The veins that crisscrossed under the skin. The spread of his long fingers. The gold ring on his hand.

"It was the best day ever," she proclaimed.

He glanced in my direction, a sad smile curving the edge of his lips.

A dangerous trembling started down in the base of my belly.

My parents had a big pond on their land, and we used to fish there when we were younger. On the rare occasion I was there alone, I used to love to find the smallest pebble I could find and toss it straight into the middle.

Because without fail, that teeny tiny pebble caused slow, rolling movement in the glassy surface of the water, and I loved waiting to see how long it would take them to reach me where I sat by the edge.

Somehow, I knew this was going to happen.

No matter how much I didn't want to face it, and no matter how much I lied to myself that we'd escape this inevitable outcome... I knew we'd have a reckoning for this thing we'd done.

The waves, tiny and imperceptible at first, were about to knock on the door.

I exhaled slowly, keeping my gaze trained outside of the window as my mind tripped over racing thoughts.

Josie would be furious.

She'd feel betrayed.

And she'd have every right to.

The house came into sight, and the trembling in my stomach spread. My ribs rattled, something trying to shake loose from where I was keeping it leashed tight.

"Can you bring Olive out into the backyard when Josie gets here?" he asked quietly.

His tone was so casual.

So unaffected.

Maybe his ribs weren't rattling, and maybe his heart wasn't knotted.

Maybe this was easy for him—doing the thing that was right, following the path in front of him that he'd decided on.

"Yeah," I said, mentally clapping myself on the back that I didn't sound like I was about to burst into tears.

"When is Mommy coming?" Olive asked.

"She'll be here soon," he answered. "I told her when we'd be home. She wants every second with you before she goes to London."

Olive nodded. "She's going to buy me a real Paddington Bear and bring home biscuits and a little red bus for my room."

Beckett's hand tightened on the steering wheel, and I had to tear my gaze away.

If she still went to London.

If she didn't change her mind in light of what we'd done.

I wasn't really surprised we'd found ourselves here. No matter how badly I didn't want to admit it, the moment he locked that door behind me, I knew that some small piece holding up the entire structure got knocked off-kilter.

A mistake.

He didn't say it, of course. He wasn't cruel.

As much as we'd promised each other the truth, that one he'd shared with me felt an awful lot like dying by a thousand cuts.

The idea that he might look back on this someday and view it in that light—view it as a selfish indulgence, view us as a mistake—was a ruthless slice of pain to the parts of me that were the most tender.

But even worse than all that, I knew that whatever was happening inside me paled compared to how he must be feeling.

Olive ran into the house, leaving Beckett and me lingering on the front porch. He braced his hands on the railing and stared down the driveway.

I stood next to him, the heat of his body close enough that I could feel it seep through my skin. I fought a wave of longing, of helpless desire to lift this burden from him.

There was nothing I could do to make this better.

Nothing I could do to take it away.

"Do you know what you're going to say to her?" I asked.

He dropped his chin and sighed. "No." After a moment, he lifted his head and pinned me with a look that I felt down to my toes. "You understand why I have to do this, right?"

Every selfish instinct screamed raw to convince him not to.

To tell him we didn't need to risk what we were building.

To slide into his arms, pour all these feelings into a kiss that might change his mind so we could stay just like this.

Me and him and Olive.

That we could take this year and build a foundation of an amazing life.

Something with love and laughter and butterflies and cats named Clarence and football games and crayons littering the kitchen table.

A sob threatened to crawl up my throat, and I swallowed it down, a door snapping shut with vicious precision in my head.

Because I saw it in his eyes, that he'd never be able to live with himself if he didn't tell Josie the truth of what we'd done.

This man would never be able to build a life on a lie.

It would be so much easier if I didn't love him.

But I did.

That was why I nodded, and as I did, my heart shattered like glass. "Yeah," I whispered. "You're doing the right thing, Beckett."

He exhaled slowly. His eyes tracked over my face, lingering slightly on my mouth.

I took a slow, measured step back, even though everything in me howled to *stay, stay, stay*. To move closer when he looked at me like that.

To take this thing we'd never allowed ourselves while we could.

Doing nothing, moving away from action in those big moments... I'd never managed it before.

But if there was any moment it counted most, it was this.

It was for him.

The sound of Josie's car cleaved through the silence between us, and Beckett straightened.

He was holding his body so tight, it looked like he might fracture into a million pieces. His eyes were frantic as they held mine.

Because I couldn't walk away without giving him something, I took a deep breath and clutched his hand in mine, stepping up to press a featherlight kiss onto his cheek. Into his ear, I whispered, "It'll be okay."

His hand gripped mine, like I was his lifeline. He smelled so good. And he felt so good.

"She knows how much you love Olive," I said quietly, pulling back to look into his face. "Just remind her of that, even if she needs to have her mad for a few days."

He managed a nod as I stepped back again.

I waved at Josie as she pulled up and then disappeared into the house.

Olive and I wandered into the backyard, her sketch pad

tucked under her arm, and through the windows, I saw Josie taking a seat at the island.

I pointed Olive to a large patch of wildflowers just past the barn, and she scampered lightly through the grass to find the best place to sit and draw.

I held a hand up to my eyes, shielding the sun so that I could see into the house.

My stomach roiled unpleasantly after only a few minutes when I saw Josie stand from her seat, her hands perched on her hips.

I took a few steps closer to the house, changing the angle just enough to see the dejected slump of Beckett's shoulders.

Josie was yelling.

He nodded his head, swiping a hand over his mouth. My lungs ached, and I couldn't pull in a full breath, imagining the pain he must be in.

When she pointed an angry finger out toward the backyard, where Olive and I stood, I laid a trembling hand over my stomach.

Beckett started saying something, his body language that of a man who knew he'd fucked up and wasn't trying to fight it.

And Josie... Josie was pissed.

I saw her swipe at her face, moving the frantic motion of her hands to point at him.

She marched toward the slider that led into the backyard and yanked it open.

Her eyes slid right past me.

Like I wasn't even there.

"Olive, come get your bag," she said. "We have to go."

"Can I finish drawing these flowers?" Olive asked.

"No." She crossed her arms. "We're leaving now."

Olive raced past me. "Bye, Greer," she called.

I pinched my eyes shut, the burn in them tremendous and horrifying.

When Olive was inside and out of earshot, I took a few steps toward the house. "Josie, I'm so sorry," I said.

"Don't," she said in a warning tone. "I can't hear this right now. I'm taking my daughter, and I will deal with the two of you later."

A sob escaped, loud and broken, and I rushed toward her. "Please don't punish Beckett for this," I begged quietly. Tears coursed down my face, unchecked and hot and unrelenting. "He's such a good dad, and this was all my idea." I laid a hand on my chest. My whole body shook like a leaf. "*Please*. He would never have done this if it wasn't for me. He just wants…" My voice cracked, and I pushed past it blindingly. "He just wants *time* with her, and he loves her so much. He never wanted to hurt you."

Josie's lip trembled as she watched me absolutely unravel in front of her.

"This was all me," I told her. My voice was hoarse, choked with emotions that I couldn't stop. "Blame *me*. Please don't punish him for this."

Beckett's face came into view behind Josie, his eyes red and his lips in a firm line. "Greer, stop. You can't fix this for me."

Josie acted like he wasn't there, and an ugly sob clawed past my lips.

"Don't you get it?" she asked quietly. "The moment you break someone's trust, it doesn't matter what your intentions were. You just have to deal with the fallout."

I couldn't stop crying. If I thought it hurt before, it was fucking nothing compared to the idea that this might have cost him a relationship with Olive.

Josie wiped under her eyes when Olive came back down the steps with her small pink suitcase and her heart-shaped sunglasses on her head.

Beckett picked her up to give her a hug, and even from where I stood, I saw the tight way he clutched her against his heart, a single tear escaping down his face.

It felt like someone was tearing my chest out.

"Bye, Greer. We can talk about Clarence when I come back!" And when she waved at me, I felt my heart crack into something unrecognizable.

I forced a smile, thankful she was far enough away that she couldn't see the tears.

Josie gave us both an unreadable look. "I'll call later after I talk to Micah," she told Beckett.

"Josie," he said.

She held up a hand. "Not now."

When she slammed the door behind her, the vacuum of sound in her wake was deafening.

Beckett's chest heaved, a choked sound of desperation

yanked from deep in his throat. I covered my mouth with my hand.

"It's over," he said, voice ravaged and weary and heavy with emotion. When I took a step toward him, he shook his head. "I need to be alone right now, Greer."

Our eyes met and held, and without another word, he turned and strode into his bedroom, slamming the door behind him.

Ten minutes later, my clothes shoved into my suitcase and my face wet with tears, I got into my car, turned it on, and started the drive back home.

# CHAPTER 26

# Greer

"I think she's broken," one of my brothers whispered dramatically. "I didn't know a human being could cry this much."

When I snatched a book from the end table and chucked it at him, I was two inches off from hitting him square in the balls.

Cameron deflected it with an incredulous huff.

Erik laughed, but his smile faded immediately when Lydia leveled him with a wife-death glare from where she sat on one side of me, rubbing my back.

Poppy was on the other side, the official holder of the tissue box.

Adaline was on FaceTime, watching everything with a sympathetic look on her face.

My mom and Tim sat on the couch, holding hands and just trying to keep their adult kids from losing their minds.

Judging by my general state, they had some more work to do.

I'd hardly stopped crying since I got back home.

There was a pile of tissues on the coffee table, and I plucked another one out of the box in Poppy's hands to blow my nose.

"How is there anything *left* in there?" Cameron asked.

"Cameron Wilder," my mom snapped. "Go outside if you can't be nice."

Tim settled back in his seat, laying his hands over his stomach and sighing. "Doesn't it feel like they're little again? You used to say that a dozen times a day."

My mom managed a tiny smile. "At least."

"Josie will forgive him," Poppy assured me. "She has to. We can all see what a good dad he is."

I rubbed the wadded-up tissue underneath my nose. "I think she will too, but at what cost? What if…?" My voice trailed off, the tears threatening to bubble over again. "What if she tries to change the custody agreement, or he gets less time with her because we did this big, horrible thing?"

"She won't do that," my mom soothed. "She might be upset for a while, and she's earned the right to be. But I don't think she'll take it that far. She knows you're both good people just trying to do right by the people you love."

I shook my head. "You didn't see her face. Or his," I whispered brokenly. "I don't think I can ever forgive myself if he loses time with her because of this."

"Do you want to get out of Oregon for a bit?" Adaline asked through the phone speaker. "Emmett will be gone for a week on that retreat he's doing with his offensive line and receivers, so I'll have the house to myself. We can eat horrible food and watch *Pretty Woman* on repeat if you want," she said.

I shrugged. "I don't know. We're so busy at work and… I have to go back to get the rest of my things." My eyes watered again. "I hope it's okay if I move back in for a while," I said to Mom and Tim.

They shared a look, and Tim patted her hand. "Of course you can. Your mom pretends she wants the house empty, but she's full of bluster."

Mom smiled.

Poppy laid her head on my shoulder. "I'm sorry, Greer. I really thought you two were…" She paused. "The dream."

Her words caused a splintering down the center of my chest, jagged and sharp. If I tried to touch it, it would make me bleed.

My mom tapped Cameron's arm. "Everyone out. Time for the rest of you to make yourselves busy, we need to talk to Greer."

Tim held up a hand. "Before you do, though, I'd like to make a statement."

We all quieted.

One by one, he looked us square in the eye. "If anyone else in this family pulls any more of this fake relationship bullshit before I die, I'm cutting you out of my will."

Cameron pinched the bridge of his nose.

Poppy sighed, squeezing my hand before she stood. Lydia took Erik's hand as she got off the couch, and Cameron gave me an encouraging look before he followed them out of the room.

Then he pointed at the skin under his eye. "You've got a

little mascara under there. You're gonna scare the baby if you look like that when she wakes up."

I flipped him off, and he left the house with an amused chuckle.

My mom shook her head. "Your kid," she told Tim.

He grunted. "I do have the worst ones, don't I?"

I watched them laugh, my chest aching from the force of how much I loved them.

"I already apologized, right?" I asked my parents.

Tim nodded. "A few times. It was hard to tell exactly how many through the sobbing, but I counted four."

"Five," my mom corrected.

Tim hummed. "Five is a nice number. I might not have forgiven you so easily if you'd only done four."

I let out a watery laugh.

He gave me a soft smile. "My sweet Greer, you were never going to learn this lesson any other way than the hard way."

"What lesson is that?"

Before he answered, he took my mom's hand in his own. "The hard comes in life, whether you do something to lessen the blow or not. And you can't make it disappear because you hate seeing the people in your life suffer through it."

I tucked my knees up to my chest, setting my chin there as I stared at him.

"When I get to sit down with your brother, which I hope will be soon, I'm gonna have to tell him the exact same thing. Parker doesn't want to look this in the face either because he feels helpless or angry, or whatever the case may be. But so do you. You just let it show in a different way than he does."

I rolled my lips together and nodded.

"You can't take the blow for Beckett with Josie because he walked into this *with* you," he said gently. "You tried because your heart loves so big and so fierce. For Olive and for him. And you can't make this last part of my life any different, any better, by trying to fix the hard parts of what's coming."

Tears slipped down my chin.

"I just wanted..." My voice trailed off. "I just wanted to give you something to make you happy."

His eyes were red. "I know. And it did. But there's no single moment in this world that tops what you and your brothers and sisters give me every day. Not a single one, Greer."

I could hardly see the room through my tears when I pushed off the couch and wedged myself next to him on the cushion while he wrapped me into his arms.

Tim held me while I cried. As he did, I heard a few quiet sniffles from him and my mom. When I opened my eyes, I saw him holding her hand.

After a few long minutes, I was spent. Drained of all huge, coursing emotions from the day. The past couple of months, really.

And my heart hurt.

Despite my parents' forgiveness, there was still reparations to be made with Josie. And with Beckett.

When I knew the tears were done, I got off the couch and

went to the kitchen for a glass of water. In the front yard, Erik and Cameron were playing a game of driveway basketball with Poppy and Lydia. Lydia simply wrapped her arms around Erik's neck, hitching her legs around his waist and clinging for dear life while he attempted a shot.

I smiled.

My mom joined me, laughing at the sight of them.

"What's next?" she asked quietly.

I managed a shrug. "Nothing tonight. He needed some space, and I understand."

"That boy feels something real for you," my mom said. "I knew it from the first night. It's the only reason I didn't say anything."

I glanced sideways. "Really?"

She nodded. "He sure didn't know what to do with you, but I figured he'd get there eventually. You have a way of wearing people down, Greer Wilder."

I couldn't help but laugh. "Thanks," I said dryly.

Mom smiled. "You know I mean that in the best possible way."

I sighed. "I don't know if he'll let himself figure it out," I admitted. "And maybe with anyone else, any other man I've ever been with, wearing them down is perfectly fine." I turned, my back to the window. "But I don't want Beckett to simply wave the white flag and say, *fine, I won't resist anymore*. That doesn't feel much like love, does it?"

"No, I suppose it doesn't."

I took a drink of water, my throat ravaged from all the crying. "This might sound strange, but the fact that he resisted so strongly is how I knew it was real. Even if he couldn't admit it." My skin flushed warm when I thought about the reception. One moment in the dark. Hopefully not our only one. "If he cared less, he would've given in earlier."

My mom's smile was soft. "We're treading awfully close to me having to hear about my adult daughter's sex life, and I make a point to never do that." She leaned in for a hug. "He'll come around, Greer. I know it."

Tim was already dozing on the couch, his stamina wiped from his daughter snotting all over him, and I watched while my mom covered him with one of the fuzzy blankets he preferred.

I took my water and wandered out onto the front porch, taking a seat on the top step to watch them play basketball. Poppy jumped in front of Cameron, kicking at his legs when he tried to dribble past her.

"Foul," he yelled, jumping out of the way of her violent defense. "Holy shit, Pops, you can't *kick* people in basketball."

"You're eight inches taller than me," she said. "How else am I supposed to stop you from scoring?"

Erik and Lydia had given up. She sat on the hood of their car, smiling up into his face as he tucked a stray hair behind her ear. My brother kissed his wife, soft and sweet, then wrapped her in his arms.

My chest hurt, so I looked away.

I wasn't sure what I planned to do about Beckett, what I planned to say when I saw him next.

I took a deep breath and stared out at the three sisters—the mountain peaks that always told me when I was home.

But tonight, even surrounded by the people I loved so much, it didn't feel like home.

That was the place I'd left just a few hours earlier, and I didn't know what to do about that.

Lydia made her way over and took a seat next to me. "Erik and I are going to go on a hike tomorrow while your parents watch Isla. You can join us if you want."

I nodded. "Maybe some fresh air will do me good. Which hike?"

"Black Butte Lookout," she said.

I was just about to answer her when the sound of a car hit my ears. The road leading back to the house was long, and it took a minute for the vehicle to come into view, and by the time it did, my heart was thundering wildly underneath my rib cage.

"Is that…?" Lydia leaned forward, eyes narrowed. Then she glanced at me, a huge smile blossoming on her face.

Cameron and Poppy stopped playing, Erik had turned toward the road, and we all watched in stunned silence as Beckett's vehicle thundered down the road toward the house.

I was fairly certain my heart had stopped beating because I definitely couldn't breathe and I couldn't think, and if I tried to stand, my legs would probably give out.

So I kept my ass right where it was, my lungs desperately trying to pull in air.

Lydia was the first one on her feet. "Everyone, inside."

Poppy sighed dejectedly. Cameron shoved her forward.

Erik paused. "Can't I do one scary big brother talk? I'm never around to intimidate anyone anymore," he asked his wife.

She pointed at the house, face unflinching. "No."

Everyone shuffled past me, and just before she followed, she stopped to squeeze my shoulder. "Good luck," she whispered.

Beckett pulled the car to a stop with his eyes locked on mine through the windshield.

He took a deep breath, never breaking the stare as he opened the door and unfolded his body.

The car door slamming echoed through the trees, and for a moment, we simply stared.

I could be patient.

I could wait this out.

Give him time to say what he needed to say, for good or for bad.

Except after about five more seconds, I heard myself say, "What are you doing here?"

Patience, as it turned out, might be a work in progress for me.

When he took a few steps closer, I saw the fire roaring in his gaze. "I'm here to get my wife."

## CHAPTER 27

# Beckett

*My wife.*

The words were out before I could register I'd said them.

Two hours in the car, countless things that I'd practiced in my head as my car ate up the miles between me and Greer. The nearer I got, the surer I was.

I'd never once practiced that line. All it took was the sight of her, and the words were there, as easy as breathing.

Her face was slack with shock where she sat on the porch.

I approached slowly and steadily, and her eyes shone with nervous anticipation as I came closer.

I didn't want to sit next to her on the porch. I wanted to face her, wanted to memorize every inch of her while I told her all the things I wanted to say.

And like she'd heard me think it, Greer carefully stood, her hand gripping the porch rail. She'd been crying, and the proof of that pain on her face sank like a blade into my chest.

"When did you come to this conclusion?" she asked in a shaky voice.

"About an hour after you left." I wanted to reach for her. Wanted to cup her face in my hands and feel her curl up against my chest as my fingers sank into her hair.

"Olive?" she asked.

Slowly, I shook my head. "Josie said she needed a day or two to cool down, and we'd talk then."

"Are you okay?" she asked.

"No." It was the only honest answer I could give her. I was terrified of a lot of things. That Josie would leave and take Olive with her out of anger. That she'd stay, and I'd lose my chance. And on top of those things, I was terrified that I'd lost Greer too.

That my initial burst of panic over what had happened cost me this incredible person who made my life better. Made me better.

"No, Greer," I said again, "I'm not okay about her. And I'm not okay about you leaving either."

Her lips twitched, but nothing else. She was afraid to smile. Afraid to trust it. But I could see that kindling of hope in her eyes, and it was enough to have me take another step.

Greer tilted her chin up, her cheeks a beautiful pale pink. "You could've called."

I exhaled a quiet laugh. "I could have."

"Why didn't you?" she whispered.

Her hands were loose at her side, and I slid my palm down the length of her arm, relishing the shiver that racked her frame when I did. My fingers curled around her wrist, and I lifted it to my mouth, pressing my nose to the satin soft skin there. Under my thumb, her pulse raced.

It matched my own, something urgent and frantic, and I forced myself to be patient.

To tell her the things she deserved to hear.

"I almost decided to wait," I told her. I pressed an impossibly light kiss to the inside of her wrist. Her fingers curled helplessly. "I could have convinced myself so easily." I moved her palm to the side of my face, exhaling heavily when she spread her hand, stroking her thumb over my cheek. I pulled her palm to my mouth and kissed her there too.

Greer just listened, her eyes fixed on mine.

"I could have made us both spend miserable days apart from each other," I told her. "Coming up with countless reasons this shouldn't work the way it does between us. I could have wasted weeks—beating myself up for all the ways I haven't done the right thing at the right time. And instead, I decided that I didn't want to waste another second, not when I know what I want."

Her eyes shimmered. "What changed your mind?"

I slid my hands up the line of her neck, her sharp inhale darting straight into my chest as I cupped her face between my palms. Her eyes fluttered shut, a tear escaping down her cheek in a quick slide. It absorbed into my skin where I held her. A small piece of Greer, just as precious as any other side of her that she'd shown.

I wanted them all.

"You." I allowed my forehead to rest on hers. "You fight for everything you want. Everything that's important. And I want to fight for this. For the family we're building together. Everything felt so empty when you left. And I knew that I'd never fill my life—Olive's life too—the way I want unless you're in it."

She exhaled a soft sob, her hands coming up to clutch my shirt in her hands.

"Can we start over?" I asked, stepping fully into her, allowing one hand to cup the back of her head, the other to wrap tight around her back. Greer sank into my embrace, her arms coiling around my middle as she pressed her face into my neck with a weighty exhale. "Start something real with me, Greer Wilder. You're the only person who I want it with."

Her hands clutched at my back, and she lifted her head to look up into my face. "If I say yes, are you going to kiss me?"

I smiled. "Yes, ma'am."

Her eyes sparkled. "Then you should know that my entire family is probably watching us right now."

Sure enough, when I glanced up toward the house, five or six bodies conspicuously darted back from the windows.

I laughed, tightening my arms around her. I slid my hand over her jaw, tilting her chin up.

"Then let them watch," I murmured before I took her mouth with mine.

Greer's lips were soft and sweet as I tilted the angle of the kiss and opened her jaw wider with a slight press of my hand. My tongue swept over hers, wet and warm, and my hand slid back into the cool silk of her hair. She whimpered when my grip tightened into the strands.

This was real, I thought. No matter how it started, or how I found her.

It was real.

And it was right.

Greer might have swept into my life like a tornado, but it was exactly the kind of destruction I needed. Because she took down everything I'd constructed before I knew she existed.

Before I knew love could feel like this—wild and fierce and fearless.

Her body against mine was warm and firm, and my hand coasted over her back, following the line of her ribs, down to the curve of her backside while she pushed up on the balls of her feet to twine her arms around my neck.

This was forever.

My arms tightened impossibly around her, the kiss deepening into something profound and seeking and endless. I pressed her backward until she hit the column on the porch. She laughed into my mouth, and with a groan, I took that sound deep into my lungs.

I wanted her everywhere.

All her sounds, every flicker of her eyes, and every smile, I wanted them inked on my skin and threaded through my veins.

With the press of my body, I deepened the kiss, changing the angle—tangling tongues and the edge of teeth and the pull of her lips against mine. We couldn't get close enough. There was no space left—no distance I could erase between our bodies, even if I kissed her like this forever.

Greer's hands clutched at my arms and back and neck, the soft whimpers that escaped her mouth into mine like a drug.

These were the things I'd been missing. And I wanted more.

I wanted everything she'd give me.

I tore my mouth off hers, sucking at the skin on her neck. Her hands shoved up underneath my shirt, nails digging into my back.

My body tightened, hard and aching and in violent need of a release. I wanted her mouth and hands and her tongue. I wanted all the places I still needed to taste and touch.

"Where can we go?" I begged. "I need you."

She gasped, tossing her head back when I rocked my hips into hers. I was so hard, and she trembled at the press of my body against her stomach.

Greer pushed gently at my chest, her eyes gleaming devilishly. "Want me to show you my make-out spot in high school?"

My chest heaved, my lungs incapable of pulling in enough air to think clearly. "How far?"

She tilted her head toward the woods behind the house. "About three minutes that way." She leaned up. "Think your car can handle it?"

I snatched her hand in mine and marched to the vehicle in question—which would *absolutely* be able to handle it—the sound of her breathless laughter had my heart hammering wildly in my chest.

I wanted to hear it every single fucking day for the rest of my life.

I wrenched the door open for her, snatching a hot, hard kiss before I smacked her ass. "Get in," I told her.

"So bossy," she muttered as I shut the door.

But the moment I was in the driver's seat, she angled in her seat, ripping her shirt off and tossing it in the back seat. "What are you doing?" I barked. "They can see you."

"If they're smart, they stopped watching a long time ago," she said, shifting forward onto her knees so she could suck at my neck, her hand starting on my belt buckle.

The engine roared to life, and I tried desperately to ignore the sway of her breasts behind the black lace as she knelt over the console.

"Greer," I said between gritted teeth. "Where the hell am I going?"

Her palm slid down the front of my pants, and I cursed.

"Back toward the road," she panted, ducking back into her seat to tug at her cotton shorts, wrangling them off her legs before I'd even put it into reverse.

This fucking woman.

There were about a thousand more romantic ways to do this, and I couldn't conjure a single one of them as she sat in the passenger seat, her insane body clad only in tiny scraps of lace.

"Turn right at that big tree," she said.

"They're all big trees," I practically shouted. Her hand was working down my zipper, and I almost drove us off the road. I snatched her hand away. "Stop it right now unless you want us to crash."

She laughed, her eyes bright. "There," she said. "This one."

There was a slightly worn path just past a massive fir tree, and I cranked the wheel.

"Stop," she said breathlessly, "they can't see us here."

"Thank God," I breathed.

I yanked the gear shift into park and practically ripped the door off the hinges. "Back," I commanded. "More room."

She was practically naked as she scrambled through the woods into the back seat of my SUV. I ripped my shorts off and tugged on her arm as I situated myself in the center of the bench seat. Greer attacked my mouth, whimpering when I speared my hand into her hair and gripped tight.

"This is not the way I imagined this," I told her between searing kisses.

She grinned. "Me neither."

I slid my hand up the toned length of her thigh as she swung it over my lap, settling her weight on top of me as I devoured her mouth.

She rolled her hips, my hand gripping her there, my fingers digging into her flesh. I ripped at her bra strap, dragging my palm over the hard tip of her breast. She shivered, tearing her mouth from mine, her eyes hazy and her breath coming in short pants.

I ducked down and pulled that soft flesh into my mouth in a hard suck, and her hands clutched the back of my head when I used the flat of my tongue against her.

Her back arched, and I licked up the line of her neck, kissing her again—never deep enough, never hard enough.

My hands trembled with the need to tear at the lace separating us, to see it disintegrate in my hands, and she worked her nimble fingers between us to shove at my boxer briefs.

"You ready?" I asked her, our eyes locked.

"I've been ready for weeks," she said, her mouth curling into a sinful smile. "You're the one who finally caught up."

I pushed my hand between our bodies, wrenching the lace to the side, two fingers sliding between her legs. With a groan, she dropped her forehead to mine, riding the motion of my hand while she chased her pleasure.

"You feel so good," I told her. "Better than I imagined."

I gripped the back of her neck, stealing another kiss while she moaned into my mouth. Her hands held my face, tilting to the side to change the angle of our mouths when I curled my fingers.

Her thighs tightened, and her chest heaved.

"Not yet," I said against her kiss-swollen lips. "Not yet."

"Beckett," she warned.

I pulled my fingers away, and she lifted herself up, sweat beading on her forehead as she slid down over me.

Perfect.

I gritted my teeth, resisting the urge to grip her waist and slam her down. She worked herself inch by torturous inch, slow rocking motions of her hips that had my eyes rolling back in my head.

"Dammit, Greer," I muttered.

She slid her tongue into my mouth, nipping at my bottom lip. That sharp bite of her teeth had my restraint snapping, a clean, precise cut.

I gripped her tight and drove my hips up.

She cried out, head tossed back and so fucking gorgeous I could hardly believe she was mine.

"That's it," I told her. "That's it."

It was heaven, soft and warm and tight, and she found a maddening rhythm that had my blood roaring. Greer worked me over, and with my mouth sealed against hers, I guided her back and forth until my skin went hot and my hands and arms shook.

I sucked at her neck and her lips, angling her back so I could lick at her chest.

She whimpered when I pushed up as she slammed down, and I knew she was close.

"Come on, baby," I said against her mouth. "Give me this one."

She gasped, her nails digging into the back of my head as she drove us both higher and higher, the sweet tight coil of heat wrapping tighter around my spine until I felt like it would burst everything around it.

"Next time, I get you in a bed," I growled. "We have days and weeks and months, and every time I wake up with my hands on you, this is what's going to happen. I'll wake you up like this every fucking day because you're *mine*, Greer."

It was enough.

With a sharp arch of her neck, she shattered. With my name on her lips, she trembled around me, the most beautiful thing I'd ever seen.

Her release triggered mine—immediate bliss in a hot spike, brutal and relentless.

I chased it with another brutal upward slice of my hips, again and again, and I stole her mouth in a fierce kiss, licking into her mouth while we gasped through the release.

She slumped over me, sweaty and disheveled, and eventually, we softened the kiss.

I slid my hand up her back, sweaty and damp, twining my fingers into her hair.

I sucked her bottom lip into my mouth, her lips curving into a smile as I did.

"Mmmm," she hummed. "Car sex is highly underrated."

I laughed, happiness springing hot and immediate from inside me.

I wrapped her up in my arms, and we sat like that for a few long minutes. She pulled back and studied my face.

"You know I'm falling in love with you, right?" she asked quietly.

I smiled. "You think I'd want to get rid of you after this?"

Greer grinned. "I'd like to see you try."

## CHAPTER 28

# Greer

**It was the hand under my shirt that I registered first. The** hard length pressed against my ass was next.

Still groggy—because *wowza* did good sex have a positive effect on my ability to sleep like the dead—it took me a second to realize the position we'd ended up in.

But this time, I thought with a sleepy smile, we could start the day very, very differently.

In our house.

In our bedroom.

In our bed.

I'd always wanted to do that thing where you casually arch your back and press your backside into the hot sleeping husband behind you, just to see what he'd do.

Especially if that hot sleeping husband was taking it as his personal mission to give you an orgasm for every single day you'd spent together that he didn't touch you.

We'd stumbled home after dark the night before, collapsing into bed where we kissed and talked for hours.

He gently pushed me onto my back the first time, holding my hands down over my head and onto the bed, rolling his hips between mine, painfully slow and so steady that I almost lost my mind by the time he let me come.

But then again, I already knew that Beckett was far more skilled in the art of restraint than I was.

He let me sleep for a couple of hours after that, generous man that he was.

Sometime around two o'clock, the moon high and streaming in through the window, he woke me up with his head between my legs.

I was incoherent after a few minutes, clutching at his hair like it was my sole tether to the earth because my back almost snapped in half when he used his tongue and teeth and fingers to shatter me into a million splinters—an orgasm so intense that I damn near blacked out.

Like the good wife I was, I returned the favor, adding in some particularly cunning use of my tongue while he gripped my hair and rocked his hips gently.

Even though I'd just had my turn, there was something addicting about the way he spoke to me in that low, smooth voice of his, the pleasant hum of his filthy words practically a narcotic.

He told me I was perfect, every part of me. I ran my hands over his rock-hard thighs, trailing up to the stacked muscles on his abs, and made him come so hard that he had to let go of my hair to fist the sheets, just so he didn't accidentally hurt me.

After that, he tugged me up his chest, his hand gripping the back of my neck so he could devour my mouth.

We passed out shortly after, his big, hard body pressed behind mine, his arms holding me tight.

It was the very best way to sleep, I'd decided.

Because now, he was mine to do with whatever I pleased.

And in my current position, whatever I pleased was to gently slide his big warm hand over my breast, rolling his palm over the tip. My back arched slightly as I did, and that's when I felt him come to awareness.

The motions of his hands took on more purpose, tugging harder, rolling the hard flesh until I ached between my legs.

Beckett tilted his hips, sliding himself between my backside, and I exhaled unsteadily.

"Good morning," he murmured against my neck, mouthing my skin as he did. His teeth pressed down on the curve of my shoulder, and his other hand tugged at my underwear. I shifted my hips to help, and once I was free, he maneuvered my top leg forward just enough that he could work himself in.

I shivered, curling my body tighter on my side, changing the angle so he could only work in short, shallow thrusts.

"This is what I imagined," he whispered hotly. "This is what I wanted to do to you, Greer."

"Yes," I panted. "Yes."

"My wife," he growled, pushing in hard.

"*Yes.*"

He clutched me to him, and I entwined my fingers with his against my chest. I could hardly move, and I loved it. There was something wildly freeing about being bound to him this way.

There was something wildly freeing about us.

About the way I'd fallen in love with him and knew he'd fallen in love with me right back, despite the odds stacked against us.

He wasn't trying to change me, had never tried to change me. And I didn't want to change him either.

It was acceptance, liberating and powerful, that I'd never experienced before him.

And it was so much sweeter because of the waiting. Patience, as it turned out, could be really fucking awesome.

By the time he slid his hand between my legs and whispered commands into my ear, I was trembling, and the slow, endless roll of my orgasm kept going and going and going while he rocked me through it.

Beckett's hips snapped harder, his body pushed deeper, once, twice, three times, and he groaned against the back of my neck. Slowly, after disentangling our bodies, I rolled over, staying underneath the shelter of his arms.

His mouth found mine immediately, and he made a satisfied growling noise as we kissed.

When I pulled away, he chased my lips for another kiss, and I exhaled a laugh. "I need so much coffee," I whispered. "I'm guessing you were a little too distracted to set it up last night, huh?"

He hummed, sucking along the edge of my jaw. "Distracted by the woman who told me to strip and screw her in the kitchen?"

I laughed. "She sounds very bossy."

"The bossiest," he whispered, sliding his hand over my face to kiss me again. "I love it."

"Do you?" I traced the bottom of my lip as he stared at me, his eyes soft and adoring.

Beckett nodded. "I kinda love her too."

My heart swelled, impossibly big in my chest. This was my life now. This was my life with him, and it could only keep getting better, no matter what we'd have to face together.

Because that was the point.

We'd have each other.

There were no battles I had to face alone, no problems I'd face without him at my side.

I kissed him, lingering and sweet, my arm wrapping around his back, my chest pressed so tightly to his that I could feel the steady thumping of his heart.

"Do you love her enough to be the one to get up and make the coffee?"

He smiled, stealing another soft kiss. "Yeah."

"Maybe make a full pot."

His smile grew. "I don't think that's necessary," he said.

I drew back. "What do you mean? Did you magically get extra sleep that I don't know about?"

He shook his head. "No. I just hate coffee."

My mouth fell open. "You...*what*?"

Beckett sucked my bottom lip into his mouth, soothing it with his tongue when he released it. "Don't drink coffee," he answered matter-of-factly.

I sat up and stared down at him. "You don't drink coffee?" I repeated.

He wedged his hands behind his head. "Nope."

"But…"

Beckett sat up and laid a hard kiss on my gaping mouth. "I had this gorgeous woman living in my house, and I wanted to do something nice for her. That's all."

And just like that, he started to climb out of bed, giving me a brief glimpse of his perfectly biteable ass before he tugged his boxer briefs back up over his waist.

*That's all,* he said.

"How dare he," I mumbled, flinging the covers off, pulling on a T-shirt, and marching after him.

Beckett had his back to me when I stalked into the kitchen, turning just as I got to him. He was laughing as I leaped at him, winding my arms around his neck, my legs around his waist, and he dropped me onto the island while his tongue twined through mine.

When I pulled away, I rolled my forehead against his, our noses brushing lightly. "You made me coffee every morning," I said. "You set out my favorite mug. Every day."

His smile was gentle, his eyes bright. "Yeah. I think maybe I was falling in love with you a bit earlier than I was willing to admit."

I exhaled a wondrous laugh. I cupped his face in my hands. "Beckett Coleman," I whispered. "You are the perfect man."

"Because I made you coffee?" he asked.

I shook my head with a laugh. "No. Because I didn't even know how to dream you up. You're better than…everything."

He wrapped me tight in his arms with a happy sigh, pressing a kiss to my temple. We sat like that while the smell of coffee filled the kitchen.

———

Later, after showers and a huge meal and no more sex because our bodies couldn't physically handle it, I was sketching exteriors for a new client while Beckett sat at the kitchen table with his laptop and a stack of paperwork.

The sound of a car broke through the silence. He glanced up. So did I.

Josie.

She and Micah got out of the car, Olive with them.

I looked over at Beckett, and he gave me a tight, nervous smile.

"She's here with them. That's a good sign."

He nodded.

I stood from the couch while he closed his laptop and took a deep breath. "Do you want me to give you guys some privacy?" I asked tentatively. I hated asking, but I knew that I might be a touchy subject for Josie for a while, and I wanted to respect that, before anything else happened.

His brow furrowed. "No." Beckett grabbed my hand and pressed a kiss to my palm. "No. You're in this with me. You're my wife, Greer."

I smiled, relief sweeping through me like a tidal wave. "I will be, as soon as the courthouse opens tomorrow."

He ducked his head, eyes intent and face serious. "You're my wife now. Whether that paper has been filed yet or not."

I curled against his chest when he tugged me in for a hug. "I like having a husband," I said quietly.

"Remind yourself of that when I piss you off," he said. "I'm sure it'll happen soon enough."

I was still smiling when Josie and Micah got to the door.

Olive burst in first, giving me a hug, and then Beckett.

"Can you go play upstairs while we talk, sweet pea?" he asked quietly.

She nodded against his neck before he set her down. She bounced up the stairs. Beckett and I locked eyes, and he held out his hand for mine. With a smile, I took it.

He tugged me into his side, dropping a kiss onto the top of my head.

"Well," Josie said quietly. "That answers one of my questions."

Micah smoothed a hand over her back.

"Let's sit," Beckett said.

They sat on the couch opposite of us, Josie openly studying our body language when I curled into Beckett's side and he laid his hand over my thigh where it rested on his leg.

"Why don't you two start again from the beginning," Micah

said gently. "I'd like to hear it from both of you, now that the shock is over."

Beckett held my gaze for a moment, then nodded.

"You know most of it," I told them. "What we told you about my dad is true, but it's the other side...for him and Olive. That's what we didn't. And I'm sorry for my part in that."

Beckett's hand squeezed my leg, and we took turns telling our story while they listened patiently.

When we were done, Josie took a deep breath. "So you're... together now."

I smiled at Beckett. He swept his thumb over my thigh, then he turned his attention back to Olive's mom. "Whether it was this week or next week or a month from now," he said, "we would've ended up right here. I was already halfway in love with her when I decided to tell you the truth."

"Only halfway?" I teased.

He smiled. "Maybe a bit more than that."

Josie and Micah traded a long, wordless look, then she nodded.

"We're glad you did tell us," Micah said. "And Josie and I agreed that we'd have one more conversation with you about it before we made our final decision. See how we felt after we'd slept on it."

Beckett inhaled slowly. "If you decide to stay, Josie, I respect that. Just...please don't keep her from me because of this."

Josie's eyes shimmered. "I won't," she said quietly. "I wouldn't," she amended. "You and I decided a long time ago that we'd always put Olive first. And I'm not going to back out of that promise now."

Beckett let out a quiet, relieved breath, and I slid my hand over the top of his.

"I'm gonna go with Micah," Josie said. "But my visits home during the year might be a little longer. Two weeks instead of one, if you're okay with that."

Beckett's eyes fell closed, his shoulders slumping in relief. "Yes, of course I'm okay with that."

I squeezed his hand, my heart near to bursting at the relief stamped all over his face. "Thank you, Josie," I told her.

She smiled. "I'm glad you two worked it out," she said. "For two people who were faking it, you did a really shitty job of not looking like you were in love."

I laughed, leaning my head against Beckett's shoulder when he wrapped his arm around my back.

"And Olive loves you, Greer," she added. "This might not have been so clear cut if she didn't."

"I love her too," I said. "She's…amazing."

Josie wiped away a tear when it slipped down her cheek. "I need you to take care of her while I'm gone. Even if it means you're pissing off the other parents at the school."

I nodded with utmost sincerity. "I can guarantee that with no problem."

Beckett laughed, smoothing a hand over my back.

They left a little while later, Josie and Beckett sharing a long, sweet hug that had me wiping quiet tears.

It's what unselfish parenting should look like.

We said goodbye to Olive, with a promise to go shopping for cat supplies as soon as Josie and Micah left for London at the end of next week.

Beckett and I stood on the front porch while they drove away, his chest at my back and his arms wrapped around my waist.

"You ready to do this?" he asked me quietly. "Me and Olive and Clarence and all the rest of it?"

I turned in his arms, my eyes closed and my heart so full that I could hardly believe it was real. It was the easiest truth I'd ever told in my life.

"I've always been ready for this. I just hadn't met you yet."

# EPILOGUE
# Beckett

**7 months later**

**Prior to Greer's presence in my life, the day of a game, I** would wake up in a quiet house. I would eat my breakfast—an omelet, some fruit, and a smoothie—in a kitchen by myself, with only the sound of *SportsCenter* on in the background.

Things were just a little different now.

"Clarence, you twisted little shit, bring that back," Greer yelled.

Calmly, I finished the last bite of my omelet, watching the chaos unfold with a quirked eyebrow.

Clarence—who was, in fact, the naughtiest cat that had ever existed—raced through the kitchen with one of Greer's bras in his mouth. When he took a corner too fast, his paws got tangled in the straps and he pitched forward in an ungainly somersault, slamming into the back of the armchair.

Olive stood on the couch, her hands braced on the back

cushion, bouncing on her toes and giggling furiously at the scene.

Greer took advantage of his bound state, snatching him up in her arms. "You are such a jerk," she breathed. "I love that one."

"So do I," I murmured under my breath.

Greer's eyes met mine, bright and happy.

My wife had a penchant for pretty lace bras, and I found that I quite enjoyed them too.

Unfortunately, so did Clarence. If they were left out on the bedroom floor, as this particular item had been the night before, it was like he had a homing beacon built into that evil little brain of his.

She wrestled the bra from his mouth, huffing in exasperation when he batted at the straps when she pulled it away. Then he nuzzled up against the side of her face, butting the top of his head to her jaw, and Greer smiled. "Don't act cute now. It's too late."

Greer set him back down on the floor, shaking her head when he darted up onto the couch by Olive, weaving through her legs and arching his back when she scratched his head.

The two of them left the family room to head upstairs, Clarence's tail twitching happily as he followed Olive to her bedroom—where he was the proud owner of the most extravagant cat tower in the world.

"I swear," Greer sighed, "that cat has it out for my lingerie."

She approached me at the island and I turned on the stool, widening my legs so she could slot herself there. My hands slid over her hips as she placed a lingering kiss onto my waiting mouth.

"He has good taste," I spoke against her lips. "I like ripping them apart too."

Greer laughed, carding her fingers through my hair. "I know." Her eyes were warm and soft. "What time do you have to head over?"

I glanced at the clock, tucking my fingers against the warm skin on her back under her shirt. "About twenty minutes."

Greer didn't ask me if I was nervous. She simply leaned back in for another kiss, slow and sweet, while her hands moved down my neck to my shoulders.

It was a big game—our divisional rival who'd always managed to sneak out the first spot in our division the last few years. We beat them the first time we met in the season, winning by a field goal as time ran out in their home stadium.

Greer had made it her mission to find a way to make it comfortable for Olive to attend games, so that I'd know I had them both there. She'd researched special headphones that would block out all the noise, but still be comfortable for Olive to wear. They arrived early, before the stadium filled, into the box I'd reserved for the family. And most of the time, Olive stayed happily tucked behind the glass.

But she was there. With Greer.

My family.

Most days, I couldn't believe that this was my life. Couldn't believe that I'd gone so many years without this type of happiness, this kind of love wrapped around all the moments that I'd never really paid attention to before.

Like breakfast.

Someone asking me what time I needed to leave for the game.

And in a few more hours, knowing that she'd be waiting for me at the end of it.

With my bag packed and the lapel of my suit jacket smoothed by a sharp-eyed Greer, my wife and daughter stood on the front porch and waved me off—clad in their Voyagers gear.

The energy at the stadium was potent, even before the fans filled their seats.

Our entire team knew what was at stake. If we could beat them today, it was almost a guarantee that we'd win our division and head into the playoffs with an advantage.

We warmed up, everyone's eyes sharp and attention unwavering from what we needed to do.

Parker and I ran routes with precision, and he tapped my fist when we passed to line up again. We both had headphones on, as did most of the guys before we made our way back into the locker room to dress for the game.

Before I left the locker room, I glanced one last time at my phone before putting it away in my bag. My smile was impossible to repress.

**GREER**

I love you, win or lose.

But please destroy them.

By the time we took the field again, the stadium trembled from the leashed energy trapped within the walls of the building. Our fans were rabid for a win, and so were we.

The roars were deafening when the ball tipped end over end on the kickoff, and I closed my eyes for a moment before I moved to line up.

I didn't know how many more years I had to play, injuries could happen at any time, or priorities could shift on a dime.

And every single time I got to play one more game, I wanted to appreciate it.

Parker and I stood side by side as we waited for the special teams to leave the field. He gave me a sidelong glance.

"We're winning today, Coleman," he said.

Despite how hard the last six months had been for the Wilders, and they had been, Parker was trying.

And whatever felt too hard for him to handle, he was leaving it all on the field. He'd been an absolute beast this season.

I smacked my brother-in-law on the back of his jersey. "Yeah, we are."

We jogged onto the field side by side, lining up on opposite sides of the offensive line, with Christian Reyes anchoring us in the middle.

And for the next sixty minutes of play, that's what we did.

Every single person who lined up for Portland played with terrifying efficiency.

Parker and I decimated their defense, Christian throwing

bomb after bomb down the field. And when the defense lined up, we stifled every single one of their weapons.

By the time we lined up in the red zone with three minutes left on the clock, we were up by twenty-one, and the atmosphere in the stadium was electric.

Our fans stomped and screamed like we were about to win the championship.

Reyes lined up in the pocket, shouting his play-call. He pointed out to the D-line, making sure his blockers watched for the blitz.

The ball snapped, and Parker shoved forward on the right, blocking the defensive end while I took off on an out route—ten yards on a dead sprint, then I cut to the middle of the field toward the sidelines. With Parker's blocking and the fact that I was easily two steps ahead of the safety guarding me, Christian hit me with a bullet into my outstretched hands about fifteen yards out, and I tucked the ball under my arm as I ran unchallenged into the end zone.

The noise was deafening as my teammates surrounded me.

The final score was 35 to 7, the kind of definitive win we'd never had.

Inside the locker room after the game, Coach teared up as he addressed our performance in front of a raucous group that couldn't quite settle down. The game ball went to Reyes, who did nothing but tap it against his chest and humbly accept all the yells and whistles from his teammates.

"Can I skip the press today?" I asked Coach after my shower.

He eyed me as I finished tugging the shirt over my head. "You got somewhere else to be?"

With a smile, I nodded. "Yeah, I do."

He waved me off, and I shoved the rest of my things into my duffel bag and made my way down to the place Greer told me they'd be.

The hallway leading to the field was quiet, and we'd done that on purpose. She stood with Olive's hand in her own, pointing to something out in the rows and rows of seats.

Before they were aware of my presence, I took a moment to watch them.

They both wore Coleman jerseys, and the sight of both of them with my last name on their backs had my chest aching. For years, I'd been missing this—and I'd hardly even noticed.

Quietly, I pulled my phone out of my pocket and zoomed in on the two of them, just as Greer crouched down to say something to Olive.

The picture snapped at the perfect time, my two girls smiling at each other with the field in the background. Greer would want it blown up and framed, no doubt, something to add to the walls of our house.

And I couldn't wait.

Greer saw me first, a smile blooming on her face as she nudged Olive's arm and then tilted her head back toward me.

Olive raced toward me, and I hoisted her in my arms.

"You were so good, Daddy," she said into my neck.

"Thanks, sweet pea." I kissed the side of her hair, holding her tight.

Greer approached, and I held out one arm so she could tuck into my side. When she turned her mouth up, I happily obliged, humming contentedly into her kiss.

"So good," she murmured.

I kissed her again, lingering for a moment longer.

She smacked my ass. "I'll show you later just how that last touchdown made me feel," she whispered into my ear.

I wrapped an arm around her shoulder with a laugh, and we left like that, with the two most important people in my life pressed against my side and safe against my heart.

There was nothing more I could have wanted.

And no matter what happened, it was the best win I could have ever asked for.

BONUS EPILOGUE

# Greer

**Six years after The End**

**I was good at a lot of things, but conceding defeat was** not one of them. Anyone who knew me would tell you that. My mother would say it with pride. My brothers would roll their eyes, but even they wouldn't be able to deny the truth. Greer Wilder was no loser, and there was not a single plan I'd instigated that did not eventually see a fruitful and satisfying conclusion—certainly not today. Or so I had thought an hour earlier when a camera crew and an NFL Hall of Famer camped out in our family room to surprise Beckett. Or they were *supposed* to surprise Beckett.

I had a plan. It was a good plan. It was going to be emotional and cute and funny, and we'd cry, and blah blah blah. Except he wasn't coming back inside our freaking house.

Which meant my husband, who I loved and adored and who would go to the ends of the earth to see me smile, was pushing me to my absolute fucking breaking point.

"Maybe we should reschedule."

My eyes narrowed as I looked out into the backyard. "No, I can get him in here."

"Didn't you already try?" someone behind me asked. It was innocent enough, but he didn't realize he'd just issued an undeniable challenge.

Bull, meet red flag.

I was, and always had been, the bull in this situation.

The steady hum of the air compressor reached the house, and I rubbed my forehead when the nail gun started.

*Thwack!*

*Thwack!*

*Thwack!*

I rued the friggin' day I had let my brothers show him how to build shit because now that was all he wanted to do. Did I have an idea that needed brought to life? In swooped my retired husband, wielding his power tools.

A casual mention of expanding a vegetable garden, and a week later, I had four new raised beds, and I'd catch him hauling soil, and building an arch, and laying rock and a cute, little stone pathway.

Don't even get me started on the animals. We'd have a fucking zoo after another five years of this man in retirement.

Don't get me wrong—it was sexy. He loved to cook dinner, and the sight of him in an apron did things to me. But right now, I didn't want sexy Beckett hiding in the barn with his tools, which is something I'd never thought I'd say in a million years.

"He looks pretty, uh, settled in what he's doing."

Yeah, no shit. I heaved a dramatic sigh and tossed my phone onto the counter. Texting the man was doing nothing. He had a firm no-phone rule when he was outside in his Man Zone, and in moments like this, it made me want to take a *chainsaw* to that Zone. Unless I sent him a picture of my tits and told him I was waiting in bed, there was very little I could do over the phone to get him inside.

My eyebrows rose slowly, and I glanced quickly down at the cleavage situation, wondering if I could sneak a dirty pic around the corner, then sighed.

In case it wasn't clear, I did not like admitting defeat, and I probably had hairline cracks in my molars from grinding my teeth so hard for the last two hours. "He said he'd be in soon, but I think he started another project."

The guy next to me, big and brawny, with excellent bone structure, peered through the kitchen window, standing slightly behind me so Beckett wouldn't see him should he happen to look inside.

He was wearing a gold jacket, the hallmark of the NFL Hall of Fame, and if Beckett would ever get his fantastic ass inside, he'd find out he'd been nominated to wear one.

I'd gone out there once just before they arrived, and he gave me a distracted kiss and told me he wanted to work on one more thing before dinner.

"I'll bring in the cavalry," I told him and gave his giant, beefy arm a consoling pat.

The guy behind the camera gave a pointed look at his watch.

Since he couldn't see me, I rolled my eyes as I took the stairs two at a time. It was saying a lot if I was the most patient person in the house.

Olive's voice came down the hallway first. "And when Dad comes in you, you say…"

"Happy birthday!"

She sighed, but I could hear the reluctant affection for her little brother. "No, James. You say, *Dad, we have something exciting to show you.*"

"He has *eyes*, Olive. Daddy will see him when he comes in." The *duh* was implied.

"I know, but your mom has a plan. And it's a good one."

See? That kid knew what was up.

I tiptoed toward the door leading into James's bedroom—the deep navy walls were a particular favorite of mine, especially with the sumptuous leather chair in the corner where he'd still snuggle with us before bed, asking for one more book and one more book, just to put off bedtime a little bit longer.

We'd transitioned him to a bed at fourteen months, much earlier than the pediatrician thought possible, because that little monster with Beckett's eyes and my penchant for trouble figured out how to climb out of his crib well before he'd turned a year and a half. Unless a pediatrician was well-versed in children with Wilder genes, they really had no idea what we were capable of.

Instead of one of those dinky kid mattresses, we went for a queen-size mattress because, some nights, we'd find him and

Olive sleeping together—when he had a nightmare, he went straight for his sister. Without fail, she'd walk him back to his bed and climb under the covers with him so he wouldn't be afraid anymore.

She was, without a doubt, his favorite person in the entire world.

Unsurprisingly, Olive transitioned into her preteen years without any of the attitude that we'd been warned about. The girl was an actual angel. She was still quiet, but much less so than when she was younger, and she'd grown into the sweetest kid I'd ever met in my life. Funny in her own way, and kind, and obsessed with every animal she ever met, and even more obsessed with her younger brother, who joined our brood the same year Beckett decided was his last with the Portland Voyagers.

He loved to play.

But he loved his family more. And once James came into the world—screaming bloody murder and with a head full of dark hair—home was the only place Beckett wanted to be.

He took to being a stay-at-home dad with a single-minded focus that made me want to bang him six times a day. He coached teams; he practiced lines with Olive when she was in a play; he helped with sets and took her dress shopping and started golfing simply because James showed an aptitude for it.

Everyone in the family was a little terrified at the thought of my child wielding a giant metal club that could break things, but they'd get over it. I heard Cameron once say that the fact that we'd only decided to have one was a gift to the universe, and I threw a golf ball right at the apex of his legs and watched smugly as it hit dead center.

After James's birth, Beckett and I decided our family was complete. Olive split her time between us and Josie, now that she and her husband had moved back to the States, and James was always his happiest when his sister was home. He probably would've loved a younger sibling, but pregnancy was hard on my body, and one felt like enough for both me and Beckett.

And in moments like this one, when I could peek through the cracked bedroom door and watch them lying on James's bed, playing with Clarence and his newest sidekick, Bumblebee (another orange-and-white menace who was sent to this world to destroy curtains and steal my sanity one day at a time), I couldn't help but marvel at the life we'd created together.

"Mom always has plans," James sighed, puckering his dark brows while he held a piece of string above Bumblebee and she tried to swat at it. He giggled, which made his sister laugh, and I almost did something ridiculous, like burst into tears watching my two favorite kids play with a demon cat.

Clarence, the little bra-stealer, had renounced the title Demon Cat when he hit four years old. He was mellow now, a very distinguished gentleman who watched Bumblebee terrorize the family with a judgy twitch of his tail.

Even though I was loath to break up the cuteness overload, I cleared my throat and poked my head through the doorway. "Can I recruit your cute, little faces for an important mission?"

James bolted up in bed, throwing his fist in the air. "Yes! I love missions."

"If you can get your dad in this house, you'll be the mission *winner*."

His eyes lit up. "What do I win?"

I set my hands on my knees and leaned down to his level. "The satisfaction of knowing you've done a good job," I told him gravely.

He deflated. "Ugh. I thought it was something good."

Olive laughed. "We already tried to get him inside. He's determined to finish."

"Yeah, and whose fault is that, Miss *I want a chicken coop like the one Uncle Cameron built*? He's in competition with my brother, and now there's no stopping him."

Olive patted me on the back. "I think this is on you, Greer. He won't come inside for anyone else."

I groaned. "Fine. Okay. But you two need to head downstairs and watch for him. Make sure you're in your places and ready."

"Happy birthday!" James yelled, standing on his bed and jumping up and down. Clarence gave a disdainful sniff and hopped off the bed. Bumblebee started swatting at James's feet.

Olive and I traded a look. "Can you…?" I gestured at the jumping child, and she nodded.

"He'll say his lines. Don't worry."

As I strode down the stairs and through the family room, ignoring the eyes of the gold-jacket dude and the crew, I ran my hands through my hair and adjusted the V of my tank top.

Six and half years into this marriage gig, and I was not above using my feminine wiles to get that man to do what needed to be done.

With that in mind, I made sure to wait until I was out of the house and halfway across the yard separating the back deck and the barn before I pulled my breasts out of the bra just a little, emphasizing the curves on display.

The nail gun was still going crazy as I turned the corner into the barn, and the sight made me stop in my tracks—not because he was building an insane chicken coop that his daughter asked for or because Myrtle the goat had wandered through the barn when she definitely wasn't supposed to be out of her pen, but because Beckett was bent over the sawhorse, shirtless and sweaty, and I swear to God, I felt my ovaries shriek in unhinged glee.

*Fertilize me*, they wailed.

I blew out a harsh breath. "Keep it together, Greer."

He hadn't seen me yet, and my eyes tracked over the defined muscles in his shoulders, the rock-hard curve of his biceps and his tanned, flat stomach with that little line of hair I loved so very, very much.

His head was bent in concentration, his gaze shifting between the plans he'd printed and the coop coming to life in front of him.

According to Olive, it would have wallpaper and a crystal chandelier because her chickens *deserved it*.

And what had my husband done? Started drafting plans and found a fucking chandelier on clearance because that's what his daughter wanted. In the same way he brought home Myrtle because James thought we had so much extra grass and wouldn't it be nice to let a cute baby goat eat some of it?

The man, in simplest terms, would do anything for us.

And I was banking on that to be true even when I pulled him from his Very Important Dad Tasks.

Beckett set the nail gun down, doing a slight double take when I came into his peripheral vision. His lips curved in a slight smile. "Wife. You've texted me six times. Is someone dying?"

I clasped my hands behind my back and sidled over, making sure my hips swayed a little bit extra as I did. He noticed. Of course he noticed.

"No, but I would love for you to come inside for a little bit. You've been out here a long time."

His dark gaze tracked over the deep V of my tank top and lingered, lifting only when I came within arm's reach. "You miss me?"

I told him the truth: "Always."

Beckett hummed deep in his throat, and even though he was sweaty, even though he had sawdust coating his arms, he slid his hands around my hips and pulled me against his chest. "Show me how much."

There was no time for this.

No time.

I had a crabby camera crew and a famous former football player chilling in my dining room, and there was no time to make out with my hot, sweaty husband in the barn. Right?

Then he stared at my mouth and licked his bottom lip.

Fuck it. There was *always* time for this.

I flung my arms around his neck and let out a decadent sigh as his mouth took mine in a fierce kiss, his tongue brushing over my own as I twined my fingers in his sweat-damp hair. Beckett gripped my ass in both hands and walked me backward until my back hit the wall of the barn.

"Beckett," I moaned, my head rolling to the side as he pushed his hand up underneath my tank top and palmed my breast underneath my bra, dragging a firm thumb over my nipple. "We can't. We—"

"Do you know how long it's been since I kissed you?" he asked in a raspy voice, the flat of his tongue following the line of my throat.

God, I couldn't think when he did that. "Do *you*?"

He stared at my mouth. "At least four hours. I can't go that long anymore. I'll be in pain."

As I cupped the sides of his face, I laughed. "When did you become so dramatic, Husband?"

He kissed me again, sweeter this time, slower this time, and my entire body melted, blood like thickened honey as it moved through my veins. "Why do you think I have to keep myself busy?" he asked, biting on my bottom lip and then soothing it with his tongue. "If I don't, I'll wander around you and touch you and kiss you, and then we'd scar our children because they'd walk in and my hands would be down your pants every fucking day."

No time.

Why didn't I have time?

I was ready to tear his shorts off and give Myrtle the most exciting eyeful she'd ever seen in her entire life. Sex in a barn would probably be messy and hot, and I'd get hay somewhere unfortunate, but it was also sex. In a barn. With Beckett.

Like she could hear my pervy thoughts, Myrtle let out a harsh bleat, and I dropped my head back on a sigh. Beckett, in all his single-minded glory, ignored the goat and tugged on the strap of my tank top in search of a breast that he could kiss.

No time.

And I was not a fucking quitter.

Even though my lady parts wailed at the betrayal, I pushed Beckett away and adjusted the strap of my shirt, giving him a quelling look. "None of that. I need you to come inside. For… something."

"Do you, now?"

"Yes," I answered primly.

His eyes gleamed. "How long do you think they'll wait?"

"Not much—" My eyes snapped to his. "*What?*"

My serious husband, who so rarely smiled, tipped his head back, exposing the long, thick line of his tanned throat, and laughed so deep and hard that his entire frame shook.

I crossed my arms and pinned him with an icy glare. "You *knew?*"

A dimple flashed in his cheek. "I saw them drive up. The gold jacket isn't particularly inconspicuous outerwear. You should've had them park at the neighbors' and walk."

"It's half a mile away," I said in an incredulous tone.

"He used to block quarterbacks for a living. He can handle a little exercise."

"I can't believe you've made us wait this long."

"It's good for you."

I gave my eyebrow a haughty raise. "Is it?"

"Patience, my little tornado," he said, dipping his head to kiss the edge of my jaw.

"I'm the most patient person ever." I kept my arms crossed, refusing to touch him even though I really, *really* wanted to.

"Yeah, I can see that. I had an over/under with myself, but I didn't think you'd last an hour before coming out here."

"Oh, you little shit," I breathed.

Beckett tugged me closer, his hands creeping from my lower back to my ass. "Call me that again. You know what it does to me when you swear."

I wriggled out of his arms, even though it was very tempting to stay. "Beckett Coleman, you come inside right now and let those men do what they need to do."

He sighed, reaching for the T-shirt he'd discarded. When his muscles disappeared beneath the soft, worn cotton, I pouted. Just a little. Beckett gripped the back of his neck.

The sexy games were over, judging by the look on his face, and vulnerability took its place in my husband's eyes.

"Feels weird, you know? I just played the game because I loved it. I never needed something like this to make me feel like my career meant something."

"I know. But it's an honor that you've earned," I told him, cupping his cheek and letting my thumb drift over the stubble there. "Let people celebrate you, Beckett. Your family loves seeing you shine. James never got to go to a game or cheer you on in the stands, but he'll get to cheer you on in this," I said quietly, watching his eyes go soft and his frame relax.

"Well, when you put it like that," he murmured. "Do we have to record it?"

"Yes."

He kissed me. "And it has to go online?"

My mouth opened on a sigh as his tongue tangled lightly with mine. He pulled back and rested his forehead on mine as I said, "Yes."

Beckett ducked his head and growled against the skin of my neck, then bit down lightly. "The things I do for you."

I was grinning when he lifted his head. "I *knew* I'd win."

Beckett laughed, and just like it always did, the sight of his smile cracked my heart wide open. "You always do, Greer Coleman."

I snuggled into his arms and sighed happily when he kissed the top of my head. "I got you, didn't I?"

"Yeah, Wife," he said fondly. "That you did."

I wished that my past self had known that love could be like this. But I'm not sure I would've believed it until he walked into my life.

That someone this good and thoughtful and humble, strong and sexy and determined could be mine. That I could build an incredible life with him, with two children who meant the world to both of us.

He was perfect—in the way he challenged me, supported me, loved me. And even better, even more miraculous, he felt the same way about me.

No matter what was planned, or unplanned, life would be met with this man by my side.

We kissed again and took another moment or two in the stillness of the barn before he wound his fingers through mine, and we walked home together.

KEEP READING FOR A SNEAK PEEK AT KARLA SORENSEN'S NEXT NOVEL IN THE WILDER FAMILY SERIES, *HEAD OVER HEELS*.

# CHAPTER 1

# Cameron

Maybe I had a hero complex—some white knight syndrome bullshit that had always been ingrained in me, or maybe I shouldered more weight than necessary—but I could not physically imagine anything worse than having to let down the women in my life.

And I had a lot of them.

No wife or girlfriend, which was probably for the best. But I had a metric fuck ton of sisters (I had four, but it felt like three times as many most days), and they kept me on my toes just enough that it was impossible to make room for anyone else who might make a greater claim on my already massive sense of responsibility.

The street corner outside my hotel in Portland bustled—cars and people and the energy of a larger city that usually made me avoid them. At that moment, though, I wanted those city noises to be just a bit louder.

Maybe they'd drown out all the shit in my head.

I stared down at my phone with a grim set to my mouth and an imaginary elephant crowding to make room on my shoulders. Two elephants, actually.

In fact, I'd prefer if someone popped in front of me and took a crowbar to my junk so that I could have a pleasant distraction from the task that awaited me.

Maybe I wasn't the eldest son in the family, but I was the one running the family business, the one proclaiming our last name proudly, and I just lost us a massive contract that would've kept us busy for at least eighteen months.

If I thought too hard about all the jobs we'd said no to for this one…

No.

I couldn't go there.

Waiting for my business partner—and sister—to pick up the phone, the elephants gained a few friends until I couldn't believe I was still standing for how they pressed down all around me.

Greer picked up on the next ring. "Sorry, I was finishing up on the other line. How'd the meeting go?"

I rubbed my forehead. "Not great." Loaded silence greeted my tight response.

Greer and I had worked together for too long for me to fake any sort of pleasantries—we'd been running Wilder Homes since we were in our early twenties. She handled the design side of things, most of the initial client interactions that locked in the schedule, and kept the communication flowing while I oversaw the construction crew, managed all the subcontractors, and built the damn houses.

And in rare cases like this, I attended an important client meeting that was about to blow the foreseeable future to fucking pieces.

"What happened?" she asked.

Before answering, I pushed my tongue into the side of my cheek and stared up at the long stretch of windows covering my hotel from the night before.

Greer booked my travel, picking an older hotel with interesting architecture, curved stonework around the windows, and eclectic decor inside. She picked it, no doubt, because she knew I'd stay somewhere cheap and nondescript, and then I'd be annoyed when I had to drive farther through downtown traffic for my meeting.

Well... I was already annoyed because a few short days ago, newspapers across the Pacific Northwest broke with the story that our client was facing allegations ranging from tax evasion to sexual assault.

Not the kind of person I'd willingly enter into business with.

But it wasn't just about me.

And because I was a masochist, I dredged up the faces of every person who worked for us, my mind racing of how we could make this right for them.

You know, considering I didn't know how to give them work.

Greer wanted to know what happened? I blew out a harsh breath.

"Our schedule is suddenly wide open," I told her. "Shit," she muttered. "So the story was true?"

"Unfortunately." I scrubbed a hand over my face. "Not that he admitted anything in our meeting, but he definitely wasn't proclaiming his innocence either."

If I'd been somewhere more private, I would've kicked at something just to have an outlet.

"He didn't seem … criminal when he hired us," she said. "He was so nice."

"I know." My jaw was tight around the words. "I know I did the right thing, but—"

She interrupted as soon as my voice trailed off. "Don't you dare feel bad about this, Cameron Marcus Wilder."

At the motherly tone—honest to God, my sisters could not help themselves—I rolled my eyes a little. "The full name wasn't necessary."

"It is if you're feeling even a shred of guilt." She cleared her throat, and the sound of a door closed on the other end of the phone. "If that story is true, and he's involved in half the things the articles are saying, you'd feel even worse taking a single penny of that man's money. If we have to lay the guys off for a couple of months until we can find a build to replace it, they'll get unemployment."

"I know," I said as my stomach churned. The trip to Portland, and the last-minute meeting with the sweet, grandfatherly old man who turned out to be involved in numerous illicit and highly illegal activities, was the last thing I needed to cram into an already insane week.

Back at home—a handful of hours away in Sisters, Oregon—we had a family fraying at the edges with my dad being sick. His decline from his third round of cancer was getting more and more apparent. As the oldest son still at home, I carried that weight too. How to step in where my dad and stepmom needed me. And for the most part, that was keeping Wilder Homes running like a smooth machine. It was the income for half our family, practically. Not just myself and Greer, but my dad and Sheila were still on payroll as minority owners—their share was worth twenty percent of the company, with Greer and I splitting the remaining eighty.

Weeks earlier, I'd promised my older brother Ian a job when he moved back home from London. He wanted to be back in Oregon because of Dad. My youngest sister, Poppy, had started helping out in the office.

Our collective grief was enough to deal with on any given day, but I couldn't help but feel a staggering sense of failure that I'd just pulled our entire company out of a job that would've been our biggest, grandest, and most visible project to date.

A four-million-dollar crown jewel, tucked away in a lush piece of property in Western Oregon.

"How did he take it?"

My answering laugh was dry and humorless. "I can comfortably say that I've never been sworn at in such a creative manner in my entire life."

She whistled. "That good, huh?"

"Yeah."

"Well, this is why we have a contract with very specific language, right? He can't sue us."

"He certainly wants to," I said. "Believe me, he threatened that with very colorful language as well."

The thought of it, undoubtedly the worst meeting I'd ever had in my life, left my bones cold and my skin uncomfortable.

I hated being stuck inside that office, knowing the consequences that came with it. Even though I knew I'd done the right thing, it left me feeling restless. A squirming itch that I couldn't get rid of until I figured out how to make this right for the people who worked for us.

The sun was bright and warm, and I tilted my face up. The pleasing heat on my skin didn't go very far to settle my nerves.

Normally, it did.

Being outside and working with my hands was my favorite thing in the world.

But even the sun couldn't touch what was happening inside me at the moment.

Even though the decision to back out of the build was right, the burden of the consequences was breathtaking.

And no one would shoulder that burden except me. "Well," Greer said slowly, and I knew she was thinking through the millions of issues that would arise as a result of this. "I'm staying at Mom and Dad's for a couple of days to help out. So I'll start crunching numbers. We had to turn down some jobs because of our calendar for the next couple of years. I'll circle back around and see if any of them still need a builder."

Some jobs? We turned down more than that. A dozen at least had inquired, and we'd said no to every single one of them, passing them on to local competitors to boot.

"Okay. Thanks, Greer."

She hummed. "We'll be okay, Cameron. We've had slow years before."

I exhaled a laugh. "When?"

"Okay fine, we haven't had a slow year since you and I took over. But we will figure this out."

The thought of heading back into the air-conditioned hotel sounded awful, and even though it was almost dinnertime, I glanced at the thick black watch on my wrist. "We can talk about it later if you want. I think I'm gonna drive back home tonight. I don't want to stay here any longer than I have to."

"Okay, but grab some food from the hotel before you leave. You're a beast when you're hungry, and I'm not talking to you about anything when you get back until you have food in your stomach."

"You know I'm in my thirties, Greer. I don't need my sister to tell me when to eat."

"Yet you forget to have lunch just about every single day on the jobsite," she said lightly. "This is why you need a wife, so that babysitting you is no longer my responsibility."

I rolled my eyes and glanced toward the entrance to the hotel, a flash of gold hair snagging my attention. She wasn't doing anything other than walking out of the building, but my throat went dry all the same.

When was the last time I'd physically lost my breath at the sight of a woman?

I honestly couldn't remember.

If it was a movie montage, one of the romcoms Poppy forced me to watch when I was home with her, they'd do something clever in a moment like this. Slow the filming of everything around us. Pipe in some heavy bass music, fill your ears with a sensual beat that left nothing to the imagination of exactly how immediate my response was.

Everything about her looked refined—sleek and tailored and elegant.

Her legs were long and tan, lightly muscled underneath the ivory skirt wrapped around her thighs.

Her hair was pulled back off her face in a severe ponytail, and around her neck was a delicate gold chain that disappeared into the V of her black tank top.

Greer was still talking, but I couldn't tear my eyes away from this woman, especially not as she came within an arm's length of me and paused. She shielded her eyes from the sun and glanced down the street with a nervous twist of her lips, and then moved her gaze past me to the building just next door. Because I just stood there—one giant, dumbstruck obstacle in the middle of the sidewalk—I was the next recipient of her attention. Who had eyes like that?

No one I'd ever seen. Not with that particular shade of dark blue with green streaks in the center.

They couldn't be real.

I was tempted to ask, but I wasn't an asshole, and also... it felt like someone jammed sawdust into my mouth while I just stood there and stared at her.

Like an asshole. "Pardon me," she said.

My mouth opened, but absolutely fucking nothing came out.

Then she smiled—polite and reserved—and walked past, leaving behind the briefest whiff of clean, fresh scent and disappearing into the tailoring shop just next door to the hotel.

"Cameron," Greer yelled.

I blinked and found my hand inexplicably rubbing at my chest. "Sorry. Got distracted."

"It's fine. Just ... don't beat yourself up, okay? I know you'll blame yourself if we're a little lean for a while. But it will be fine. I promise."

"Right." I blinked again. "Thanks, Greer. I'll, uh, talk to you when I get home."

I continued to stare at the ornate black door to the tailor's shop, not quite sure what had just happened.

It wasn't like I was immune to a beautiful woman. But for years, I simply didn't have the space in my head to take on a relationship.

Blinders went on to everything that wasn't work or taking care of my parents and siblings.

When you lived in a small town, which we did, most of the single women there knew me. Knew my family. The fact that I'd had those blinders on didn't go unnoticed by any of them.

I wasn't the guy knocked speechless at the sight of a pretty face and pretty eyes.

I was usually the guy who didn't notice them at all because I was too damn busy and too damn tired to think about it.

Maybe that was part of my problem.

# ACKNOWLEDGMENTS

A massive thank you to all the usual suspects: my husband and my kids, my mom, for stepping in and picking up the slack when I entered into one of the craziest deadlines I've ever attempted in ten years of writing.

To Georgana Grinstead, Holly Ingraham, Jocelyn Travis, and the team at Sourcebooks Casablanca for making quite a few author dreams come true, I'm so very thankful.

Kathryn Andrews, Piper Sheldon, Kandi Steiner, and Brittainy Cherry, for being wonderful cheerleaders and motivators for this book.

Najla Qamber and the Qamber Designs Media team, for being amazing and having the continuous ability to read my mind.

ME Carter and Nicole McCurdy for giving me their time and energy to make the story as strong as possible, as well as Jenny Sims and Julia Griffis for cleaning the mess afterward.

Tina Stokes and Colby Robbins for keeping the Team Sorensen ship running smoothly. And my readers—you are the very best in the world, and I adore you. Thank you for letting me continue to tell stories in the way that I love to tell them.

> *God is our refuge and strength, an ever present help*
> *in trouble. Therefore we will not fear, though the*
> *earth give way and the mountains fall into the heart*
> *of the sea.*
>
> *Psalm 46:1–2*

# ABOUT THE AUTHOR

Karla Sorensen is a #1 Amazon bestselling author who refuses to read or write anything without a happily ever after. When she's not reading or avoiding the laundry, you can find her watching football (British AND American), or HGTV. With a degree in Advertising and Public Relations from Grand Valley State University, she made her living in senior healthcare prior to writing full time. Karla lives in Michigan with her husband, two boys and a big, shaggy rescue dog named Bear.

Website: karlasorensen.com
Facebook: karlasorensenbooks
Instagram: @karla_sorensen
TikTok: @karlasorensenbooks